CLERIC OF APHRODITE

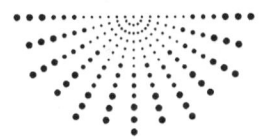

ARK HORTON

To everyone who is motivated by spite and likes to swear.

You're my kind of people.

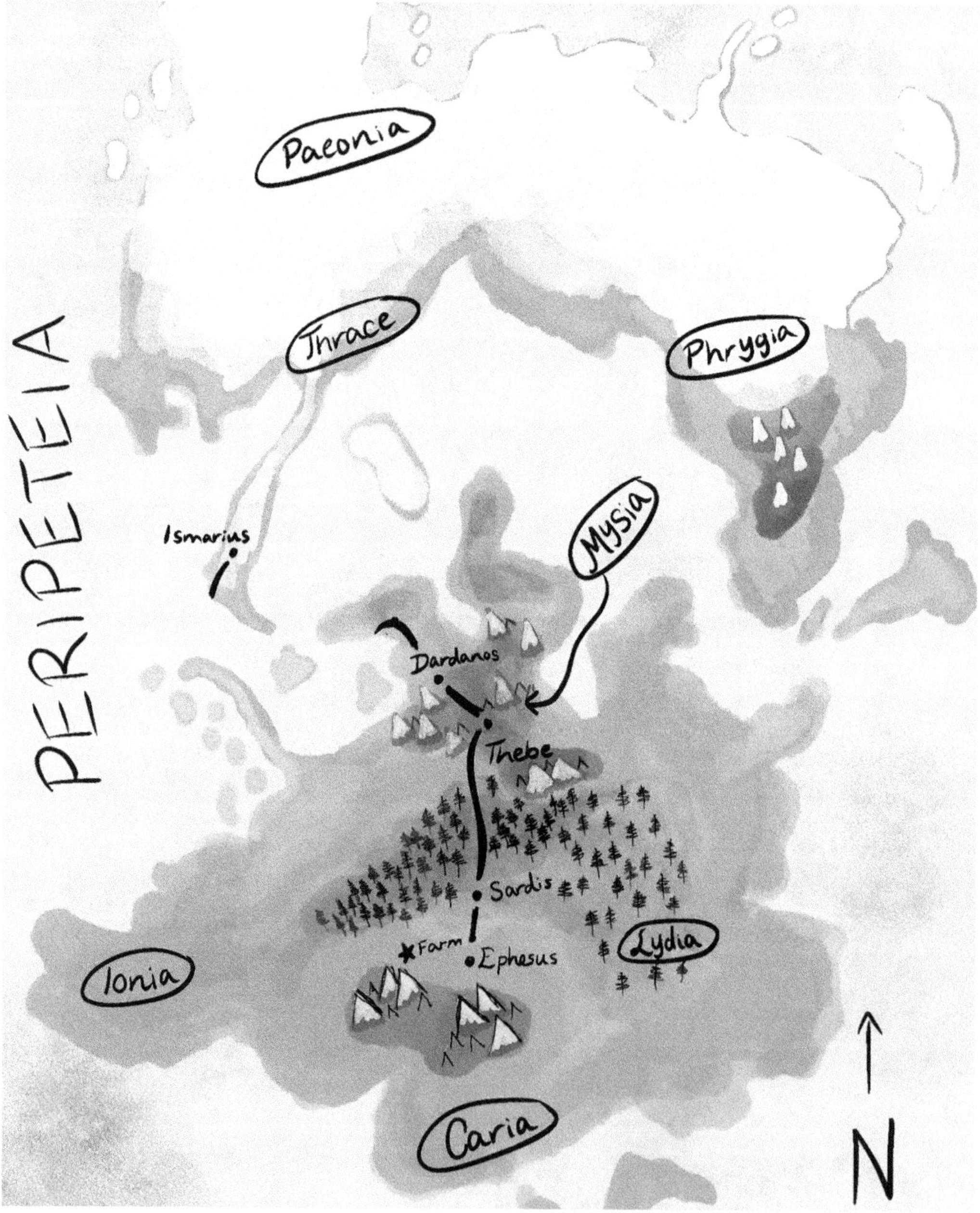
PERIPETEIA
Paeonia
Thrace
Phrygia
Mysia
Ismarius
Dardanos
Thebe
Sardis
Farm
Ephesus
Lydia
Ionia
Caria
N

CLERIC OF APHRODITE PLAYLIST

Alrighty Aphrodite — Peach Pit
Running Up That Hill — Bard to the Core
Dear God — XTC
Soldier Girl — The Polyphonic Spree
The Book of Love — The Magnetic Fields
Fight Like Gods — Chelsea Wolfe
My Type — Saint Motel
Crush — Tessa Violet
Human — dodie, Tom Walker
Woman — Wolfmother
Live And Let Die — Paul McCartney
Persephone In The Garden — Aidoneus

Extended Playlist — https://tinyurl.com/coasongs

CONTENTS

A SPECIAL NOTE BY THE AUTHOR

LitRPG is a fantasy and science fiction subgenre I've enjoyed reading for a long time. When I mentioned my interest in writing it at a conference, an expert in the subgenre told me that only men like LitRPG and they don't buy books from women authors or with women protagonists. He told me I would fail because of my gender.

So, of course, I didn't listen to him.

See, when someone tells me I can't do something, it becomes my mission to prove them wrong. I decided to not only write LitRPG but also focus on a very feminine character, write in a romantic subplot, make it LGBTQIA inclusive, and add in a whole lot of *emotions*—all things I was told don't work in this subgenre.

Why? Because I like both LitRPG and the story elements I just listed, and I know I'm not alone. This is a book for readers like me. This is a story for *you*.

CHAPTER ONE

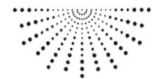

Mom always told me I could be anything I wanted. Bullshit.

Okay, that's too harsh. Mom's been sick a lot recently. Yet, she's still taking me to the movies and calling me up for long chats about our favorite TV shows.

I'm sure being the single parent of a "gifted" child wasn't easy, either. I could always counter all her rules like I was an experienced lawyer. I acted out in school a lot because everything was too easy and boring. But she took it all with a smile, making it seem effortless when I *know* it wasn't.

Mom means it when she goes on about how special I am. That doesn't mean she's right. Skills, experience, and hard work mean fuck all when luck isn't on your side. Besides, this isn't like one of the fantasy RPGs I play. In the real world, we're not heroes on an epic quest, and we don't level up simply by trying.

I'm sure Mom meant for her words to encourage me to stick to a successful life plan that involved choosing an impressive job, getting married, having kids, and buying a house. And I've tried; I've really *tried*. But adulthood doesn't come with gold stars and glowing report cards like school did. The pizza lunches my job provides instead of pay raises don't have the same appeal as the free personal pan pizza I got for reading a hundred books. My motivation to achieve anything has all but disappeared without consistent external validation.

Yes, I have a college degree, but I took a while getting it because I kept changing my mind about what I should major in. Now, I have a bachelor's in art history. *Art history.* I'm not going to be the doctor or lawyer that would make a parent proud.

While I stay employed, I get burned out with any job I take. I've only been doing tech support for three months now and I already feel like quitting and getting a teaching certificate to become an art teacher.

Jesus, Lauren, get a grip. You'd quit that job on day one.

As far as getting married and having kids? There's my live-in boyfriend, Doug, but...well...I mean, he's Doug. He's like the first car I ever drove: familiar, easy, and still sticking around eleven years later. Another thing they have in common is that neither of them are working right now. I've been taking the train to work for three days, while Doug has been at our house doing nothing for the last two years, four months, and six days. Not that I'm keeping track of how long all the bills have been on my plate or anything.

I spent all day getting yelled at by people who don't understand how to use my company's software program. The ride home wasn't a breeze either. My extreme social anxiety *hated* that the train was fuller than usual. I'm pretty sure the man six seats down from me on the Yellow Line was masturbating while talking to himself. Even with my giant pink cat headphones on, my entire being was on high fucking alert. The ten-minute Uber ride from the station to my apartment complex was also a nightmare. My driver wanted to know if I'd found Jesus. If I wasn't so averse to talking to strangers, I would have asked him how long Jesus had been lost.

But there are two things to look forward to when I get back home: there's an unopened bag of cheese puffs waiting for me in my pantry, *and* I got paid today, so I can finally preorder that new, hyped-up, single-player fantasy RPG *Legends of Sacrifice.*

I open the door to my apartment, expecting to take advantage of these two things and then binge-watch my favorite show. However, the first thing I see is Doug sitting at my computer with a completely empty bag of cheese puffs next to him.

I should know better by now. Keeping my expectations low means I'll never be disappointed. I'm not disappointed right now, though. I'm angry.

Doug barely notices my presence. There was a time when he'd rush to see me at the end of the day and tell me how pretty my caramel blonde hair and gray eyes were. Now he's too absorbed in grinding the starting area of the same MMO he's been playing since high school to care that I'm back. The game, *Straying Tempest,* is actually how we met. We didn't go to the same school, but we both loved dungeon crawling online with other kids our age. It was fun back then, but it felt like a slog after a few years. So I've moved on to other games, while he lives in the past.

I put my purse up before walking over to him and clearing my throat.

"Just a minute, babe," he says, not even blinking in my direction. "Almost done culling these corrupted rats."

Breathe, Lauren. It's just a bag of cheese puffs. This is your boyfriend of eleven years. You know he does dumb stuff like this sometimes. You just need to communicate.

Doug licks his bottom lip as he kills off the last rodent for his quest. Then he turns to me with the Labrador puppy smile that he usually uses in an "ask for forgiveness, not permission" kind of way. I'm about to be even more pissed at him. I can tell.

"Oh, hey, I used your card to buy the new *Straying Tempest* expansion," he says. "Hope you don't mind."

I clench and unclench my hands in an effort to keep my anger out of my tone. "Doug, you have that card in case of an *emergency.*"

"Well, I mean it was fifty percent off today, so it was *kind of* an emergency."

"How much?"

Doug shrugs. "I think seventy-five."

"*Dollars?!*" I can't be hearing him right.

"Well, I mean, that's after tax, but—"

"Doug! I don't have that kind of fucking money!"

Holding his hands up defensively, Doug gets up from his seat and backs away from me. "You just got paid, Lauren."

"Yeah, and all of that is going toward bills," I say. "You know what bills are, right? It's how I keep a roof over our heads, make sure we never lose electricity, and keep a fully stocked kitchen."

My gaze flicks over to the empty bag of cheese puffs on my desk. Orange dust is all over the place, especially on the W, A, S, and D keys of my keyboard.

"And you ate all my cheese puffs!" I half-shout, half-sulk. "I pay for all our food. Could you at least ask before you eat my stuff?"

"I didn't realize snacks were only for *you*," Doug says. "I guess since I lost my job, I don't *deserve* to eat."

He's using that same "I'm the victim here" tone I've tolerated for years. It usually works on me, making me feel like *I'm* the asshole for simply reacting to the bullshit he's pulled on me.

I don't know why today is different. Maybe it's because of the sad realization that a bag of junk food was going to be the highlight of my day. Perhaps it was learning that I wasn't going to be able to preorder *Legends of Sacrifice*. It could even be because that dude on the train was trying to make eye contact with me when he put his hands in his pants. Whatever the reason, I've had *enough*.

"Out," I say, pointing at the door.

Doug just stands there, looking at me like I spoke to him in an alien language.

So I elaborate. "O.U.T. Out. Get your stuff and get the fuck out of my apartment."

This breaks him out of his stupor, and he crosses his arms. "*Our* apartment, Lauren. My name is on the lease, too."

"Okay, fine, I'll let the landlord know that I'm leaving, and it's all under your name now," I say. "Good luck paying your rent with no job."

"Lauren, babe—" he starts, but I'm not about to let him continue the false apology he's about to improvise.

"Doug," I say, with a calmer tone than I've been able to muster in months, "I want you to listen to me and understand that every word coming out of me is sincere. You haven't pulled your weight as a room-mate for as long as we've lived together."

"Babe, I can—"

I hold up a finger, stopping him immediately. "That would be okay if

I thought you were even trying. Hell, even if we'd had sex at any point in the last eight months. But you sit around my house all day doing the same bullshit you've been doing since high school. Also, you should at least mute your phone when you're masturbating in the bathroom. I *definitely* didn't need to know what kind of porn you're into. Not to kink shame, but...Bugs Bunny? I don't get it."

"W-well," Doug blubbers, eyes wide and cheeks blushing with embarrassment. "I could say a lot about you, too, you know. All you do is work and then come home in a bad mood."

I don't even have a response to his boneheaded words. Honestly, how can anyone be this obtuse? Instead, I pull my phone out of my back pocket and open up my contact list.

"What are you doing?" Doug asks.

"Calling Pete," I answer.

Doug knows he's in for it now. Pete's his big brother, the one who always has to bail Doug out of his messes if I'm not around. He's the last resort, though, because once Pete's involved, so is their mother, and that woman certainly knows how to guilt-trip her children.

Doug tries to snatch my phone from my hands, but I dodge away in time. Pete answers right away. He knows that if I'm not texting, something's really important.

"Lauren, everything okay?" he asks in greeting.

"Nope," I say. "I need you to come pick up your brother and grab his stuff. I'm done."

"*Done*, done?" he asks.

"One hundred percent."

Pete's sigh of resignation rattles the line with static. "Well...I guess that's that then. Let Doug know I'll be there by eight. I gotta finish up work first."

"Will do. See you then, Pete."

"See ya," Pete says before he hangs up.

Doug's crying now. "You're gonna be so sorry you did this."

I shake my head. "No, I'm sorry it took me this long."

"You're going to be so lonely once I leave," he says. "No one will ever love you like I do."

That stings a little, because I'm pretty sure he's right. I haven't been happy in our relationship for a long time, but I've stuck with it because I believed Doug was the only guy who would ever want to be with me. As I look at Doug's entitled and outraged expression, though, I'm willing to throw away any chance I might have at romance.

"Yeah, I don't mind if I'm single for the rest of my life," I say. "At least I'll be able to eat my cheese puffs in fucking peace."

CHAPTER TWO

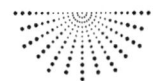

When I told Doug I didn't mind if I was single for the rest of my life, I don't think I really meant it. However, as I lean over my kitchen counter, scrolling through his Instagram feed, I'm convinced that I couldn't have been more correct. He's moved on suspiciously fast. It's been a month, and he's already taking selfies with some brunette all over town.

Is that what he's been up to while I'm at work? Chatting up another woman and *leaving* the house? He never took me to bars, restaurants, museums, or parks. Not that I ever wanted to go out anywhere. I mean, there are *people* out there.

It would have been nice to be asked, though.

She's so thin compared to me. There's a photo of her with a sleeveless top, and I can tell she works out because her upper arms are so toned. Her skin is clear. There aren't any dark circles around her eyes. There isn't one picture of her with headphones on because she doesn't need them to deal with crowds. Her smile shines, like she isn't just pretending to be happy; she actually is.

Looking at the twinkle in her eyes makes me ponder when I last experienced genuine joy, and...I can't remember. When Doug and I moved in together, maybe? That was four years ago. Goddamn that's sad. What's even sadder is that we'd already been together for seven years when we did. Eleven *wasted* years together before we ended things.

Never once did we talk about marriage. But there's a ring on her finger. His grandmother's. The one his mother showed me at Doug's high school graduation party. I wonder what she thinks about Doug's new girlfriend—sorry, *fiancée*.

Doesn't matter. Miss Brunette can have him and his fucking snack-stealing, job-avoiding, couch-farting ass. Because love isn't just over-rated; it's a trap.

I could have had a cat! A black one with giant green eyes, waiting for me when I come home from a hard day at work. But Doug was allergic, so I never got to have one.

I walk up to the whiteboard in my kitchen and update my to-do list. *Adopt a cat.* This list used to be where tasks went to die, but not anymore! Now that Doug is gone, I'm a new woman. I get shit done!

Like right now, I'm waiting for the bread to finish in my oven because I bake now. I've also taken up crocheting, as is evident by the overflowing basket of yarn by my recliner. Even better, I'm back to painting. I was fantastic at it throughout college and high school, but at some point, I gave up, and I can't remember why. No, that's a lie; I was too tired after working all day and then taking care of Doug.

I'm saving a lot on my grocery bills now, so I was finally able to preorder *Legends of Sacrifice*, and—

Hold up. What's that smell? Is something burning?

Before I can even finish processing what's happening, my smoke alarm goes off. I put on my mitts and pull the charred bread out of the oven. How is this even possible? It's only been in the oven for fifteen minutes.

I look at the dial. It's on broil. I remember now that when I leaned over the counter, my butt bumped into something. That must have been it. Jesus *Fucking* Christ.

I turn off the oven, turn on a fan, and open the nearest window. As I wave the smoke out, I look at the people walking down the sidewalk three stories below me. From up here, the world doesn't seem so bad. It's too much when I'm down there in it. I only go to work because I have to, and even then, I put on noise-canceling headphones to survive the train ride home. Fortunately, my car's fixed up now, so I can take a break from sitting shoulder-to-shoulder with strangers.

Just wish I had some friends...

Doug was my only social life. Maybe that was why we didn't break up sooner. He was familiar and predictable, which could be comforting sometimes. Now he's gallivanting everywhere, and it's dawning on me that maybe he stayed cooped up in our apartment because I needed him to be here. That was the trade-off, and probably a depressing one for him. Could that be why he went without a job for so long? Depression?

No, it's because he's a lazy asshole.

Once the smoke is clear, I take a steak knife and scrape off the burned top of my loaf like I would with a piece of toast. Below the char, it's still under-baked. I've really fucked this up. Maybe baking isn't my thing. I'll stick with crocheting and painting, as well as what I'm already accustomed to: computers and gaming.

Just the thought of gaming brings me a sense of peace. It's true that I can't handle loud noises, crowds, and action, but it's different when it's on my PC. Just like the people walking on the sidewalk below my apartment, it's at a distance. There's a screen between me and the digital worlds I explore. I control my experience there, and I can actually do something other than tolerate what's happening to me. I can whip out a sword or fling a bolt of lightning.

I read somewhere that anxiety is a byproduct of the modern world screwing up our natural fight or flight response. When someone on the phone is yelling at me because my company's software isn't working for them, I can't reach through the phone and punch them; I can't even run away. Instead, I sit there letting it happen while faking a patient, customer-service tone.

When I game, though, I can smack the shit out of monsters. I'm *really* looking forward to doing that in *Legends of Sacrifice*. The game's beta forums are public now, so I've been lurking around and reading the posts. And what I've seen is right up my alley.

Because Mom loved reading them to me growing up, I've always been interested in Greek myths. Even though this game is apparently *really* loose with its interpretation, it seems to be pulling out all the stops with its monsters. There's even a labyrinthian dungeon with a minotaur boss. The graphics in the trailer look incredible, too. I've always been more interested in gameplay than story elements, but from what I've read, the characters and their backgrounds are really compelling.

I can't wait to get lost in that world because, quite honestly, this one *sucks*. In the meantime, I'll be playing this cozy game Mom got me on my PlayStation. I may not be able to bake bread for shit in real life, but I'm a baking prodigy in *Kawaii Boulangerie*.

Speaking of baking...I sigh as I toss my disaster of an experiment into the trash can. Then I look up the Domino's website and order pizza.

Before I can submit my order, Mom's number pops up. I almost flick it away, but then I remember all the times she's been there when I was down. She's probably calling to check up on me, and I sure could use her kind words as I get over my failure as a baker.

"Hey, Mom!"

"Is this Lauren Spivey?" asks a woman who definitely isn't my mother, causing alarm bells to sound off in my head.

"Um...yes..."

"I'm calling from Northside Medical," the woman says. "We have a woman here who can't seem to remember her name, but it looks like she calls you all the time from this phone. I was hoping you could come here and help us figure out some stuff."

"She's my mom. What's wrong? Why is she there?"

"We'll tell you everything we know when you get here," she answers. "She's not in danger, but we do need to talk to someone about what's going on."

⇧

COMPARED TO HOW FRIGID NORTHSIDE MEDICAL WAS, THE hospice feels like a warm bath. That should comfort me. I'm sure that they meant for it to. The point of hospice is to make the last days of your life nice, right? But nothing can make this any fucking easier.

Early onset dementia. That's why she forgot who she was. It's really uncommon for a woman in her fifties to have dementia. However, it turns out all those times she thought she was dizzy because of a cold or something were actually signs of a stroke. Her MRI showed that she'd had five. *Five.* Five times I've failed her when she's never, not once, let me down.

Where was I when she wasn't well? Pouting about my loser ex and obsessing over a video game that isn't even out yet. Creating disasters in my kitchen and wishing I had a cat. I even let her pay for our movie dates. Jesus Christ, I'm the worst daughter in the world, just as bad as the sperm donor who walked out on her once he knocked her up with me.

Dementia alone wouldn't have landed her in hospice care. You can live for years and years with it. But after suddenly getting pneumonia, Mom's condition has progressed so fast that she qualifies for hospice. It's been a week, and already she can't say much. She sometimes manages a short sentence that doesn't make sense, but she mostly just stares into the distance with a blank expression.

And she's grown so thin. Growing up, I often heard her complaining about how fat she was getting, but I always thought she was the most beautiful woman in the world. Now she's wasting away because she can't eat without help.

Mom knows my face, though! She knows my name! Even with her illness, when I come to her room, she says, "Lauren," and lifts her trembling hand when my cheek gets near enough to touch. She has trouble reaching all the way, though, so I hold her palm against my cheek and try not to cry because she can't smile anymore.

Today, she had fever and chills. They told me somehow she'd gotten sepsis. How? *How?!* These are trained medical staff. It's "under control" now, though.

I don't believe them. I want to fight them. I want to stay in her room.

But I can't. I have work in the morning, and they have rules.

I can't sleep. I lay in bed thinking about how her eyes are bright in the *wrong* way—glossy with illness and vacancy. "Lauren," she'd said when I visited her today, but nothing more, and I imagine that maybe there *was* more to say. So much more. That she's screaming it all in her head, but her brain won't let her say anything other than one word anymore. I can't tell if I love or hate that it's my name.

If I was a hero in one of my games, I could save her.

Wait...games...What day is it?

I grab my phone to look. 1:23 am, Saturday, August 5. *Legends of Sacrifice* just released an hour ago.

Working in a tech support call center means my hours accommodate our customers. So, my weekends are Thursday and Friday. I don't have time to play my new game now, but...

Fuck it. I'll call in sick. I just need a day to forget the way my life has gone to shit in the last couple of months.

I go through all the steps to download the game. Every second that passes, that progress bar seems to take longer and longer to fill up. At last, the menu comes into view, and I press play.

The prologue cutscene is glorious. Dramatic music plays as Peripeteia, the fictional land inspired by Greek mythological locations, spreads across my screen. A fire-breathing dragon chases after a Pegasus over an orchard of golden apple trees.

Wait, do dragons fly in Greek myths? Lauren, just enjoy this. It's inspired by mythology, not married to it. Let the game makers have a little creative freedom.

The viewpoint changes, and there's now an incredibly handsome man staring at the chase scene in the distant sky. His dark features are melancholy. Ash, mud, and blood cover his armor. He tosses his sword to the ground and falls to his knees weeping.

A beautiful woman in regal attire picks it up. He lifts his face to look at her. "Never again," she says, her voice seething with the same fury I can see in her eyes. She steps away from him and into a hall of marble floors and columns. There are others that dress in robes like her, all of them sitting on thrones.

"There will be more," a man says in a consoling manner.

"I hope so," she says, sitting on the throne next to him. Her eyes are now filled with deep sadness, and she gazes upon the bloody sword she'd just taken from the man. "If not...Oh, Zeus..."

He squeezes her hand and looks at the others. "There will be other heroes eager to fight in your name," he says in a voice that commands their attention and respect. "You must aid them. Without their offerings, Olympus *will* fall."

The scene fades away as the music swells in an even more epic and thunderous beat. The title, *Legends of Sacrifice*, appears with the play button underneath it.

My hands shake with excitement as I move my mouse to click on the button. My breath becomes quick and shallow with impatience while I wait for the loading screen to hurry up already.

Finally, the character creator comes up. "Welcome, adventurer!" a voice greets. "Who are you?"

Immediately, I'm overwhelmed by all the options on my plate. Character creation is one of my favorite parts of the RPG experience, but I get analysis paralysis every time. Everything has to be perfect, *everything*.

I go through every class, deliberating what would be the most fun. Usually, I play a caster. Who doesn't love flinging fire spells at baddies? But I'm not feeling it right now. It's not enough. I want to hurt some digital monster as much as the world is hurting me. For that reason, I choose pugilist monk because goddamn, I want to throat punch someone, even if it is just pretend.

Now, I need to decide on a race. They all have different strengths and weaknesses, which seems racist as fuck, but whatever. It's a game. The more I look at my options, the more I scoff. Halflings? Really? I thought this was supposed to be Greek mythology stuff. I remind myself it's the most hyped game for a reason, though.

Orcs seem to align best with monks, but I just can't do it. They're so ugly. Call me a vain little girl, but if I'm going to stare at my character running all over the place, I want her ass to be spectacular. Elves are *beautiful* of course, but they're built for spell casting, not fist fighting. In the end, I choose the vanilla option and go with playing as a human. *Yawn.*

I make her as pretty as possible. I choose the supermodel body preset and give her the very-not-human traits of purple hair and eyes. Sticking with the color theme, I name her Violet.

When I hit the *"Time for Adventure"* button, the loading screen comes up again. This time it seems to take even longer. What the fuck is the issue? I just want to play already. The moment I see a peek of a grassy field, the game crashes on me.

I throw off my headset. "God fucking damn it!" I yell at my computer, like it can hear me. "Can't I just have this? Please?"

I take a deep breath.

Lauren, it's just a game. Sit back down and reload it.

I take my inner voice's advice, and it works. The world pops up again. There are green hills as far as I can see. There's a farmer reaping his wheat. He waves at me, but a quest notification to head to the tavern steals my attention.

So far, this seems more like any other fantasy RPG than one that incorporates Greek mythology, but it's *gorgeous*. I don't think I've ever seen such realism in a game before.

Maybe that's why my PC crashed. It can't handle this game.

I head to the tavern. It's packed with locals drinking, eating, and socializing. I'm grateful this is just a game because in the real world, I'd be *noping* right out of there, quest or no quest.

Leaning against the wall on the far left side is the same handsome man from the prologue cutscene. He's moping over his drink. There's a glowing blue orb above his head that I assume means he's the person I need to talk to.

I click on him, and he says, "Hello, there! I haven't seen you here before. Are you an adventurer?" I read the caption below his face. His name is Alexander, and the answer options are:

1. *Yes.*

2. *No.*

3. *I'm a chimera, actually.*

I choose the first option.

"I was once an adventurer," he says, "but the gods have cursed me to never lift a blade again."

I remember the cutscene. So that's what that was about.

"Because of Phoebe," Alexander continues. "She was the most beautiful woman I've ever seen, but my thirst for glory made me careless. When I set fire to the nest of harpies, I didn't realize they had kidnapped her and hidden her there. Now, she's dead and by my hand. For my sin, I can never touch my sword again."

Yikes. That hits hard.

My mind flits to earlier in the day, watching Mom stare vacantly at the TV in her room. I'd put on that competitive dancing show she and I liked to watch together. It might as well have been off. I didn't realize she'd been having strokes. If I had known...If I had known...

I shake myself out of it. This game is supposed to be a distraction.

"My love had a locket," Alexander says. "It's still in the ruins of the harpy's nest. Can you retrieve it for me? Without my sword, I cannot fight any beasts that may arrive, so I have no way to get it myself."

Yes, Alexander. I absolutely fucking can get that locket. I can't do shit in real life, but in your world, I'm capable of anything.

Time to throat punch a harpy!

CHAPTER THREE

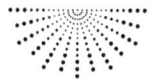

In my experience, fictional men are superior to real men. They don't stink up my couch with their farts or eat all my favorite snacks while I'm at work. They certainly never call me a bitch while they pack up their stuff and leave. Sure, I can't have sex with the men from video games, but that's what my toy drawer is for. If anything, my sex life has *improved* since Doug left.

When it comes to sexy fictional men, Alexander is way up there. He's a tortured Greek hero. He has a brooding allure, dark tousled hair, and mournful brown eyes that only light up when I talk to him. He's also *stacked*.

One thing I'm definitely set on doing in this game is helping him get over Phoebe's death so I can get in his digital pants. Once I finished that super easy beginner harpy quest, I found new dialogue options with him. He opened up about how much he loves dandelions because they remind him of his happy childhood.

So, last night, I found every dandelion I could and gave them to him. Yes, I've been looking forward to bashing baddies for months. However, there's something heart-fluttering about a man with a tragic backstory and a chiseled jawline.

Before going to sleep, I looked him up on the *Legends of Sacrifice* wiki to find out all his likes and relationship-level events. Then I made a promise to myself that I'd do more than stick around in the starter zone flirting with a string of code. Quest first, seduce NPC second.

But this morning, I'm already thinking about how I'm halfway to the fourth-level relationship event where he calls the player "remarkable" while blushing. I'm still only level two as a monk, which is pretty pathetic since I really only have to punch one more monster and I'll be level three. That doesn't matter, though. I just want to have fun and *forget* about all the shit going on in the real world.

I sit down at my computer, take a big gulp of hot coffee from my "*Mana Potion*" mug, and click "*Continue*" on the *Legends of Sacrifice* menu. Then, I watch in horror as my screen becomes a solid expanse of bright blue before turning off completely.

"*Fuck!*" I shout.

I press my hand on the PC tower. Sure enough, it's hot. I think back to last night, wondering if I noticed anything was up, but I was too distracted by Alexander's puppy dog eyes to pay attention to anything else.

Since heat is the key symptom, I open up the PC tower and investigate. The first thing I check are the cooling fans. I need not go any further. It takes me no time to know they're *definitely* the problem.

There's a thick coat of cheese dust on the fan blades. It must have gotten moist at some point because it's gunked up in some areas.

Doug. That fucking asshole!

It's all those bags of *my* cheese puffs that he ate at my desk, leaving his mess for me to clean up. Even now, his slobbery is making my life miserable.

There's only one thing I can do, and it's the *last* thing I want to do right now. I need to go to the store and get new cooling fans.

I run a comb through my honey-blonde hair, brush my teeth, wash my face, and change out of my pajamas into the first t-shirt and leggings I see. Getting ready is usually the hardest part about leaving the house, but I'm still dreading going to the store, where some dude will inevitably try to advise me on what parts to buy.

In those situations, I always want to channel my inner Ron Swanson and say, "I know more than you." But that's the kind of thing that Doug always told me makes me seem like a bitch, and I don't want him to be right about *anything*. I also don't think I have the energy to do more than nod at people in reply, and not just because I stayed up too late playing last night. My mind keeps jumping out of the fantasy and back to the reality where my mom's life could end any day.

I decide to visit her after I go to the store. I don't want to. I'd rather wrap myself up in a blanket and forget everything. But I'm going out anyway, and I'm going to hate myself if I don't take every chance I have to see her before she's gone for good.

I grab my purse and a water bottle on the way out the door. I have a feeling I may need to take a long gulp of *something* before heading to the hospice, and water is a better option than hard liquor since I'm driving.

When I arrive at the store's parking lot, I reach behind my seat to grab my pink cat headset to deal with the overwhelming chaos of any store on a Saturday. But it's not there. Is it in my purse? I rifle around in the gigantic bag that I sling over my shoulder whenever I leave my house. Sometimes, I feel like there's a portal in here where I can find everything from a tarnished penny to a skyscraper.

They're not in there either.

Fuck. I'll just have to suffer through this trip.

This will be the "sacrifice" part of my experience with *Legends of Sacrifice.*

I take a long swig of water and tell myself I can do this.

Fortunately, there don't seem to be many people milling about the store. I easily find the fans I need and head to the cash register. I sigh with relief, knowing that I can leave this store now, visit Mom, and get some gaming done when I get home. Maybe I'll do more than pick dandelions this time.

"That will be $36.62," the cashier says.

I dig around through my giant ass purse for my wallet, but it's not there.

Jesus. It's probably sitting somewhere like my kitchen counter. Oh wait! Maybe it fell out of my purse when I was trying to find my headset.

My cheeks burn with embarrassment as I say, "Sorry, I think my wallet must have fallen out into my car. Can you hold onto that while I look?"

The cashier nods and sets the cooling fans to the side so he can help the next customer.

I sprint out of the store, expecting to pop right in and out of my car.

But I don't see my car. I don't even see a parking lot. All I see are trees—a *lot* of them.

Maybe I went out the wrong entrance?

I turn around to re-enter the store, but it's not there anymore, just more trees. I'm in the middle of a forest.

"Fuck."

CHAPTER FOUR

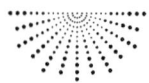

I'm a tech support worker by day and a gamer by night. No matter what time it is, I'm sitting at some desk somewhere. Hiking is not my thing, and nature belongs on my computer screen. I am *not* made for this. On top of that, my heart is pounding a million beats a minute because I'm freaking the fuck out about suddenly being in a forest. No matter how much I pinch or slap myself, I can't seem to wake up.

My legs and my brain aren't equipped to get me out of this forest right now. My only other choice is to sit around hoping someone will rescue me, though. Since it seems my cell phone has run off to wherever my wallet and headphones are fucking hiding, I don't have any way to reach out for help. Even then, could I tell them where the hell I am?

So I head where the most light filters through the leaves.

Not even thirty minutes into this, I'm already regretting this plan. The hard ground gives way to murky patches of swamp, exposing the trees' woven and gnarled root system. So, of course, a woody knot introduces itself to my toes.

"Holy fuck!" I scream as my clumsy ass falls into the mud, intense pain radiating up my twisted ankle.

Panic floods me to the point of hyperventilation for a spell. But then a strange peace settles over me. It's like someone popped a Xanax into my mouth and made me swallow. I'm fuzzy all over, wanting to touch and taste everything I can.

Did someone at the store drug me? Is this all a hallucination?

Another bolt of pain shoots up my ankle.

I'm not imagining that!

When I was a teenager, I took a job as a lifeguard at a community pool to make enough money to buy some games on my wish list. To get the job, I had to be first aid certified. Ten years later, I still remember everything I learned.

"R.I.C.E. Rest, Ice, Compress, and Elevate," I mumble to myself. I look around at my swampy surroundings and call out, "My kingdom for an ice pack!"

Well, I'll do what I can for now and then see what I can manage *if* I get out of here. Rifling through my purse produces some breath mints, a few crumpled receipts, a broken hairpin, and a plethora of other useless items. There *is* aspirin though, and I swallow two pills dry.

There's nothing to ice this sprain and nothing to compress it...Except...

I groan at the cliché solution.

I'm not attached to the t-shirt I'm wearing. It's just what I wear when I'm behind on laundry. It was a misguided gift from Doug—or maybe a thoughtless one is a better way to describe it.

Early in our relationship, he'd somehow gotten it into his head that I was a big fan of this anime about girl superheroes labeled by their favorite flowers. I'm not sure if I said something that got blown out of proportion, or if he just thought I was a fan because all the girls he knew loved it. So, across my chest is a picture of the show's main character, Star Lily, winking and flashing a peace sign with hearts and butterflies forming a halo over her yellow hair.

Sorry, girl. It's you or me.

I attempt to tear my shirt, but the material is thick. As ugly as the shirt is, it's made from high-quality cloth. I can't tie the whole shirt around my ankle, though, so I keep trying, and it finally tears...right down the middle, exposing my bra and stomach.

Goddamn it! Now I'm injured and my boobs are out.

I know I can tear the cloth now, though, so I take the shirt off all the way and tear at it until I have a reasonable length of cloth to wrap around my ankle. I'm tempted to throw the shirt away, but the light coming through the forest is starting to dim, and there's a chance I could fall again, so I stuff the tattered thing into my purse.

With great effort and a lot of swearing, I get up and hobble on as best as I can. Because of my injury, I move at a snail's pace. By the time I finally break free of the forest, it's tar black outside, save for the bright stars in the sky.

I haven't seen a night sky like this since I was a kid.

Being a homebody means that I'm seldom out at night. Even when I do go out, I live in a light-polluted city. The constellations above me now aren't familiar at all. They've become strangers since I stopped caring about what was in the sky. I wonder why I did. They're breathtaking, almost unreal.

I scan the area and laugh when I see the glow of lamplight through a house's window, knowing someone there might be able to help.

THIS LAST PART OF THE TREK WAS THE MOST PAINFUL. MY swollen ankle desperately needs to be elevated and iced, and my aspirin has worn off completely. That strange sedation that calmed me before has vanished. So when a burly man with a mop of brown hair and a friendly smile opens the door, I cry with relief.

"Oh, thank God," I say, wiping the tears off my cheek. "Sir, I need your help. I'm injured." I motion to my ankle, which now looks like a red balloon.

The man doesn't look. Instead, he moves out of the way and says, "Please, come in."

Because it was so dark outside, I hadn't gotten a good look at the exterior of the house, but the interior isn't what I expected at all. It looks as though someone built it from mud. There's a fire in the clay fireplace and a pot of *something* bubbling over the flames.

It's all one room, too, with a bed in the corner and what looks like *might* be a kitchen next to the fireplace because there's a table with some fruit on it.

"Lovely home," I say, trying to mean it, or at least sound like I do. I don't want to be rude to this gracious man.

After another glance at my host, I realize he's a little odd like his house. He's wearing a tunic made of what looks like burlap, cinched with a leather belt.

He must notice the questions in my eyes because he says, "Sorry for the way I look. Farming makes me sweaty."

Oh, he's a farmer. I guess that's why everything's so rustic.

"I haven't had a guest in a long time," he continues. "I'm not used to making myself presentable."

These words remind me that I'm standing in his house without a shirt on, and I cross my arms over my chest.

The man doesn't seem to notice, but I'm sure he's just pretending. I don't want to brag, but my tits are hard to ignore, even when they're *under* a t-shirt.

"I'm Celeas," he says. "It's nice to meet you."

"Likewise. Can I sit down somewhere?"

"Make yourself comfortable."

There are only two places to sit: on a stool by the table or on the bed. Seeing as I need to elevate my leg, the bed seems the more reasonable choice. It feels impolite, though.

"Is...is it okay for me to sit on your bed and prop my leg up?"

"Make yourself comfortable," the man says again, as he stirs the liquid boiling over the fire.

"Okay..."

There's a small, lumpy pillow on the bed. It feels incredibly rude to use it to elevate my foot, but Celeas told me twice to make myself comfortable. I lay back with my foot propped up the two inches the pillow can provide. It isn't much, but it's worlds better than traipsing all over the forest.

"I hate to intrude on you any further, but do you have any ice?" I ask.

"You can buy supplies at the temple," Celeas answers.

"Yeah, it doesn't look like you have a fridge. Thanks, anyway."

Celeas moves from the pot and sits on the stool where he stares through me silently. I feel a strange tug of familiarity in that action and the tilt of his head.

Déjà vu.

"Can I use your phone? I just need to get a ride home so I can leave you in peace."

"Make yourself comfortable," Celeas says again.

His response gives me the creeps for no reason I can explain. I take a steadying breath, trying to shake away the strange feeling that something's wrong. This is the only person around as far as I can see in the dark. He's done everything he can to, well...*make me comfortable.*

"You don't have any tech? Are you Amish or something?"

"I'm a farmer by trade," Celeas answers.

"Yeah, you mentioned that earlier."

I swallow down an anxious lump in my throat. Every true crime podcast I've ever listened to is playing through my brain. Staying at this man's house until daylight doesn't seem like a good idea, and walking around in the dark hoping for a ride home is an even worse one.

I'll lie down for a bit to rest my ankle. Maybe it'll feel somewhat better soon, and I'll have a solution.

I lay my head down, and the fuzzy feeling from before washes over me again. It helps with the pain in my ankle, but it's making it so I can barely think at all, and my eyelids grow very heavy.

Within minutes, I'm dreaming of a beautiful woman caressing my cheek. "You've done well," she says. "Bring me an offering, and I will reward you."

Then a disembodied but clear voice says, "Cleric of Aphrodite: Level 1. Spell Gained: Healing of Minor Wounds."

CHAPTER FIVE

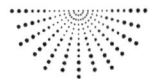

I wipe the sleep from my eyes. "Where the fuck am I?"

As I wake up and take in my surroundings, I realize that last night hadn't been a strange nightmare fueled by recent events. If anything, this is a sustained hallucination. That's the only way a parking lot could disappear, landing me in the middle of the woods until I could crash at some Amish dude's house. It also would account for some voice telling me I leveled up.

What's almost as weird is how great my mental clarity is within minutes of waking up. I haven't even had coffee yet. I'm sharp and aware of everything, but that's not necessarily a good thing for someone with my special brand of anxiety.

I've been so focused on the ren faire quality of the room I'm in that I take a while to realize something very important. My ankle feels fine. I lift it slightly and gasp when I see it. There's no more discoloration or swelling. I can stretch my foot this way and that without even a twinge of discomfort.

Where'd my t-shirt scrap I wrapped it with go?

No matter how much I look around, I can't find it anywhere, and there aren't exactly a lot of places for it to hide in this one-room hut.

Did the farmer take it? Did he touch me *in my sleep?*

A shiver rattles up my spine. My imagination certainly cooked up a total creep with Celeas.

I pinch myself, trying to snap myself out of this illusion. All it does is hurt a little. I slap my cheeks. Nothing. Everything seems too *real*—from the scratchiness of the bed to the smell of manure coming from outside.

What if I was coming out of my hallucination when I arrived at Celeas's place? That would explain a lot. If so, I definitely want to get as far from here as possible. Nothing in me wants to stay in a weird stranger's house a second longer.

Sadly, I still don't have a shirt to wear. I have to go outside with only a bra and leggings on like I'm doing the Walk of Shame.

I grab my purse and steel myself for judging eyes. I just need to get home. No one's going to arrest me for only having a bra as a top. It's the old ugly one that covers more than a bikini top. It's not like I'm breaking some nudity law. *Right?*

When I open the door, I realize I don't need to be afraid of people gawking at me. The only person around is Celeas, and he's busy ineffectually swishing a scythe around in one spot of a small patch of wheat immediately to the right of his hut. I know the polite thing to do is to thank him for his help before leaving but...

Fuck being polite. That dude gives me the fucking creeps.

I'm not sure I can simply sneak away without going through the forest again, though. There's a seemingly endless expanse of rolling green hills around me. If he pays attention to anything other than his mindless activity, he'll spot me. I decide to try it anyway and crouch as I turn the corner, keeping my eyes trained on Celeas as I do so. I should have done a better job looking where I was going because I stumble into an empty barrel and fall with a loud thud.

"Shit!" I shout on instinct and then immediately clap my hand over my mouth.

The farmer doesn't say anything or even look my way. He just keeps robotically swishing his scythe around. He has no clue I'm even there.

Did I die and become a ghost?

To test my morbid theory, I walk right up to Celeas and wave my hand in his face. He keeps his eyes focused on the wheat he's failing to reap, despite all his effort.

"Hello?" I say like it's a question.

At that, Celeas turns to face me.

"Hello," he says. "Sorry for the way I look. Farming makes me sweaty."

"Yeah, you said that before. Look, thanks for letting me crash at your place last night."

Celeas smiles. "I haven't had a guest in a long time. I'm not used to making myself presentable."

Déjà fucking vu, Mr. Serial Killer Vibes.

"Well, thanks again for letting me stay. You even let me sleep in your bed."

Without missing a beat, Celeas says, "Make yourself comfortable."

"Okay, I'm saying goodbye now!"

The farmer returns to swishing around like an idiot.

Jesus Fucking Christ, I need to get home.

I scan my surroundings, seeing nothing but a narrow dirt road stretching from another patch of woodland to the distant hills. No rideshare service would come out here. Not that I can get a ride without my cellphone.

The moment I groan at my situation, a small group of people around my age walks out from the trees. My first assumption is that they're part of the Amish community, but when they get closer, I see that they're dressed in cosplay. They're probably passing through like me.

On foot and in costume?

They're more prepared for whatever their journey is than I am, though. I look down at my bra. It's the comfy beige one with stains that I wear when I know there was no chance in hell I'm getting laid. Which is pretty much always.

At least one of them *has* to have a cell phone. So, as embarrassing as it is, I cross my arms over my chest and walk over.

It's a motley crew. There's a short young woman with chin-length black hair, a swarthy complexion, and hazel brown eyes. Based on her all-black clothing, she seems to be cosplaying as a ninja, sans the face covering. There's a redhead who looks a lot like if a Viking and a super-model had a baby. She's wearing a suit made entirely of animal skins. The third person is a black woman with a sweet smile and a pastel pink afro that reminds me of cotton candy. If not for the leather armor, I'd assume kawaii trinkets from her favorite animes filled her house.

There are also two men. One is lanky with pale skin, black hair, and blue eyes, and he holds a sword. He's exactly the kind of guy who would show you his sweet katana moves if you made the mistake of going to his house. The second one is handsome in an "I have a wicked sense of humor, but I can do more than make you laugh" kind of way. He looks a lot like a young Ryan Reynolds, but he's wearing robes and has a staff on his back instead of dressing up like Deadpool.

I hurry to them as best as I can without uncrossing my arms. "Hi! Can you help me?"

The cosplayers look at each other for a moment.

"Think this is an escort mission?" the redhead asks, sounding a lot like Regina George from *Mean Girls*. "I hate those."

"Escort? I just need—"

"She's wearing skimpy clothes," the guy with the sword says. "She might be a romanceable NPC. We're taking this quest."

"Don't be such a perv," the Ryan Reynolds lookalike says.

My cheeks burn with both embarrassment and anger. "Hey! Stop with your geeky role-playing! You're not at whatever con you're going to *yet!*"

Everyone stops talking to each other and stares at me.

"I just need to use someone's phone," I continue. "I got hurt yesterday. I lost my phone and had to stay in that creepy dude's house last night." I point at the still-swishing farmer and shudder.

"Celeas?" the woman with the pink hair asks. "He's not creepy. That's a great spot for a long rest."

"Y'all, she clearly has no idea what's going on," the ninja lady tells her friends. She turns to me, giving me the non-smile you give someone when you've got bad news, but you're trying to soften the blow by looking nice. "You're not in Kansas anymore, Dorothy."

I shake my head. "What the fuck are you talking about?"

"She's definitely not another NPC," the redhead says. "Not with a mouth like that."

"NPC...?"

"You're in a game," the pervy guy says. His friends glare at him. "What? Just ripping off the Band-Aid."

I roll my eyes. Obviously, they don't care about my situation and just want to keep dicking around. "Wow, okay, have fun at your con. You've all been *incredibly* unhelpful."

Ninja Lady grabs me by the arm before I can walk off. "Look, I know that's hard to swallow, but listen." She points at Celeas. "Didn't you notice anything weird about that farmer? Like he kept repeating the same stuff over and over?"

I don't answer, but the "yes" must be all over my face, because the woman nods.

"Was there something familiar about him, too?"

"Yeah..."

"Think," the woman says. "Where might you remember him from?" With her free hand, she motions to the surrounding scene. "Where might you remember any of this from?"

I search my mind. I've never been anywhere like this. The closest I've come to the countryside was a field trip I took to a petting zoo. Then, I notice dandelions swaying in the breeze on top of a nearby hill.

Oh, fuck. Oh, fuckkkkkk.

I feel like I should puke or pass out in a situation like this, but unfortunately, I'm as clear-headed as I was when I woke up.

"He's the farmer..." I whisper. "The first guy you meet in *Legends of Sacrifice.*"

⇧

After pacing around while repeating, "This can't be real" for a while, I finally calm down long enough to accept their invitation to join them at a tavern. I don't normally follow strangers to secondary locations, but they promised to tell me all they've learned about what's going on over some food, and I'm hungry now. I mean, my stomach is *growling*.

They introduce themselves along the way. Tara is the one wearing a ninja-like outfit, Cait is the redheaded cavewoman, Sylvia is the pink-haired chick, Joshua is the lanky dude, and Guy is the man wearing robes.

I laugh at the name Guy. When Guy looks confused, I explain that Ryan Reynolds played an NPC named Guy in a movie about being in a video game. When he still doesn't get it, I explain that he looks just like him. No one else seems to agree.

Seems like I'm the only purveyor of quality entertainment here.

When we reach their destination, everything feels even more surreal. The very fact that we're at a *tavern* is strange enough, but we're also surrounded by more NPCs. The only thing normal about this situation is that being in a crowded building is causing my social anxiety to rile up. Every time the NPCs lift their mugs and drink them in unison, it gets harder to breathe.

I thought I was doing a good job hiding it, but Joshua looks at me and then says, "They have outside seating where there are less NPCs. Let's sit there."

I'm incredibly thankful for his surprising kindness and sensitivity when, a minute later, there's a wall between us and the rumble of pretend conversations. A barmaid takes our orders. Every time one of us tells her what we want, she responds with, "Coming right up!"

"Gimme some of that milk!" Joshua says and honks as he mimics squeezing her breasts from several feet away.

Was this the same guy who helped me out when he saw a panic attack coming for me?

"Coming right up!" the barmaid responds in her chipper tone. Joshua snorts as he laughs.

Cait smacks him on the arm. "Stop that! It's stupid!"

Joshua laughs even harder at that. "She's just an NPC! She doesn't have feelings or anything."

"How do you know?" Tara asks. "I mean, we're in a video game. Nothing makes sense anymore. NPCs could have feelings, and we wouldn't know because they're stuck saying the same thing over and over."

"Besides, we're all a little tired of you being so pervy," Cait says.

Joshua looks to the only other man in the group for support, but Guy looks back at him with a stone-cold expression.

"Oh, come on, Guy!" Joshua says. "It's not like you're innocent. I've seen you glancing at Lauren's tits."

Guy ducks his chin down as a blush spreads over his olive skin. "No, I haven't."

I cross my arms over my chest again.

"Can we move on from this?" Sylvia says. "We have a lot to tell Lauren." She gives me a sympathetic smile. "Though, I think the first thing we need to do is figure out your class so we can get you something to cover yourself with."

Cait half grunts, half laughs. "Better hope she's not a bard like Joshua. The female version of that getup is pretty much what she's wearing right now."

"I don't know what my class is," I say.

Sylvia squints at me. "You don't? You should have been assigned a class and deity on your first night here."

"On the way here, you said you felt drugged last night," Tara interjects. "Is it possible you thought you were dreaming or something?"

The previous night's dream comes back to me, and I groan. "Fuck me," I mutter.

Joshua smirks, and Cait smacks him on the arm again. He looks at her incredulously. "What was that for?" he asks.

"I think you know," she says.

"But I didn't say anything."

Cait narrows her eyes at him. "But you thought it."

Tara glares at them. "This is important. Let Lauren speak."

"I'm a fucking cleric," I say. "A Cleric of Aphrodite."

The whole group brightens up.

"*Thank God!*" Guy cries out. "We've needed a healer so bad. I can barely make it out of a fight alive!"

"That's a great class. Why do you look so sad?" Tara asks.

"I hate playing healers," I explain. "I did it for a while in an MMO, and other players always treated me like absolute crap during raids. DPS is more my speed."

"Well, we won't be mean to you!" Sylvia says with a bright smile. "If you travel with us, we'd be really grateful."

Cait looks at me with knowing eyes. "I know what you mean. Sometimes tanks pull way too much aggro and then there's always some asshole who runs off and gets himself in hot water. But *I'm* the tank of this group, and before I got here, I usually played a healer class, so I know how to work with clerics."

"Well, actually, I'm the tank," Joshua interjects.

"Not this again," Guy groans. "Joshua, you may have a sword, but you're a bard. You're support DPS. Cait's a barbarian."

I listen to the group squabble for a bit over their dynamics, while I sulk over my assignment. It's not fair. I want to beat up bad guys, not be everyone's nurse.

"How did I even get assigned this class?" I complain. "Why didn't I get to choose?"

Tara shrugs. "Well, we don't know for sure, but we have a pretty solid hypothesis."

"Elaborate."

Tara goes into a long, eye-opening explanation. She thinks we went into the game without a class or deity, and our actions that first day determined our assignments. On Tara's first day, she'd stumbled into an area rife with monsters, so she hid for a long time until she could sneak out. Once she made it to a village, she was starving but didn't have any money. So, she stole food from vendor stalls until she could get money with her first quest.

"So, on my first night, I was given the title Rogue of Hermes," she says.

"Me next!" Sylvia says with a beaming smile. "I came through the woods, and there was this puppy cornered by wolves. I couldn't just let the puppy get eaten up! So, I started throwing rocks at the wolves."

I gasp. "How are you alive?"

"I have great aim. Of course, it only made them dizzy. So, I had to scoop up the puppy and run out of there before they could chase after us. Now I'm a Ranger of Artemis."

"You *really* lucked out," Cait says and then she sighs. "I didn't. When I got here, I walked right into a giant wasp nest and got stung all over."

I wince. "What did you do?"

"I screamed and beat the nest with a branch like it was a piñata."

I stare at her open-mouthed.

"What? I wanted to make sure the wasps died," Cait explains.

"I think I would have just run away."

Cait nods. "Yeah, that's probably what I should have done, but it seems I go with the fight instinct when it comes to fight or flight. Anyway, I'm an Axe of Ares."

"The first people I saw here were a bunch of women warriors," Joshua says. "I thought they were LARPers, so I showed them my sick sword-fighting skills with a stick, thought maybe I'd get laid. Anyway, they weren't pretending like me; they were Amazonians. They seemed to think I'm funny, though, so now I'm a Bard of Pan."

So far, every single one of them has a story that suits them perfectly. *Especially* Joshua.

I turn to Guy. "What about you?"

"Well, I don't remember much," Guy explains, his eyes fixed on his ale. "I...I was pretty drunk when I wound up here, so it's all kind of a blur, but I'm a Mage of Dionysus."

I can picture Guy being some kind of frat bro waking up after a keg party, not knowing what the fuck happened while a voice tells him he's a Mage of Dionysus. It's kind of a cute image for some reason.

"What was your first day like?" Tara asks me.

"Well, I was lost in the woods, and I hurt my ankle," I answer. "So, I took some aspirin and used my shirt to wrap up my sprain."

Tara nods. "Makes sense you'd be a cleric. Not sure why for Aphrodite, though. I mean, Hermes makes sense for me because I tried to steal something. Artemis makes sense for someone who could clock some wolves with rocks. Ares chose Cait because she fought the wasps attacking her. Pan chose Joshua because...well...probably because he's horny. And Guy was drunk, which is kind of Dionysus's whole thing."

I think through the previous day's experiences. All I'd done was wander around with a sprained ankle, swearing even more than usual. Then it hits me.

"Holy fuck," I mutter.

"God, you really curse a lot," Cait mutters.

At the same time, Guy chuckles and says, "You don't hold back, do you?"

"No, that's the answer," I explain. "I said that when I hurt my ankle. Who else would answer to *Holy Fuck,* but the holiest of all fucking, the Goddess of Love and Sex?"

The barmaid returns to the table with platters of food.

My heart sinks, because I realize I can't pay. Guy notices my distress, and says, "Don't worry, I've got this covered."

He taps at some invisible points in the air, and then the barmaid sets everything on the table.

"What was that?" I ask.

Guy squints. "What do you mean? I just paid her from my inventory menu."

Sylvia smacks herself on the forehead. "Oh! She hasn't set up her UI yet. She probably slept through the voice's instructions on that."

"UI? Like how I'd see things in a game?" I ask.

Sylvia nods. "Say something like 'Menu up' or 'See my settings.'"

"Uh... Show me my settings."

Too many words and symbols pop up at once, blocking my entire scope of vision. "What the *fuck*?"

Cait groans. "Can you at least *try* to watch your language?"

"Now say 'Give me default settings,'" Sylvia says.

"Give me default settings," I parrot.

Suddenly, most of my vision is almost as clear as it had been a moment ago, except that now I see details that hadn't been there before. For instance, above everyone's heads are their assigned class and deity. I tap on the top of my head as if I could feel the label above my own.

"Do I...?"

Sylvia shakes her head. "No, you don't have your title turned on. Tell it to turn on your title if you want other people to see it."

"Is there a reason to have it on?"

Guy shrugs. "I have mine on in case I bump into other players. Sort of, like, 'Hey, I'm one of you.'"

That makes sense to me, so I say, "Turn on my title."

Guy smiles and gives me a thumbs up, confirming it worked.

I redirect my attention to the bottom of my vision. Just like in *Legends of Sacrifice*, I have a row of twelve spell slot boxes at the bottom. Only one of them has a symbol in it. I tap on it, and a disembodied voice says, "You must choose an appropriate target before you can cast Healing of Minor Wounds."

"Who *is* that?" I ask.

"The voice?" Sylvia asks. "Yeah, I don't know who that is, but they kinda help you in the game. They're who taught me how to do all this UI stuff. Like I said, you probably slept through that part."

"Oh, well...I guess I have a spell called Healing of Minor Wounds, but I need to select a target to cast it."

Tara rolls up her sleeve to display a nasty bruise. "Got this when we were fighting some rock elementals this morning. Point at me and then tap the spell. Just as a forewarning, you'll notice that casting a spell will make you feel a little tired. There's no limit on how many spells you can cast, but the lower your level, the fewer spells you can cast before you pass out."

I gulp. "Pass out?"

"It won't happen at once," Tara clarifies. "You'll feel worn out first. It's your sign to stop spell casting before you really do pass out. I don't think casting your one spell on my bruise will do much, though. Give it a try."

I do as I'm told and then watch in awe as Tara's bruise simply blinks away. Just like she said, I feel a slight loss of energy, kind of like I want to curl up in a more comfortable chair.

The Rogue of Hermes sighs in relief. "Thank God," she says. "I really didn't want to be in pain until we could take a long rest."

"So there are long rests here, too?" I ask.

Everyone nods.

"You all learned a lot fast."

"We've been here for ages," Joshua says.

"But...the game just came out yesterday."

"We were beta players," Tara explains. "Not that it clears up much. I mean, how is any of this possible?"

"Give it a rest, Tara," Cait whispers.

Tara rolls her eyes. "Fine. I'll stop making y'all *think*. You can put your blindfolds back on."

"We can get philosophical when we're not struggling to survive," Cait says. "For now, let's just focus on getting our offerings to our deities."

I remember my dream again. The beautiful woman who talked to me must have been Aphrodite. She'd said something about rewarding me if I brought her an offering. "What kind of offering?"

Guy shakes his head. "We don't really know. Something our particular deity would want. We just go around doing the quests they give us and hoping we get a clue because they'll reward us whatever we ask for if we get it right."

Quests? I search around my peripheral vision until I see a little glowing blue box that says, "*Quest Log.*" I tap it and there are two quests listed. One is struck through to show it's complete: *Heal Wound.* The other one makes me blush: *Inspire Lust.* Then I watch a line cross through those words. I barely hold back a gasp before I look around at my tablemates. None of them are leering at me, not even Joshua, who seems distracted by the barmaid's bottom as she leans over another table.

Before I can figure out whose lust I inspired, another quest pops up: *Speak with Alexander.* I really do gasp this time and look up to see the romanceable NPC I swooned over during gameplay. He's leaning against the back fence with a blue orb over his head.

And he's looking straight at me.

CHAPTER SIX

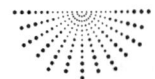

My new acquaintances chatter noisily about something. I don't know if they're always this talkative, or it's just because I'm around. I don't care. Alexander, *the* Alexander, is waiting for me to talk to him. So, I get up from my seat, ignoring everything but his handsome face.

Because of the UI, I can see a small, glowing blue orb above his head. When I played the game, that marked an NPC with an available quest. Given what's in my quest log, I assume it means the same thing here.

As beautiful as he was as an animation in a video game, he's drop-dead gorgeous in living flesh. A stubborn lock of his dark hair brushes the edge of one serious eyebrow. His brown eyes somehow communicate the pain in his heart, as well as his interest in speaking with me.

When I get close enough to speak to Alexander, I can see his chest hairs peeking through the V of his tunic. There's also a hint of his pectoral muscles that the cloth mostly obscures. I tilt my chin up to look at his face, knowing it will give him a full view of my blushing cheeks.

"H-hello," I whisper.

"Hello, there!" Alexander says. "I haven't seen you here before. Are you an adventurer?"

Ah, yes. We're at this part.

Remembering that he's another NPC douses the flames burning in my chest and on my cheeks. He's programmed to gaze at every player this way, not just me.

"Um, yes, I am."

"I was once an adventurer," he says, "but the gods have cursed me to never lift a blade again."

"Because of Phoebe..." I mutter to myself.

"Because of Phoebe," Alexander continues. "She was the most beautiful woman I've ever seen, but my thirst for glory made me careless. When I set fire to the nest of harpies, I didn't realize they had kidnapped her and hidden her there. Now, she's dead and by my hand. For my sin, I can never touch my sword again."

I take a moment to think about how best to respond to his backstory monologue. I could ask him if he needs my help. That would lead to the first quest, which is finding Phoebe's locket in the ruins of the harpy's nest. I could also take some time to get to know him, which would mean a lot of rehashing conversational points.

Is there a Skip Dialogue option somewhere on my UI?

Alexander's face holds the endless patience that NPCs exhibit while players deliberate over the best course of action. His dark hair is so shiny and healthy, not at all digital in appearance. I bet if I stroked it, my fingers would feel like they were combing a gentle stream. His eyes absolutely smolder with regret and longing. He looks like every guy I ever crushed on but never had the guts to approach. For a moment, I wonder just how far his NPC coding goes.

Lauren, you need to do the quest. Getting back to Mom is more important than seeing if you can romance an NPC in person.

"Do you need my help?" I ask.

"My love had a locket," Alexander answers. "It's still in the ruins of the harpy's nest. Can you retrieve it for me? I cannot fight any beasts that may arrive, so I have no way to get it myself."

"I'll do that for you."

The blue orb above Alexander's head turns yellow. My quest log's glow also turns yellow.

I return to the table, feeling heavier than I had before. It was unreasonable of me to want Alexander to speak with me in an authentic, unscripted way. He's a video game character. Still, it reminded me of what I realized when I broke up with Doug. I'll never find real love. My choices are heartbreak or fiction.

"Harpy quest?" Cait asks.

"Yeah."

"Well, it's a necessary one to get through to the better ones," she says and then sighs. "It's super boring, but we'll help you out with it."

"It should give you enough money to buy some beginner equipment," Sylvia chimes in. "You'll need a mana-enhancing robe and a staff."

Everyone around the table discusses the fastest path to level me up. They have months of experience on me, and they need me to be as prepared as possible to heal them on their higher-level quests. Tara's silent, though. Every time I glance over, she's studying me intently.

Suddenly, she interrupts the conversation. "We're not rushing her off to any quests today, y'all."

Cait blinks. "Why not? It's an easy quest."

"Look at her," Tara says, pointing at me. "She just found out she's in a game, but it hasn't sunk in yet. That's going to happen soon, though, because a major character just proved himself to be nothing more than an NPC with better dialogue options."

"So?" Joshua pipes up. "We all had to go through the same thing, and we didn't get a break from the game to do it."

"Because we were alone; because we didn't have a choice," Tara counters. "She has *us* though. Why make her go through what we went through? Let's help her get used to this world before we throw her into combat."

Sylvia nods. "I agree with Tara."

"Well, what about what Lauren wants?" Guy asks. He turns his deep brown eyes to me. "How do you want to do this?"

I consider my options. Taking the day to contemplate my situation tempts me for a moment, but it gives me anxiety just thinking about how much thinking I've yet to think.

Does that make sense?

I don't want to confront reality—or whatever this is—yet. I'd rather jump into quests to distract myself from how scary my situation is.

"Cait, how fast do you think we can get this harpy quest done?" I ask.

Cait twists her lips to the side and taps her chin. "Well, it takes about fifteen minutes to walk there and about twenty minutes to find the locket in all the ash. There's a mini-boss battle with a surviving harpy. Took us maybe three minutes to finish her off last time. Then it's fifteen minutes to get back here and turn in the quest to Alex."

"So, about an hour," I say. Then I turn to Sylvia. "Let's do this. If you help me with stuff like this, I'll be your healer."

Everyone cheers, especially Guy.

Poor mages. They're like tissue paper in a fire. I better learn more than Healing of Minor Wounds if I want to keep this handsome man alive.

⇧

GETTING PHOEBE'S LOCKET FROM THE HARPY NEST IS THE ONE *Legends of Sacrifice* main quest I completed before my computer died. It was a pretty quick one, only requiring me to dig around in the ashes for a while, pluck out the locket, and take care of the surviving harpy who showed up. That *had* been easy while playing it on a computer as a monk. In "real" life on a rainy day as a cleric with only one spell, however...?

"What the fuck?!" I shout.

The harpy shrieks from above, her raptor-like claws extended. I don't know whether the harpy wants to use those claws to rake me across the face or guts. Maybe she wants to snatch me from the nest and drop me from a great height. Whatever the case, with no defensive or offensive spells to use in the situation, I *need* to get out of the nest ruins and run away!

However, I'm right in the middle of the nest, and it was like crossing over a dune to get here. The paste of damp ash on my hands and feet is crystalizing and producing a painful heat.

Why does it burn? Does ash really do this when it goes from wet to dry? Stupid programmers!

Getting out feels impossible. I'm not at all helpful in this situation. Honestly, I'm probably holding them back. Every time I try to take a step out of this muck, the pain of my efforts causes me to wince and grab

Cait's arm. She can't do what she needs to do because I'm clinging to her like a toddler having a tantrum.

"Duck!" Cait shouts, pushing me off her, and she dashes in front to block me from the monster swooping down on us.

The screeching creature with the face of a woman and wings of a buzzard reaches out to grab Cait, but the barbarian pulls out a great axe from thin air at the last moment and cleaves the harpy's leg from her body. Rusty brown liquid pours from the monster's stump. It's beyond disgusting, but of course, Cait's somehow still fucking gorgeous covered in its blood.

Still, the harpy isn't dead. As shrill as she'd been before the attack, her screams are even more ear-splitting now.

The harpy rises high in the air. For the briefest moment, I think she might be retreating. But the wound only caused the harpy's wrath to intensify, and she's readying for another attack.

"Sylvia, get your bow ready!" Guy calls out, as he produces a ball of lightning in the hand he isn't holding his staff with.

The archer gives a curt nod in response, but her eyes never leave the harpy. Just as Cait pulls her great axe out of nowhere, Sylvia knocks a flaming arrow onto it.

"Sylvia, no!" Guy shouts. "The ash may still be flammable!"

"But it's wet!" Sylvia calls back.

"Don't risk it!" Cait shouts. "A regular arrow will do. Now stop talking and get ready to attack!" Under her breath she mutters, "We'd be done with this already if not for the—"

The harpy swoops down on us again. This time, though, she curves her flight path at the last second so that she's behind me. Before I can turn around to face the monster, an arrow and a bolt of lightning strike it. A health bar pops up above her head, showing that they've taken half her life away—not enough to give me peace of mind.

"Get behind—" Cait starts.

Joshua comes dashing in front of me, shouting, "Leeeeeeeeeroy Jenkins!"

"Oh, for Pete's sake," Cait grumbles, as Joshua swings his sword wildly at the harpy.

Joshua slices the harpy's stomach. It looks gruesome, but it seems to be only superficial since the health bar barely nudges. He juts his sword forward, puncturing the monster. This time, his attack is effective, bringing her almost all the way down. Unfortunately for him, she responds to that by clawing at his chest.

Screaming, Joshua buckles to his knees, leaving me face-to-face with the harpy. The creature's eyeballs are entirely red, even the sclera. They glow with rage, searing my face. The harpy moves to bite me with her sharp, blood-stained teeth, but another of Sylvia's arrows strikes the beast, this time in her temple.

The harpy's eyes lose their glow, and she falls the few feet she'd been hovering from. Slumped on the ash, she doesn't seem as large or terrifying anymore. Death has taken the monstrosity out of her. That, more than the attack, shakes me. I've only ever seen death once: when I came home from school to find my cat curled up under my bed. This is different. This looks almost like a person.

For a split second, I see Mom's face. I hear her soft whisper of my name. The illusion passes faster than I can register it, but now I'm consumed by one thought: this will be Mom soon.

I need to get out of this game.

"Ugh! Can someone cover her up?" Cait asks, sneering at the corpse. "I mean, why did the game designers have to give harpies such big breasts that they don't even put a bra over? Tired of seeing their nipples all over the place."

I stare at Cait in horror. "There are more of them?"

Will I see Mom's face in each of theirs?

"Oh, yeah," Cait answers. "There's a whole quest line of ridding them from this series of islands called the Strophades. It's such a snooze. I hate grinding."

"Helps bump that XP way up, though," Tara says, climbing down the ash dune.

"Where were you?" Cait asks.

Tara shrugs. "Hiding until you needed me for a sneak attack, like a rogue should."

"Can our cleric make herself useful?" Joshua groans in pain. "Please?"

I shake myself out of my emotional turmoil and bend over the bard. "Sorry, still getting used to this. Let me see your injury."

Joshua pulls up the tatters of his blood-soaked shirt, exposing deep claw marks in his chest. Everyone winces in unison.

"That looks like more than a minor wound," Sylvia says, her voice soft with empathy.

I tap on my one spell, anyway.

"You must choose an appropriate target before you can cast Healing of Minor Wounds," the disembodied voice says.

"But I chose a target!" I respond. "I thought it would at least help a little bit."

Guy shakes his head. "That's not how it works. If your spell doesn't do exactly what the situation calls for, it doesn't do anything at all. The right target would have a minor wound, and this is a major wound."

"We need to get him to a temple," Tara says. "Gonna be hard carrying him out of all this ash in his state, though."

"Let me see if I can do something to at least stabilize him so we can get him out of here." I rifle through my purse, finding the part of my torn shirt I didn't use yesterday and pressing it to his wound.

"Didn't you say you had aspirin?" Cait asks. "Give that to him, too."

I shake my head. "That will inhibit clotting. That's the last thing he needs." I size Cait up and down. She's built for cheerleading, not the life of a barbarian. Yet, she did one hell of a job with the harpy. "Does your class make you really strong?"

"Yeah, of course."

"Is it possible for you to carry him over the dune while I keep a firm press on his wound?"

Cait nods. "That shouldn't be too hard."

"Well, let's get going, then. It's going to take us at least half an hour to get to the temple since we'll have to walk slowly."

Guy's lips form a grim flat line, making my heart sink. He's upset about his friend being hurt, and if I hadn't been so quick to jump into this quest, maybe Joshua wouldn't be in this state. I hardly know this group, but it matters to me a lot that I make them happy. Especially Guy, for some reason.

C'mon, Lauren. You know it's because he's hot.

I promise myself that I'll figure out how to acquire spells and be fully prepared before doing any more questing.

THE WALK TO THE TEMPLE GOES THROUGH THE VILLAGE. IN ANY location from the world beyond, we probably would have drawn as much attention as a parade would receive. Here, though, the NPCs are oblivious. Their wordless chatter acts as background noise for their cycle of activities. They examine items at merchant stalls, walk in and out of buildings, and mill about aimlessly on the roads. Two men even get into a fight that ends with them both on the ground before they right themselves and begin again.

It's way too much for my social anxiety, which is almost comical. These aren't people. They don't even know I'm here. I would have to be the one to establish any interaction with them, and I'd control the whole thing.

Yet, I desperately wish I had my pink cat ear headphones, and I'm grateful when Tara insists we don't stay long enough to shop there for my supplies. She says I need a long rest before making decisions like that.

When we get to the temple, none of the NPC priestesses even notice our entrance until Guy tells one by a back door that Joshua needs healing.

"Let's see what we've got here," the priestess says.

We don't need to lift the cloth; the priestess's programming tells her exactly what the problem is. She waves her hands over the wound, and a pale yellow light spreads over Joshua's chest.

In an instant, Joshua's facial features, which had been twisted together in agony, relax, and he says in a dreamy voice, "All better."

I take the makeshift bandage off, revealing a chest that doesn't appear to have ever suffered a wound. This is the magic common in video games, but it still stuns me that I can't even see a trace of a scar.

Cait slowly sets him down until his feet solidly plant on the ground. Then she slaps him across the face.

Joshua winces and rubs at the red spot on his cheek. "What was that for?!"

"You idiot!" Cait yells. "What were you thinking running in like that? You even did that whole Leroy Jenkins schtick again. Did you forget you can actually *die* here?"

I gasp.

We can die?

"We don't know that for sure," Tara interjects. "People don't *respawn*. They could be alive outside of the game."

Cait growls at Tara, who in turn lifts her hands in surrender.

"Come on," Joshua says. "That quest is so easy for players our level that I thought I'd have a little fun with it."

"Battles aren't for fun!" Cait shouts in exasperation.

"Well..." Guy says with a shrug. "We're all here because a game like this is how we had fun. I mean I get to do *magic* during our battles. That never gets old."

Cait crosses her arms, turning her glare toward Guy. "Yeah, it was a good time *then*. Back when we could just go back to our last save when we died."

Sylvia nods. "Or pause a battle to drink a healing potion when we got injured."

"Ehhh..." Tara says with a non-committal shrug. "I mean something like this could have been how Joshua found out what his offering should be."

"Whatever," Cait says rolling her eyes.

I raise my hand like I'm in school and wait for the group's attention before saying, "We can die here? Like really die?"

There's a mixed reaction from the group. Cait's face darkens with pain, Joshua and Guy look down at their feet, Tara nods solemnly, and Sylvia looks at me with the most compassionate expression I've seen since a doctor told me about Mom's strokes.

Sylvia pats my upper arm. "I keep forgetting you're brand-new. You haven't seen the things we have."

"It's why we're so happy to find a healer," Tara adds.

"And I rushed us into a battle when I wasn't prepared." I shake my head, disgusted with myself. "I should have gotten a robe and a staff and learned at least one more spell before we went there."

"It's not your fault," Sylvia responds. "Joshua was right that this quest is easy for us now. You should've been able to grab the locket and leave while we handled the harpy on our own. Joshua made his choice, knowing that you only knew Healing of Minor Wounds."

Guy nods along to Sylvia's statement and adds, "Besides, you were able to use your head and help Joshua even without having higher-level spells. That's pretty impressive."

I want to believe what they're saying, but it's a struggle. I feel so useless. This is part of why I don't like playing a healer class. I can't really do much to battle the bad guys.

However, as I remember the way the harpy had lain on the ground lifeless, I'm not sure if I could have killed someone even if I was a class that specialized in offense. I know it was either going to be my life or the harpy's, but the creature had a human face, one that reminded me of Mom. I can't help but wonder if she really was a monster or just a grieving woman that wanted people to leave the ruins of her home alone.

Sylvia puts a hand on my shoulder. "Let's get you a bath, some food, and a long rest. You need time to process everything that happened today."

I don't want to process *anything*, but I know Sylvia's right. I give her a slow nod and let the group lead me to their camp on the outskirts of the village.

It's a lot grander than I expected. Perhaps because they've been in this world so long, they have a large tent that reminds me a little of the kind you see with traveling circuses.

In front of it is a fire pit. Tara collects firewood, which Cait chops up and tosses into the pit. Guy uses a small flame in his palm to light it. Joshua plays his fiddle to lift everyone's spirits, while Sylvia cooks up a pot of stew over the fire. The smell of it is the only thing that keeps me awake as I soak in the bath that Sylvia drew for me.

Afterward, we all sit around the fire and eat. The group chats away. I don't know about what, and I don't really care, as I chew my food in silence, thinking about the dead harpy and the wound I couldn't heal. Despite this cycle of disturbing thoughts, I fall asleep within a minute of resting my head on the straw-filled pillow Sylvia gave me.

However, before I drift off, I hear the disembodied say, "Cleric of Aphrodite: Level 2. Spell gained: Healing of Major Wounds."

CHAPTER SEVEN

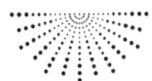

The next morning, my new friends convince me to get actual clothing before turning in my quest to Alexander. Now that the shock of my new situation has settled, it doesn't take much to persuade me. I can't believe I charged right into a dangerous quest wearing a bra and leggings. At breakfast, Tara explained to me that my hasty decisions were probably an emotional response to my shock over the situation. I'm going with that excuse instead of admitting I'm a dumbass.

Now, we're back in the starter village, walking down a row of merchant stalls lined up against the temple's stone wall on the right. The background noise of wordless chatter has risen to a roar as we navigate the dense throng of shoppers and traders. Once again, I wish I had my noise-canceling headphones or that I could sit somewhere away from it all. I feel like I might cry as I notice how much more crowded it is up ahead. On a good day, I struggle with sensory overload, but I'm already overwhelmed by my current situation. How am I going to survive this?

I turn to Sylvia and ask her if there's a way to control volume levels in the game. Sylvia offers me a sympathetic frown and shakes her pink-haired head.

Guy rushes up to my side. "No, but I can create a small silencing spell." He taps on his ear before pointing at mine. "May I?"

Normally, I don't like anyone touching me. The few exceptions to this are Mom and Doug. Well, I guess it's just Mom now because I'd knee my ex-boyfriend in the groin if he came in for a hug now. This is different, though. I need as much help as I can get if I want to survive this situation. If that means letting someone touch my ear to shut off the current source of my torture, I won't complain. Besides, Guy is pretty hot. So, I nod, and he leans in close.

Guy traces the shell-like curve of my ear, while tapping a few places on his personal UI with his free hand. His finger tickles pleasantly, sending little tingles along my scalp. Then he tugs at my earlobe, and suddenly the world is jarringly silent. I can do more than take shallow, painful breaths now, so I gulp down a deep lungful of air.

"Thank you," I whisper.

"You're welcome," he says.

Guy's voice is so much clearer without the useless babble of NPCs competing for my subconscious attention. It's calm and breathy, like a nurse checking on your vitals in the middle of the night. My pulse slows, no longer at the bidding of my anxiety. If we ever make it back to the real world, he should make his own ASMR channel on YouTube.

"How can I hear you?" I ask.

"Silencing spells are used to nullify enemy spells in battle but allow party members to speak to each other."

I tilt my head. "We're party members?"

"I just put you on my party list in my menu." Guy licks his bottom lip subtly enough that he could have just been thinking, but it makes something hot coil deep within me. "Hope that's okay."

"That's okay," I say, more breathless than I intended. I clear my throat. "You'd make a better healer than me."

That earns a chuckle from Guy. "And give up spitting out icicles from my palms? No way!"

If I were him, I wouldn't want to make the trade either. There's nothing badass about wrapping a t-shirt around an ankle.

At last, we make it to our destination. I hadn't noticed this when we went to the healers in the back the previous day. At first, it looks like any other stall in the market, but then I see that within the tent is a doorway into the temple.

"Why is the shop in the temple?" I ask Guy.

Cait answers before Guy can. "Where else would a cleric get their gear?"

I huff. "Well, why didn't we go through the temple entrance from the beginning?"

"They're at prayer on the other side," she answers.

"Are you *actually* concerned about interrupting some NPCs during their fake worship?"

"I'm not, but Tara will pitch a fit." Cait points at our rogue with her thumb. "She's got this theory that the NPCs have actual emotions, but they can only do and say the same things they're programmed for."

"Just hedging my bets is all," Tara responds. "If the AI suddenly shifts, I don't want to be targeted as one of the jerks who treated them like garbage."

Tara nods in Joshua's direction. He doesn't notice her as he pulls down a shopper's pants and laughs. God, he's a moron sometimes.

We make our way inside, and I see that the shop is a long hallway with a door at the far end. A merchant waves at me and shouts something, but I can't hear a word thanks to Guy's silencing spell.

"Oh, great, how am I going to shop if I can't hear what the shop-keepers are saying to me?"

"I'll handle it," Guy answers.

Cait crosses her arms and shakes her head. "She'll still need to hear Aphrodite, and you can't add a god to our party."

At the mention of Aphrodite, a familiar calm washes over me. It feels fuzzy, like what I'd experienced on that first day while I dealt with my sprained ankle. Only this time, it doesn't sedate me. In fact, I feel invigorated.

"I think maybe it's different here in the temple," I tell Guy. "Try removing the silencing spell."

Guy arches a brow. "You sure?"

Embarrassment floods me. He thinks I'm too weak to know what I can handle.

"She knows her own mind, Guy!" Cait says in a commanding—dare I say Karenish—tone. With her whole Viking look, it comes off as sexy instead of bitchy, though.

49

Am I...bi? No, I can just appreciate that hot people are hot.

"Turn off the spell and let her handle this!" Cait continues.

Guy's eyes widen in shock, but after a beat, he responds with a slow nod and taps a few spots on the UI only visible to him. Suddenly, the world comes back to life. Worshipful chanting on the other side of the wall drifts over to our side. Their muffled words praise every major god in the pantheon. When I hear "Aphrodite," another wave of that delicious fuzziness caresses me. I may not like being a cleric, but I certainly appreciate that Aphrodite somehow has a hand in easing my anxiety.

My quest log box dings, and I open it up, reading, *"Pray to Aphrodite."* I puff out a breath, letting my lips blubber as I do.

"What's wrong?" Sylvia asks.

"Looks like I'll need to pause our trip and join worship," I answer.

Sylvia chuckles. "The temple is always open for players to pray, even when the NPCs have stopped for the day. You have plenty of time to get gear beforehand. Besides, I'm not sure your deity will take kindly to you showing up for service in your current getup."

I look down at myself. My designated comfy bra has sported sweat stains for years, but now it's brown from drying harpy blood. My black leggings are stiff with blood as well. The image of the harpy's lifeless body ambushes me. Mom's blank stare flashes alongside it. I almost disassociate, but I know I can't survive if I keep spiraling like this. So, I shake myself out of it before it can get worse, shoving down that grief as deep as I can force it.

I take a deep breath. "Yeah, you're right. Who do I talk to about a robe?"

"Robes are with the man on the right who's wearing yellow," Sylvia answers, gesturing in his direction.

"Don't forget your staff," Guy reminds me. "You'll need one if you want to cast without having to poke at things in your menu."

Oh, so that's why it seemed like they were actually fighting against the harpy, instead of tapping stuff in the air. Apparently, using gear we're proficient in can take the place of a menu so a staff would do a lot to help speed up my reaction time. Well, once I have some proper spells that I can use during combat, that is.

I get to the man wearing yellow and see that he has a simple robe on a mannequin behind him. There are no other garments in sight. Will he magically produce alternative selections out of thin air, or this is the only outfit a cleric can get in the starter village?

"Can I see your robes?" I ask him.

"You may purchase the robe behind me for four copper pieces," he answers.

Well, that answers that question. I'm a little disappointed. It's so ordinary. Also, it's white. I don't foresee that staying clean for even a day. Still, it's a far cry better than what I'm currently wearing. Plus Guy said earlier that wearing a robe makes it so that I'm far slower to wear out from spell casting.

Since I haven't turned in the locket to Alexander yet, I don't have any coins on me. Fortunately, Guy promised that morning he would purchase my gear until I could pay him back. Four copper pieces don't seem like a lot, but when I look at the details of the locket quest, I see that I'll only get twelve when I turn it in. I really hope the staff isn't a fortune.

The NPC merchant takes the cleric robe off the mannequin and hands it to me. I look around the hallway, hoping there's a changing room somewhere.

"Look at the top right corner," Sylvia instructs. "There should be a button there that says gear. Tap it and then tap the button for armor. This isn't technically armor, but it goes in the same slot."

I do as I'm told, and suddenly I'm no longer wearing the tatters of an already frumpy outfit. To my surprise, the white robe fits me nicely. It's a loose chiton made of linen, with a gold chain cinching the waist, creating a flattering drapery. I swear it hadn't looked like that on the mannequin.

Sylvia presses her hands together below her tilted chin and looks at me the way my mom did whenever I did something cute as a child. "You look so beautiful," she says.

I scan the faces in my group. "Yeah?"

They all nod with genuine expressions on their faces. Even Joshua looks at me with a smile instead of a pervy smirk. I feel a little better about the sole choice given to me for attire.

"Let's get you a staff," Guy says, and he ushers me further down the hall until we're face-to-face with a woman in red standing in front of a row of four staffs bearing gems of various colors at the tips.

Thank God! I get more than one choice here.

"Can you tell me about your staffs?" I ask the woman.

"We have four cleric staffs," the woman answers. "All four heal, but each grants a different additional spell. The staff with a red gem can cast a fire spell of your choice, the yellow gem can cast a smiting spell, the green gem can cast a poison spell, and the pink gem can cast a charm spell."

I suck in an indecisive breath between my teeth. "Ooh, that's a hard choice."

"Well, what are you gravitating toward?" Cait asks me, sounding a little impatient with me. As gorgeous as she is, I don't like it when she's grumpy with me. For some reason, I don't exactly *hate* it either. It suits her.

Fire spells are a lot of fun but can be pretty dangerous in the wrong setting. Poison is good, too, but...

I turn my gaze from the staffs to Cait. "Are there any poison-resistant enemies in this game?"

Cait shrugs. "I've only encountered a few."

With a nod, I turn to the merchant. "I'll take the staff with the green gem."

The woman smiles and extends the staff in my direction. "That will be nine copper pieces."

I wince, but Guy produces the copper right away. I'm going to owe him even after Alexander pays me for the locket.

When I reach to grab the staff, my peripheral vision grays out and red words in all caps appear: *"Not proficient in poison magic."* The staff disappears from the merchant's hand and returns to the row behind her. The nine copper pieces jingle as they return to Guy's pocket.

"Okay, then," I say. "Guess, I'll go with the red gem staff."

Once again, I'm not able to grab the staff presented to me. Turns out, I'm not proficient in fire magic either. The yellow gem staff gives me the same issue. That leaves only the staff with the pink gem. Out of all the staffs presented, this is the one I want the least. In fact, I don't want it at all. Charm magic isn't my thing. I'd rather beat a monster's head in than persuade it to let me pass by.

I think back to the harpy's shrill cry as she dove at me, claws ready to rake off my face. I remembered her bleeding stump and pierced temple.

Who am I kidding? If I could have charmed that harpy into giving me the locket, I would have taken that option.

"Well, let's try the pink gem," I say.

This time, the exchange works.

"That was so weird," Cait says. "Those were all cleric staffs. They all should be available as an option."

"Maybe it's because she's a Cleric of Aphrodite," Sylvia chimes in. "She doesn't really do violence. She gets what she wants by other means."

I think about mentioning that she had an affair with Ares, the god of war, but I have a feeling that might upset my patron deity.

"Well, a staff is a staff, and now I won't have to use my menu in a fight," I say as I place my new purchase in the weapon slot on my menu.

The staff poofs out of my hand, and I sense its weight on my back. I grab it and easily pull it forward until it's in front of me. Then I return it to my back, and it snaps into place like a magnet. That's going to be so much easier than carrying it around all the time.

"I think you're ready to pray now," Sylvia says. "Just so you're not surprised like I was, you should know that you're going to be given the option to change your appearance."

I blink. This is a game changer. "You mean like in character creation mode in *Legends of Sacrifice*?"

Sylvia nods.

"Can I be any race I want?"

"Of course," she says with a smile.

Oh, fuck yes!

I picture myself as an elf. I'd wanted to play one when I first started up the game, but they were terrible for playing pugilists. An elf would be perfect for a cleric though. I look around my group and realize that they'd had the option to be whatever race they wanted but had all chosen to stay human.

"Did any of you choose to change your appearance?" I ask.

I look first at Cait because she's a total knockout, but she shakes her head. "By the time I got to this stage, I was so sick of other players being surprised that I was a barbarian that I felt like making a point about it. So, I stayed how I was IRL."

God, she's blessed with great genes.

"Well, I made it so my hair is always pink, but I enjoy being kind of fluffy," Sylvia says. "My girlfriend used to say she loved cuddling with me because I was so squeezable." Her eyes dim. "I miss her so much."

"Oh, yeah, I definitely changed my appearance," Tara says. "I'm a rogue. I wanted to be as inconspicuous as possible. Also, halflings give you great buffs for stealth."

"You're not human?" I ask. "You look human."

Tara laughs. "That's because you haven't seen my feet."

"Isn't it kind of weird that there are halflings in a game inspired by Greek myths?" I ask, and everyone groans.

"Don't get Tara started about how none of this makes any sense again!" Cait gripes.

Tara says nothing but winks at me conspiratorially. Apparently, we're on #TeamQuestionEverything together.

"What about you?" I ask Guy.

He shrugs. "I changed one thing, but this is pretty much me outside of the game, too."

"I didn't change anything about myself," Joshua says. He motions down his body and raises his chin up with pride. "I mean, who would want to change perfection?"

Cait fails to stifle a laugh, and he glares at her.

"Tell her the truth," she tells Joshua, and he responds with a sigh.

"I kinda got bored praying and skipped past most of it," he says, his eyes cast to the ground. "So, I didn't realize I'd missed that bit until it was too late."

Oh, so you can *skip parts!* I file that away to ask about later.

"Thanks for all the info," I say to Sylvia. "I'll be back whenever Aphrodite is done with me."

"We'll meet you at the tavern," Guy responds.

As we part ways, the sound of chanting on the other side of the wall grows louder, as if greeting me.

⇧

I'm not sure what to do at first, so I watch the NPCs. Along the walls, there are twenty statues almost the height of the temple. Worshippers kneel before them in clusters, obviously aligned with the god they're closest to, most of them huddling around a statue of Zeus. Some walk away looking non-human—a few elves, a gnome, a halfling like Tara, and two orcs.

Like Zeus, some of the gods I recognize. Hermes and Dionysus are pretty obvious because of their distinctive outfits. Athena is wearing a helmet like a crown so that her face is still exposed. Small clues help me figure out who most of them are, and I narrow the last two statues down to Hera and Aphrodite. I *really* don't want to choose the wrong one because I'm pretty sure neither goddess wants to be mistaken for the other.

They're both so beautiful, though. Eventually, I decide Hera must be the statue next to Zeus since they're married. The other statue is between Ares and Hephaestus. Given that Aphrodite was married to one and in love with the other, it makes sense that it's her.

Like the other worshippers, I kneel before her, closing my eyes and clasping my hands below my chin. Mom wasn't a religious person. The only time I ever went to church was when my grandmother took me to a Christmas Eve service, so I don't have much experience praying. I hope I do this right.

Around me, the other worshipers are chanting, but that doesn't feel right. It's more like an invitation to join the quest, not what I should be doing. The quest said to *pray*, not chant.

Well, fuck it. Let's wing this.

"Dear Aphrodite," I say, sounding like a child to myself. "I'm uh... here...praying. I'm not sure what for, except to say that I'm pretty sure you're the one who helped me not freak out when my ankle got sprained...and some other times. So, thanks for that. Um..."

"Cleric," a clear, familiar, feminine voice says. "You've come as bidden."

My eyes flash open, and I scan the room. I had expected maybe a voice in my head, but it sounds like she's right there next to me. But she's not next to me, she's above me. The statue of Aphrodite is looking down at me with a smile.

"Oh, uh..." I say. "You're talking to me, like *talking to me*, talking to me."

"Of course," she says. "You are my cleric, one of the few I have chosen to bring me an offering. You're one of my cherished children."

"Can I ask why you chose me?"

"Why do you think?"

"Because I yelled 'holy fuck'?"

Aphrodite chuckles. "That helped."

Her spirit pulls away from the statue and shrinks down to my height. She's even more beautiful in this celestial form, a breathtaking woman formed by galaxies of pink stars with her hair splashing around her like ocean waves. Though it took me time to deduce which statue belonged to her, she's unmistakable in this form. She exudes love and sex.

With a wave of her hand, the temple disappears, and we're standing on a beach made of what looks pink Himalayan salt. The sea sparkles under a bright blue sky, and small white flower petals drift along on an ocean breeze.

To my surprise, Aphrodite takes my hand and squeezes it affectionately. You might think the touch is seductive, her being the Goddess of Love and all that, but it's more reassuring than anything. She knows this has been a hard journey.

"I can't tell you why I chose you," she says. "Not yet. But one reason I'm glad you belong to me is that I know you've given up on love."

That makes no sense to me. Shouldn't that be exactly why she *wouldn't* want me? Besides, she's wrong. "No, I gave up on Doug. I can still feel love."

Aphrodite cocks an amused brow. "I know you can still *feel* it, but you're resisting it." I open my mouth to speak, but she holds up a finger to stop me. "No, a scripted romance with an NPC doesn't count. Love isn't a dream. And what you felt for Doug wasn't love; it was obligation."

"So why do you want me, then?"

"Because while you've given up on love, it hasn't given up on you."

Aphrodite nudges my chin up, so that I'm gazing at the sky. At first, it's too bright, but the blue shifts to black, and I see millions of stars. The goddess beside me somehow plucks one from the sky and then another from much further away. In her palms, they're soft, glowing orbs that fit just right.

"You see, that's you," she says, lifting one palm higher than the other. "And that's your soul mate." She lifts the other to the same height. "Well, one of them, anyway."

One of them?

The stars all look identical to me, but I trust that a goddess can see more than I can. My heart dances at the thought of a soul mate (*and possibly more?*), and I realize she's right. There's something deep down inside me that longs for love.

"Bring me the right offering," Aphrodite says, "and I'll bring you and your love together."

I thought back to what Guy had said. The gods would offer us whatever we asked for with the right offering.

I need to see Mom before she dies.

"What if I would rather go home?" I ask.

Aphrodite looks at me with tender disappointment. "Then I will grant that, but you would never be happy. Not truly." Her smile returns. "Besides, who's to say this person isn't where you came from?"

That's true. Perhaps, by uniting with my soulmate, I'll come home as well. But still...

"Any hint as to what offering you'd like?"

"You'll know it when you see it," she says. "It will show that you truly worship me."

Well, that's the vaguest answer in the world.

My frustration must be on my face, because she throws me a bone—a small one, but it's something. "Follow the quests given to you, and you'll see it," she says.

"Is there a level I need to be to see it?"

"You can get up to level 100 here, but you really don't need to be high at all to find it."

That will have to do. At least I don't have to level up one hundred times to get home.

"Would you like to change your appearance?" she asks.

I nod. "I'd at least like to see my options."

Aphrodite winks. "I know it's one of your favorite parts of any game."

Just how long has she been watching me? Is she why I wound up here?

The world shifts again. This time, I'm standing on a platform in what looks like a changing room. I'm in front of a mirror, butt naked. My arms clap over my privates with impressive speed but then I realize I'm alone. Aphrodite has vanished. Except for the exit button, my menu is only related to appearance and race now.

After my pulse stops thundering, I take a long look at myself. I'm not awful to look at. Many people remark on how beautiful my honey-blonde hair is. I've got gray-blue eyes, which I've been told are pretty, though I've always secretly wished were a brighter blue. I also have a smattering of freckles across my face that kids used to make fun of but everyone thinks are cute now.

My body has some curves, with pretty large breasts. All that does is make me look boxy when I wear a t-shirt, though. I'm pretty average in weight, which is to say my doctor likes to remind me I should be more active since my BMI isn't perfect. I always wanted to chew him out when he said stuff like that, but deep down, I wanted to have the svelte body I saw in weight loss ads. A body like Cait's. After considering all my features, I decide there are a lot of things about me I want to dabble with.

First things first, unlike most of my player friends, I'm not content with staying human. If I have a chance to play an elf, I'm taking it. I choose it from the dropdown. My ears point at the end, and a caption at the bottom of my vision states that I have an extra 15 percent buff to magic stamina now.

Nice.

I get to the eyes category, and it presents a series of boxes to choose from. I try out all the blues, but none of them look right on my face. They belong to a stranger, and it freaks me out. When I return to my original gray, I sigh with relief. I try out all the other changes I consider with my face, but they all make me feel the same as changing my eye color did. So, I leave my face the way it was.

Then, I try out the different body presets. They're all beautiful— some are athletic, some are reed-like, some remind me a little of Jessica Rabbit. None of them feel right at all, though. It's like I put my head on a Barbie doll's body. Returning to my original body gives me a new appreciation for it. Perhaps it doesn't belong to a model, but it's mine, and I love it just the way it is. I understand better why most of my new friends stayed the same, or at least close to it.

The only thing I really want to change is my race. Somehow, being an elf makes me feel more like *me*. Plus, it's really going to help a lot with spell casting.

I still think racial buffs are racist, though.

I hit the exit button, and I'm once again surrounded by worshippers in a tall stone temple. I touch the tips of my ears. Sure enough, they're pointy. As I make my way to the tavern, I wonder how my new friends will react. I decide it doesn't matter because I look exactly how I want to.

CHAPTER EIGHT

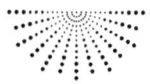

The tavern is packed when I arrive, and not just with NPCs. There are many players here, looking as confused as I've been feeling over the last couple of days. They must be new like me because a lot of the people in the line winding around the tavern's fence are looking at Alexander with doe eyes.

The cacophony of their conversations causes my heart to race and my breath to hitch. I squeeze my eyes closed and hold my hand over my tightening chest. Then I feel the stroke of a finger on my ear, and like someone flipped a switch, the world goes quiet. I open my eyes to see Guy mere inches away from me.

"Thanks again," I whisper.

"No problem," he says. "Let me know if you want me to turn it off so you can talk to people outside of our party."

I sweep my gaze over all the other players crowding the area. How many of these people will die? I decide I don't want to find out. There are more than enough people I'm becoming attached to over here. I don't want to compound my odds of future grieving.

Except I definitely will grieve when Mom dies.

Guy and I take a seat with the rest of our group. I'd expected them to hound me with questions about my experience in the temple, but they're all staring at the milling newbies.

I try to sound lighthearted when I say, "Busy day," and nod in Alexander's direction.

"Yeah..." Cait responds.

I notice that she's staring at the crowd with a concerned expression. In fact, everyone at the table looks like they're trying to solve a difficult puzzle.

"Is that weird or something?" I ask.

"These days it is," Cait answers. "It's like this in the zone we left last week, but it hasn't been crowded in the starting zone since, well, since I arrived."

"You said the game just came out, right?" Tara asks me. When I nod, she continues, "That must be why. Fresh meat. Beta had started when we all wound up here. Not that any of this makes sense..."

No one shushes Tara this time. Apparently, everyone's philosophical now. I've had all these questions burning my tongue since I found out where I am, but I've been more focused on logistics than anything. After talking with Aphrodite, though, I'm thinking more like Tara. Why and how are we here? What makes us different from any of the other gazillion players? I decide now's the best time to push the subject, even if I'm still recuperating from walking through the mass of strangers.

"I snooped the beta forums when they became public," I say. "I never noticed anything weird. There were so many players. Even days before I got the game, there were hundreds and hundreds of them chatting. There are probably close to a million players or more now that it's out. So, it's not like everyone winds up here. Why us?"

Everyone tears their attention away from the newcomers to gaze at me with weary eyes. This is a question they don't have an answer for, probably one that runs circles around their brains every hour of every day.

"We don't know everything, Lauren," Guy says. "If we did, we wouldn't be back at square one trying to see if we missed anything."

"I know, but—"

"Look at us," Guy continues. "We have so little in common. I'm not even an experienced gamer. My roommate was the beta player. He just let me fiddle around with it one time. Then one day, I fell asleep drunk in the bathroom and woke up here."

"I didn't even like the game," Joshua chimes in. "It was so glitchy, but I wanted to make sure I could give the designers lots of notes."

"We're all different," Tara says with a nod, "but you all know my theory."

Joshua groans. "But you're wrong."

"What theory?" I ask.

Tara looks at me with a shrewd glint in her eyes. "I think we're here because we didn't want to be *there*, in the real world."

"Well, I certainly didn't want to be here," Joshua says. "I already said I didn't like this game."

Tara raises an eyebrow at Joshua. "Yeah? So you're saying you'd rather be sitting at your desk selling insurance than ogling NPCs?"

This silences Joshua. He leans back in his chair and crosses his arms, before turning his gaze back to the crowd.

"Still, that doesn't fully explain it," Guy says. "A lot of people don't want to live in the real world, especially gamers. Why us? What makes us so special?"

Cait sighs. "Doesn't matter. We're here. Might as well make the best of it and work on getting our offerings."

That reminds me of what I planned on talking to them about when I left the temple. "Aphrodite said something about giving me a reward in return. I always thought it would be us getting to go home, but she told me..."

I trail off, realizing I'm about to tell them more than I'm comfortable divulging. Do I want them knowing I'm some unlucky in love loser?

"That she'd help you find true love or something?" Sylvia guesses.

"How—?"

"Because she's the Goddess of Love," Sylvia answers before I can finish my question. "Artemis offered me my own forest kingdom."

"Hermes said he'd make me the richest person in this world," Tara says.

Cait rolls her eyes and huffs out a laugh. "Thousands of soldiers under my command. Ares certainly knows what women want."

Joshua side eyes the group long enough to say, "Pan said I could make any woman want to sleep with me."

"Dionysus offered me a party that never ends," Guy says, wrapping it up.

"We can have whatever we want," Sylvia explains, "but that's what they say we really want. They certainly don't think we want to go home."

Cait crosses her arms. "They'd rather give us anything but that, even though that's what we all want." She hitches a thumb in Guy's direction. "Except him."

I squint at Guy. "Why don't you want to go home?"

"What's waiting for me there?" he asks. "Exams? Bills? Here I can wield magic and see fantastic things."

"And die," Cait interjects.

Guy lowers his gaze to the table. "You can die over there, too."

The crowd of new players seems to form little groups as they stagger out of the tavern, probably to battle the harpy and get a locket.

"I better go turn this in," I say, rising from my chair. I turn to look at Guy. "I'll have your money soon."

He waves his hand dismissively. "Keep it. I've got so much gold that I can't possibly spend it all."

I don't like feeling indebted to someone, but I don't want to seem ungrateful. "You're too nice."

Guy chuckles. "No, I'm not. Consider this payment for being our healer. Trust me. We'll be keeping you busy once you get enough spell slots filled."

I eavesdrop on the conversation between Alexander and the last newbie to receive the locket quest. The NPC repeats the same words to this new person as those he'd said to me yesterday. The player is looking at him with such a love-struck expression.

Is that how I looked when I received the quest? How pathetic.

Tara claims that it's possible the NPCs feel emotions but can't express them. I have a hard time believing that when he gives every player the same sorrowful words and mournful expression.

Back home, I played through enough of the relationship quests with him to know he's about to look at me with appreciation. I wonder how many other players get that same treatment. I'd prefer him to not feel anything than for him to regard everyone the same as he does me.

I realize that I've been hungering for something for years now. I want to be *special* to someone. It wouldn't even need to be for a lover. I'm so mediocre in every facet of my life—my art, my tech skills, even my gaming and hobbies. Maybe this is why it took me so long to choose a major and why I've never stuck to one job for more than a few months.

Is it possible to fit in everywhere and nowhere at the same time? I'm the "good enough for now" until the "just right" comes along. The high school sweetheart you settle for until you can put a ring on a thin brunette's finger.

Oh God, am I making this about Doug again?

Aphrodite must've really gotten under my skin. There are way bigger things to worry about than my lousy ex.

Alexander's looking straight ahead when I approach him. His face is neutral, as if he hadn't just been pouring his heart out about his dead girlfriend. When I say "hello," it captures his attention, and he looks at me with relief.

"You're back! Did you have any luck?" he asks.

I pull the locket out of my purse and hand it over. "And the last harpy is dead, too." I wish I hadn't said that because I can't shake the image of Mom's face on the harpy's dead body now.

"Thank you, adventurer! You are a true hero!" He looks off into the middle distance. "One that I can never be."

I roll my eyes. Did this really make me swoon when I was playing the game?

Give me the money already.

"Here," he says, retrieving something from the pouch on his belt. "It isn't much, but it's all I have."

He holds out the twelve copper pieces, and they disappear in a blink. I hear a ka-ching, and a number twelve next to a brown circle appears at the top of my UI.

"Thanks," I say. "Well...see ya." I know he'll give me another quest if I ask for it, but that one will only open up the relationship quest chain. There won't be any money in it, and the XP is minimal.

Wait. How does XP work here? I need to talk to the group about leveling up.

I turn and walk back to my group, but I only make it a couple of steps before I hear him call out, "Wait, adventurer!"

I glance back to see Alexander staring at me with a desperate expression.

This is new.

Out of curiosity more than anything, I walk back to him with my arms crossed and my head cocked. "What's up?"

"May I travel with you?"

I groan. Of course. I guess I don't even need to ask here to initiate this quest.

"I don't think that's a good idea, Alexander," I tell him. "You have a lot of fans who'll be back later with lockets."

"Please?"

Despite knowing he's a string of code, something in me stirs when he looks down at me with his puppy dog eyes.

Get a grip, Lauren. You and your group don't need an NPC standing by the fire repeating the same lines over and over.

Alexander's manly eyebrows tent together in the most pitiful way. His soft lips are slightly parted. He combs back the lock of hair curled over his forehead, but it falls back into place.

Ugh. Fine.

"Let me talk with my party," I tell him. "This isn't up to me alone."

"I'll be here, waiting," he responds.

I nod, forgetting that NPCs don't pick up on visual communication. When I return to my group, I see that they're all getting ready to leave. Jesus, how am I going to broach this subject?

"So, uh..." I freeze. Am I seriously about to ask them if we can keep an NPC like a pet?

Tara puts her hand on my shoulder. "He doesn't eat any of the food. He helps with a couple of battles. Then he leaves when you tell him you're not interested in a romantic relationship."

They knew exactly what I was going to say. That's how predictable all of this is.

"Is it worth it?" I ask.

Cait shrugs. "I mean, at our level we don't really need him for the battles, but maybe having him around could remind us of something we missed from our first go around here."

I'm embarrassed at how easy it was to get permission to bring the NPC I crushed on into the fold.

"How does this work?" I ask. "I mean, he can't very well leave the tavern when there are other players."

"Oh, this one won't," Sylvia answers. "Another version of him will pop up at our camp when we get there."

"You mean...there are other Alexanders walking around?"

"Oh, totally," Cait says with a nod. "They're everywhere, like little, sexy, brooding ants. God knows where they all hide when players are done with them."

Done with them. Another reminder that Alexander isn't real. Maybe having him in the camp is a big mistake. This world is already surreal enough. Do I really need a constant reminder that sentient beings are the minority here? Still, if there's a chance he might help us figure out what offerings we need to make, I'll deal with it.

"Okay, I'll go talk to him," I say.

"Ask him for the next quest, while you're at it," Sylvia says. "We gotta get you trained up before we do the Nessa quest. That's a pretty tough escort mission for being so low-level."

Guy nods. "Way too OP for that area."

Great. The harpy was scary enough. Good to know things can only get more traumatic from here.

CHAPTER NINE

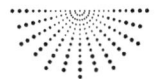

W e're on the crest of a hill, overlooking a field full of cercopes. They're interesting creatures, like children with pointed ears and a hairy tail, sort of like if an elf and a monkey had ugly babies. But the cute kind of ugly.

They're dancing and laughing with each other, an utter delight to behold. So, of course, I'm really worried about why Alexander brought me here. None of my new friends are saying anything about the quest because they don't want to "ruin my game experience with spoilers."

Despite the fact that we're all trying to get out of this world alive, everyone is still enamored with the idea that we're actually playing a game. And, honestly, so am I. I mean, yes, I'm not over the dead harpy thing, and I desperately want to get home to Mom. But there's a reason I play video games. It's more fun than real life!

"Okay, so what's going on with the cercopes?" I ask Alexander.

His eyebrows are way too serious, and his chin is way too firm in contrast to the childlike laughter in the field below. "These cercopes are a menace," Alexander says. "They've been stealing tools from the villagers. Blacksmiths are without their tongs. Stable hands are without their pitchforks. Farmers are without their hoes."

Joshua snickers and calls out, "Where my hoes at?"

I give Joshua a lot of grief, but I have to hand it to him. The contrast of his words against Alexander's earnest expression is perfect. There's a reason he's a bard. I mimic a chef's kiss in his direction, and he responds with an exaggerated bow.

Alexander doesn't notice Joshua's tomfoolery and continues his monologue. "Zeus's son Hercules has been tasked by his queen to kill them, but the cercopes' mother has asked me to capture them and bring them to her."

"Mother?" I look down at the field. There are dozens of them down there. "Busy woman."

"Alas, the gods have cursed me to—"

"Never lift a blade again, I know," I say with a sigh. "Wait...You said I just need to capture them. This doesn't require you to lift anything sharp."

"Oh, hun," Tara says. "Trust me when I say that a weapon might come in handy right now. Your staff should do, though. It might be enough to herd them."

"Herd them? Like sheep?" I ask.

Tara shrugs. "Yeah, like sheep. If sheep were tiny assholes that like to bite and pants people."

"Ugh, don't remind me about the pantsing," Guy groans.

"Okay, so how do I capture them, and how do I get them to their mom?" I ask Tara.

Sylvia steps over and answers me instead. "You're not capturing anyone. We need to be smart about this and play the game in a way that works best for you. *Legends of Sacrifice* the video game has some big differences from how this all works here. Just like you don't choose your class, you don't choose your spells and skills. You earn them with the actions you take during quests and key moments."

"So, I need to do cleric stuff instead." I rub my chin, wondering just how badly these people will need healing. Though, being a cleric isn't all about mending wounds. Maybe I could somehow buff them, like grant them guidance or some shit.

Sylvia nods. "Yeah, so you'll join Guy and me on the perimeter while Cait and Tara rush up to the cercopes from behind. When they try to spread out, we'll shoo them back into the middle so that they're headed in the direction we want them to go."

"And I'll play my fiddle so that they follow me into that cage over there," Joshua adds, pointing toward something shining in the distance.

"That's a cage?" I ask. "Seems pretty far away."

Cait finishes stretching her legs. "Yeah, it's gonna be some cardio for sure."

We all get into position. Tara and Cait are to the west of the cercopes. Joshua is to the east, like the far-off cage. Sylvia is to the north, while Guy and I are to the south. With how spread out we are, how far away the cage is, and how many cercopes there are, I can't imagine how difficult this quest must be for newbies choosing to play solo.

"So how do we do this?" I ask Guy.

He holds out his hand, and in a blink, his staff disappears from his back and poofs into his hand. "Just swing your staff at them and make loud noises."

I raise an eyebrow. "That works?"

"Usually," he answers. "Sometimes, you have to chase after them. That's why I'm glad to have you on my side. That way you can keep fending off the stream in case I need to grab a stray cercopes."

"What about Sylvia?" I ask. "She's on her own."

Guy laughs. "No, she's not."

He points across the field, and Sylvia waves at us. Then she taps at what must be her UI, and a wolf appears at her side.

"Jesus Christ!" I yelp. "I thought she didn't like wolves!"

"It's not that she doesn't like them," Guy says. "She'll just do anything to protect animals who are being attacked by anyone. And that wolf isn't just some wolf. That's the *puppy* she rescued."

My eyes strain from how wide open they are. "*That's* a puppy?"

"Well, he used to be," Guy answered. "We've been here a while, and he's grown a lot."

The thought of a helpless puppy growing into a snarling wolf does more than amaze me, it makes me ponder. If this wolf comes from the game, shouldn't he have stayed a puppy? Do NPCs age here? Do players?

Don't think like that. You'll be out of here before you can answer that question.

Suddenly, Cait's running at full speed holding her great axe over her head practically roaring at the cercopes. Tara's racing beside her, screaming at the top of her lungs to scare the herd in the right direction. The two of them are terrifying, even to me, and I'm their ally. The cercopes definitely feel the same way because they've stopped laughing and started fleeing.

Just as everyone told me they would, the cercopes try to disperse in every direction. It takes me a moment to snap my attention away from Tara and Cait. As soon as my mind is on my mission, a growling cercopes dashes in my direction. Now that they're closer, they're not as cute. In fact, they're fucking scary.

I let out a blood-curdling scream. I suppose it sounds like I'm trying to intimidate the cercopes, but it's really just my knee-jerk reaction to its bulging eyes and needle-like teeth. The little guy doesn't know that, though. He shrieks and turns tail, rushing back to the middle of the field. As soon as he's there, his eyes fix on Joshua.

Joshua's playing the fiddle as he twirls and frolics in an eastward direction, completely in his element. The cercopes that just ran at me a moment ago is dancing now, too, as he follows our bard.

I should have been paying less attention to Joshua and more to my job, because another cercopes leaps at me. I swing my staff and hit him like he's a baseball. He goes limp and drops to the ground.

"Oh, God!" I cry out. "Did I kill him? Oh God, oh God, oh—"

The cercopes springs back up, eyes bright with the light of vengeance.

"Oh, shit!" I fight the instinct to run away and hold my staff out. "Fuck off!"

That does absolutely nothing. He lunges at me with his mouth wide open, and I swing my staff again, but he dodges it just in time. Then he jumps up and buries his sharp teeth into my arm.

"Fuck!" I shriek. "You little fucking fucker! Get the fuck off me!"

Guy bops the cercopes on the head with his staff and flings the creature into the middle.

I stare in horror at the cercopes's prone body. "You killed him," I whisper.

Guy shakes his head. "No, you can't kill the cercopes. If you could, this quest would be next to impossible. Sometimes the only way you can get them where they need to go is with good old-fashioned violence."

"I see now why Alexander wasn't able to—"

I'm not able to finish that sentence because a searing bolt of agony rushes up my arm to my shoulder. I look where the cercopes bit me. It's red and swollen. Pus is bubbling from the little punctures the creature's teeth left in me. Well, shit. It's infected. I might even be poisoned.

"Heal Minor Wounds!" I shout. Nothing happens. "Heal Major Wounds!" That doesn't work either.

Before I can process this information, another cercopes is dashing in our direction. I try to lift my staff, but my arm is too weak now. I turn toward Guy to ask for his help, but I see he's fending off two cercopes now. Shit.

The little terror is gnashing his teeth as he sprints over to me. Panic clutches my heart, but suddenly, the familiar peace from my first day rushes over me, giving me the ability to think. Now that I have a moment of clarity, I realize that there's a way to work smarter instead of harder in this situation.

I focus on the pink gem in my staff. I never asked how to do this before, so I'm just winging it when I shout, "Charm!" and point it at the cercopes.

He stops in his tracks. His eyes turn pink, and he has a dazed expression on his face as his head sways back and forth.

"Follow him!" I command and nod in Joshua's direction.

Without hesitation, the cercopes turns around and marches eastward, keeping his hypnotized eyes on Joshua the whole time.

When I turn to look at Guy, I can see that he's tossed one cercopes back into the fray, while the other one is trying to yank Guy's staff away. I point my staff at the little thief and once again shout, "Charm!" His body goes slack, and he loses his grip on Guy's weapon. That's all Guy needs to give the cercopes a good thwack, sending the little guy hurtling back into the center of the field.

"Well, that's handy!" Guy says, laughing. "Keep it up!"

Blinding pain flashes up my arm again, and I nearly fall to my knees. Neither one of my healing spells worked before, and I realize now it's because I'm not trying to cure a wound. I need to cure a poisoning condition. Before another burning pang can attack, I thrust my purse at Guy.

"Is there anything left of my t-shirt in there?" I ask.

Guy rifles around in it. Then shakes his head at me.

"Fuck," I mutter. "Um...what about a water bottle? Oh, shit, no. I left my water in my car."

"You need water?" Guy asks.

I nod. "To flush out my wound."

Guy points his staff at my arm, and a snakelike stream of water leaves its tip before wrapping around my arm. It's cool against my skin, literally washing me with relief, as it soothes my pain. I watch in awe as I see the pus dilute and leave my wounds.

"That enough water?" Guy asks.

"Yeah, looks like it is."

He takes my arm to inspect it. Satisfied that my wound is clear of any pus, he flicks his staff away, and the water splashes onto the ground. While it didn't get rid of the wound, it cleaned it out, and I no longer feel the searing pain of the poisoning condition.

"Heal Minor Wound," I say, looking at the small punctures still on my arm. They close up, and I sigh with relief, just before fatigue makes gravity that much harder to fight against. I can only keep this up a little longer, but I'm sure Guy won't let me pass out.

"You're really getting the hang of this!" Guy says. Then, he nods toward the herd of cercopes. "Looks like they're all under Joshua's spell now. All that's left for us to do is follow along."

Just as Guy said, other than having to make such a long hike, the rest of the quest is a piece of cake. Within an hour, we trap the cercopes in a cage where their mother has been waiting for them. To my great surprise, she's quite beautiful. She's an Oceanid with black curly hair and a sheer chiton that shows off enough to make Joshua visibly pleased.

Unlike the locket quest, this one puts me in a good mood. We're all feeling festive, in fact. Once we're done setting up camp and Sylvia comes back from fishing from the nearby stream, we make ourselves a little feast of her catch. Joshua plays his fiddle for us, and holy shit...If the Devil ever comes down to *Legends of Sacrifice*, he shouldn't go head-to-head with our bard. Mr. Satan would lose for sure.

With a full belly and a lightened spirit, I lay my head down and close my eyes. Before I can drift off to sleep, I hear the disembodied voice say, "Cleric of Aphrodite: Level 3. Spell Gained: Restoration. Skill Gained: Strategy Under Duress. Stats Unlocked: Strength - 8, Dexterity - 14, Constitution - 14, Intelligence - 17, Wisdom - 15,

Charisma - 16, Faith - 10. Favors Gained: Beguiling Eyes, Soothing Grace."

That's *a lot* to process when I'm this tired, so I promise I'll look into it in the morning. I'm sure I'll have a lot of questions for my companions.

The sounds of Cait and Sylvia clanging about outside of the tent wakes me. They must be making breakfast because I can smell a campfire and rosemary. I'm still bone weary from the long herding quest from yesterday. However, after several minutes of trying to return to sleep, I'm certain that I'm awake for the day. So I leave my dozing companions behind to step outside.

My head is buzzing with the questions that haunted my dreams last night. It's disorienting. All my thoughts dissipate before I can make sense of them, like soap slipping from my hands in the bathtub. However, when I leave the tent, I'm greeted with the crisp mountain air of Peripeteia, and it brings me clarity.

Last night, the voice told me I'd leveled up, and today I realize there's a ton of information about what that means in my UI. I'll need to read it all and see if my friends can help me make sense of it all. But first, breakfast.

Sylvia cracks eggs onto a flat slab of rock next to some fish and sliced-up turnips roasting over a campfire. I used to watch Instagram reels of people camping out in the wild like this. It was intriguing, therapeutic even. Seeing someone do it right in front of me has me in awe, even after watching her do it several times already. How did she learn to do it? Was this a gift given to her as an Archer of Artemis?

"Can I help?" I ask her, but she shakes her head.

With a kind smile, she says, "Honestly, one of my favorite things to do is cook breakfast alone before everyone wakes up."

Cait chuckles from her perch on a boulder where she's weaving reeds. "That's her nice way of saying you need to get out of her way and be quiet." She pats the expanse of rock next to her. "Come sit with me where we can whisper and gaze at this fantastic scenery."

That sounds like an amazing idea, and Cait seems to be in a rare, non-grumpy mood, so I climb up and join her. Our vantage point from the tent is already breathtaking. We're high up enough that villages look like dollhouses in the green valley below, but the mountain peaks are still a little further up. The ones above are craggy and snowcapped. The ones on our level are smoother with greenery.

Legends of Sacrifice is supposed to be in a fantasy version of the Aegean area and its surrounding regions. I wonder if this is what the real Greece looks like or if this is just how the game engineers imagined it. Whatever the answer it is, Peripeteia is beautiful, and Cait has picked the perfect spot to admire our current high altitude.

"God, this is gorgeous," I whisper.

"It's the only part of this game that hasn't gotten old for me," Cait responds. "The mountains, the islands. The valleys, villages, and farms. All of it. If I leave—*when* I leave—I hope I can go to the Mediterranean Sea and go to places like this again. But with my friends and family and all the people I miss."

Cait's eyes lower from the mountain range, and I can tell she's thinking about her loved ones. I wonder if Mom is okay. Is time the same here as there? She may not have noticed I'm gone yet. Or maybe it's been months already, and she's assumed the worst.

She could be dead already.

I hope I can get back soon so that I can give her a big hug. But before I can do that, I need to figure out this game and win it.

"I leveled up last night," I say.

"Oh?" Cait asks. "What level? Two?"

"Three, and I got a whole of lot of notifications about it," I answer.

"That comes with level three," Cait says. "By that point, the game or gods or whatever have figured out enough about you to give you stats. And at every level up you get some other stuff. What did you get?"

I bring up my menu and read my new stats to her. She winces.

"Are those bad?" I ask.

"They're not bad per se, but..." She hesitates. "It's just...as a cleric, your wisdom should be higher than your intelligence, and your faith should be a lot higher. You're spec'd more like a wizard."

"How do you know all this?"

"Well, like I told you before, I've played a healer a bunch, and I'm familiar with their ideal stats in other games," she explains. "As for your faith stat, that's more of an assumption on my part. You're a cleric, the holy servant of a deity. You'd think your faith would be kind of a big deal. Ten is the minimum without taking a penalty."

"So that means I'm going to take a penalty with strength?" I ask.

Cait nods. "Yeah, anything you need to do that requires strength will tire you out quickly now and make all your other actions suffer."

Well, I guess I should avoid anything related to that. Thankfully, I'm with a group that seems to work well with collaboration.

"How do they figure out these stats?" I ask.

"They evaluate the way you've handled quests and go from there." She must see the anxiety on my face because she continues, "Don't worry, they tweak them at levels five, ten, and twenty. So, you have time to nudge things in the right direction."

That's a *gigantic* relief. I like a challenge when I'm playing video games, but I'd like to make my experience here as easy as possible so I can get home. Having the wrong stats could really be a hindrance.

"Did you get anything besides your stats?" Cait asks.

I close my eyes, trying to remember what I can without going through my menu first. "I got a spell, a skill, and two favors."

Cait's eyebrows shoot up to her hairline. "*Two* favors? Already? People don't usually even get one until level four or five. Having two this fast is impressive, especially with a low faith stat."

Ah, so that's what the faith stat does. Cait's right, then. I wonder why I got so lucky.

"Well, go on, tell me what all you got," Cait prompts.

"I remember I got Restoration, probably because I got rid of a poisoning condition," I say. "If there are more poisonous creatures, that should be really helpful."

I look next to my spells to find my skills. "I got the skill Strategy Under Duress. That must be because I figured out a solution for the poisoning while the cercopes were attacking us."

Cait nods. "And why your intelligence is so high. You were thinking strategically. A good thing in the moment, but you'll need to counterbalance that by finding ways to use wisdom. Sylvia can help with that."

"As for my two favors, I have Beguiling Eyes and Soothing Grace."

"Figures Aphrodite would gift you with Beguiling Eyes," Cait says. "That'll be handy when we get to cities. Not sure what Soothing Grace is, though."

I shrug. "The only way to find out is to use it. It sounds positive. Would you let me try it out on you?"

"Favors aren't spells, they're features," Cait says. "It's a boost that helps you in certain situations. You won't need to cast Beguiling Eyes if you're trying to sweet talk someone into something. Persuading others will just come more easily. You may never know what Soothing Grace is because it might make a subtle difference that you don't notice."

"Hey, guys!" Sylvia calls out to us. "Can you rouse everyone so we can eat before this food gets cold?"

Cait responds with a nod.

As we head back to the tent, I notice Alexander gazing at the mountains in the distance. Shit. I was so excited about surviving that cercopes mission last night that I totally forgot to turn in the quest.

I tap Cait on the shoulder. "Hey, I gotta go talk to Alexander. Can you take care of waking everyone without me?"

Cait laughs. "I can handle shouting at everyone to wake up."

We part, and I head over to Alexander. His eyes don't leave the mountain range until I say, "Hello."

"Hello, traveler," he greets back.

Being called "traveler," "adventurer," and "wanderer" by every NPC I meet is getting old. I wonder if there's a way to change that.

"Can you call me Lauren from now on?" I ask. "I mean, is that an option I can choose?"

He blinks at me like he doesn't understand. That's...strange. He's an NPC. He should respond with something pre-generated, *if* he responds at all.

"Hello, Lauren," he says after a pause.

Whoa! It worked.

"I got the cercopes to their mother."

Alexander smiles. "Oh, she will be most pleased. Now that their mother has them contained, Zeus will not allow their deaths. Here is your reward, Lauren."

The two silver and five copper ka-ching into my inventory and then he holds out something I didn't expect because he hadn't mentioned it when giving me the cercopes quest. It's a cornflower blue cloak with a golden clasp. There's a subtle sparkle to it, like it's imbued with magic.

"This is a gift from Aphrodite," he says. "It will offer protection from even the most bitter cold."

"Cold?" I ask as I put on the cloak.

"Winter is coming," he says.

I snort. "Okay there, Eddard Stark."

Alexander, of course, doesn't notice my little pop culture reference and continues his explanation. "And Aphrodite wishes for you to visit Khione the Snow Nymph to the North. You must bring her news of her child, Eumolpus."

"That's an oddly specific quest that sounds like it's just for me," I say. Surely, my party would have told me if the next quest was related to my deity.

"You must plead with Khione to claim her son, as he is returning to Thrace in a bid to become their king," he says. "If she does not, he may die."

"Why does Aphrodite care about any of this?" I ask, not expecting an answer.

"Because Poseidon is one of her lovers, and he is Eumolpus's father."

Twice now, Alexander has acted more autonomous than another NPC would. Given that this is such an Aphrodite-specific quest, I wonder if she's using him as some kind of conduit. Why not give the quest to me directly in my menu, though?

"Okay, I'll do that," I say. "Are there any other quests I should know about?"

"Spiders have woven a tapestry above a village to the north called Sardis," he says. "It is so thick that the villagers can no longer feel the sunshine. They need a hero to destroy the web and drive away the spiders. Make sure not to kill any of the creatures. We don't want to make Arachne angry."

He's right there. The last thing I want to do is piss off a woman with eight legs and a grudge against the gods.

I return to my friends who are all happily eating the breakfast Sylvia made.

"So, did you get the spider quest?" Cait asks as I sit down to eat.

I nod. "And another one, too."

Cait raises an eyebrow. "Another one?"

I scan the group. Their features scrunch with confusion.

"I think Aphrodite wants me to do a special one for her," I say. "In Thrace."

"Thrace!" Guy shouts. "It's almost winter. It's going to be so cold there."

"That must be what the pretty cloak is for," Tara says, pointing to Aphrodite's gift in my arms. "Where'd you get that from?"

"Alexander gave it to me when he gave me the quest."

Tara lifts a brow. "Must be nice to have a goddess giving you seasonal wear."

"I can try to do this one alone," I offer.

Sylvia shakes her head. "No, we work together as a group. That's the only way to survive in this game. Besides, we've already done all the quests from level one to level thirty. It will be nice to do something new."

"And maybe find clues about our offerings," Joshua interjects.

"Guess we'll need to do some shopping once we fix the spider issue," Guy says.

I feel so guilty about how much I'm costing this group. "I've got some money. I—"

Guy puts his hand over mine. "Save your money. I've earned so much I don't think I could ever run out."

I notice a subtle blush on his cheeks, and I have a realization. When I had gotten to know this group at the tavern, I'd received a quest to Inspire Lust. It must have been an Aphrodite-specific quest. It had no reward other than a tiny XP bump. But I hadn't even needed to try because as soon as I noticed it, it was complete. I hadn't figured out who it could be.

With all that had happened since then, I'd almost forgotten about it entirely. Guy had been there, though, and he'd been more than generous ever since. Could a dude as hot as him have a crush on me?

No way, Lauren. Girls like you don't get that lucky.

CHAPTER TEN

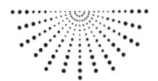

I like spiders—love them, in fact. Did you know some cultures consider them to be lucky? Back in the real world, I used to enjoy watching videos about spiders, especially the close-up ones where you can tell they're super adorable. I used to beg my mom to let me have a tarantula as a pet but wound up having to settle for her not killing the house spiders. None of them are like *these*, though.

They have the spindliest legs the length of my arms. Each spider has three mouths—one on their heads, one on their abdomens, and one right next to the area they spit their silk from. Why the butt mouth? To help them cut their webbing while they're eating with the other two mouths.

Their plethora of eyes aren't beady like regular spiders have. No, no, my friend! These are *people* eyes, with whites and pupils and irises of various shapes. I don't even know how many eyes each has because there are too many to count when I'm trying to not die!

Just like Alexander said, they've woven a web so thick over this village that it's dark as night down here, even though it's the middle of the day. There are torches and such lit, but they do little to cut down on the shadows.

When you start playing a video game on your PC, you can adjust the brightness setting so that it's comfortable on your eyes. I always make it as bright as possible because I want to see everything clearly. You can't adjust any video or audio settings when you're actually in Peripeteia, though, and I'm night blind as fuck despite being an elf now.

There are about a dozen of them. That's how many I can tell there are, anyway. There could be more lurking in the shadows. All the villagers are hiding inside, probably have been for a while. I can't blame them, but shit, that's no way to live. How soon until they run out of food or need a healer? This is a bigger problem than I'd imagined when Alexander gave me this quest. I feel terrible for the people here.

Lauren, they're NPCs. They're not going to starve to death.

One spider skitters down the side of the Temple of Athena, making clicking noises with the mouth on his head as he does. I squeak in terror, which is a big mistake because he turns all of his baby blue eyes in our direction. Then he licks his jagged teeth with a long, forked tongue. Fortunately, he doesn't seem to see us because he turns back around.

"Holy dick in a cunt bucket!" I scream as I back up. "It's got a goddamn *tongue*! What kinda fucking spiders are these?"

"Language!" Cait hisses as she steps in front of us. "And keep your voice down. We don't want to attract attention."

"Especially from them," Sylvia whispers and points at the three that are click clacking at each other conversationally under the dim torch-light down the road.

"Y'all, this isn't that hard of a quest," Tara says. "We've done this one five times, once for each of us. We just have to run past them, climb up the webbing, and burn it down. Then Joshua plays his little intimidation song, and we hightail it into that mountain cave we passed a while ago."

"Right," Guy says with a nod. Then he turns to me. "Remember we can't hurt any of them, or we'll make Arachne angry."

I respond with a nervous chuckle. "I don't even think I could hurt them if I was trying."

We make a mad dash down the road, drawing closer and closer to the three spiders who are busy chatting. I'm putting a lot of trust in my new friends since they're veteran players and want their healer to survive. Still, I'm having doubts about whether we can dodge these monsters when they take up so much of the road and can jump thirty times the length of their body. That's pretty far, considering that their diameter is around eight feet.

Before we catch their attention, Guy waves his staff, and suddenly we're nothing more than an undulation of the scenery. We look like people-shaped versions of the heated air above a fire. With another wave, our steps are silenced, as well as our ragged breaths. However, this is a time-capped spell and it's clear that it's taking a huge amount of energy from Guy, so we need to be fast.

The three spiders on the road don't notice us as we flee past them, but when I take a quick glance up at the temple, I see the spider there squinting his eyes in our direction. He must be trying to see through the optical illusion Guy's created. I send a panicked, silent prayer to Aphrodite.

Please don't let me die! I promise Thrace is my next stop!

To my dismay, we turn a corner, heading straight to the temple. I want to ask why, but I realize the answer quickly enough on my own when Tara jumps on the side of the building and starts climbing up. This is the part of the web we're supposed to take to the silken canopy above.

We're going to haul our butts up right beside the horrible beast that was just licking his chops in our direction minutes ago.

Jesus. Fucking. Christ.

Climbing up isn't the same as running down the street. It's slower and more difficult. I have to yank my feet upward when the web sticks to it, and every movement sends a slight ripple through the whole structure. Mr. Forked Tongue may not be able to see us, but he can sure as hell feel us.

Arachne's terrifying child turns his attention from the street, snapping his head in our direction. Even though I know he can't see us, it looks like he's staring straight into my eyes.

It's just a coincidence...right?

We just about reach the top of the temple, where there's a small opening in the web above, when Guy's invisibility spell wears off. It may be dark, but I can still see the torch-lit expressions of horror on my friends' faces when they all realize that time is up. Tara's cool as a cucumber, though. She waves her hand to get our attention and makes a crisscross with her pointer fingers. My companions all nod, seeming to know what she's trying to communicate. Guy tugs my arm and nods to our left. He wants me to follow him, and I do.

Our climb is no longer just a vertical challenge. We're spiraling around this temple in opposite directions from each other: Guy, Joshua, and me to the left; Tara, Sylvia, and Cait to the right. This is enough to confuse the spider. For the first time since we approached the temple, I feel a glimmer of hope. We might just make it!

Tara reaches a small opening at the peak of the temple. It's just wide enough for a heavy-set person to squeeze through. She climbs above it and then extends her arm to pull Sylvia through. Sylvia helps Joshua up, who then helps Cait. When Cait helps me, she's so strong that I practically slam into her chest. Heat rises in me as I take in the leathery scent of her armor.

"You gonna help Guy or what?" she asks.

I shake myself out of my body's unexpected reaction to Cait's body and help Guy.

When I finally lift my face upward, I'm blinded for a moment by the midday sun. Everyone else seems to be as well, judging by the sounds of moans and winces around me. After a few blinks, my vision returns, gradually normalizing. I almost sigh in relief, but then *he* comes into view—the spider that will haunt my nightmares for eternity.

"Where are you t-t-tuh going, t-t-tuh trespassers?" he asks in a scratchy voice.

Bastard on a biscuit! The spider can fucking talk?

I hold my hands up in surrender. "Look, mister, please let us go, and we'll leave you alone!"

The spider cocks his head at me. "Mister? Can you not see that I am female?"

Seriously? Shit, I've been misgendering this fucker the whole time. Do I just assume that someone who wishes me physical harm is always a man? I need to explore that further.

When I'm no longer trying not to piss myself!

"Sorry, sorry," I say. "I call everyone 'mister.'" I look at Tara. "Right?"

Tara nods desperately. "All the time! Every one of us, no matter what we've got in our pants!"

Miss Webby Magoo narrows her blue eyes in suspicion and clicks in thought. "Why should I t-t-tuh let you live?" she asks me. "We know you've t-t-tuh come here to t-t-tuh destroy our home."

"Your...home?" Well, that's new information.

"We were living here t-t-tuh peacefully, when these t-t-tuh *humans* cut down our forest and t-t-tuh built their town," she says. "They kept taking t-t-tuh more and more and more. And we've had *enough*! So, t-t-tuh we're reclaiming what's t-t-tuh ours."

Well, fuck. Now I feel bad. Urban sprawl is causing habitat loss here, too.

"Really? I'm so sorry. We were told that the opposite was happening."

The spider clicks some more. "Of course, t-t-tuh you were. The same people who t-t-tuh took our t-t-tuh homes are looking for t-t-tuh help."

I frown, pondering. What happened to Arachne's children was unfair. They may be "monsters," but they don't deserve to be exterminated for simply existing. Just like the far less terrifying spiders back home. On the other hand, there are people—*children*—down there who deserve to live, too. Who do I side with?

Why choose one or the other, though?

"I don't want you to lose your home," I say. "You deserve to live here. But the people below built here so that they'd have a place to raise their families. They can't just pack up and leave everything behind. Is there a way you can both get what you want?"

The spider tilts her head. Without human facial features, it's hard to tell how she's reacting, but I *think* she might be considering my words. It hits me that she and I have been having a conversation this whole time. This doesn't feel like I'm prompting pre-generated responses from an NPC.

First Alexander with that special quest and now this? What is going on?

"Families?" she asks. "Humans have t-t-tuh families?"

Sylvia steps over. "Yes," she says. "They have children, too. Like your eggs and spiderlings, they need protection but for even longer. They need sunlight to grow their crops. In fact, their health can suffer greatly if they don't receive enough time in the sun."

All (*twenty?*) of the spider's eyes look downward. "I didn't realize t-t-tuh." She lifts her eyes and squints again. "But they threatened our t-t-tuh families by taking our home!"

"What if you shared a home?" I ask. "What if they turn their Temple of Athena into a Temple of Arachne?"

"T-t-tuh...A temple to our t-t-tuh mother?"

I nod. "Yes, and I bet there are other ways they can help you. How you can help *each other*."

The spider clicks. "Talk to the humans t-t-tuh," she says. "Let me know what they t-t-tuh say to this idea."

"Absolutely!" I agree.

We all turn toward the gap in the webbing we'd just passed through, but the spider jumps ahead of us. "I'm not t-t-tuh stupid. Just *you* t-t-tuh can leave. The rest of your group are t-t-tuh staying with me."

My friends all grow pale.

Damn, is Joshua crying?

I don't have a choice. We wouldn't stand a chance in a fight against this daughter of Arachne. Even if we did, we can't hurt her without risking a goddess's wrath. I give a solemn nod to the spider and then to my friends before making my way downward in silence. As I descend, I hear my quest log ding. I open it the moment my feet hit the ground. *"Negotiate Peace,"* it reads.

Well, I better get on that, then.

IT TAKES A WHILE FOR MY EYES TO READJUST TO THE DARKNESS below, but when I do, I see all the spiders gazing upward. I suppose they've been wondering where their friend went, especially now that some fucking elf girl is coming down.

Most spiders are solitary creatures, but obviously Arachne's children are the rare kind that live in colonies. Maybe their community is more of a hive. One of the random factoids I know from pursuing so many unfinished degree programs is that in South America, there are spiders called *Anelosimus eximius* who cooperate using a hive mind. If Arachne's children are like that, they can communicate telepathically and understand what happened above with their friend. I hope.

I gulp and make my way down the temple webbing, then walk down the road with cautious steps and my hands held up in what I hope is a sign of peace and not antagonization.

"I-I've come on behalf of your friend up there," I say. "Sh-she w-wants me to talk with whoever is in charge of the humans down here."

A chorus of clicking echoes around the town. It's so loud that I realize there are many times more than the dozen spiders I'd seen before.

Don't shit yourself, Lauren.

One approaches me. "Uttu sent you t-t-tuh down here?" they ask.

"To negotiate on your behalf," I answer.

"T-t-tuh, the human you are seeking t-t-tuh lives inside t-t-tuh the Temple of Athena."

"Okay," I say. "I'm going back there now." I duck my head as I swivel toward the temple and whisper to myself, "Please don't fucking eat me."

"Eat you?" the spider asks.

Shit, they heard me.

I gulp and turn around. The spider looks like they're going to puke at the suggestion. I am *certain* that's not a predetermined NPC reaction.

"We don't t-t-tuh eat humans," the spider says. "We eat the dead t-t-tuh animals we t-t-tuh find in the forest."

So, they're scavengers—beneficial, even. Because of these creatures, humans wouldn't have to deal with animal carcasses themselves. This is something I can use when I negotiate.

"Seems there's a lot that humans don't know about Arachne's children," I say. "And vice versa."

"Elves, t-t-tuh too," they say in response.

I turn around and head to the temple. Before we'd come to the village, Alexander had explained to us how it was laid out. He'd mostly spoken about the temple, though, because he was certain that the spiders were here seeking vengeance in their mother's name.

Athena had punished Arachne for daring to believe she was a better weaver. The spiders seemed to prefer being spiders, though. So far, they'd made it very clear that they thought humans were gross. If Arachne hadn't become a spider goddess, her children would have been humans, too. Why would they seek revenge? Still, I'm sure it was a slap in the face that the very people who took their home put up a temple in honor of their mother's enemy. I hope whichever human I speak to is amenable to changing that.

It's no surprise that when I try to open the temple door, it's locked. I knock, timidly at first, but when no one answers, I pound on the door. "Hey, I'm not a spider! Let me in!" I shout.

"Go away!" a man shouts back. "We're not opening the doors for anyone."

"What about the person coming to rescue you?" I ask.

I'm greeted with silence, but after a nerve-racking minute, there's a scuffling of footsteps and numerous clicks from the other side of the door. A man peers at me between the half-inch crack he's made in the doorway and gasps upon seeing the way I'm dressed.

"A cleric! Thanks be to Athena!"

Oh great, this guy's the religious type. Convincing him to make this a temple to Arachne might prove difficult.

He yanks me through and slams the door shut behind me. As he clicks all the locks back into place, he says, "My name is Andreas. I am the head priest of this temple."

"Well, then you're the exact person I need to talk to," I respond.

"Come, follow me," he says, motioning for me to walk down a hallway.

What I see when we reach the end makes my heart sink. There are dozens of people here, mostly women and children. By the dark circles around their eyes and slow movements, I can tell they're unwell. There's coughing, the small, high-pitched kind that babies and toddlers make.

"It's such a relief that you're here," Andreas says. "We've been trying to eat as little as possible, but it's almost gone. We have a few days at most."

"Sounds like many are sick as well," I say.

The man responds with a grim nod and asks, "How do you plan on getting rid of the spiders?"

I clear my throat. This isn't going to go over well. "I'm not."

Andreas backs away, anger flashing in his eyes. "You lied! You just wanted to eat our food and—"

"Stop," I say. "I didn't lie. I *am* here to rescue you from the spiders. Just not in the way that you're thinking."

"Then...how?" Andreas asks.

"Let's find somewhere to sit. This is going to take a while to explain."

Andreas leads us to a bench near the altar, which is clear of any would-be eavesdroppers. As clearly as I can, I tell him about my conversation with the spider named Uttu and what her point of view is. I describe her reaction to learning about the humans and what they're going through. I also tell him that the spiders don't want to eat humans, but that they can help get rid of dead animals that otherwise could spread disease.

"So," I say, "Uttu has asked that you reach an agreement with her and the spiders. She will take down the web and help the village in any way that she can on two conditions."

"What are they?" Andreas asks. "We'll do anything!"

"Stop taking away their forest habitat," I say.

"Done. We don't need to expand."

"And make this a Temple of Arachne."

Andreas stares at me in horror. I've asked him to do the impossible, to betray his goddess. This isn't just changing the temple to another deity. Athena would surely abandon him if he honored one she had punished.

"I...cannot. Athena—"

"Did nothing while a bunch of giant spiders took over your village," I say, completing his sentence in a way I'm sure he didn't intend.

Andreas stares down at his lap. I stay quiet, letting him take his time to consider everything I've said. I get it; this is a big ask. But there are only a few days of food left for the villagers here, and so many are sick already. It's either betray Athena or watch those he clearly cared for die a slow, agonizing death.

Just like everywhere in the village, it's dark in this temple, but I can still see the silent tears sliding down his cheeks. He isn't like me. He chose to worship Athena, to spread her word and blessings. This choice is painful, like cutting off a family member or a part of himself.

Going down that train of thought makes me once again think about how NPCs are starting to act less like NPCs around me. The man sitting with me is having a crisis of faith. I was just supposed to destroy a web. Negotiating with him, sharing such a deep moment...This should be impossible.

I decide to break the silence. "I'm asking too much of you. I'm sorry."

Andreas shakes his head. "No, what must be done *must* be done. It doesn't matter what I want, when so many might die. Let the spiders know I will agree to their requests. I just hope that Athena forgives me."

This stuns me. I was certain just a moment ago that I was going to fail. Yet Andreas relented. Without lifting a blade or casting a spell, I'd fulfilled the conditions of my quest.

CHAPTER ELEVEN

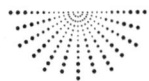

When I returned to Uttu, everything went even smoother. I watched as she climbed through the gap in the webbing, then all of us followed her and witnessed Arachne's children and the humans reach an agreement. Without fire, the *hundreds* of spiders in the village unraveled their web. The sighs of relief from the humans were like a song.

Now that we're back at camp, my friends are looking at me like I'm superhuman. Though Sylvia is busy building a fire to make dinner, she keeps glancing up to stare at me. When she notices me looking back, she returns her attention to her task. Joshua taps his chin as he stares. He doesn't care when I make eye contact with him. Guy gazes at me like a lovesick puppy. Cait and Tara are at my side as I walk toward Alexander. They have a lot to say about the day's events.

"That Beguiling Eyes favor really came in handy today, huh?" Cait says.

Tara pulls thoughtfully at a strand of her chin-length dark hair. "No, it's more than that. This is *not* how this works."

"How do you know?" Cait asks. "Maybe this was an alternate method we never encountered while beta testing."

"No, I agree with Tara," I say. "The NPCs aren't acting like NPCs. They weren't regurgitating canned responses. I could hear actual words as they talked to each other. The priest was interacting with me genuinely while I mediated his discussion with that spider lady. But I don't understand why."

Cait's red brows press together, making her look both stern and perplexed. "No, it must be a uniquely programmed result," she says. "Otherwise, that would mean...I don't know what it would mean, but this is a game, not real life."

I ponder all this as Alexander's features become clearer. There were a few times I'd wondered if he was acting strangely, like he was a "real boy" and not Pinocchio. Was there something new, something unexpected, going on?

"Hi, Alexander," I say when I'm face-to-face with him.

"Hello, Lauren," he responds. "Have you freed the village of their curse?"

"Lauren? He knows your name?" Tara asks. I can see the gears turning behind her hazel-brown eyes. She's thinking this is another sign that something's up with the NPCs.

"I asked him to call me that," I say and then return my attention to Alexander. "Arachne's children removed their web and have returned to the forest."

Alexander squints, like he's confused instead of just analyzing the data I've presented. I wonder if I've broken him. After too long of a beat, he says, "They left of their own volition?"

"Yep."

"And none of them were harmed?" he asks.

"Correct."

Alexander's mouth parts slightly in surprise. Then he looks off into the middle distance, and I can almost see him calculating whether this unexpected outcome fulfills the quest's requirements. Eventually, he looks back at me.

"Thank you for freeing the village of the spiders and their web," he says. "Here is your reward, as promised."

I don't even look at his extended palm. What's the point when I know that I'll receive the money before I can even attempt to grab it.

There's a ka-ching as coins pop into my inventory.

"What next?" I ask him.

"There's a lorekeeper named Nessa in the village," Alexander says.

"She needs an escort to the king to deliver an important message to him."

Cait groans. "Ugh, I hate escort quests."

"Is this the hard quest you told me about back at the starter village?" I ask.

Tara nods. "Unfortunately, this one isn't a side quest. Even if it was, you know we agreed to do *all* the quests in case an answer comes up."

"I know, I know," Cait grumbles as if Tara was telling her this instead of me.

I smile at Alexander. "We'll rest for now and get supplies tomorrow. We can take Nessa to the king after that."

Cait and Tara are already on their way to the fire where Sylvia is cooking when I take a step away.

"Lauren," Alexander says.

I turn around. "Yes, Alexander?"

"I...I never knew someone could do what you've done," he says with a tone of admiration. "You've surprised me."

I'm embarrassed by how pleased I am that I've impressed an NPC.

He almost seems truly human, until he blushes and says, "You're remarkable."

Well, wouldn't you know it? I unlocked that relationship scene I wanted so badly when I was in the real world. I didn't even need to pluck one dandelion. Yet, the enjoyable warmth that had just been spreading across my chest cools. This is Alexander following his coding, not breaking it.

So little is real here in Peripeteia. The romantic fantasy I'd had sitting in my living room back home is so false, so artificial. I wish I had taken the time to enjoy what was real while I was there. I could have spent more time with Mom and tried my hand at baking again. Practice makes progress, right? I even could have adopted a black cat. Though, now I'm glad I didn't do that. Poor thing would have been all alone.

Laughter from the fireside catches my attention, and I remember that there *is* something real in *Legends of Sacrifice*—the players. I should spend time with them, not listen to the relationship progression speech Alexander was programmed to give.

"Goodnight, Alexander," I say and walk back to my friends.

"Hey!" Guy calls out to me when I get close. "Heard you got the escort quest. Cait's gonna hate it."

I laugh with him. "Yeah, I remember her thinking I was an escort quest when I met you all." I stop to consider those words. "I guess I wound up being one in the end."

"Well, technically we *are* escorting you on your quests," Cait says and then sighs. "Though, I guess this one isn't so bad."

"Gee, thanks..." I respond.

Cait rolls her eyes. "Okay, maybe I *like* being around you. Sometimes. I'm glad you joined us."

A delightful sensation buzzes through me, and I feel warm tears pricking at the corners of my eyes. I really needed to hear that. "Really?"

"Me, too," Joshua says. "Even if you aren't a hot NPC who will bang me."

Cait elbows him in the ribs.

"Hey!" he cries out. "I was being nice!"

She chuckles. "Yeah, you actually kinda were."

"We're all really glad you're here," Sylvia says.

"Yup," Tara agrees. "And not just because you might help us find out what our offerings should be."

I nod. "Yeah, I know. It's because I'm a healer."

"No," Guy says, his voice soft and low. "Because you're our friend."

Though there are still strands of web draped over rooftops, carts, and various other surfaces, the village looks like an entirely new place. The biggest reminder that anything happened here is that the NPCs look haunted, not so much by the spiders, but by all they had to go through to survive.

We're here to shop for supplies, but it's becoming clear that this isn't at all feasible. The few merchants setting up their stalls today have little they can sell. Where would they get their goods from when they'd been cut off from the rest of the world? This is a big problem because we'd counted on this stop to get us to the next one.

Joshua gazes at it all, perplexed. "This is so weird. When we did this before, there was a celebration, and all the merchants had plenty to sell. This time it's just...sad. I hate it."

"Guess I'll be making good use of my foraging and hunting skills,"

Sylvia says when we pass by another grocer who has nothing left but half-rotted root vegetables. "I *hate* hunting."

"Isn't Artemis the Goddess of the Hunt?" I ask.

"Yeah, but she chose *me*. I didn't ask to be a hunter. I hate seeing them die."

This vibes with what I've learned about the archer during our time traveling together. Like me, she seems misplaced. I want to pack a more powerful punch, while she wants to play more of a supportive role.

Thinking back to yesterday, though, I realize that I would have hated to battle anyone to get the job done. Not so much because I was scared or reluctant to fight, but because I genuinely cared about everyone involved. I'm grateful for my Beguiling Eyes favor and high charisma score. Without that, things could have gone in a much more tragic direction.

Though Guy walks beside Sylvia and me, he's in an entirely different mindset.

"Joshua's right," he says. "When we did this before, everyone was happy. Now, they're all shell-shocked. NPCs don't get shell-shocked, do they?"

"Again, we've never solved the quest in this way," Cait responds. "Perhaps because Lauren fulfilled the mission in an empathetic way, we're seeing a more emotionally compelling outcome."

Joshua and Guy have a point, though. This isn't just a different mood from what they'd expected. The NPCs seem so real. Their background chatter is close to overwhelming me because I can actually hear the words.

Guy must notice that because he gestures to my ear. I'm tempted to take him up on it, though I turn his offer down, instead. Silencing other people's pain feels disrespectful.

We pass by a mother and her two small children sitting on their front doorstep. One is just a baby, feeding from her mother's very realistic breast. The other is a toddler leaning against his mother's legs. Tears had left a trail down his dirty face, but he's not weeping now. His eyes are dry, haunted, not a child's eyes at all, more like what you'd see on a soldier's face after a devastating battle.

"It will be all right, love," the mother whispers, and she runs her fingers tenderly through her son's hair. "I'm sure your father is...somewhere. And the hunters have promised to bring food later today. The spiders have even offered to help."

At the mention of spiders, the boy freezes up, and his eyebrows press together in an expression of agony and terror. A strange, high-pitched, primal sound resonates from him. It's not a scream or a shout or a cry. I don't know what to call it. I feel it, though.

His mind is lost, and his instincts are taking over. It sounds like he's channeling a spirit of grief and fury. He's just a little boy. He's so young that he may never remember a time when he experienced normal.

Except he isn't real, right? NPCs don't experience trauma.

They're not supposed to stray from their programming either, though. What if Tara was right at the tavern when we first met? Could the people from Peripeteia *feel*? Prior to this, were they incapable of expressing their emotions?

Are these NPCs just a string of code in the most realistic and immersive video game ever? Or are they something more? What purpose does it serve the game to have us witness all of it?

I need to stop dwelling on this. Aphrodite is waiting on some mysterious offering. That needs to be my focus because I've already done what I could here. As difficult as it is to walk past all this suffering, I can't take their trauma away.

So I turn my attention back to my companions. "There may not be fresh food here, but I don't think clothing can rot within a few weeks of sitting around a shop. Let's at least get some warm stuff to wear before we pick up our escort quest."

"You're right," Guy responds. "I think I remember the tailor's shop being somewhere near the temple."

"Let's head that way, then," I say.

But I turn my head to look at the woman again. She's looking straight at me. There's something in her eyes that doesn't invite conversation, but it sends a message just the same. The quests exist for the players. If not for us, there would be no conflict or loss.

Stop it, Lauren. She's not real. It's just a game.

The mother unlatches her baby from her breast. The infant cries immediately. She responds to the child with a gentle shush but soon joins in her crying.

It's just a game.

CHAPTER TWELVE

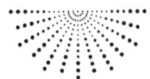

Lorekeeper Nessa is annoying. Whenever we stop for even a moment, she says the same thing: "We must get to the king." Not a "hurry up" or nagging so much as a reminder that we have a mission. It was incredibly grating when we sat to eat lunch. For an hour, every other minute, she'd parrot that line.

The good thing about it, though, is that she's behaving like an NPC. I don't have to worry about whether she has feelings. The woman is robotic and predictable. I want to throttle her, but at least my heart isn't weeping at the sight of her.

"We must get to the king," Nessa says as I take off my shoe to shake a rock out.

"I *know!*" I shout and groan.

"See why I hate escort missions?" Cait asks.

"They're a pain in the butt on video games," I say, "and even worse like this."

"Yes!" Cait responds. "Like we get it, Nessa! We have a quest!"

"It's the fucking worst," I say, nodding.

Cait frowns and squints at me.

I hold up my hands defensively. "Sorry, it slipped. Swearing is my mother tongue."

With a sigh, Cait says, "I'll try to ignore it, but you really should clean up your language."

"Can I ask why it bothers you so much?" I ask. "They're only words."

"Taking the Lord's name in vain breaks a commandment," she answers.

"Wait, are you, like, a hardcore Christian or something?"

Cait crosses her arms. "Would that be so surprising? It's not like we're an endangered species."

"But you're fulfilling a quest for a Greek god! Surely that's shaken your faith a little."

"Ares?" Cait laughs. "You believe he's an actual god? That any of them are? We're in a *video game*. They're NPCs like the others. They're part of the end game so that we can go home."

I wonder how she can hold on to her religion so tightly and so flippantly disregard our tangible reality. Nothing here makes sense, and the whole situation is beyond surreal, but we're walking through Peripeteia. I just had to take off my shoe because a real rock was bothering me. There's a stitch in my side from the jog we had to make to get past a pride of lions before they spotted us. This certainly feels more real to me than a God who has a problem with people saying "fuck."

"Well, agree to disagree on that," I say. "I hope we can still be friends even if I don't live in a way that's Christian-approved."

Cait cocks an amused brow. "If I couldn't get along with non-Christians, would I hang out with this group? I mean, look at Joshua. He's constantly breaking some commandment, and we're friends."

"You're friends?" I ask.

"Of course we are!" she answers. "Why wouldn't we be?"

"I've always thought of you as simply tolerating him. You're always getting on to him about being a perv."

"Just like I'm always getting on to you about your language," she says, which is a great point. "I nag because I see the best in you. Joshua *is* a perv, but he's also the first person to lift our spirits. I know he acts like a fool sometimes. It's easy to write him off as an annoyance at first. Yet he'll put off taking care of himself to play us music or tell a bunch of jokes when we've had a hard day because deep down, he cares about his friends."

96

That was all true. I recalled those moments he showed a sincere side as well. Maybe he acted like a weirdo, but who am I to judge? I'm sure I'm annoying as hell to some people, too.

"Well, I'm glad we're friends," I respond and then put my shoe back on.

"We must get to the king," Nessa says.

"We know!" Cait and I shout in unison.

Then we both laugh and share a look. Maybe Cait actually likes having me in the group. She's been grumpy with me so much in the past, but that could just be her personality. And right now, she's looking at me like...

Is that admiration? That can't be right.

While we've been chatting, everyone else has continued marching toward our quest objective. However, the moment I'm ready to catch up with them, I see Guy up ahead with his hand up to indicate everyone should halt.

"Looks like the sun is going to set any minute now," he says. "I think I recall there being an ambush area not far from here. We need to rest before we get there."

"We must get to the king," Nessa says.

"How can we rest when she's constantly popping off like that?" I ask.

Cait, who had moments ago shown some level of softness, shrugs and says, "Deal with it or don't. Better to try for a rest now than get ambushed while worn out."

Guess she's back to being a grump.

Though I'm grumbling aloud about how annoying our guest is, I'm a little more worried about something else. I didn't hear the voice last night. I don't know that I expected to level up or anything, but I hoped I'd at least get *something* for saving an entire village and establishing negotiations between Arachne's children and the humans that lived there.

Did I do something wrong? Did I break the system, and the consequence is that the game didn't recognize my accomplishment? I remind myself again that this is just a game. I don't actually even need to level up or whatever to accomplish my goal of getting home. Mom needs me. That's so much more important than a gold star for my efforts.

But if I broke the game, seeing Mom might not be possible.

Tara and Sylvia wander off into the woods to hunt and forage before it gets too dark. Cait and Joshua work together to set up camp. That leaves Guy and me to keep watch over Nessa. We obviously have the hardest job out of all of them.

"We must get to the king," Nessa says, looking at the horizon.

I groan, and Guy laughs. "Just think of her as a parrot," he says. "Her words are meaningless. Plus, by the time we're done with dinner, she'll be asleep. Even the NPCs have a power saving mode."

"I just wish your silencing spell could work on her."

"Sorry, any NPC we escort is temporarily part of our party. That's how it works."

This reminds me of what's been bothering me about the village we just left. "Did you notice that there wasn't any wordless background chatter when we were searching for supplies?"

Guy nods. He has a gentle smile, but I can see the seriousness in his eyes. "That's unusual, but I'm thinking it's probably because you unlocked a rare achievement. Consider it as opening up a storyline, maybe. Like a prize for accomplishing what so many others couldn't."

I think about the haunted eyes and tearful, trembling conversations. If that's a prize, I wish I'd lost.

"I'd rather level up or get any kind of spell, skill, or favor out of what I did yesterday," I respond.

"You didn't?" Guy asks.

I shake my head.

"Well, it gets harder the higher up you go," he continues. "I've been level thirty-one for twenty-four days now."

"Yeah, but *nothing*?" I ask. "Not even a skill about mediation or something?"

"We must get to the king," Nessa says.

I imagine her following that up with a caw, a whistle, and a "Polly wants a cracker." That makes me giggle. Guy is right. If I just think about her as a parrot, she's not so bad. This is enough to put my worries on the back burner. I'd like to enjoy the moments we have in between quests.

The smell of the campfire reaches me, and I'm already salivating.

My Pavlovian response makes me impatient for Sylvia and Tara to return.

"We haven't been the best guides for you on this journey," Guy says out of nowhere. "There's so much we haven't told you yet. I think we just keep forgetting stuff from this early on until you're already there."

I respond with a dismissive wave. "That's okay. Without you, I would have had to learn all this on my own. I'd also be running around mostly naked and starving so..."

"The mostly naked part wasn't so bad," Guy says with a chuckle.

I smack his arm. "Joshua's a bad influence on you."

Guy gives me a crooked smile that I'm sure he means to look rakish, but it leans more on the shy side. "You're a Cleric of Aphrodite," he says. "Surely, you've picked up that I'm attracted to you."

Even though I didn't believe it at first, it doesn't take Aphrodite to clue me in on that. Guy has blushed so often and given me so many admiring glances, I'd have to be clueless not to notice. I don't know what to make of it, though. He's sweet and attractive, so I should probably hop on him right now. But the last time a guy liked me, I wasted more than a decade of my life on someone who didn't really love me. If I wasn't good enough for Doug, what makes me think Guy won't get tired of me in a few days? Things would be so *weird* in the group.

Besides, I need to get back to Mom. I was so eager in the real world for a distraction from my pain over her imminent death. Now that my life is full of distractions, I don't want them. They could be the difference between seeing Mom one last time and not.

I look at Alexander, who's staring off at the burning orange line narrowly separating the horizon from the starry sky. When I first booted up *Legends of Sacrifice* on my computer, I was immediately besotted with him. I was far from his only fan girl, but I think it was more than his purposefully designed heart-throbbiness.

Yes, I was the one who broke up with Doug, but it still broke my heart. The dream of love died when I realized it was only going to get worse for the two of us, so real relationships scare the hell out of me now. Guy is real; Alexander is not. While my attraction to an NPC is laughable and depressing, it's risk-free. I can leave this game and Alexander without regrets. I can go back to Mom without breaking anyone's heart, including mine. Someone like Guy could devastate me, especially with how fragile I am right now.

I need to be honest with him. Though not *too* honest. As much as I like everyone in my party, I'm not ready to divulge what's going on with Mom right now. It's too...*vulnerable*. I decide to just tell him about Doug.

"Right before I came here, I ended a really long relationship with a guy I'd loved since high school," I say. Already I can see realization dawning on Guy's face. He knows he's about to be turned down. "I don't get why Aphrodite chose me because love fucking terrifies me."

"I get it," Guy says. I can tell he's trying to sound casual, but his smile is forced now. "The feeling isn't mutual. That's okay."

He begins to get up, and I realize how lost I'll feel if he leaves right now. Just last night, I'd stared at Alexander, and it dawned on me how much I long for authenticity. Even if it will probably gut punch me, eventually.

I grab Guy's arm. "Stop."

Guy stares at me with astonishment for a moment and then sits back down.

"I'm not saying I want you to be my boyfriend or anything," I tell him. "We barely know each other, but..."

"Yes?"

I can't believe what I'm about to say. This is so opposite of where my thoughts were turning just a moment ago. "I was already living in a dream world before I stepped foot in Peripeteia. I'd like to feel something *real* for once, even if it's just a flutter or a good fuck. Even if we realize we're not a good match, or you can't stand the sight of me anymore."

"Are you saying you'll give me a chance?"

Guy looks so earnest right now, but I don't know much about him except he's hot and generous. So far, at least. I hope I don't break his heart.

Lauren, if anyone's heart is going to break, it's yours.

"Just promise me you won't hate me if things don't turn out how you want them to be," I say. "I may not be the person who lives in your head."

"I promise," he says.

He better mean it.

⇧

ONCE AGAIN, CAIT AND I TREK CLOSE TOGETHER AS WE ESCORT Lorekeeper Nessa to the king who lives north of her village. This should be the last day of this voyage, barring anything awful happening. I've had social anxiety my whole life, so it's weird how natural it feels to gab with her.

In high school, she was the popular mean girl, and I was the weird loner kid. She's no-nonsense and a little judgmental; I have very little self-confidence and the mouth of a sailor. We shouldn't get along this well. I guess gaming brings all types together, though. Besides, our conversation is enough to distract us from the constant loop of "We must get to the king." It also takes my mind off the blisters forming on my feet.

"Okay, so you haven't leveled up in a couple of days," Cait says. "That's not super concerning. Turning in quests is usually how that happens, and you've only turned in one since you leveled up last time."

"Yeah, that's what Guy said," I tell her. "I was still a little worried, though, and I'm pretty relieved that I finally heard the voice last night."

Cait nods. "Title gains are an interesting acknowledgment from the game. Kind of an 'I see what you did, and now other people get to know about it, too.'" She points to the new title I earned under my name, goddess, and class. "Risk Taker, though? Surprised that you didn't get that from seeking peace with Arachne's children. What on earth did you do yesterday besides follow Nessa?"

There's only one thing it could be, and I don't know if I want to tell Cait. On the one hand, Doug is the only person I've ever dated, and it's kind of exciting to try it out with someone new. On the other hand, our social circle is more of a speck. Do I really want everyone in our business? How would they even react? A romance in our group could spell disaster if it went sideways.

I decide Cait's probably going to figure it out eventually anyway. I might as well get the satisfaction of getting some potential schoolgirl-type giggles out of it.

"Um, so...last night something happened," I start.

Cait cocks an inquisitive brow and smirks. She knows I'm about to dish out something juicy. "Go on."

"Guy and I were talking, and, well…I think we might be kinda dating now?" Ending my statement as a question reminds me of how ambivalent the whole situation is. I'm still scared as fuck that I'll get hurt, but I'm not mad at the idea that I might make out with a hot guy soon.

Cait freezes. Every feature on her face flattens. "I see."

"What?"

"I'm not sure how that was a risk for you," she says, practically growling out the words.

I don't know how I expected Cait to react, but I'm a little stunned that she seems even grumpier than usual.

"It is a risk," I continue. "I've only ever dated one guy before, and he broke my heart."

Cait responds with a jaded chuckle. "Oh, I don't think your heart is the one to be worried about. You're a Cleric of *Aphrodite*. The game is practically beckoning you to play around with everyone else's feelings."

The fuck she say to me?

"I'm not playing around with feelings!"

"Sure, Lauren," she says. "Not yet. Not on purpose at least."

"What the fuck are you—?"

I don't get to finish that question, though. A chorus of howls stops us all in our tracks. Even Nessa shuts the hell up.

"What was that?" I ask Cait in a whisper.

"Lycanthropes," she answers.

"Lycanthropes? You mean like werewolves?!"

I turn to look at Guy, who's standing very far ahead. I glare at him, hoping he can read the, "You said you were going to tell me this stuff ahead of time" in my expression. He winces and offers an apologetic shrug that I'm pretty sure means, "Sorry, I got distracted the moment you mentioned being naked."

Cait squeezes my hand reassuringly, which surprises me almost as much as the howling. She went from pissed at me for no good reason to friendly fast.

"It's going to be okay, Little Red Riding Hood," she says. "Just stick next to me and keep your spells ready. I'll protect you from the Big Bad Wolf."

Maybe she's trying to come off as sarcastic, but damn, her promise of protection is kinda sexy. I might appreciate it more if I wasn't scared out of my damn mind.

Cait puts an arm around my trembling shoulders and whispers, "Seriously, don't worry. They're not as scary as they sound. I promise."

The calm, reassuring look in her eyes settles my nerves. I remember that I'm surrounded by veterans. This is a level two quest, and they're all in their upper twenties and lower thirties.

There's another wave of howls, which sound closer this time.

"We must get to the king," Nessa says.

"Now for the hardest part of an escort quest," Cait says with a sigh. "For more than a day now, I've hated this woman, and I'm going to have to keep her alive, even when she does something stupid like run up to a wolf."

"Well, I guess that's what I'm here for," I say, wishing I had more confidence in my healing spells.

Cait nods. "If she doesn't stay alive, it's not the end of the world. She'll just respawn, and you can choose whether you want to redo the quest or abandon it."

"Wait, you can abandon quests?"

Terrifying creatures with patchy fur, long claws, and red eyes prowl out from the forest. Their howls have turned to growls of hunger and blood lust.

"More on that later," Cait says. "Let's kill these guys first."

A werewolf lunges right at Nessa. I suppose it correctly sized her up as the weakest prey. That or the game is programmed to make escort quests a pain in the ass. Nessa screams and falls to the ground. There are long claw marks on her arms. A health bar pops over her head and is instantly down by half. Fuck.

"Heal Major Wounds!" I shout as I point my staff at her.

Nessa's health bar goes up some, but there's still a quarter-sized chunk missing from her health bar. At least the claw marks seem to be gone. That doesn't do anything about the werewolf hovering over her and about to strike again, though.

Sylvia looses an arrow, and it flies straight into the werewolf's temple, dropping it to its side. I squeak as its body rolls my way. Fortunately, it stops before it can touch me.

Another werewolf dashes forward, this time at me. Cait springs into action. She raises her great axe over her head, cleaving the very center top of the beast's skull. The werewolf makes a wounded puppy noise, and I fight a maternal response to soothe it as it falls the moment Cait dislodges her axe.

"Told you I'd protect you," she says smiling down at me like a radiant angel of justice. Only blood-splattered.

Goddamn! How can she make gore look so hot?

Four more werewolves rush out from the woods, but Sylvia and Guy work together, her with arrows and him with rapid-fire spells, making short work of the monsters. Sylvia's wolf, Marshmallow, also gets involved, going for the throat of anyone who gets close to his pink-haired friend. Joshua and Tara keep pulling Nessa away from the monsters, which makes it a lot easier to handle the job. Just like the one that attacked me, the werewolves Sylvia and Guy kill make pitiful sounds as they slump to their deaths.

There's one werewolf left, the big guy, the obvious boss. He huffs, more like a bull than a canine. A thick rope of slobber hangs like a pendulum from his growling mouth. His red eyes fix on Nessa.

Like a complete idiot, Lorekeeper Nessa frees herself from Joshua and Tara and races toward him, shouting, "You'll feel the true smite of Zeus now, King Lycaon!"

Wait...Is this the king she's supposed to meet? I thought she was supposed to give him some important message. I guess "eat shit and die" is what she came here to tell him.

I don't have time to question it any further because now King Lycaon and Nessa are barreling at each other like the most terrifying game of chicken I've ever witnessed.

"Ignite!" Guy shouts, and flames immediately engulf the werewolf. Guy slumps forward a little from the moderate energy sap.

Fortunately, this werewolf doesn't let out plaintive yips on his way to the ground. Instead, he screams like a real person, which isn't great either. As he does, he shifts from wolf to man. To my horror, his eyes turn to me during his final moment. I loved Indiana Jones when I was a kid. Hell, I wanted to *be* him when I grew up. But I always thought the scene where the Nazis' eyes all start melting was a complete fabrication. It wasn't. Your eyes can literally melt when they're on fire.

Jesus shit-on-a-biscuit Christ.

Then Nessa does something even more boneheaded than before —*she runs into the fire!*

"Goddamn it!" I shout at her. "You stupid fucking asshole!"

I dash in her direction as Joshua pulls her away from King Lycaon's flaming corpse and Guy casts his water spell over the flames lapping up her long skirt. She's got maybe a fifth of her health bar left.

"Heal Major Wounds!" I shout, sounding more annoyed than powerful as I cast my spell at her. This gets her health bar up to a third full.

Cait joins Joshua, and together, they're able to keep her completely contained. For such an old woman, she sure is strong. Guy uses his water spell to douse the fire currently using the king's charred corpse as kindling.

With the fire no longer a threat, Cait and Joshua can let go of Nessa, and she runs back to King Lycaon. From out of nowhere, she pulls out a staff of lightning and hammers it into the dead werewolf's skull. "You'll terrorize the good folk of this land no longer," she cries. "Zeus has put an end to his curse so that others might live."

Then, Nessa gingerly walks over to me with a broad smile. "Thank you for your help, adventurer. Sorry that I didn't tell you the truth before. I wasn't sure you'd take the job. Here's your payment."

With a ka-ching, nine silver pieces enter my inventory. The annoying old lady proceeds to walk away from us back toward her village, completely alone. Now that the threat of werewolves is over, she doesn't need our protection anymore.

"I *hate* escort missions," Cait grumbles.

I whirl around, anger at my other friends replacing my annoyance with Nessa. "What the *fuck*?" I shout at them. "Think you could have told me a lot earlier that we were going to be battling goddamn werewolves?"

"Guy didn't tell you?" Cait asks.

I shake my head.

Cait huffs and sneers at Guy. "I guess he was busy doing more important things."

Guy steps toward me, his eyebrows tented apologetically. "I'm sorry, Lauren."

"Sorry doesn't cut it!" I scan the group, pointing an accusatory finger at everyone, including Alexander, who did *nothing* to help during the battle. "You need to keep me in the loop ahead of time. I haven't been here for months like you. This is all new to me. I shouldn't be surprised by werewolves when you've all done this before."

They all stare at me with open mouths and guilty eyes, completely silent because they know there's nothing they can say to redeem themselves.

"Now make camp!" I command.

"But it's midday..." Sylvia says.

"And I'm fucking tired from healing that Nessa bitch over and over!" I yell back. "We're resting until tomorrow, when *hopefully* my nerves won't be so rattled!"

I storm away until I realize I don't have anywhere to go to. The forest? No damn way. There might be more monsters lurking there. Everything else is just a long road for as far as I can see. So I find a large rock on the edge of the path and plant my butt on it with a huff.

My friends set up camp as I insisted. Occasionally, they look at me with chastened expressions. My rage cools down, but I fight the urge to forgive them out of pure stubbornness. When the smell of roasting meat reaches me, I relent. My hunger reminds me just how much these people have done for me.

Even though my stomach growls, I take my time walking back. I don't want to seem too eager to make amends. When I get close, Guy jumps up from his seat by the fire and guides me to the campfire.

As he does so, he whispers, "I really am sorry. I meant to tell you last night, but I forgot all about it."

I shrug. "Yeah, I guess I get it."

"I'll do better," he says. "I promise."

The sweet sincerity in his voice and expression convinces me. "Ugh, fine. I forgive you."

We sit next to each other, and Sylvia passes me some roasted rabbit and stewed greens of some kind. It smells amazing. Without Sylvia, I'd probably be eating dangerous berries in the woods.

"Thanks," I tell her and to the rest of the group. "Thanks for taking care of me, even when I'm yelling at you."

Joshua smiles. "Hey, you've put up with me this long. Plus, you're right. We need to do a better job preparing you for stuff." Everyone nods, and Joshua continues, "For instance, Guy farts in his sleep. So maybe don't fall asleep cuddling after sex."

Guy blushes in horror and drops his face into his hands. "Oh my God, I'm so sorry. I was so excited, and it just came out of me. I'm sure you didn't want anyone to know, but I—"

He's just so damn cute right now. I don't think anyone's ever crushed on me, not even Doug in the beginning. But Guy likes me; he *really* does. It's like he thinks I'm more than a Cleric of Aphrodite, like I'm the Goddess of Love herself. And honestly, that's really doing it for me right now.

So, fuck it.

I pull Guy's hands away from his face and tilt his chin so that he can look at me. "It's okay," I say, then I kiss him on his still-blushing cheek.

Except for Cait, who has a scowl on her face, the group choruses some celebratory whoops, while Guy smiles at me giddily. We take a moment to gaze at each other. Then, he pulls me to his side so that my head rests happily on his shoulder. This could be fun—maybe even great. We'll just have to see.

"Back on topic, though," Cait says in an all-business tone. "You should know that eventually we're going to have to kill a demon lady. Fortunately, that's after we go through a town first with only a few side quests."

What a relief!

CHAPTER THIRTEEN

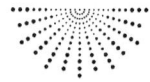

W hen I got my cleric robes, I bemoaned the fact that they were white and would get stained in no time. The magic in its cloth must be keeping it clean because I'm grimy from head to toe, but my outfit is spotless. Sylvia tells me it won't be enough for Level 3 quests, though. So part of our aim in the bustling town of Thebe is to get me new cleric robes.

That will have to wait until after we all take a long bath. When we were in the starting zone, we had easy access to clean water. On our journey on the road from the spider village to this town, though, we were nowhere near a water source. Every drop on hand needed to be conserved for drinking, and that needed to be rationed carefully.

I practically lusted for a long, hot soak, and Cait told me there's a bathhouse in Thebe that's worth every copper piece it requires. However, the attendant told us it's two silver for the bath alone, more if you want anything extra like *soap*. It hits me then how poor I am.

"I've got you covered," Guy tells me.

"You need to stop paying for everything," I say. "I don't want you thinking I'm your sugar baby."

He smirks. "And what would be so wrong with that? I like the idea of spending money on you."

"Mm-hmm…" I respond. "You just don't want me stinking so bad when we get intimate."

To my surprise, Guy puts his arms around me and smells my hair. So far, he's been very reserved, always letting me take the lead with physical touch. I don't know if it's because he's trying to respect my boundaries or he's trying not to scare me off. Right now, though, he's showing a side of him I haven't seen before.

"Even covered in dirt, you smell good," he whispers. "Like sugar and campfire smoke."

"Liar," I playfully chide, while secretly tingling from his breath on my ear.

I think back to when he touched my ear for the silencing spell. It tingles pleasantly. I wonder how it feels when he touches other places.

I better take that bath.

There's a ka-ching, and I see an entire gold piece show up in my inventory. I gasp. Holy shit! Is Guy *rich*? No wonder it didn't bother him to spend a few coppers on my basic gear and food.

"Get anything you want," he says as he steps away. "They've got roses and everything. I'll be on the men's side of the bathhouse."

I nod, probably looking like an idiot as he walks away. When I turn toward the women's side of the bathhouse, I see Cait looking annoyed with me.

"What?" I ask.

"You're wasting time," she gripes. "We need to get our baths and get you upgraded gear. Also, like I told you earlier, there's another temple here. Our deities will want us to check in."

"That doesn't mean we can't enjoy ourselves a little," I tell her. "Chill."

I want to tell her to yank the stick out of her ass, but that will only make her more abrasive. Cait's such a hot and cold person. I'm glad she's my friend, but Jesus, she can be a pain in the ass sometimes.

When we get to the women's side, I take a gander at the menu and realize I'm going to have money to spare.

"I'll take the exfoliation, the soap, the rose petals, the hair wash with scalp massage, the extra rinse of hot water, and the pedicure."

When the attendant leaves to get supplies, I squeal at Cait. "They have pedicures here! I've never had one before."

Cait gasps. "You've never had a pedicure?"

I shake my head. "Nope. I mean, I've obviously clipped my toenails, but I've never even stepped into a nail salon."

"Why on earth not?"

"I don't know," I say. "Just seemed like something only pretty girls got to do."

Cait rolls her eyes. "Oh my God, Lauren. You *are* a pretty girl!" She sighs. "I've changed my mind. Our main objective today is to have a girls' day out. After we're done here, we're getting you some nice accessories and getting your hair done. Fortunately, the game designers remembered to cater to us vanity players, too."

The attendant returns and guides us to a changing room, where we store our clothing in lockable boxes. I expected to be given a bathrobe or something, but no, we're completely naked. The differences between my body and Cait's are extremely clear now. While she's svelte and toned, I'm plump and about as far from muscular as a person can get. I try not to look at her, but it's hard not to. She's *right there* and just about the prettiest person I've ever met. Practically lickable.

Get it together, Lauren. You're exploring things with Guy, and Cait is definitely straight.

Two women guide us to large marble slabs, elevated so that we can lie on them without having to crouch first. I expect the stone to be cold, but it seems they've heated it somehow. It's surprisingly comfortable. One woman uses a salt scrub on every inch of my body, except for the more sensitive areas. It feels so good that I almost fall asleep.

Once the scrub is over, my personal attendant washes me off and leads me to a hip bath made of terracotta. The water inside is light pink and milky with rose petals scattered on the surface. It looks like something out of a travel magazine's spa destination article. I lower myself in and find that it's the perfect temperature. The smell of roses is strong but not overwhelming. It's heaven.

Because it's a hip bath, the water covers only my lower half. So, I grab the sponge on the table next to me and squeeze the water over my shoulder and chest before lathering it up and cleaning my body completely. Throughout the whole bath, Cait is in the tub next to me. Thank goodness for the privacy screen between us. Without it, I'd be too distracted to chat with her about our plans for the day. Even with the divider, I can't forget that Cait is naked just a few feet away. All I'd have to do to see her is lean forward and crane my neck.

My experience in Peripeteia has been a roller coaster. Overall, this entire experience has overwhelmed me in one fashion or another. I've been confused and in denial, not to mention missing Mom more and more every day. And I'm still trying not to think about that dead harpy. When we completed the cercopes quest, I felt victorious and celebrated. The spider quest terrified me, then made me feel proud, but ultimately, I'm still in despair that I'm so powerless to help the villagers move on. Now I feel romantic stirrings with Guy and a little lustful toward a pretty bitchy barbarian. It's all just so much.

One thing I never expected to experience here is giddiness at the prospect of a self-care day with a gal pal. This is like the fantasy RPG version of *Pretty Woman*, except I won't be prostituting myself to some millionaire.

Okay, so it turns out that Guy is rich, but it's not like I'm exchanging sex for gifts.

Wait...does he expect sex after this?

"Hey, so about Guy," I say. "You've known him a lot longer than me. He seems like a great person, but I mean...I don't know how to ask this."

"Are you asking me if he's secretly a jerk? Because he isn't."

"No, I mean..." I sigh. "He's paying for so much. Back home, girls say if a man spends a lot of money on you, he expects something in return."

My friend laughs, almost *guffaws*. It's so deep and loud that it's unnatural coming from someone so completely feminine. "What did he give you for this spa day? A gold coin?"

"Yeah."

"That's *nothing* for him," Cait says. "He rarely spends any money. Not because he's tightfisted but because he just doesn't care about anything that costs money and isn't strictly necessary for questing. Honestly, I'm surprised he's at the bathhouse, too. He usually just finds a stream or something and cleans up with a cold dip."

"Oh, so, he's not rich?"

"I didn't say that. He does a lot of the side quests for fun, so he makes more money than we do."

"Oh, well, I guess I don't feel so bad, then," I say.

But this doesn't settle my nervousness at all. No one's ever pursued me like this. I don't know how to respond to it.

"It's okay," Cait says with a sigh. "Don't get me wrong. I still think it's a bad idea for you two to get romantic. You barely know each other, and this could turn into a Yoko Ono situation if you two aren't careful."

"I promise we'll be smart about things," I say. "We've already discussed being mature about things if it turns out we're not a good match."

"Did you talk about what might happen if someone else in the group develops feelings for you?" Cait asks.

"Well, no. But I don't think that'll happen."

"You really don't think you're attractive?"

I motion in her direction, though I know she can't see through the privacy screen. "Cait, look at you. You're *perfect*. I'm...well..." I look down at myself. "Even Doug used to call me squishy."

"Doug?" Cait asks.

"My ex."

"He sounds like he has turds for brains," she says. "Lauren, you're..." She goes silent for a long beat. "There was this cartoon that I saw once at a friend's house. It's the kind of movie that my parents would *never* let me watch. I really shouldn't have, but I couldn't look away. It was so good."

"What was it?" I ask.

"*Wizards,*" she says. "It was by this guy named Ralph Bakshi. One of the main characters is a fairy. She's so round. All curves everywhere. If she were a real woman, people would call her fat." A small sigh escapes Cait. "You could see through her clothes to her breasts. Lauren, she was so beautiful, so *sexy*, and you look so much like her."

I can tell I'm blushing because my entire face is as hot as a stovetop. "Oh. Well, I'm sure that's not many people's taste."

"Even if it's not, remember that you're a Cleric of Aphrodite. People are going to be drawn to you romantically and sexually. And you're going to be mostly around our party. Even if someone isn't looking for love, they might accidentally tumble into it with you."

"You think Guy...?" I trail off.

What if he's not really into me, and it's just Aphrodite's power? My heart plummets. I may not be looking for anything serious right now, but I *am* attracted to him, and I don't want our entire relationship to be a lie.

Cait shakes her head. "No, he's really into you. I've known him for months. Not only are you hot, but you both have a lot more in common than you know."

That's a huge relief. So much so that I close my eyes and even my breathing for a moment.

Our attendants return, ready to rinse me off and then take me to get my pedicure. My thoughts once more return to how the rest of our day will unfold.

"Girls' day out!" I call out to Cait as she's escorted back to the changing room.

She responds with a big smile and a thumbs up. "We're going to have a blast!" she promises.

I DIDN'T HAVE MUCH TIME TO ENJOY GUY'S APPRECIATIVE GLANCES when I finished with my bathhouse pampering because Cait whisked me away. To my delight, when we bumped into Tara and Sylvia, they decided to join us as well, even though earlier they'd chosen to clean up with fresh water using our camp's wooden barrel bathtub.

They both seem refreshed from their clean ups. We're fortunate that video game logic means our entire camp's worth of supplies and furniture are stored in some mysterious nether space until we need them. All they have to do is snap their fingers, and every item is available for us to set up.

This town is a pleasant change of pace from our tents, though. It's bigger than the last two villages we've gone to. The temple stands tall and grand within a concentric circle of roads. On the very outer edge are roads for the homes, then inward from those are the basic shops, and the more elite stores stand closest to the temple.

We walk the innermost roads as we shop for the best accessories and clothing. None of this is just for show, of course. It's a video game. We can't wear stuff that doesn't serve a purpose. My new chiton grants me the ability to light up dark spaces. That would have been *really* helpful in the spider village, but I try not to dwell on it.

My earrings grant me the ability to communicate with a partner who wears a matching pair. We decide to give the other pair to Tara so she can let us know what she spies when she lurks around our enemies. My new bangles add enough of a strength boost to negate my penalty. I also get a small, delicate laurel of tiny brass leaves. This brings my wisdom score to seventeen so that it's even with intelligence. Cait still prompts me to train in wisdom, however.

After that, we all get an updated hairdo. Cait usually keeps her hair in a practical ponytail until we're relaxing at the end of the day, when she brushes it out. However, she lets the hairdresser give her braids that make her seem even more like a Viking princess. It is, of course, incredibly hot. Sylvia's hair gets teased and manipulated so that her pink afro takes on the shape of a cloudlike mohawk with gold hair pins keeping it in place. Tara gets her dark hair trimmed so that it is chin length.

As pretty as I know my golden blonde hair is, I rarely do anything with it. Like Cait, it's usually in a ponytail. But my friends prompt me to do something special. And why not? Maybe it will only last for the day, but today's my day to feel *girly*. So, I give in to that urge all the way.

The stylist makes a crown of loose braids at the top of my head, a perfect place to perch my laurel. The thin layer of hair not braided is curled into wispy spirals that brush against my shoulders. This will be a bitch to undo later, but I don't care because of how good I feel when my friends gasp and fawn over how pretty they think I am.

After all our vanity shopping is done, it's time to head to the temple where I'll get an upgrade on my staff and check in with Aphrodite. I wonder what my deity will have to say, but I'm more interested in presenting her with a list of questions of my own.

First, how do I improve my faith and wisdom scores? How likely is it I'll accidentally attract people? Is it a good idea for me to date *anyone*, let alone someone in my party? Most importantly, what's up with this personal quest she's given me?

All of my thoughts pause the moment we enter the temple. It's more like a tourist trap than a place of worship here. Crowds of players and NPCs alike have packed every inch of the place. With so many real people in there, the sound of their chatting is too much for me.

I clap my hands over my ears and shake my head. "I can't."

Cait nods and guides me out of the temple, while Sylvia and Tara follow us. We make our way to an alley that's relatively quiet compared to the interior of the place of worship. I lean against the wall with my hand over my heart as I count breaths until they're even.

When I finally feel somewhat normal again, I nod at my friends. "Thanks."

"No problem," Cait says. "It was overwhelming for me, too."

"I guess the newbies caught up with us," Sylvia says.

"How?" Tara asks. "There was no one within sight of our whole trip here. They all were just starting the harpy quest when we left the starting zone."

"Because they didn't have anything slowing them down on the way here," Guy says from behind, surprising us all.

We turn around to see him and Joshua. Guy's mouth drops open, and his eyes might as well be heart-shaped with the way he's looking at me.

"God, you look good," he whispers to me and strokes one of my curls with his index finger. I warm under his praise. "Better than good. You look like Aphrodite herself."

Cait shushes him. "Are you dumb or something?" She points at the temple while glaring at Guy.

Guy drops his hand and looks at the building nervously. "That was a joke," he says. "No human could come close to being as beautiful as Aphrodite." But then he turns back to me. "But *wow*, you're gorgeous."

"You're so sweet," I say, blushing.

"What did you say about nothing slowing them down?" Tara asks, bringing us back to reality.

"While you were out shopping, Joshua and I came here to check in with our deities, and we had to wait in line for a long time," Guy says. "We eavesdropped on the people near us. Seems that the spider village quest is glitched."

"Glitched?" Tara asks.

"Yeah, there's no web, and no one needs saving," Joshua answers. "They're all rattled, but living regular lives. So, the newbs all skipped that one and went straight for the escort mission. That cut out a couple of days of work for them."

We're all silent for a moment, each of us wondering the same thing. Did we break that quest when I helped Arachne's children make peace with the villagers? That shouldn't be possible. It should have reset once we were out of sight. The web should have been back, and the humans should have been cloistering in their homes in fear.

I should be horrified that the game can be changed that way. If a quest can glitch, what else can? What if a boss just *never* shows up for a battle? What if enemies respawn the moment a player vanquishes them? Worst of all, could we all suddenly die for no reason?

Despite all that, though, I'm happy. I don't want the spiders or the villagers going through any of that all over again. I *want* to have impacted their lives positively for good, even if that's foolish. They're NPCs for fuck's sake. They don't have feelings or know they're in an endless loop.

I think back to that mother and her two small children. What if they do? What if I should stop assuming that this game's NPCs are just like those in a normal game? I'm *in* Peripeteia. Many of the video game's rules completely changed the moment I stepped foot here. The fact that I'm here at all doesn't make sense. Is it such a leap that NPCs have lives of their own?

"Maybe Tara's right," I say, breaking the silence. "Maybe the NPCs have feelings but are coded so that they can't express them."

"That still doesn't explain why the quest didn't reset," Guy responds.

"If you felt something strong, like terror or grief, wouldn't you fight anything holding you back from expressing that?" I ask.

Tara taps her chin thoughtfully. "What if all it takes to help them break through their coding is to break the quests?"

"Should we be more careful, then?" Cait asks.

"Fuck no!" I shout, earning a gasp from everyone. "Sorry, but I'm *glad* we actually helped those people. Imagine living in terror like that, getting a quick break from it, and then being thrown back into the dark? And then not even being able to tell players they can't take it anymore?"

Cait nods and then the rest quickly follow.

"You're right," Cait says. "If there's a chance that these NPCs are more real than they seem, we need to do everything we can to help them. Even if it means breaking the game."

"*Especially* if it means breaking the game," Tara says. "What if that's the offering our gods want from us? What if *that* is how we get back home?"

It's as good a theory as any, but we have no way of knowing whether or not it's correct. There's too much we can't explain, too much we don't understand. But there's one thing I *do* know: if we're to have any hope of getting out of here, we have to figure out how we're able to break things at all.

CHAPTER FOURTEEN

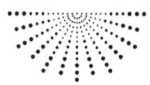

We wait at our camp until it's late at night so it's less likely other players will be in the temple. Then we head back to check in with our deities. Even at midnight, there are some stragglers. They look weary, probably because they've waited all day to do this. That makes me feel extra spoiled by my shopping trip and time at the bathhouse.

Fortunately, there's only one other person in line at the Aphrodite statue. I guess people aren't doing very sexy or romantic things on their first day in Peripeteia. Not that I did. She's my deity because my "holy fuck" amused her.

The guy in front of me is big on expressing his thoughts through hand waving. I can't hear Aphrodite's side of the conversation, but he definitely has a lot to say to her, most of it not good. He's griping about how he can't complete the "Inspire Lust" quest because women are too picky and don't like "nice guys." He sounds exactly like guys I block on social media. I absolutely hate that he and I share the same deity.

"Okay, I'll keep trying," he says in a sheepish tone, making me think he got berated by the Goddess of Love.

He turns around to leave. Of course, I'm the first person he sees when he does. He waggles his eyebrows and bites his bottom lip.

"Looking for a bang?" he asks.

I cross my arms. "Sorry, I'm already dating a really nice guy."

He rolls his eyes and mutters, "Slut," before walking away.

I stick my tongue out at him behind his back and step up to Aphrodite's statue. "Dear Aphrodite," I say. "I've come to check in with you and offer my thanks."

The breathtaking goddess pulls away from the statue and shrinks down to my height. "Your gratitude is most welcome after my last worshipper," she says and takes a moment to glare at him as he exits the temple. Then a wicked smile spreads across her face. "I'm going to make his manhood fall off tonight."

Yikes. Note to self: do not piss this goddess off.

"Well, I'm certainly thankful," I say. "Beguiling Eyes seems to have helped me in the spider village."

"Oh, no, that was all you," she says. "Your charisma score helped, of course, but Beguiling Eyes has only lowered vendor prices for you so far."

"I...I really negotiated that on my own?"

Aphrodite nods. "I'm thrilled about that, by the way. I've been holding it over everyone's heads at Olympus. So far, only one of *my* worshippers has found another way to fulfill that quest."

"I think I broke it," I say.

"I know! Isn't it marvelous?" Aphrodite's smile is bright, and her eyes gleam with excitement.

"Well, I'm happy the villagers there don't have to go through that again," I say, though I'm not sure I want to discuss that quest anymore. She may not take to my thoughts about freeing NPCs of their programming as kindly.

"As for the quest Alexander gave you," she whispers. "That's still very important, but don't skip out on your other quests. Trust me when I say you'll want to level up as much as possible before you get there."

"Why?" I ask.

"You'll see," she answers and then brings her voice to a normal volume. "In the meantime, I have things you'll need to do while you're here in Thebe."

"Should I take notes?" I ask, even though I have nothing to take them with.

"No need," she says. "I'll put them in your menu with as much detail as needed. Don't let anyone tell you they're unimportant side quests. If you want to improve your faith score with me, these need to be completed."

I nod. I *very* much want to improve my faith score. According to Cait, it makes it much more likely that I'll get favors.

Cait believes the gods are also NPCs, but Aphrodite clearly knows this is a game. All our interactions are organic. I wonder how she and the other gods wound up here. I think about asking, but I have a feeling that would cause her to put up walls between us.

Aphrodite has had plenty of information to share with me, but I still came here with a list of questions that I intend to get answers for. Working up the nerve to request anything from a goddess is difficult, so I clear my throat and take a deep breath.

"I have a few questions," I say. "Is that okay?"

"Of course," she says.

"I'm kind of dating a party member."

She tilts her head and crosses her arms while smiling. Is she impressed? "That was quick. Especially given that you were so against love when you came here."

I shrug. "I'm still not love's biggest fan," I say, prompting a sigh from Aphrodite. "But if I could die any day, I might as well enjoy myself."

"Die?" she says, her eyebrows pressing together in confusion. "I won't let you die."

"But Cait says—"

Aphrodite waves a dismissive hand. "I'm sure *some* gods are fine disposing of their followers, but I'm not—and definitely not one that's special like you."

"I bet you say that to all the girls," I say with a laugh, not wanting to admit how good it makes me feel to be special to a goddess.

Until this point, her tone and expression have been sweet, appreciative even. As though she was talking to her teacher's pet. However, my response to her calling me special flips her from lighthearted to stern in a flash.

"Do not question my words, even in jest," she says "If I tell you that you are special, that is the truth. You have achieved something that no other player has before, and you're the top contender for bringing me the offering I wish to receive."

I consider asking her for a hint about what offering she wants, but she looks cross already. I don't want a body part falling off me like that dude who just left.

"Okay, I believe you," I say, holding up my hands in surrender.

"What question do you have about your romantic life?" she asks, suddenly as sweet as she was just a moment before she got onto me.

I'm grateful that she's redirecting our conversation back to my questions. I don't want to press the matter after getting on her nerves.

"Well...is it wise? What if things end badly?" I ask. "I'm supposed to be working with this group, and a falling out could spell disaster."

Aphrodite laughs. "I think I've slept with half of Olympus. Yet, we still rule this world and work together on many things. You can do the same."

I really hope she *only* means that I can still work with someone I've been romantic with. As great as my friends are, I don't want to sleep with all of them. This brings me to my next question, though.

"Am I able to control whether people are attracted to me?" I ask. "I can see life getting difficult for me if I'm constantly having to turn down suitors."

The goddess sighs. "Yes, that's a problem that I understand. You'll find that it is not your association with me or even your gifts that will cause this, though. *Anyone* may be pursued by those they don't want in return."

That wasn't what I was hoping to hear, and by the look on her face, it's clear that she understands that, but she offers no comfort. This is just a fact of life that I'll have to learn to deal with, hopefully not within my party.

"Did you have any other questions?" Aphrodite asks.

"Well, I was wondering about the quest to see K—"

Aphrodite snaps her fingers, and suddenly my voice is gone. I touch my throat on instinct. Nothing's missing, she's just silenced me. And she looks...scared?

"There's a reason I gave you that quest in that fashion, why I refer to it as Alexander's," she whispers. "We will not go into details here where anyone can hear you. If you have questions about it, direct those to Alexander. Nod if you understand."

I nod obediently, and she snaps her fingers again.

"Sorry," I say. "I didn't know."

"There's much I won't tell you. Even more that I *shouldn't* tell you. You will simply need to trust me on these matters."

"I will," I say, as I bow my head.

"It's very late," she says in almost a motherly way, "and it seems your friends have already finished speaking with their deities. Go to your camp and rest. You will have much to complete, and you'll need all the energy you can get."

In a blink Aphrodite is gone. I turn to see my friends milling about the exit. Cait's leaning against the wall, playing with her nails. Sylvia is sitting on the floor with her head resting against the wall and her eyes closed. Joshua is tuning his fiddle. Guy and Tara are playing some sort of coin flipping game.

I walk over, and they all sigh with relief when they see me. Guy rushes over to give me a peck on the cheek, acting like he hasn't seen me in days. How long was I talking to Aphrodite?

"How'd it go?" Tara asks me.

"Well, she really seems to like how we handled the spider village," I answer.

Tara arches a brow. "Interesting."

Cait shakes Sylvia's shoulder. "Time to go, Sleeping Beauty."

Sylvia responds with a weary nod. "I can't wait to leave such a crowded city."

I wince. "Well, about that..."

"Oh, no, what?" Sylvia responds.

"Aphrodite says she has stuff I need to get done for her in Thebe."

Joshua laughs. "Oh, that? Yeah, all the gods give you Thebe quests, but they're not really important."

"Hey, now, they're fun!" Guy says. "Let's take a break from all the danger and just enjoy ourselves while we're here."

I remember what Aphrodite said about not believing it when people say these are just side quests. Given her tone and overall secretiveness, I feel like I need to take her word seriously on this matter.

"I *really* need to improve my faith score," I say. "It's at bare minimum now, and that's not good enough if I'm going to be an effective healer for you all."

Sylvia nods. "I hate to say it, but she's right. As much as I'd rather be out in nature, XP is XP, and we need to do everything we can to ensure

Lauren's scores are where they need to be as a cleric. Besides, maybe we'll find a clue we missed the first time we did the side quests here."

"But first, sleep!" Tara says, waving her hands in the exit's direction. "Hermes gave me quests, too. Can't hurt for us all to get some XP having fun. What quests did she give you?"

"I haven't even looked yet," I say. "Let me bring up my quest menu." There are four new quests waiting for me and...No, this can't be right. Surely, Aphrodite would know I'm the wrong person for tasks like this.

"What's wrong?" Cait asks.

"I'm supposed to make people believe in love again," I answer. "How the fuck do I do that?"

Cait shrugs. "I guess just tell them all the reasons love is great or something."

But how am I supposed to do that when love isn't great?

WHAT GAMER DOESN'T LOVE A GOOD SIDE QUEST? WHO WOULDN'T want a break from saving the world or whatever to chase after chickens or collect herbs? In every game I've played, I've gotten so sidetracked by easily ignorable tasks that it takes me five times longer than it should to make progress in a game.

However, this is my actual life now, and I can't afford to do that, so it's tempting to skip these altogether and move on to main game stuff. But is that my strategic mind thinking or the part of me that dreamed about Mom dying alone last night? It doesn't matter. Aphrodite was clear. I have to do this. I need the XP and to improve my faith score, otherwise I won't be able to make progress on the main quest. And if I don't, my chances of seeing Mom again are nonexistent.

Today, I have four almost identical quests. I have to make people believe in love again. The only difference between the quests is that each of them involves a different person and has an alternate component.

Amalthea was seduced by Zeus a long time ago. Unfortunately for her, she caught feelings for him in record time. Zeus being Zeus, he moved on pretty much the next day, breaking her heart. Since she's in charge of keeping the local temple spotless, she's constantly reminded of his rejection. I have to take over cleaning for a day and convince her to accept the advances of the handsome food vendor across the street.

Gelasius is the oldest of five brothers, making him the heir to one of Thebe's most powerful council elders. It's important for him to get a wife with the right connections. To him, love is a work of fiction, and marriage is a transactional obligation. But if he'd just turn his head a little, he'd find there's an absolutely beautiful maid who has a huge crush on him. I need to help him collect all the scrolls his father needs and somehow get him alone with this maid.

Dolius is a traveling merchant. He's too busy hustling to have time for love. Besides, he's never met a woman who ever stirred anything in him. That's because he's gay and hasn't realized that yet. I need to help him hawk his wares and hopefully inspire his "I like dudes" breakthrough.

Phemie is a widowed mother of eight and grandmother of twenty-six. Her husband was an abusive asshole that she truly thought she loved when he was courting her. Because of him, she decided love was an illusion. She's spent decades telling her kids and grandkids not to believe in it. I need to deliver gifts to each of her adult kids and show her how much she's hurting them with her bias.

The problem is that I'm no good at selling what I don't believe in, and I *don't* believe in love. Aphrodite knows this. We've discussed it. It's clear that she's trying to sway me to the romantic side. I can't blame her. It must be vexing to have a cleric like me, but then again, she chose *me*, not the other way around.

As we sit around the campfire eating breakfast, I read out my side quests to the group.

Guy winces. "That's a lot of work, and our camp is a good thirty-minute walk to town. There's no way you're getting this all done today."

"Yeah, I know," I say, closing my menu.

"I suggest we budget about four days here," Sylvia says. "One for each quest. If it gets done faster, then all the better!"

"What's our main quest again?" I ask. "I've been so focused on what Aphrodite wants from me that I forgot all about what the next step is for the game."

"Oh, we gotta defeat this empusa who's been killing travelers to the north," Tara says.

"What are empusas, and how gory is this going to be?" I ask. "I want to be fully prepared this time."

"Demons," Tara explains. "Usually, they look like pretty ladies. Since there are a lot of people trekking north from Thebe, it's hard to spot her, but if you see anyone with wonky legs, that's probably her. As far as gory, don't worry. We just hurl insults at her."

"What? We just bully her to death?" I ask.

Cait nods with a weary expression. "It's honestly really boring. It gets depressing, too, because she starts crying when she gets down to half of her health bar."

Are the game developers sadists? This quest sounds absolutely miserable for everyone involved. She's killing travelers, though, so I guess it's necessary. Still...

After putting my dirty dish in the bucket of water that Sylvia uses for washing, I take a moment to look toward the city while stretching. Of all the side quests, Phemie's sounds like the easiest one to manage. I just need to deliver eight gifts and then tell her that she can't tell her kids love doesn't exist just because her dead husband was a dick.

I click on the quest and look at where it is on the map. It's blessedly on the outskirts of town nearest to our camp. Maybe I can finish this one in time to start another.

"I'm heading out," I say, waving at my friends.

Guy jumps from his seat by the fire and rushes over. "How about I help you?" he asks.

There's no rule stating that I have to do these quests alone, and having an extra pair of hands could prove helpful.

"Sure," I say. "I'm going to Phemie's house first. It's not far."

Everyone wishes us good luck, and we make our trek to town.

"You still look so good," Guy says, once we're out of earshot of our group. "Even after spending a night in a tent."

I smile, pleased by his flattery. "You're not bad to look at yourself."

Guy responds with a smirk. "I wasn't fishing for a compliment, but I appreciate it."

"You really do look like Ryan Reynolds," I tell him.

He laughs. "I don't see it, but I'll take it."

Guy twines his fingers with mine. I look down at our clasped hands and then at him.

"I thought it might make the trip to town a little nicer if I was touching you," he says.

The wholesome act is so genuinely sweet, adorable even, that it endears me to him. It feels...right.

I'm fucking terrified.

CHAPTER FIFTEEN

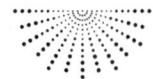

Phemie's house isn't grand, but it's comfortable and well-kept. When I knocked on the door, I wasn't sure what I'd see or how I'd be received, but the woman seemed to have been expecting me. She'd sent for a delivery service the day before, and she assumed I was with them since I was offering to take her gifts to her kids. In a way, I *am* the person she'd requested, since her request was just a quest prompt created by whoever developed this game.

For someone who doesn't believe in love, she certainly is friendly and gracious. She sits Guy and me down at her table to eat some stew, telling us she doesn't want us getting weak roaming all over town.

The stew is phenomenal. There are so many ultra-real elements to this game, but the one that always surprises me the most is how I can actually taste the food. It even sustains me. Video games shouldn't do that. Then again, NPCs *shouldn't* have feelings, and I'm beginning to think they do.

When I hear the ping of a notification, I'm reminded that there are still unrealistic elements to this experience. I tap to see what the notification is for, and I'm pleased to see that Phemie's stew has given me a speed buff. Because we ate it, we'll be able to dash all over town without wearing out. Nice!

When we finish eating, Phemie grabs the packages for us to deliver.

They're each conveniently in their own bags, but they're also on the weightier side, which is annoying. We can transport an entire camp from spot to spot like magic, but I gotta lug this heavy stuff for a side quest? This must be part of the challenge. Once again, I wonder if the game developers are sadists.

Fortunately, Guy is with me, and he takes half of the packages so that we're each only carrying four of them. Still, this feels like when you grab all your groceries from the trunk of your car at once, and it takes too long to get them in your house—except that I'll be doing this all over town.

It doesn't take long for my fingers to go numb from the bag handles digging into my skin. I find a clean place to set my packages down and stretch my digits to get blood flowing to them. Guy sets his next to me and does the same thing.

"This is a lot harder than I thought it would be," he admits.

I nod. "Even with the speed boost, this will take us all day if we have to keep stopping like this." I sigh. "There's gotta be a 'work smarter, not harder' solution to this."

I close my eyes and think, tapping at my temple like I can nag my brain into coming up with ideas faster. After a moment, I give up that tactic and look around.

We're in an alley, and there isn't much to see. Just some trash and pigeons. Then an old man walks past us. His back is crooked, probably from a life spent bending over as he worked. He's rail thin and unsteady on his feet. Fortunately, he's got a pretty sturdy cane. Then it hits me.

"Get your staff out," I tell Guy.

He raises his eyebrows in confusion but doesn't ask why, simply takes it off his back where it's held with some kind of magical magnet that the game provides for every player's weapon of choice.

"Do what I do," I say.

I loop two package bags on each end of my staff and then use both my hands to hold the staff across the back of my neck and shoulders. Guy smiles in understanding and does the same.

"Oh, this is so much better," he says. "Good idea."

"I'm grateful for that Strategy Under Duress favor."

"Well, you're pretty smart without it."

Guy glows at me, and my stomach does a flip.

"Let's get going."

A few minutes later, we find one of Phemie's children. He's selling food across the street from the temple. The moment I lay eyes on him, I hear a notification ping, and I check it, expecting to see that I'm one step further into this side quest. To my surprise, that's not the only one.

"Weird..." I mutter.

"What is?" Guy asks.

"This is the same man I need to hook up with the chick in the temple," I say.

"Well, that's convenient," Guy responds. "Want to make a quick pit stop at the temple before heading to Phemie's next kid?"

I consider that for a moment. A lot of times in video games, they lump side quests together so that you can get them all done in one go. But this isn't like other games. I can't clean up a temple and deliver packages at the same time.

"No, I'll have to come back later," I say. "Amalthea's quest might be an all-day thing with how busy that temple gets."

We greet the man, and he smiles when I tell him that his mother has a package for him. Wanting to know just what I'd been hoisting on my shoulders, I stick around to see him unpack it. The man weeps when he does. He lifts a large woolen cloak and two smaller ones.

"She's always thinking of us," he says and then looks at me appreciatively. "Winter's coming. Since my wife died, it's just been me and my little girls. She was a tailor, but now that money's gone, and it's a lot harder to make sure my children have what they need."

The man digs into his pocket and pulls out some coins. I hear a ka-ching and see that he's given me a few copper pieces.

"For your trouble," he says.

I know that the game is simply rewarding me for completing this step in the quest, but I can't accept money from someone who just told me he doesn't have enough money to give his kids what they need.

"Please take your money back," I tell him.

The man stares through me with a blank face. I can see his little NPC gears grinding to a halt. I almost leave, thinking that he won't respond to me since this isn't an option to take with this quest. Then he snaps out of it, and his eyes meet mine.

"You'll let me keep the coins? Why?" he asks.

"Your mother is already paying me, and I want to make sure that money goes to helping your children," I answer.

The man wipes a tear away. "You're too kind."

"Honestly, it's no problem," I tell him.

He looks at me with large, admiring eyes. "I will never forget this," he says. "I already thought you were beautiful, but I didn't realize your heart was even more so."

Uh oh.

"Um...thanks. Gotta dash!" I give an awkward laugh and lift my package-laden staff onto my shoulders again. "Let's go," I whisper to Guy, before I scurry away from the street food vendor. The moment we're out of earshot, I ask, "What the fuck was that?"

Guy shrugs. "Appreciation?"

I shake my head. "No, that NPC just hit on me. He's supposed to be the love of Amalthea's life. My job is to get them together. I let him keep some copper, and suddenly he's telling me I'm beautiful?"

"Maybe he's just being nice," Guy offers.

I side-eye my friend. "Do you really think that?"

Guy doesn't say anything, but I see the doubt in his eyes when he glances down in thought.

Fortunately, three of Phemie's daughters are in the same place. They all work as maids for some rich dude. Each one of them is quite pretty, with perfectly coifed dark curls and big, brown eyes. One of them is truly stunning. She has long lashes, bee-stung lips, and an hourglass frame.

She gasps when she opens her package and shows it to her sisters. "Look, new cloaks! Oh, and they're so lovely. We'll be warm and fashionable this year," she says with a giggle.

Her sisters nod in agreement.

"She even packed some for your little ones," the young woman tells them.

A handsome man walks down the hallway, and the beautiful woman's attention shifts immediately from her present to the man. Her eyelashes flutter as she sighs wistfully. The man doesn't notice her at all, causing her smile to drop.

A notification pings, and I open it up. Not only does it show that we're halfway through our deliveries, it indicates that I'd found both Gelasius and the maid crushing on him.

"Again?" I say and then turn to Guy. "I guess they really intend for us to do these in tandem. That man who just walked by is another one of my side quests. I have to find some scrolls for him."

"Maybe you can find them really quick while we're here," Guy whispers. "If we run out of time, we can always come back."

I nod. This quest would probably be a lot faster than cleaning up an entire busy temple.

"I would love to have kids of my own to give cloaks like this to one day," the young woman says to her sisters. Frowning, she continues, "I guess I should just marry the stable boy. He's...nice."

Ouch. Poor stable boy.

"Don't settle!" I say. "You're beautiful! One day, the right man will come along."

The woman shakes her head and looks at the doorway Gelasius just left through. "My mother keeps telling me that love like that doesn't exist. And, well...I haven't had cause to disbelieve her."

"I'm really fucking up this quest," I mumble.

Her eyebrows press together. "What do you mean? You're not at fault."

"No, it's not that, it's..." I trail off.

Once again, an NPC has responded in a way that doesn't make much sense to me. She's supposed to pine over Gelasius so that he can fall in love with her. Now, she's responding to my muttering that wasn't in any way directed at her.

"You might be surprised," I say. "As long as you stay patient, that is."

I deal with finding the scrolls as quickly as possible, barely interacting with Gelasius as I do so. I'm in such a rush that I forget to talk to him about the maid until I'm pretty far away. I decide to come back the next day and talk to him then.

The next two packages are easy, because they're for two brothers who work together as blacksmiths. I almost sigh with relief when the whole interaction is uncomplicated. There's no connection to any of my other quests with those two.

However, when I walk away, one calls out to me, "Please let our mother know we appreciate this, and we'll come by for dinner soon."

I nod at their request and wonder why the game would find it necessary for me to pass such a message along. Of course, I have my suspicions. So far, every NPC I've interacted with today has had actual conversations with me. Though I'm not doing all that much, I seem to be chipping away at something holding them back from truly communicating.

The next package is for a woman. She's the oldest of the daughters we've met so far, and possibly where a third of Phemie's grandchildren come from. They're everywhere—running around, screaming and crying, wiping their snot on everything. Some of them appear to be trying to climb up their mother.

This clearly overwhelmed woman's face goes from beleaguered to delighted the moment she learns her mother has sent her a gift. When I take her package off my staff, I suddenly feel weightless. It's no surprise that there are a ton of cloaks inside of it. As the woman passes out the cloaks, she's sweet as sugar to each of her kids.

"You're a great mother," I tell her.

She looks at me as if she might cry. "Thank you," she says. "It's nice to be recognized for what I do. Though, I learned everything from my mother." She lifts one cloak to demonstrate her point. "As you can see, she's very generous."

I think of Mom, and all the gifts she's given me and how she's gotten me through so much. I think of how she still knows my name...or at least she knew it when I was in the real world.

Is she still alive?

I shake away those thoughts. Worrying will do me no good. The best way to get back to Mom is to do these quests and give Aphrodite whatever offering it is she wants.

We finally reach the last of Phemie's children. Just like everyone else, I get a ping notification that I've made progress in this side quest. For the third time today, I also see that I've managed progress with another quest.

This man is Dolius, the traveling merchant. His eyes light up when he sees us approach with a package. "Are these the travel supplies I ordered?" he asks.

I shake my head, "No, it's a gift from your mother."

Dolius gasps. "Even better!" He tears into his package like a raccoon with a bag of burgers from a drive through. "Oh, this is perfect," he says, as he examines his cloak. "I set out tomorrow to sell my wares in other towns. With winter coming and me heading to the north, I'll need this to stay warm."

A horrible realization hits me. "You're going up north?" I ask.

He nods. "Yes, I want to get to Thrace before the first freeze of the year."

"No, no," I say in haste. "Wait just three more days."

Dolius blinks. "Why?"

"There's an empusa up there targeting travelers," I tell him.

"And you think it will be any different in three days?" he asks.

"Yes," I answer. "Some heroes are going to kill her then."

"How would you know?" he asks.

I struggle to answer this, but Guy jumps in. "Can't you tell she's a Cleric of Aphrodite? The Goddess of Love has gifted her with visions."

"*Visions?*" Dolius seems truly surprised but then sighs. "But empusa or not, if I don't make it to the next town's market day in time, I won't have enough money to get up to Thrace."

An idea jumps out at me. "What if you can sell enough here tomorrow? Will you hold off traveling if you can?"

Dolius squints at me. "I suppose so, but I don't know that I'll be so lucky."

"I'll come here tomorrow and help," I tell him. "I'll work hard all day if it helps you stay safe on your travels."

"You...you would do that for me?" he asks. "Why?"

For the XP? The chance to improve my faith score?

No, there's a better answer, the real one.

"If you die, I'll never forgive myself."

"Well, in that case, I'll meet you here tomorrow at dawn," he says.

"Perfect!" I shake his hand, startling him.

Then Guy and I put our staffs back on our backs and hightail it back to Phemie's house.

As we're running, Guy asks, "You realize you just agreed to wake up before dawn so that you can meet him here to help him sell his stuff, right?"

Ugh, he's right. I *hate* waking up early.

"It's worth it! I don't want the poor guy to die."

"But he'll just respawn, Lauren," Guy says. "He's an NPC."

I stop and take a moment to study Guy's face. "But what if he doesn't respawn? What if I've already broken this quest?"

"Do you really think—?"

"Guy," I say, putting my hands on his cheeks so I can focus his gaze on mine, "you can't tell me that those didn't feel like organic conversations. Do you really think that there's a coded response to me saying someone's a good mother or you telling someone I'm a Cleric of Aphrodite?"

Guy says nothing for what feels like a long stretch of time but is probably just a few heartbeats. He stares at my lips. I've unintentionally put us in a very intimate position by pulling his face so close to mine. The part of me that wants to drive my point home retreats, and the part that heats up every time he flirts with me comes front and center.

I rise to my tiptoes and press my lips to his, soft and slow. He licks the crease between my lips to part them. Once my mouth opens to him, he delves right in, and thunder booms above. The sound of a coming storm seems like a soundtrack to the kiss we're sharing, the first one that feels real. However, just as I tilt my head to deepen it further, a sudden deluge of rain soaks me in a split second.

I scream, and Guy giggles. We clasp hands and rush back to camp. As tired as I am from crisscrossing all over Thebe, this trip doesn't wear me down because we're laughing and chatting the whole time. For a little while, my brain isn't half-focused on quests and how Mom is doing. I'm just thinking about how Guy stirs feelings in me I thought weren't possible. Doug never made me feel giddy in the rain.

When we get back to camp, we can't get a moment alone, and I'm afraid more kisses will result in sexual frustration. Instead, I tuck myself under Guy's arms, and we carry on playful whispered conversation as we eat Sylvia's excellent meal of roasted vegetables. After dinner, I drift off to sleep with happy thoughts and then the disembodied voice says, "Cleric of Aphrodite: Level 3 Maintained. Spell Gained: Near Future Vision. Skill Gained: Negotiation."

CHAPTER SIXTEEN

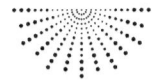

Being on the phone with strangers yelling at me all day is my idea of hell. Unfortunately, it was the highest paying job I could get back in my home world. Now, I'm trying to sell stuff from a merchant stall in a fantasy game developer's under-researched idea of an ancient Greek city. This may be a close second in the miserable job department.

Of course, that might be partially due to how fucking tired I am. I'm not able to block out any background chatter because I must talk to people outside of my party to sell stuff. The road is crowded because of a music festival, and everyone's heavy use of musk is giving me a headache. Even the unexpected and blessed arrival of Aphrodite's calm isn't enough to make this job bearable.

Did the developers have to make these NPCs so nasty? I'm just asking people if they want to buy some jewelry. A simple "no" would do, but they gotta go a step further and admonish me for it.

This woman is literally looking down her nose at me. "Why would I want such a cheap-looking necklace? I've got plenty of high-quality gems at home."

"I understand," I say in my best customer service voice and with my most pleasant smile. "Enjoy your day!"

"You should be ashamed of yourself," she continues. "You're out here peddling junk when you should be married and taking care of children."

It's past lunch at this point, and I'm nowhere near earning enough money for Dolius, but I've *had it*.

"Are you married with children?" I ask her.

"Of course I am!" she huffs.

"My condolences to your family," I say.

Her eyes are so wide, and her face is so red that I'm surprised there isn't steam shooting out of her ears. I guess Karens are timeless. "Ex*cuse* me?"

"I'm sure you have much more important things to do than hang around my stall," I tell her. "I mean, if I were you, I wouldn't want to be caught looking at such tawdry wares while talking to a harlot."

She opens her mouth to give a retort, then closes it again. Then she gives an indignant, derisive "hmph" and storms away.

The man hawking housewares in the stall next to me laughs. "I wouldn't have the nerve to talk to someone like that," he says.

Of course, he wouldn't. He's an NPC. Though none of the NPCs I've met today have acted like one.

"It helps that I'm only working this stall today, and I'll be long gone from here in a few days," I tell my neighbor.

"Oh, that's too bad," the man says. "I could use the entertainment."

"It's not really my stall," I explain further. "I'm helping a man named Dolius."

The man's eyes light up at the name, and I hear the quest notification ping. "Dolius? I didn't realize I'd nabbed the stall next to his. Wh-why isn't he here today?"

"He's getting ready for a trip to Thrace," I answer.

Disappointment droops all the man's features at once. "Oh."

"Are you friends?" I ask.

He laughs, but it's as sad and forced as the fake smile on his face. "We once met at a market day in Athens," he says. "I doubt he even remembers me. He was very busy that day."

"Maybe he does," I say. "After all, you remember him."

He shakes his head, and it hits me what the man is actually trying to say. That ping was probably about progress in my side quest to convince Dolius to believe in love. My neighbor here has had a crush on Dolius for a long time, but he doesn't even know this man exists. Could this be any more like my middle school experience?

"What's your name?" I ask him.

"Cyrus," he answers. "What's yours?"

"Lauren."

He tilts his head. "What an unusual name!"

I laugh. "Not where I'm from."

"Where's that?"

Oh, boy. I don't know enough about Peripeteia to make something up, and I can't exactly tell him the truth. *Wait, why can't I?* I'm already breaking the damn game by having this conversation. What's another crack?

"America," I tell him.

I might as well have told him I was from Jupiter. He's never heard of America. Why would he have? It's not in the program. The only world these NPCs know about is Peripeteia.

"How far away is that?" he asks.

I sigh. "Too far."

This prompts countless questions from Cyrus. He wants to know if I miss it or if it's anything like Thebe. I tell him what I think is just enough to settle his curiosity without giving too much away, but I only create more questions on his end. What is a phone? Is it magic? What do you mean everyone has one from where you're from? Is everyone in America a mage? You mean you can just travel around in carts without animals to pull them?

Maybe I should have lied about where I come from.

To my relief, Dolius shows up before I have to admit that Peripeteia is a work of fiction that I'd accidentally stumbled into.

"How are sales?" he asks me.

Ugh...

I search my mind for the most positive way to spin that I've only earned about two silver all day and just pissed off a woman who's likely spreading word that Dolius's stall should be blacklisted. I don't need to say anything, though. He's nodding his head, like he can tell just from my facial expression.

With a sigh he says, "Well, you tried."

"The day's not over," I say.

Dolius shakes his head. "I've talked to several merchants, and they're all having bad days. It's unlikely that there will be any sales in the last few hours."

"I'm sorry," I say. "Please don't leave until the empusa is taken care of, though."

"Empusa?" Cyrus asks. "Where?"

"On the road heading north from here," I answer.

Cyrus leaves his stall to talk to Dolius directly. "Empusas are dangerous. You should do as she says."

"I can't," Dolius explains. "If I don't make it to the market day in Dardanus, I won't have enough money to get to Thrace."

"How much do you need?" Cyrus asks. "Perhaps I can help."

Dolius eyes almost pop out of his head. "Three gold," he answers. "You don't have to—"

"I'll give you five," Cyrus interrupts.

I gasp in unison with Dolius. Five gold is *a lot* of money. Cyrus must *really* like this man.

"Why would you be so generous?" Dolius asks.

Cyrus blushes. "We merchants stick together, right?"

Dolius chuckles. "That's the biggest lie I've ever heard. We're all in competition over the same customers."

"But you and I don't have to be," Cyrus says.

"You should take his offer," I tell Dolius. "Like I told you, in just a few days, the empusa will be gone."

"How do you know that?" Cyrus asks me.

"She's a Cleric of Aphrodite," Dolius answers for me. "She received a vision of the future."

"A Cleric of..." Cyrus says and trails off, though his eyes remain on me, like I may be the ticket to a dream come true.

Now's my chance to complete this side quest.

"Dolius, this is Cyrus," I say. "He was at the Athens market the same day as you."

"You were?" Dolius asks him.

Cyrus nods. "You don't remember me. That's fine. You were very busy that day."

Dolius tilts his head, examining the man, and then recognition registers on his face. "Oh, yes, you sell housewares, right? You had long hair and a beard back then."

"Y-yes..." Cyrus responds.

"This is a much better look on you," Dolius continues. And then I see something new on his face. Is he realizing he's attracted to men? Then he sighs. "I can't accept this much money from you. What if there's an emergency, and you need it?"

"Maybe you could travel together," I offer. "That way you could share the costs and help each other in case something unexpected happens."

Cyrus smiles and nods his head enthusiastically. "That's an excellent idea!"

Dolius gazes at Cyrus. There's a note of admiration in that look, though I'm sure he's mostly considering the pros and cons of the idea. "All right," he says. "I suppose some company would be pleasant on the road."

I hear another ping, and I hold back the urge to fist pump. This is it! I've completed this side quest. I bring up the menu, then groan when I see the update. Instead of it showing as complete, it's amended the quest. Dolius doesn't believe in love *yet*, so I will need to escort Cyrus and him to Dardanus and help the two merchants get closer.

Another fucking escort quest. Cait's gonna kill me.

"My party is also heading that way in a few days," I say. "We can join you until we all get to Dardanus. Strength in numbers, right?"

Cyrus looks annoyed at my suggestion, and I give him a look that I hope communicates that he should trust me. *This is for you, dude. I'm trying to get you laid.*

"Fine," Dolius agrees with a nod. "Talk with the others you're traveling with, and let's plan tomorrow. I'll be here all day." He gestures at his stall.

I leave the market, relieved that I at least convinced Dolius to hold off on traveling and helped Cyrus secure some quality time with his crush. My day isn't over, though. I need to go talk to Phemie.

My arrival surprises the woman at first. Then she remembers that I never returned for my payment yesterday and invites me in so she can find where she's hidden her coins. I wonder if the ancient Greeks didn't have banks, or if that was just an assumption that the game developers made.

I take a moment to look around her house. Despite the cooling temperature outside, her house is warm. The scent of stew boiling over the hearth fire has me salivating. All of her children glowed when they learned their mother had sent them something. It's hard for me to believe that this dear woman doesn't believe in love when so many love her.

Phemie returns with a handful of coins ready for me. "There you go, my dear," she says.

A ka-ching tells me the transfer of money is complete, but I know the quest isn't.

"Your children are all so delightful," I say. "You did a wonderful job raising them."

She waves a dismissive hand. "I'm no better than any other mother."

"I've known many people whose mothers hurt them growing up," I tell her. "Your children had nothing but beautiful things to say about you."

"They did?" Phemie asks.

I nod in response. "I hope this isn't getting too personal, but... Well, I heard you've been telling them love isn't real."

Phemie frowns and crosses her arms. "Who said that?"

There was a show Mom used to watch called *Touched by an Angel* about an angel who went around changing everyone's lives for the better. There'd always come a point where her subtle nudges weren't enough to get the job done. So, she'd reveal her true identity, and the people would be in such awe that God had literally sent a divine messenger to set them on the right track. It worked every time. I decide to take a cue from that.

"Aphrodite," I answer. "I'm her cleric. She sent me on a mission to help those who have turned away from love."

"Hmph!" Phemie's manner has shifted from warm to cold in a blink. "She can take her 'help' and shove it up Hera's ass! Fat lot of good either of them have ever done me."

Maybe mentioning Aphrodite was the wrong tactic.

"I understand," I say. "You thought you'd found a love match with your husband, but he turned out to be a monster in disguise. No one could blame you for resenting the Goddess of Love and the goddess of marriage. But giving up on love? That's only hurting yourself."

"I'm an old woman," Phemie says, her tone still just as irritated as when she cursed two goddesses. "Can I not enjoy this time of my life without feeling pressured to be with some man?"

That's a fair point, but my side quest wasn't to hook her up with anyone. I'm here to prove to her she shouldn't let her past ruin her children's happiness.

"You're absolutely right. Wanting to be single is perfectly fine."

Phemie chuckles. "Be careful. Aphrodite might make your lady parts fall off."

Wow, sounds like the Goddess of Love has a pattern. I wonder how that incel is doing.

"Trust me, I'm not saying anything she'd be unhappy with," I tell Phemie. "I'm not saying you should go out and get a man. I don't think you should forgive and forget what your husband did to you. But I've met your children. The love you share with them is so obvious."

"That's not the same."

I shake my head. "It's not the same love, but it's still love. If that kind of love exists, isn't it possible that romantic love can be real, too? Even if your husband turned out to be lying about his feelings?"

Phemie's silent now. She's spent decades believing that romantic love doesn't exist because she's never received it herself. But my words are still getting through to her. I can see the doubt in her eyes, the way her crossed arms are loosening.

"I suppose my daughter Erianthe has been happy enough with her marriage," Phemie says at last. "She and her husband certainly can't keep their hands off each other. Ten babies and another on the way!"

"And that's even with you telling her that love doesn't exist," I say. "But some of your other children are taking it to heart, and it's hurting them."

"It is?"

I nod. "Three of your daughters are maids, and one of them is ready to marry some stable boy she doesn't have feelings for just so she can be a mother. And it's all because she doesn't believe that the man she yearns for could ever love her. She even said love doesn't exist."

"Ione said that?" Phemie uncrosses her arms and sits down at her table. Her eyebrows knit together in worry. "My youngest child, the one with the kindest, sweetest heart. I've failed her."

I sit on the chair next to Phemie. "No, you haven't. You've been a wonderful mother, even when your husband spent his life hurting you." I squeeze her hand. "And it's never too late to tell her to take a chance on love."

Phemie nods as a tear makes a slender path down her cheek. "I'll talk to her," she says. "It's not dark yet. I can get to her house and be home in time to eat and sleep."

To my surprise, the woman hugs me. I stiffen with shock but then relax into the embrace. I forgot how good it could feel to be hugged like this. Since Mom's mind started deteriorating, I hadn't experienced a good motherly touch. I cry. No, not just cry—sob.

"What's wrong, dear?" Phemie asks, releasing her hold on me to look into my eyes.

"I really miss my mom," I answer and hope she can understand what I'm saying since my words are wavering with despair. "She's sick, and I don't know if I'll ever get to see her again."

Phemie wipes away her own tear and places her palm against my cheek. She may be an NPC, but her fingers are calloused from years of work. It feels good, though. It feels *real*.

"You'll see her," she says. "Maybe not how you think, but she'll be in your dreams or on the whisper of a cool breeze. She'll show herself in a field of her favorite flowers. You'll feel her when you hear a certain song and when you eat a meal she used to cook for you. That's what I tell my children, and I'm sure she'd want you to know that."

As sweet as those words are, they make me cry even harder. Phemie is right, but I don't *want* to see Mom like that. I want to sit beside her and lay my head on her shoulder. I want her to know I'm okay.

"Let me get you something to eat," Phemie says, patting my hand.

I wipe away my tears and sniff. "Sorry, I can't stay. My friends are waiting for me back at camp."

"Then, I'll pack it up for you," she says as she walks to the pot boiling over her hearth fire. "How many people are in your camp?"

"You don't have to—"

"I asked how many people are in your camp," she responds, "not whether I have to do this. I know don't have to, but I *want* to."

"Six, including me," I answer.

Phemie gets a pot and takes the lid off. She ladles generations portions of stew into it and then puts the lid back on. Then she tightly binds it all up with twine and puts it into a bag.

"Take this and eat well," she says, handing it over. "And know your mother's wish for you to be well is answered this day."

CHAPTER SEVENTEEN

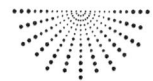

Last night, everyone shared their side quest experiences. Joshua made one hundred copper coins busking and helped a bunch of travelers find their way to important areas of town. Sylvia trained some women in archery. Cait got a side quest busting pickpockets, which made Tara sweat a little until Cait promised she would let her off the hook. That was good for Tara because her side quest was to get two hundred copper coins from pickpocketing and turn it in to the leader of Thebe's Thieves Guild. Guy was the only one who hadn't done a side quest yet because he was busy with me.

When I updated them, I left out the part about the future escort quest I'd unfortunately stumbled into. I'd tell them all later, when it was too late for anyone to talk me out of it. However, Dolius was expecting me to come back to him with details about the trip.

I'm thinking about this as we sit around the campfire to eat breakfast. If I choose my words carefully, I can figure out enough to tell Dolius. Probably.

"I think after tomorrow, I'll be ready to head out of town," I say. "What about you?"

Tara responds with a shrug. "I'm good whenever y'all are. Now that I know there's a side quest to bust pickpockets, I'm gonna stick around camp."

Cait sighs. "I told you we'd let you off the hook," she says. "Besides, I finished that quest."

"Yeah, tell that to the newbies who probably have the same quest," Tara says.

"I'd like to stay longer," Sylvia says. "I think Lauren's onto something about missing hints by skipping out on side quests. Besides, I've made friends here, and they want to learn more about leveling up as archers."

"That should only take today and tomorrow, right?" I ask.

"Why the rush?" Joshua asks. "I'm still having fun here."

Guy answers for me. "We were talking to a merchant yesterday, and he said if we don't head north right now, we won't make it to Thrace before the first hard freeze of the year."

"Yikes!" Tara exclaims. "Maybe we should leave now. Lauren can always come back and finish her other side quests."

"No!" I shout.

Everyone looks at me with stunned expressions.

I clear my throat and continue, "Look, the NPCs are breaking their programming here, and these quests might not be available when we get back."

Joshua nods. "Yeah, I've seen the signs, too. Yesterday, I told an NPC she had nice tits, and she actually *responded*."

"Did she smack you?" Cait asks.

"No, she just called me gross," Joshua answers.

"Shame," Cait mutters. "That might have taught you a lesson."

"Well, we bought enough winter gear to travel, at least," Sylvia says. "Though I still wish I could spend more time with the archers here."

"There's still that empusa to take care of," Joshua reminds everyone. "It might be worth staying a few more days to grab some XP before fighting it. I'm *so* close to leveling up. I can feel it."

I shake my head frantically.

Tara taps her chin. She's always been the one to see right through me, and I can tell I'm not fooling her. "There's something you're not telling us, Lauren."

They all study me. The weight of their stares threatens to flatten me. I really wish I was better at withholding information.

"It's just that one of my side quests changed a little," I explain. "I was supposed to convince Dolius to believe in love, but now I'm supposed to hook him up with this other merchant..." I take a deep breath and let the rest of my words tumble out of my mouth at record speed. "By escorting them to the next town."

Cait groans. "You took an escort mission?!"

"I *have* to!" I say.

"It's just a side quest!" Cait insists.

"No, it isn't," I respond. "Aphrodite told me—"

"That's what they *all* say!" Cait shouts. "It's how they convince you to get sidetracked from the main quest line, but you'll see in your menu that it's labeled as a side quest. We've all gotten them, and we've all skipped them."

Cait's glaring at me, and I'm glaring right back. "Maybe that's why you still haven't figured out what your offering should be," I say, unable to keep my anger out of my tone. "Maybe your gods were trying to be as obvious as possible." I get to my feet and straighten my chiton. "Well, I have a busy day ahead of me," I tell everyone. "I'll let Dolius know I'm leaving the morning after tomorrow. Whether you come with me is up to you. I don't care if I have to go alone to keep him safe and help him find true love."

"Fine!" Cait calls out and gets up herself. "If you're going to be so bullheaded about it, I'll help you with your side quest. I'm not letting you get eaten up by monsters or something. *But* we're working on the rest of these side quests together."

That last statement came out of fucking nowhere. Does she think I'm incapable of getting these done?

"Why?" I ask.

"Because apparently, when you do it on your own, you accidentally wind up with more side quests," Cait answers. "I'm going to keep you on track, so we don't have to travel through a blizzard or something. Where are we going today?"

"Um...the temple."

Cait marches toward town and calls back to me, "Hurry! I want to complete whatever this quest is as soon as possible."

CHAPTER EIGHTEEN

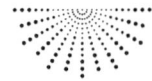

When we meet Amalthea at the temple, she seems annoyed that we weren't there sooner. Apparently, today is supposed to be a special day, and it needs to be spotless.

"What's the event?" I ask.

"The Council of Elders will be here to honor our gods," she answers. "They're holding a grand ceremony that all the wealthiest families will attend."

The Council of Elders? I wonder if Gelasius is coming. Maybe I can get a little progress on that side quest while I'm here.

"Where do you want us to start?" Cait asks, keeping us on task.

"Block the entrances to the temple and polish the floors," Amalthea tells her. "I don't want anyone coming in here messing anything up."

I bet the newbie players are going to hate that. Whatever. They can find something else to do today.

Cait doesn't even respond. She walks over to a group of people milling around the Zeus statue. "Shoo!" she says to them, waving her hands like she's trying to get rid of a housefly.

"What's your problem?" one man, an elf by the look of him, asks. "We have as much right as you to be here."

"We're cleaning up for a grand ceremony, and we don't need your muddy shoes messing things up," she tells them.

The elf rolls his eyes. "You can clean around us, little girl. No one orders fighters of Zeus around."

I've seen Cait mad, even go berserker in battle. I've *never* seen her like this, though. Her eye twitches, but that's the only thing on her face that's moving. The rest of her features seem carved in stone.

Normally, she gets really loud when she's upset, but her voice is low now. "Did you just call me a little girl?"

The man doesn't even answer. He laughs and *pats her head*. I hope he already fucking prayed to Zeus because he's going to need all the divine intervention he can get.

Cait grabs his hand from the top of her head and bends it unnaturally. There's a crack, and the elf screams as he falls to his knees. One of his friends lunges forward. I don't know whether he wanted to take on Cait or help his friend because he doesn't get far. Cait turns her steely gaze on him and grabs his hair with her free hand.

"I. Said. SHOO!" she growls in his face.

God, why is growling so sexy to me?

I once again remind myself I'm with Guy, and I don't want to stir up drama in our group.

The man can't hide the panic in his eyes as he says, "C-can I get my f-friend first?"

Cait lets go of the first man's hand. "Get him and go," she says. "I never want to see your stupid faces again, *newbs!*"

After helping their friend up from the floor, they all scurry away. Then Cait scans the others in the temple. They're all looking at her in horror after witnessing what she just did.

"Anyone else want to be next?" she asks them. "Or do you want to leave the temple while you still can?"

No other prompting is needed. Other than myself and Amalthea, every single person in the temple flees as fast as possible.

"Your friend is scary," Amalthea whispers to me.

I chuckle. "You should see her when a harpy is attacking."

Amalthea's eyes widen. "*Harpy?*"

"Lauren, go put up some chairs at the entrances!" Cait calls out. "I'll make sure no one takes them down while you polish the floors."

As frustrated as I was with Cait at the camp this morning, I'm really glad she's my friend right now. Without her, this quest would have been a pain in the ass. I would have had to keep cleaning up everyone's footprints.

Because the temple has to house so many colossal statues, it has a *lot* of floor to polish. However, I get it done in a couple of hours. To my relief, that's all that Amalthea wants from me, and I can see that this part of the side quest is checked off in my menu. Now for the hard part.

"Um...why don't we go get some lunch?"

Amalthea squints at me like I'm the dumbest person she's ever met. "The Council of Elders will be here any minute! Now's not the time to leave the temple."

"Just trust me on this," I plead.

"Why would I do that?" Amalthea asks.

Cait sighs. "Lauren is a Cleric of Aphrodite. The Goddess of Love wants you and one of the street food vendors to fall in love and make babies or something."

Amalthea laughs. "That's the most ridiculous thing I've *ever* heard. I'm a *priestess*! I take care of the gods, not consort with street food vendors."

"At least meet him," I say. "What's the harm?"

She rolls her eyes but then those same eyes land on Zeus, and her pain is obvious. To love a god and not be loved back must hurt like hell. Settling for a street food vendor is almost an insult when she made love to someone so powerful.

I can't help but compare Amalthea to Mom. Like the priestess, my mother fell hard for a man who abandoned her and was never able to move on to a new relationship again. This left me as her only close relationship, which means that now she's got *no one* to visit her.

"Aphrodite told you I should be with him?" she asks.

I nod. "I talked to the guy yesterday. He's got a giant heart."

After a moment of studying Zeus, Amalthea says, "Fine, I'll meet him just to appease Aphrodite." Then she looks at Cait. "Don't let *anyone* in. I'll take care of receiving the elders when I get back, because I am *not* going to suddenly fall in love with some street food vendor."

"You got it," Cait says.

I lead Amalthea out of the temple and across the street where

Phemie's son is busy selling his roasted chicken on sticks. When he spots me, his face lights up. I have a moment of panic. Yesterday, he made it clear that he thought I was hot stuff.

Then his gaze shifts from me to Amalthea, and his mouth opens in awe. He looks like he might melt onto the pavement.

"This is Amalthea," I tell him. "She's a priestess. Amalthea, this is..." I realize I never got his name.

"Hektor," he says in a breathy voice. He's full-on blushing now. I can practically feel the heat coming off his cheeks.

"It's nice to meet you," Amalthea says. She's timid, but I can tell she's enjoying the attention. After years of being ignored by the last dude she slept with, this must be a pleasant change.

"Why don't you two get to know each other after the grand ceremony is—"

"You're the most beautiful woman I've ever seen in my entire life," Hektor says.

Amalthea giggles and twirls her dark hair around her index finger. "Oh, you don't mean that."

"I swear on my life," he says. "Are you sure you're a priestess and not a goddess?"

"You're making me blush!" Amalthea doesn't even sound like herself now. She's not the stern priestess bossing people around.

Hektor gets on one knee and takes her hand in his. "Would you let a humble man such as myself kiss your knuckles? Such a blessing would likely bring me happiness for years to come."

"Um...I see some rich-looking folks heading to the temp—" I begin.

"You may," Amalthea tells Hektor as she flutters her eyelashes.

"The Council of Elders is waiting to be let into the temple!" I shout.

Amalthea's eyes don't even leave Hektor's as he lays his lips tenderly on her knuckles. Still not looking at me, she waves dismissively in my direction with her other hand. "I'm sure you've got this. You're a Cleric of Aphrodite, after all."

A notification pings, but it's amended, too. Goddamn it! I've got to help the Council of Elders with their fucking ceremony now. I don't know how to do that! Cait's going to murder me!

⇧

"I ONLY LET YOU OUT OF MY SIGHT FOR TWO MINUTES, AND YOU still screw it up," Cait says in a seething whisper.

"I swear all I did was introduce them!" I say. "It's like all I have to do is stand near an NPC, and everything breaks."

Cait sighs and pats my shoulder. "Okay, well, what's done is done. Let's just get this over with."

"But I have no idea what I'm doing!"

"Neither do I, but does it matter?" she asks. "Does it say we have to do a good job or that there's stuff we have to achieve in the ceremony?"

I shake my head. "It just says to help the Council of Elders."

"Okay, so if they tell us to do something, we do it and nothing else," Cait says. "Then we go back to camp." She leans closer and locks my eyes with her serious ones. "And you think about what you've done."

I decide not to debate with Cait any further about how I'm not at fault. She's already barely tolerating me as it is.

We let the Council of Elders in, and they all look pissed as hell. It's not just them, of course; they've all come with their own entourages, and there are attendants waiting behind them. Because of my quest with Amalthea, everything is running late.

Gelasius is one of the many funneling into the temple. I wonder if I can find a moment to talk to him before he leaves. I dismiss that idea when I consider it might make his side quest go sideways as well.

Then I see Phemie and her children and grandchildren come in with the common citizens. The only one of her family that isn't there is Hektor. I assume he's off eloping with Amalthea or something. I take a moment to go over and greet her.

"Lauren!" Phemie says with a big smile. "I suppose I shouldn't be surprised to see a Cleric of Aphrodite here!"

Phemie's youngest daughter, Ione, gasps. "She's a Cleric of Aphrodite? I thought she was just delivering packages."

"Seems Aphrodite tasked her with a divine message," Phemie tells her daughter with a wink. "She's here to help us all learn about love."

This catches Dolius's attention now. "Learn what about love?" he asks.

But I have no time to answer because one elder clears his throat, and the whole temple silences in response.

Phemie and her family hustle to their seats. The elder who brought order to chaos without even saying one word glares at me. I assume he wants me by his side, and I make my way to him. However, the moment I'm there, I realize how wrong I was.

"Sit *down*," he hisses.

"I-I'm supposed to be helping you," I say.

"Then, you're doing an awful job of it," he whispers.

I gulp and find the nearest empty chair available. Fortunately, it's right next to Cait, who's been saving it for me. To my surprise, on the other side of the chair is Gelasius. Both Ione and the man she's crushing on are in the same place. I'm tempted once again to wrap up two quests in one day, but I've really messed things up so far. I can't afford to rock the boat.

Gelasius is focused on the elders, so I don't expect it when he greets me as I sit down. I'd watched him pass right by Ione like she wasn't even there. He seems like the type of person who can't be bothered to social-ize, yet he's talking to me.

"Your friend told me you're a Cleric of Aphrodite," he whispers. "I'm arranged to be married to a young woman who will arrive here tomorrow. Would you be willing to give her a fertility blessing?"

Oh, fuck. He's getting *married* tomorrow? Well, now I have to speed up my process. Feels like I should have done his side quest today and Amalthea's tomorrow. Then I wouldn't be stuck working at this stupid ceremony.

"Um...sure," I whisper back.

Cait elbows me in the ribs and nods at the elder in charge. He's glaring at me again. Did he hear me chatting with Gelasius?

"Now the *cleric* will give her blessing," the elder says, clearly repeating himself.

Shit. I've never blessed anything or anyone. How does this work?

I think back to the times I had dinner at a religious friend's house. They always did a blessing before they ate. How did it go again? Ah yes, it was the Johnny Appleseed song!

I get up and stand next to the elder, then clear my throat and try not to waver as I sing. "Oh, the Lord's been good to me! And so I thank the Lord for giving me the things I need, the sun and the rain and the apple seeds. The Lord's been good to me! Amen. Amen. Amen, amen, amen!"

The blank stares as I finish cause embarrassment to wash over me like ice water. "I mean...the *gods* have been good to me, of course."

I don't even look at the elder as I scurry back to my seat. I know he's probably fantasizing about the assassination he's going to order on me.

Cait's biting her bottom lip to stop herself from laughing, but I can still see that her chest is shaking from the giggles trapped within. She's been so grumpy all day that this is a welcome sight.

"Shut up," I whisper to her, but I'm fighting back a chuckle myself.

"I haven't made a peep," she whispers back.

"You know what I mean."

Cait smirks at me. "Did you really just sing the Johnny Appleseed prayer to a temple of NPCs who worship the Greek pantheon?"

"I panicked, okay?"

Fortunately, my dismal failure means that the elder no longer calls on me to do anything at all. I have no idea what this grand ceremony is for, but it's quite boring. I struggle to stay awake the entire time. When it finishes at last, I hear the notification ping and sigh with relief that this side quest is now complete.

Now to make a miracle happen for Ione. Gelasius gets up and moves to follow the elders out. Not thinking, I grab him by the wrist. "Wait! We need to talk about tomorrow!"

He stares at me like I'm some weird bug that he almost stepped on. I guess my poor performance changed his opinion of me.

"Sorry, I've changed my mind about blessing my union," he tells me. "Please let me go."

"No, it's not about that," I say. "Well, I mean, it kinda is, but I'm not going through with the blessing."

Gelasius pulls his hand from mine and wipes it on his pants. Are my hands really sweaty or something?

"Then, we're agreed. Please, leave me alone now," he says and walks away.

"The bride you intend to marry will make you the unhappiest man in Peripeteia!" I call out to him.

This time, I don't need to grab him to make him stop. Gelasius turns around, and I can see in his eyes that I've touched on a genuine worry of his.

"How would you know that?" he asks.

"Aphrodite gave me the favor of sight," I say.

It's not a lie like when Guy said it to Dolius. I have Near Future Vision now. It wouldn't tell me if someone would be happy in a marriage long term, but he doesn't need to know that. Besides, that doesn't matter. He should be with Ione. If he's with the wrong woman, he really will be unhappy.

Gelasius is still looking at me like I'm a weirdo, so I continue, "I know I messed up the prayer. I wasn't supposed to help with the ceremony today. Amalthea thrust it on me last minute. Aphrodite doesn't task me with stuff like blessings. I'm in Thebe to give certain people important messages about love."

This causes a laugh to ripple from Gelasius who has been far too serious every time I've met him. "Are you telling me that Aphrodite cares about my love life? Love is a story we tell children, and I don't have time for that."

"Love is *real*," I insist. I'm shocked at the words coming from my lips, the conviction in them. Am I this desperate to end this quest chain, or am I actually starting to believe in love again? "I've seen it happen first-hand, and you will soon, too. But hopefully, it won't be too late."

"Is this what your goddess has told you?" he asks.

"Yes," I say. "I even know who it is. I know she pines for you every day, but you've never even noticed her. You're too focused on what you must do as an elder's heir that you're not taking time to do what you must for yourself."

"Fine," he says. "I'll play along. Who's the woman?"

"Ione!" I call out, hoping that Phemie's family hasn't left yet and also that I'm heard over the chatter of the crowd.

Probably only a second has passed, but it feels much longer. Then, I hear, "Yes, Lauren?"

I turn to see Ione, looking just as gorgeous as ever. Though she's addressing me, her eyes are on Gelasius. Somehow, she seems even more smitten than before.

Gelasius turns his smug face away from me to see who I'm talking to. The shift in temperament is instantaneous. His smirk drops, leaving his lips parted in awe. His eyes are wide with surprise. Within a second, he shakes himself out of it and chuckles. Then he looks at me.

"Just because she's beautiful doesn't mean this is love," he says.

I shrug. "I guess you'll never know unless you learn more about her," I say. "She comes from a very loving family, has yearned for even a second of your attention for years, and knows your family inside and out."

"How?" he asks.

"Because I'm one of your maids," Ione answers.

In the time that I've been talking, Ione has come closer. She's now close enough to make out the pretty pink blush of her cheeks and smell the subtle floral scent of her perfume.

Gelasius scoffs. "A *maid*! You want me to give up a proper marriage for a *maid*?"

Ione winces, and I wish I could hug her. Gelasius is such a snob. What does she even see in him?

Phemie storms over, a wrathful expression on her face. "You would be *lucky* for anyone to love you, you stone-hearted boy! And though being a maid is nothing to look down on, Ione isn't *just* a maid. The girl is in school learning to be a mage. Top in her class, as a matter of fact!"

So, this world has mage schools. The developers really copy-pasted a standard fantasy game instead of doing their due diligence on studying Greek history and mythology.

Gelasius seems stunned again, looking at Ione with more than lust. Now she's earned his respect. "You're going to school?" he asks.

Ione nods. "The same one you went to. I-I saw what you could do, and I wanted to learn to do it myself. You're so talented. I hope to even come half as close..."

"If you're top of your class, I'm sure you're much more than half by now," Gelasius says. He looks at the floor, seeming almost humble for a moment. Then he lifts his eyes to hers and puffs his chest with pride. "Well, if you want to be as good as I am, I suppose I must mentor you."

"You'll mentor me!" Ione exclaims.

"Starting tomorrow," he says.

"Aren't you supposed to be getting married tomorrow?" I ask him.

"Perhaps it's best I hold off on marriage," he admits and then looks at Ione. "At least until I find the right woman to marry."

A notification pings. I open it, worried that some new wrench has been thrown into my plans. To my relief it says that this side quest is complete. The only one left is to escort Dolius and Cyrus to Dardanus.

"Let's go," I tell Cait. "I need to work out travel plans with Dolius."

CHAPTER NINETEEN

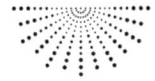

When Alexander had given me the cloak from Aphrodite, the prospect of a seasonal change seemed so distant. A few days later and Alexander is still uselessly looking off into the distance at the edge of our camp but the air has shifted. It pricks along my bare flesh, and the wind whips locks of my hair out of the ornate updo I just got a few days ago. It was already a little disheveled from days of wearing it, so I pull out all my pins and brush it as I gaze at our camp's glorious view.

We'd positioned our camp just south of Thebe on the crest of a high hill, so I can see the road leading north from the city. It bisects a mountain range and reminds me of the skyscraper-lined street I used to walk to get from the subway station to my job. Wind would funnel between the skyscrapers so forcefully that I didn't dare wear a skirt. I'm suddenly more grateful than ever for my new cloak.

Sylvia is boiling grains. It doesn't smell all that appetizing, but having a belly full of something warm and substantial is the perfect way to start a day traveling in the cold. Cait approaches me, wearing a full suit of leathers in addition to a woolen cloak. I'm jealous. As a barbarian, she gets to wear stuff made of thick material, while I'm basically wearing a sheet. Despite her much warmer clothing, I hear her teeth chatter as she sits next to me.

"I'll never forgive the game developers for the newbie quest chain," she says. "Why do they make everyone go *north?* This is supposed to be a game inspired by Greek mythology. We should be eating olives on a rock overlooking the sea while basking under the Mediterranean sun."

"Well, there's a *lot* that doesn't gel with the game's theme," I say. "I mean, players can choose to be an orc. Those don't exist in Greek mythology. Elves don't either."

With a nod, Cait adds, "It's like some guys said, 'Let's take a fantasy RPG and toss some gods and myths in. No one will notice if it doesn't make sense.'"

Cait's impression of the devs is so over-the-top and comical that I can't help but laugh. She smiles at my reaction, clearly pleased with her own joke. Even with her heavy barbarian gear, it's hard to forget that she's the popular mean girl type. How does someone like her wind up someplace like this?

"Who were you?" I ask. "Before Peripeteia."

"A liar," she answers. My confusion must be evident, because her chest bubbles with a silent chuckle. "I was pretending to be someone my parents trained me to be my whole life. I'm the only daughter of five children. My mom was *so* ready to have someone to do girly stuff with. And, mostly, I enjoyed it. I mean, look at me." Cait gestures at her perfect body with a slow wave of her hand. "This takes effort, but..."

"But?"

"Girls are *only* supposed to be into choir and makeup and boys and stuff," she says. "They're not supposed to like sports and video games. At least that's what my mom told me."

"And you felt differently," I say with a nod of my head.

Cait shakes her head. "No, I thought she was right, and that there was something wrong with me. I *enjoy* being a girly girl. I *like* getting dolled up and gossiping with my friends. It just isn't what I *love*. There's so much about me that doesn't fit, so I spent my whole life hiding it."

"That sounds awful."

"It was." Cait looks off into the distance, deep in thought, probably remembering her life before Peripeteia. "I was twenty-four, a virgin, and had no interest in marrying any of the bachelors my parents tossed my way before I wound up here. My mom was over at my place all the time, inspecting it for any sign of promiscuity or unfeminine behavior. Even out of her house, I couldn't get away with gaming."

"Then, how did you wind up here?" I ask.

"One of my brothers," Cait says with a playful smirk. "Elijah is only a year older than me, so it's felt like we were almost twins our whole lives. With him, I never feel like I have to pretend. So, when he got an invitation to beta test *Legends of Sacrifice*, he let me play it at his place." The affection on her face and tone shifts in a melancholy direction. "I wonder what he's up to now. I wonder if he misses me."

Until now, I haven't wanted to open up to anyone about Mom, but Cait's being vulnerable with me. I decide to do the same for her.

"I miss my mom," I tell her. "She's the only person I really feel close to. Because I have social anxiety, I don't really go out there making friends. But Mom? She and I would do all sorts of fun stuff together. Well, we used to..."

"Used to?" Cait asks.

I nod, and to my frustration, a hot tear trails down my near-frozen cheek. "Right before I wound up here, she had a stroke. Apparently she'd had a lot of them, and...now she's in a hospice." I shake my head, wipe away my tear, and offer Cait what I hope looks like a genuine smile. "Anyway, we need to get ready to go."

I move to get up, but Cait grabs my wrist. "Lauren, I—"

"Breakfast's ready!" Sylvia calls out.

Tilting my head toward the campfire, I say, "Food first, chitchat when we're traveling and bored out of our minds."

With a nod, Cait gets on her feet, and we walk together. I see Guy there, his eyes lit with appreciation as I draw near. I feel a twinge of guilt. He's so all in with me, but Cait's the one I finally revealed my deepest pain to.

Guy pats the space next to him by the fire. "I've got your bowl," he says, holding it up for me to grab as I sit down.

I take it with gratitude and dig right in the moment my bottom touches the ground. Sylvia's mixed some honey and cream into whatever these grains are. It's...delicious? Honestly, I thought this was going to be bland, but it's hardly a chore to eat.

Within a minute, I've slurped the whole thing down. I consider going for a second bowl, but I'm already quite full. If I eat any more, I'll be groggy and uncomfortable all day.

"We need to wrap this up," Tara says, tossing her bowl into the washing bucket. "We have to meet Dolius in two hours. It's time to clean up, pack up, and head out of here."

Everyone nods and murmurs in agreement, and we all set about getting ready to leave.

Once I hand Tara my bowl, I head into the tent. I let out a long sigh of relief. It's so perfectly warm in here, and I wish I didn't have to leave.

I roll up my sleeping pad and tap the button on my menu that will send it to whatever realm it lives in while we travel. As I do so, Guy enters behind me and strokes my back. I startle at his touch.

"Whoa, everything okay?" he asks.

I catch my breath and say, "Sorry, I didn't hear you come in."

Guy crouches next to me. "I was hoping we could get a moment alone."

"We don't have time," I tell him. "Like Tara said, we need to hurry and get to Dolius."

"Just a second," Guy insists. "Just long enough to—"

Joshua comes stomping in, grumbling under his breath. He rolls up his bedding and shoves his personal items in a bag.

"Do you need help?" I ask.

"I *need* someone to take the stick out of Cait's ass," Joshua answers. "All I said was that I like what the cold does to..." He trails off, his eyes widening with realization. "Never mind."

"Does to what?" I ask.

Guy stands and crosses his arms. "Yeah, Joshua, does to what?"

Cait walks in at that moment, takes a quick look at our faces, and asks me, "Did he tell you how much he likes how your nipples look in the cold?"

Mortified, I slap my arms over my chest in a flash. I hate this flimsy fabric.

Shaking his head, Guy says, "I wish I could say that I'm surprised, but this is getting predictable. You're lucky I like you, man. If you ever talk about Lauren that way again, though—"

"I meant it in the most complimentary way!" Joshua protests. "I'm not gonna try to touch them or anything. How is this any different from saying her hair looks nice today?" He turns to me. "It does, by the way. You should wear it down more."

"Enough!" Cait interjects. "Joshua, just don't talk about our bodies, okay? That's the best way to make sure no one's mad at you."

Joshua rolls his eyes, but says, "Fine." Then he looks at Guy. "Can you help me take down the tent?"

Guy gives me a wistful look with his big puppy dog eyes. When I don't respond to him, he nods at Joshua. "Sure."

Cait and I leave the tent, and I'm slapped in the face with a bracing breeze.

Ugh, why?

I pull the cloak tight, but it's not enough. My cleric chiton might as well be tissue paper, but if I wear anything else, my healer stats will drop dramatically. No one designed this game with the player's comfort in mind because we're supposed to be in the comfort of our own homes.

"You're miserable," Cait says in a tone so warm that I wish I could feel it, not just hear it.

"It's not fair," I say. "Everyone else gets to wear real clothes."

Cait taps her chin. "Hold on," she says. "Let me look through my inventory."

I watch her scroll through the menu that's only visible to her. Her face lights up when she spots whatever she's looking for. A heart-shaped locket appears in her hands.

"Put this on," she says, holding it out. "Ares gave it to me forever ago."

"What is it?"

"The Heart of Ares," she says. "It apparently holds a flicker of the love he feels for Aphrodite. It used to give me a boost to my Courage skill, but that skill was strong enough on its own, and I found a strength boosting collar. Anyway, the flame keeps the locket warm, and I bet it will create a sort of heat bubble under your cloak."

I reach for the locket and feel the heat radiating from it before I even touch it. My frozen fingers fumble with the clasp.

"Here," Cait says.

She takes it from me and does the job for me. Her hands are calloused and warm as they touch the back of my neck. When she's finished, I'm immediately disappointed by her retreat. I wrap my cloak over the locket, and in mere seconds, there's a pleasant shift in temperature. It's like the Heart of Ares is creating a tiny sauna under there.

"Better?" Cait asks.

I nod. "Better."

"Good."

Cait's smile is bright. Just looking at it makes me feel even warmer. I think back to yesterday when she went berserk and beat the shit out of those sexist assholes. Then a breath later she was ordering me around and nagging me to death. How can she be that person and also one of the kindest people I've ever met?

⇧

I HAD BEEN FRUSTRATED WHEN MY QUEST TO MAKE DOLIUS believe in love updated to an escort quest. Now I'm fucking elated. Every day I've been in Peripeteia, we've had to traipse everywhere on foot. Since I'm not a fucking hobbit from *Lord of the Rings*, my feet haven't been happy at all. So when Dolius expected us all to get in his carriage to guard his merchandise, I wept with joy.

"What's wrong?" he asks.

"I thought we were going to have to walk," I answer.

Dolius grimaces. "Walk? All the way to Dardanus? Hermes preserve us! I'd be cruel to expect that of anyone."

While Joshua, Cait, and Sylvia help pack Dolius's merchandise, Cyrus arrives. He's got his own carriage, which he'd already packed himself. After the two men exchange greetings, they discuss logistics.

"Perhaps half of our guardians should sit in your carriage and half in mine," Dolius suggests.

Cyrus strokes his short-cropped beard. "There's an odd number of them, though."

"What do you mean?" I ask. "There are six of us."

Cyrus squints. "I see seven."

"There's Cait, Guy, Joshua, Sylvia, Tara, and me," I say, demonstrating by putting up a finger with each name. "That's six."

"And him," Cyrus says pointing behind me. "That's seven."

I turn and see Alexander. Because he's always out of the way, I often forget about him. It's so odd knowing that a couple of weeks ago, I'd practically been obsessed with this perfect but fictional hottie. Now, he's a sort of accessory. Yeah, he's lent an occasional hand and given us details on major quests, but mostly he's been useless.

"So weird," Tara mutters. "He should have said goodbye and returned to wherever the Alexander copies go by now."

"This is the end of his quest chain?" I ask Tara and she nods.

"Maybe he just needs you to tell him you're heading to Thrace."

That makes as much sense as anything. So far, he's needed me to be very direct, or else he just stands there staring into the middle distance.

"I'll go take care of it," I tell Tara and leave her behind.

As I approach Alexander, he turns his attention from the pair of carriages to look at me. This is strange, of course, because NPCs aren't supposed to notice you unless you initiate contact vocally. However, the unusual is becoming the usual.

"Hey, Alexander," I say like I'm about to give bad news to a child. "We're all about to head to Thrace. So, you know, you can do whatever now."

"I shall accompany you," he responds.

I guess I broke him, too. "You don't have to," I tell him. "It's not part of your quest chain."

"My quest is to help you with your quests," he says.

Oh, I see. "Did Aphrodite assign that to you?"

Alexander squints. "No, this is what *I* want. You helped me, and now I will help you."

Help me? How does he think he's been helping me? I mean, he hasn't been a burden. He doesn't eat or drink. He doesn't even require company or protection. But he hasn't exactly been an asset.

"We're fine, really," I say.

"No," he says, shaking his head. "In the mountain pass ahead, we will encounter a monster, and I must fight at your side."

I shouldn't feel frustrated with an NPC, but this makes me groan. "Really, Alexander? You've never once fought by my side. You *can't*, remember? The gods won't let you. You've given the occasional tip and pointed us toward our next location, but we've all pretty much had to do things on our own."

To my surprise, Alexander looks down in shame and says, "You're right. I must make up for that. The gods have cursed me to never again lift a blade, but there's more I could do."

"Like what?" I ask.

Then Alexander looks at me. I mean he *really* looks at me. His gaze lands directly on mine as he considers his response. "I will throw my body in front of yours if I have to. I will pull the enemy's attention away from you so that you can attack him from behind."

"That's suicide!" I shout. "Alexander, if you can't fight back, you'll die!"

"It would be worth it to protect you," he says. His voice is low and breathy, like he's admitting a secret. His responses have been formulaic the entire time I've interacted with him. Now he seems *genuine*.

"Why?" I ask. "We've barely spoken a word to each other in days."

"That doesn't matter," he says. "Not when you're my savior." He gestures at Cyrus and Dolius and then at the NPCs walking up and down the road. "*Our* savior."

What does he mean by that? For a moment I wonder if he's cognizant of my personal motivation to free NPCs of their programming. That kind of realization seems like too much to believe from any NPC. No, this must be some "You are the Chosen One" quest line I unlocked somehow.

"Well, okay," I say. "But you gotta talk to Cyrus and Dolius to see which carriage you're riding in."

"It shall be done," he says and walks over to the two merchants.

"What was that about?" I hear Cait ask from behind.

I turn to face her. "Not sure what you heard, but Alexander has insisted on staying with us."

"No, he's staying with *you*," she says. "Yesterday, you said that it felt like you just had to be around NPCs for them to break. What if you were right?"

I shake my head. "That doesn't make any sense."

"No, listen," she continues. "What if when you broke the quest with Arachne's children, you created some kinda...I don't want to call it a virus, but that's the best I can come up with. And now you're walking around, carrying it wherever you go."

Thinking of myself as the Typhoid Mary of Peripeteia wasn't all that flattering, but what Cait suggested made more sense than anything else I've thought of. That would make it incredibly easy for us to undo all the programming keeping the NPCs stuck in the same patterns day in and day out.

I'm about to ask Cait how she thinks that might influence future quests, when a trio of players walks by. They're venting to each other with raised voices.

"Every quest, *every single one* has been broken!" a curly haired halfling man exclaims as he comes around the corner. "How am I supposed to level up if there's no wedding for me to collect flowers for?"

"Tell me about it!" an orc player responds. "I'm supposed to fight off some thieves coming after a street food vendor. But the vendor's not even there! Some NPC said he'd run off with a priestess!"

A human woman walking with them wipes at her teary eyes. "How am I supposed to get home if I can't even do Demeter's quests? I just want to see my friends again!"

The orc puts his arm over her shoulders. "It'll be okay. We'll figure out whatever's causing this and stop it."

When the three are out of earshot, Cait and I stare at each other in horror. We're fucking up the game. Yes, we're helping the NPCs, but we're screwing over the players. And if they figure out it's because of me...

"Load in!" Tara calls out to us. We walk over to the carriages, and Tara continues, "Cait, you're in Cyrus's carriage with Sylvia, Joshua, and me. Lauren, you're in Dolius's carriage with Guy. And Alexander for some reason."

Cait and I nod at each other before parting. Guy's as excited as a Labrador puppy to have me in the carriage with him and Alexander. "Finally," he says. "Just the two of us."

I nod in Alexander's direction. "And him."

Guy laughs. "An NPC hardly counts." He bites his bottom lip. "He's not going to care what we do."

He pulls me to sit next to him and strokes my cheek before he rests his forehead against mine. "I know you want to take it slow, and I'm fine with that. I just need time alone with you. For us to get to know each other, for me to look at you as long as I want."

Guy's words are so sweet and sincere that I feel myself blushing from my scalp to my toes. I truly believe he would wait forever if he had to. We don't have forever, though. I need to get back to Mom, and that means leaving him behind.

I'm too much of a pussy to bring that up. We've only dabbled with our physical connection. I can't stop thinking about how it feels when he touches my ear to silence everyone outside of our party. My lips still tingle from the kiss we shared in the rain a couple of days ago. We haven't had any alone time since then.

Once everyone's loaded in their carriages, my lips brush against Guy's as soft as slipping on a silk dress. He moans against it, and I feel a pulse of lust between my legs. Yes, this can't last forever, but wouldn't it be nice if there was hot sex in the meantime?

Guy weaves his fingers into the hair on the back of my head and kisses me back. It's a little firmer than mine, but he's not getting carried away. "God, if we weren't in this carriage..." he whispers.

I chuckle. "I just bet."

The carriage hits a bump, and we knock into each other. Somehow in the bustle, Guy's hand reaches my breast, and he pulls it back immediately. "Sorry, sorry..."

"It's okay," I say, but then my eyes flicker to the person I'd forgotten about in our carriage. Alexander is blushing, like he's embarrassed. No. I shake that notion away. He's an NPC with more extensive dialogue options.

But this isn't that game. This is Peripeteia, and I'm changing it with every choice I make.

CHAPTER TWENTY

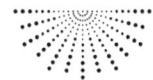

Dardanus isn't as far from Thebe as Thebe was from Sardis, but our current trip is still long, and we didn't head out until midday. So, we still need to make camp tonight.

As I had predicted, the wind is harsh here. Actually, "harsh" doesn't even come close to describing it. Ever been in line for a rollercoaster that has a warning sign about every five paces about how you shouldn't get on it if you have any health problems at all? You think the signs are there to warn off your grandma with the heart condition, but as you come down from the very first peak, you wonder if you have unknown health problems. For a solid second, you wonder if you might die.

Well, the wind is like that, but I'm not wearing a seat belt.

When I exit the carriage, my cloak is useless—an impediment, really —because now it's not covering me but catching the breeze and dragging me away with the gust. I don't dare take it off, though, because I'm sure I'll lose it for good, and the crunch of frozen grass beneath my feet reminds me that much more than icy gusts are on their way.

Fortunately, Guy grabs me by the arm and flings me around to the side of the carriage so that we're blocked from the frigid wind. "Let the folks with the high strength stats take care of setting up camp," he says.

I shake my head. "And then what? Our tents will fly off, too."

Guy laughs. "A magical camp that floats along in the ether until we call on it isn't so easily controlled by the weather. How do you think it stayed warm inside the tent last night?"

"Body heat?" I suggest with a shrug.

Guy says something, but I can't hear him because a gale howls so loudly that I have to slap my hands over my ears. When it dies down enough to for my mind to clear, I say, "Any chance your silencing spell can get rid of the sound of wind?"

"I'll do you one better. There's a silencing dome that can help everyone."

Like a hare-brained idiot, Guy rushes around to the other side of the carriage where I can't see him. "Guy!" I call out. "What are you doing?" But it's useless. The wind carries my voice away.

Suddenly, the loud gusting chorus is gone, which is weird because the wind is just as strong as ever. Guy staggers to my side of the carriage. He's holding on to the carriage with an iron grip but still looks likely to fall. So I grab him and yank him to me.

"Thanks for the help. That spell took a lot of my energy," he says, his hand clasped to his gasping chest.

"Why did you have to leave me to do it?"

"I wanted to get to the center of our group so that everyone would fit under the dome."

There's Guy, being the most considerate person I've ever met again.

Cait comes over to us, red in the face, looking like she might murder someone. "What did you do?" she asks Guy.

"I cast a silencing—"

"You *idiot!*" she shouts. "We can't hear anything Dolius and Cyrus are saying! They're freaking out!"

"I'll go explain to—" Guy starts.

But Cait's not done ranting. "And now you've made it *super* easy for anyone to sneak up on us and attack during this obviously magical windstorm!" She growls in frustration, and I know I need to intervene before she reduces poor Guy to a blubbering mess.

I get between the pair and hold up my hands in surrender, keeping my steady gaze on Cait's. "He was just trying to be helpful. He probably didn't realize it would cause issues because it's hard to think with all this wind."

Cait presses her eyebrows together and swallows. I almost breathe a sigh of relief, thinking I've diffused the situation, but then she narrows her eyes at me and says, "He isn't thinking because you've clouded his head with lust."

Stunned, I can't say anything, only gawk at her, my mouth agape.

"I'm going to set up our tent and help the merchants set up theirs," she says, then gives Guy a pointed look. "The silencing spell better be down by the time those are up."

She storms off. Despite her svelte frame, she strides through the strong gale as if it's nothing but a playful breeze.

I turn to Guy, seeing my confusion mirrored in his scrunched features.

"What was that about?" he asks.

"You tell me," I say. "She was *your* hot-headed friend first."

"Yeah, but not like that," he says, shaking his head. "She's never taken anything so personally. Why should she care about whether I—Oh..."

"What?"

Guy blushes and scratches at the nape of his neck. "She's been weird with me ever since she realized I had genuine feelings for you. I think she's jealous."

"Of me?"

"Well, I mean, there was a minute before you came along when she was kind of...well, flirting with me."

"Guy, she's told me herself that she doesn't believe in people messing around in this group," I explain. "She thinks it can lead to drama."

"She asked if I would be fine with a relationship with her, but I was scared of ruining our friendship."

I'm so astonished that it takes a beat before I realize my eyelashes are fluttering wildly. "Why didn't you tell me?"

Guy has the intelligence to at least look sheepish, with his eyes lowered and his mouth in an awkward grimace. "I didn't think it was that important. She and I never got anywhere because you entered the picture."

"Did you want to have a relationship with her?" I ask.

Guy says nothing.

"So, you were considering dating someone who probably doesn't believe in sex before marriage," I say and then mutter more to myself than to him, "No wonder you're cool with taking things slow."

"Hey, now, I actually care about you," he says.

"Why? We hardly know each other!" I shout.

At that moment, Sylvia peeks around the corner and greets us with an embarrassed smile and an awkward wave. "Hi, so because of Guy's silencing spell, there's no noise to muffle your discussion."

"Fuck my life," I say, closing my eyes as I plant my face onto my palm.

"So, like, maybe fight after the spell is over?" Sylvia's plea lifts at the end like she's asking a question instead of making a request. "I don't think any of us want to know more about Guy's romantic life. Cait can't even look anybody in the eyes."

"Sorry," Guy whispers to Sylvia.

"Tent's up!" Cait calls out and then continues, "Also, I'm not jealous of Lauren! I got over you, Guy!"

Guy sighs, and I lift my face in time to see him raise his staff. Suddenly, the wind is back to keening. I don't mind it as much now. I'd rather listen to that than Guy's excuses as to why he didn't tell me about his history with Cait. It doesn't matter that they had a thing. It's not like I was single all that long before we met, but he should have been open with me.

Guy approaches me, his eyes apologetic and his hand outstretched like he wants to touch my cheek. I lift my palm and shake my head to stop him. "We'll talk later," I say.

I move to walk away, but then I hear something that chills me even more than the bitter weather. I'm not sure how I picked up on it. The wind is bellowing, and *this* is subtle—a faint rattle and hiss.

Not daring to make a sound, to even breathe, I mouth to Guy, "Do you hear that?"

Guy responds with a slow nod. He already has his staff out, and now he shifts to a defensive stance, though he's clearly shaking from exhaustion since he cast and uncast a powerful spell. I also get into my stance. Whatever this is, I hope I can charm it or something.

I look around wildly, trying to match a shape to a sound. I suspect a snake, maybe multiple snakes, but when I finally spot the source, I know we're much more fucked than that.

Beyond the brush a hundred yards away, I see her. She's gorgeous, with the face and tits of a porn mag's centerfold. That's not enough to distract me from the fact that she has dragon wings on her back and a long serpent's tail where her legs should be. My *Jurassic Park*-inspired hope that staying still and silent will keep us off her radar is dashed when she snaps her startling blue eyes on me.

"Guy," I say, edging closer to him as I back away from the monster, "is that the empusa you were telling me about?"

Guy shakes his head. "No, the empusa looks a lot more human. Th-this..." Guy gulps. "This is a dracaenae. A descendant of Echidna, the original dracaenae, the mother of all monsters."

"Son of a Titfucking Asshole," I mutter under my breath.

I wonder if the rest of the party is aware. She's on our side of the carriage, and I'm pretty sure everyone is trying to ignore us because of our rather embarrassing argument. If they don't know, we have to warn them somehow. But I'm afraid to take my eyes off her. She's got me locked in a hypnotic stare, and that may be the only thing keeping her from racing over and sinking her now-evident fangs into my flesh.

Guy is too weak to fight her, and all I can do is defend myself. We need help *now*.

"Go," I tell Guy. "Warn the others. I'll stay here."

"Lauren, I can't—"

"Go!" I command.

Guy stands there for the briefest moment, then dashes to the other side of the carriage. The dracaenae's intense stare flickers in his direction but returns to me, this time with a wicked smirk. He's left me alone. I'm now an easier morsel to pluck off the buffet table.

Fuck. Did I just make a huge mistake?

The dracaenae speeds toward me, fangs fully exposed and taloned hands outstretched. There's no charming or negotiating my way out of this situation. I probably just used my Strategy Under Duress skill to send Guy over to warn the others. There's nothing to protect me other than a staff, and that might as well be a fly swatter in this situation.

"Fuck, fuck, fuck!" I shout.

I try to run, but as soon as I turn the corner, the wind actually pushes me *toward* her. Her fangs are so close now that I smell her last meal. I squeeze my eyes tight, hoping that'll relieve me of at least a portion of my impending death's horror.

Then a strong arm circles around me and pulls me back from the monster. I lean into whoever my hero is, but the moment I feel tempted to see who it is, there's a wicked hiss against my ear.

"Back off!" My hero growls, and I know it's Cait.

She doesn't let go, simply pulls me further away from my would-be murderer. Somehow, she fights off the dracaenae while keeping me pinned to her side. When I finally open my eyes, I see her snarling face and wrathful eyes. There's the promise of death in the glare she gives the monster, which she makes good on in a heartbeat.

Cait's great axe swings with fury, slicing the dracaenae's head clean off her body. I watch in horror as the creature's head rolls onto the ground, its fangs still bared, and its eyes wide open. The monster's body collapses next to it, and blood oozes from its headless neck. The wind halts, just as dead as my attacker is.

It reminds me of the harpy, and I have to turn away to keep from screaming. When I do, I'm face-to-face with Cait. Her face is splattered in the dracaenae's blood. That should be disgusting, disturbing even. But in this moment, my hero looks like a glorious angel fresh from battle. In an instant, her expression flips from wrathful to worried. No, more than worried. She's looking at me like I'm a treasure she almost lost.

"Are you okay?" she asks in a desperate whisper, cupping my face in her hands so she can study me closely.

Our lips are so close now that it would only take an inch of craning my neck forward to kiss her. The temptation is stronger than I care to admit.

"Did she bite you or scratch you or anything?"

"I'm fine," I say. "She didn't touch me."

"Oh, thank God," Cait says. Tears well in her eyes and then she hugs me tight. "I thought—" Her words halt, replaced with gurgling.

Cait lets go of me and staggers backward. Her eyes widen as she grabs her throat with one hand. At first I think she's choking. Then I see dark blue spidering up from her collar to her chin. There are ragged claw marks on her indigo-colored arm.

Shit.

I lift my staff. "Restoration!" I shout. Nothing. Why? This is clearly poison of some sort.

Cait falls over; her whole body spasms on the ground, but she makes no sound. I'm not sure she can even breathe.

Desperate, I get on my knees next to her and press my palm against her arm. It's as hot as a pot pie despite the bitter gusts that had only now stopped battering us.

"Restoration won't work! It's a curse!" Guy calls out as he rushes over from wherever he went. "Remove Hex," he says with a wave of his staff.

Cait makes a choking sound and then draws in several deep, rasping breaths, clutching at her chest. She rolls over onto her side and vomits up something as blue as her arm. That's when her skin returns to its normal hue.

There's still the gash though, so I shout, "Heal Major Wound" and the jagged claw mark disappears. I stroke Cait's arm where the wound once was as she takes long, steadying breaths, then I look up at Guy. "How did you know? This had all the markings of poison. It *still* looks like she was poisoned."

"Because we've met one before," Guy says. "In Paeonia. They're much higher-level monsters than you find in this area."

Cait grabs my arm and uses it to get to a sitting position. Her skin is still so hot. Is the hex truly gone? Does it take a while for its physical effects to alleviate?

"Are you okay?" she asks me in a croaking whisper.

"Are you kidding me?" I ask. "I'm perfectly fine! You're the one that needs tending."

At this point, the entire party has reached us. I wonder what took them so long, but I'm grateful that Cait was there as fast as she was. A second longer and I might not be here to help her to her feet.

"She'll need a bath," Sylvia says, putting an arm over Cait's shoulder.

"I'll heat some water," Tara says and runs off.

Joshua looks at Cait with a pained expression. "You should have let me handle it. I'm wearing metal armor."

Cait shakes her head at him. "You were all too far. There wasn't enough time. I..." She looks at me and then lowers her gaze. "I couldn't take that risk."

Well, fuck my heart. I want them both now.

⇧

GUY WAS RIGHT. THE WIND DIDN'T KNOCK OVER OUR TENT. IN fact, it was cozy and warm inside. Dolius, not having a magical camp like ours, wasn't as lucky. His tent was in tatters within an hour of us setting everything up. Cyrus had been smart, though. He attached his to his carriage on the side blocked from the wind. He was gracious enough to let Dolius stay with him.

This morning, we're all far better rested than any of us could have expected. Cait seems fully recovered, too. When she tells everyone good morning, it's in her usual popular girl voice and not in the hoarse rattle from last night.

And Dolius and Cyrus? Well, they're both smiling as though they'd won the lottery. Maybe they did. I check my quest log and sigh. Nope, I still gotta take them to Dardanus, and I don't see anything about Dolius's feelings on love. I squint at the back of his head and think *really* hard about love in a pathetic, impatient attempt to make him have feelings already.

There's a chilly breeze, but it's nowhere near as violent as it was. Something light might fly away if we're not careful, but my aching legs don't have to struggle against it like they did last night. I remember how it halted the moment Cait slayed the dracaenae.

Cait...

I watch her fill her bowl with Sylvia's new batch of boiled grains. She seems so normal right now, when last night she'd shown what a complete badass she could be. That wasn't her typical battle rage. She'd put herself between me and certain death and *saved* me. She was...She was...

So hot.

Cait looks up from her breakfast at me. Our eyes meet, and my breath stops. She smiles and waves. I return the gesture and then she turns her attention back to her breakfast. A delightful shiver runs from my head to my toes.

It's just my luck that my bi awakening came from falling for a prim and proper chick who hates swear words. What the fuck is wrong with me? Cait would probably puke at the thought of a woman being into her. Plus, things were just starting to heat up with Guy.

That is before he admitted that he and Cait had a sort of thing.

Or maybe Cait would be *really* into being with a woman and I could find out just what those gamer girl fingers are capable of...

"Hey," Guy says as he puts a hand on my shoulder.

I jolt out of my fantasy and force a chuckle. "Sorry, my mind was miles away."

Guy frowns. "Thinking about the dracaenae attack?"

"Yeah," I say. It's only half a lie. Technically, I was thinking about hot lesbian sex because Cait had saved me from the monster.

"I should have stayed with you," he says. "I could have blasted her back, at least. A big enough flame would have gotten Cait's attention."

"I told you to leave," I say. "And I have that whole Beguiling Eyes favor that makes it hard to say no to me."

"It's hard to tell you no even without Beguiling Eyes," Guy responds with a wicked smile.

"Where was everyone else, though?" I ask. "Cait and I were alone for a while."

Guy looks embarrassed. "Apparently, they took a walk in case you and I got into it again."

"Except for Cait?" I ask.

"Yeah, she wanted to finish getting the tent up."

"Thank God for that," I say.

"Look, about all that stuff with her..." Guy says.

I sigh. "Later, okay? I just don't have the mental energy for that right now."

Guy nods with obvious reluctance. "I'm getting breakfast. Want me to grab you a bowl?"

At that moment, Alexander walks up to me carrying a bowl of grains himself. "You're eating?" I ask him. I've never seen the NPC eat even one bite of food in the days he's spent standing around camp.

Alexander shakes his head and extends the bowl to me. "This is for you, Lauren."

"Did he just call you Lauren?" Guy asks.

"Oh, yeah," I say. "I guess Cait and Tara are the only ones I told. I told him my name and asked him to call me that instead of 'traveler' or 'adventurer' or whatever."

I put a spoonful of the grains in my mouth and moan. Somehow, it's even better than last time. There's a little kick to it. "What's different about this?"

I don't expect an answer, but Alexander provides me with one, anyway. "I found some ginger root this morning and added shavings to the mixture."

"Well," Guy says, a hint of jealousy in his tone, "our token NPC is making himself useful. That's not weird at all."

Sylvia whistles and waves for us to join everyone by the fire. "Okay," she says once we're all seated and paying attention. "Dolius says that the Dardanus has another market day tomorrow. So, he can still make some money before heading to Thrace. We need to get him there before sundown so he and Cyrus have time to prepare. Because the road is likely to be more crowded today, and we still have an empusa to get rid of, that means we need to hustle."

I almost forgot about the empusa. I just survived one monster, and now I have to encounter another.

Across the fire, Cait catches my eye and mouths, "Don't worry."

She's right. The dracaenae had been a high-level fluke. The empusa was the right level for a player like me, and it's supposed to be a bloodless battle. You just belittle her until she's defeated. Honestly, I feel bad for the lady. Having worked in customer service for as long as I had, I knew how much being verbally harassed sucked.

Guy gives my shoulder a comforting squeeze. "You can't make me leave you behind this time," he whispers. "No matter what you say."

"Good to know you'll be by my side as I lay the verbal smackdown," I say with a laugh.

But Guy doesn't respond jovially. Instead, he blinks, like I've just slapped him across the face. "I know it's not the same as standing up against the dracaenae, but she's still a difficult monster for a level 3 cleric. And I'll be here for you when we face even worse. Please," he says, his apologetic eyes pleading with me for forgiveness, "trust that I won't let anything happen to you."

I respond with a slow nod, not knowing what to say. I hadn't realized my joke would hurt him. Apparently, he felt worse than I thought he had about splitting when the dracaenae attacked last night.

When I squeeze his hand to assure him all is fine, I feel his body relax. He's been pent up, half expecting me to break his heart this morning. I glance across the fire at Cait. Her gorgeous emerald eyes burn right through me, but there isn't a frown on her face, no hint of disappointment. Just *intensity*.

Guy's kisses were lovely yesterday. I bet he's great in bed, too. But right now, I don't want to think about him; I want to think about *her*.

CHAPTER TWENTY-ONE

The closer we get to Dardanus, the more people we see on the road. It's probably because of market day happening tomorrow. That's what makes it perfect for an empusa. Who can tell if one person in a crowd has a wonky leg? All she has to do is wait for someone to wander off the road a little and follow them.

I'm still shaken by our encounter with the dracaenae last night. I know the other party members said that the empusa is a lot easier, but they also said the harpy would be a breeze. The harpy's lifeless eyes and the dracaenae's decapitated body consume my thoughts. Why are so many Greek villains just pissed off women who are part monster? As a woman who can get a little hangry sometimes, I'm starting to take this personally.

The traffic is so slow that the two merchants' carriages are plodding along at a snail's pace. Since we want to spot the empusa as quickly as possible, we decide to walk along the road while scanning the crowd.

Guy and I are in the middle of the others. Being the easiest players to kill, no one wants us to be too easy to nab off the side of the road. Joshua is all the way over on the left side of the road, and Sylvia is walking through the forest near him. Cait is all the way on the right, and Tara is lurking in the shadows beyond the brush. I still have the earrings on from Thebe that help me communicate with Tara, so if she spots the empusa, I'll be able to rush over there and help her.

I *hope* it will be her, because otherwise, I may not complete the empusa quest. My companions seem to recall the monster being on that side of the road, at least. Still, I'm not getting my hopes up. A lot of quests and monsters aren't behaving the way the game programmed them.

"She'll walk with a limp," Guy reminds me.

"Why?" I ask.

"One of her legs is made out of copper," he answers.

I blink at him. "So, you're saying we're going to hurl insults at a woman who has one real leg and one copper leg? I'm just gonna say it. This seems very ableist."

"Take it up with the game developers," Guy says with a shrug.

"If I ever meet those assholes, I'm gonna have a lot more to complain about than that," I respond.

He laughs.

"I wonder if they know that there are actual players in here," I say. "Like was this planned, or is there some magical, secret reason?"

"Questions like that go through my head all day, every day," he says. "Why is this happening? Why us? How did it happen? What about all the other players? Is this real? Am I in a coma?"

I nod. "Yeah, I toy with the coma theory a lot, too."

Guy smiles at me. "If it is, I'm having the best coma dream ever because just *look* at you."

He weaves his fingers with mine as I blush. I've got to hand it to Guy. Sometimes he can be *really* smooth.

"Lauren," I hear Tara whisper through my earrings. "I see her. She's got some man with her. And they're—oh my. Well, if he dies, he'll die happy."

"How far away are you?" I ask, grateful that things are going as planned. At least so far.

"Not far. I can kinda see you from where I am," she answers. "Just head to your right, and you'll find her once you get past the trees. But *be quiet*. We don't want her to bolt before you can confront her."

"Got it."

Looking at Guy, I tilt my head to the right so he knows to follow me in that direction. The road is so crowded now that it's pretty difficult to get to the side of the road. It feels like I'm trying to change lanes in LA traffic. We " 'scuse me, pardon me" past all the NPCs until we reach the tree line bordering the road to Dardanus.

Compared to the shuffle of feet, clopping of hooves, and squeaking of wheels on the road, the woods are silent—eerily so. I tiptoe, knowing that just a crunch of leaves could give me away.

Soon enough, I see her and damn! If she's a monster, then I'm...I don't know what. Not anything good. What's uglier than a monster? Because that would be me.

She's got a perfect hourglass figure, and the golden scrap of fabric she's wearing is leaving very little to the imagination. At least on her upper half. A long skirt hides her bottom half. Her hair is like a long, shimmering river of ink, and lashes frame her big onyx eyes. The mysterious blue tattoos on her pale arms intrigue me as she beckons her victim deeper into the woods. The man can't keep his eyes off her pouty, blood-red lips.

"Not much farther," she says in a sultry voice. "I just don't want anyone to hear me. I can be...loud."

She winks, and the man groans.

"You're killing me," he says. "I feel like I'm going to explode in my pants right now."

She lets him catch up just enough to stroke his obvious hard-on. The moment he tries to touch her back, she laughs and sprints just out of his reach. That's when I notice her limp and get a glimpse of her copper leg. This is definitely the empusa.

"I feel bad for her victim," Guy whispers to me. "Either he's going to die at her hands or of blue balls. Maybe both."

"Blue balls are a myth," I whisper back. "Anyway, we've got more important things to worry about than whether he's going to go to bed lonely tonight."

After creeping closer, I can see her face better. She's truly striking, and she seems *really* into this. If I didn't know she was just looking for lunch, I'd believe she truly wanted to ride this guy until dawn. Then I get a peek of her long, pointed canines. Are empusas like Greek mythology vampires?

I catch sight of Cait half-hidden behind a tree on the other side of the empusa. She nods at me, and I know it's time. Holding up my staff, I dash in front of her would-be victim. The empusa startles and turns to run, but then Cait reveals herself. Tara and Guy appear as well, and the empusa realizes she's surrounded.

"Shit," she mutters. "There's a lot of you."

The man grabs me from behind. "I'll save you!" he tells the empusa.

"You idiot, I'm trying to save *you*!" I yell at him as I try to wriggle out.

"Finally," the empusa says and sighs with relief. Her mask of innocence drops, and she looks at me with an expression that's all business. "Okay, let's get this over with. I'm *so* ugly and *so* evil. Yada yada."

"You're beautiful, my love!" the man cries out to her.

The empusa waves at him dismissively. "Thanks, Vas. That's very sweet of you, but I'm afraid you're getting cockblocked now."

Yada yada? Cockblocked? This woman sounds like a player, not an NPC.

"Wait!" I say. "Who are you?"

"I'm the empusa," she answers. "Duh."

"Empusa?!" the man shouts and then drops his hold of me so he can run away screaming his head off.

I tidy my cloak where his arms had just rumpled it and walk toward her, saying, "Okay, but you don't *talk* like an empusa. You talk like a player."

"Yeah, well, that would be because I *am* a player," she says and then narrows her eyes as she continues in a bitter voice. "Or at least I *was* a player. Word to the wise, don't piss off Hekate. Being one of her warlocks was great until I told her I didn't feel like killing this giant named Clytius."

"So she changed you into an empusa?" I asked. Suddenly I feel like Aphrodite making genitals fall off is one of the kinder punishments the gods can inflict.

"Yep," she says and claps her hands together. "Okay. Let's do this. It's been a long day, and I need a nap."

Guy joins my side, squinting at the empusa. "Wait a minute," he says. "You *want* us to kill you?"

"Well, I mean, I don't actually die," she answers. "I just get sent to this weird black space until I respawn. It's actually pretty peaceful there. I've never slept so good in my life."

"Is that where all the monsters go when they're killed?" I ask.

The empusa shrugs. "I suppose so. I don't see anyone else when I'm there, but they could have their own little pocket of nothingness."

It occurs to me she may have information that could be helpful. I know I need to finish this quest but...

I walk over to the empusa and extend my hand, "My name is Lauren. What's yours?"

The empusa looks from my face to my hand with suspicion in her eyes. After a beat, she puts her hand in mine and shakes it. "Komiko," she says. "But my friends call me Miko. Or at least they did before I wound up like this. Then it was like they all forgot I existed or something."

"That's Guy," I say, pointing at him. Then I point at my other two nearby companions. "That's Cait and Tara."

"Hi," Miko says as she waves at them. "Nice to meet you."

"Sorry, if I ever killed you," Guy says, wincing and scratching the back of his head in embarrassment.

Miko chuckles. "That probably wasn't me. I haven't been doing this for more than a few months. Even if it *was* me, it's okay. It doesn't hurt or anything."

"What happens if you don't get caught?" I ask.

She points up the hillside. "I get to my cave up there and then Vas goes back to the crowd. I usually make a snack from the food the Hekate worshippers leave me before I start the whole rigamarole again."

"That sounds really boring," I say.

"It so is," she says with a nod. Then she gestures at herself in a way that suggests she's ready for a fight. "Anyway, fire away with the insults."

"No," I say and cross my arms. "This is stupid. You're not hurting anyone. You should join us."

"Lauren, seriously?" Cait says, looking at me like I just sprouted horns.

"Pretty sure that would make my goddess mad," Miko says.

"Seems like that's already happened," Guy says with a shrug. "I suppose you don't want things to get any worse, though."

"Understatement of the decade." Miko crosses her arms. "Please, just kill me. Just talking like this might end badly for me."

The resignation on her face hurts my heart. One look at the rest of the group tells me they feel the same. How can we do this to another player?

Guy looks up at the sky and says, "Okay, yeah, I'm using that boon."

"Boon?" I ask. "What are you—"

Before I can finish that question, a grape appears in Guy's hand. "Eat one," he tells Miko, presenting it "If you do, you're promising Dionysus that you will be one of his heroes. He can protect you from Hekate."

"And what does being one of his heroes entail?" Miko asks.

"Mostly getting drunk and having a ton of sex," Guy answers honestly. He looks at me. "But not always. He's letting me take a break from some of that stuff right now for, uh...personal reasons."

"So, like, partying?" Miko asks.

Guy nods, and Miko swipes the grape from his hands and pops it into her mouth without a second thought. She closes her eyes and moans orgasmically. The blue tattoos on her arms disappear, and her skin exchanges its porcelain quality for a fawn complexion.

"Oh gods," she calls out, breathily, "this feels *amazing*! I'm me again! I'm—" She stops and looks down. "*Seriously?*"

"What's wrong?" Guy asks.

Miko points at her legs. One of them is still copper. "I guess that's here to stay. I suppose it was too much to ask that my real leg would magically grow back."

"Grow back?" I ask. "You mean you lost the real one? I just thought it was encased in copper."

"Oh, no," Miko said, shaking her head. "She cut it off and put this sucker on."

My companions and I wince in unison.

Miko waves a dismissive hand. "It is what it is." Then she looks at me with an apologetic expression. "Sorry, you didn't get to complete this quest. Another empusa might come along if you wait."

"Can't," Guy says. "We need to finish our escort mission first."

The mention of the escort mission reminds me that sometimes my objectives change. I bring up my quest log, and sure enough, the empusa quest is no longer there. Instead, it says I completed an alternative objective to persuade her to give up her evil ways.

"This quest is complete," I tell everyone. "Let's get to Dardanus."

CHAPTER TWENTY-TWO

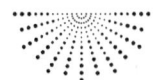

I wonder what the Dardanus from Greek mythology is like because there's no way it's like this. The people here look even more like they came out of a typical fantasy RPG than in any other city we've traveled through. I mean, seriously, there's a bard playing a violin in the center of the market.

I need to let this go, but the part of me that spent half a semester as a world mythology major is having such a hard time with all this. How did a world so rich and full come from people who were so lazy with their research? Though, I guess Peripeteia is its own thing, and I have to give them one thing at least: the most visible mountain I can see from here is definitely Mount Ida, and it's even more breathtaking than in photos.

My quest log updates the moment we set up Dolius's table next to Cyrus. I long for that "complete" notification and groan when it says, "Talk to Dolius about his feelings for Cyrus." Just how stubborn is this guy? It was abundantly clear to everyone this morning that they were digging each other. I wouldn't be surprised if we were witnessing the afterglow that comes from a night of sex.

I have to do it, though. My main quest here hasn't even popped up yet, and I'm pretty sure it's because I haven't finished this one. Fortunately, my companions know exactly what I need to do. It's a rescue mission, which is a nice change of pace from killing lady monsters and convincing people to give love a chance. Though the premise is disturbing.

Princess Idaea is fleeing home from the kingdom where she once lived with her husband. Something bad happened to her there, but when she brought justice to those who hurt her, it backfired. Now her husband wants her dead, and apparently, so does her dad.

What is it with this game and women? Why can't I rescue a man or fend off a *male* monster? I'm so tired of it. If I ever get out of *Legends of Sacrifice*, I'm calling this bullshit out. They slack off on a ton of Greek mythology, history, and geography, but they got the sexism *just right*.

I stick around Dolius to help him ply his wares. He's told me several times already that I don't have to. I know I don't. Honestly, I may even be holding him back from making more sales simply because I'm taking up space he needs to rummage through his merchandise. But I need to talk to him, and that means I can't let him out of my sight yet.

Fortunately, a brief lull in shoppers arrives, and Dolius relaxes a smidge. Now might be my one chance.

"So, uh...Cyrus is really nice," I say.

Dolius nods as he tidies up his displays and puts more merchandise on his table. "Yes, he's a good man."

"Kinda handsome, too," I continue.

"What do you mean?" Dolius asks, squinting at me. "Are you interested in a relationship with him?"

I laugh. "No, I feel like he's not exactly interested in people like me." I gesture at Dolius. "I think he's more attracted to people like you."

"Ah, I see," Dolius says. "Well, I suppose so."

"You suppose? Isn't it obvious to you?"

Dolius returns his attention to his booth, fussing with the angle of a rather expensive-looking necklace. "Men sometimes find pleasure in each other, but it's nothing serious."

Jesus Fucking Christ. Is Dolius one of those dudes who thinks it's not gay if it's just a one-night stand? No wonder this quest isn't complete yet.

"Dolius, stop," I say. "Let's be serious for a moment."

"I *am* serious," he says, huffing. "I have more important things to do than talk about who Cyrus wants."

"No, you don't," I insist. I take his face in my hands and force him to look at me. "One day, you won't be able to travel all over the world and ply your wares. One day, you'll be old and need to rest, but you'll have been so focused on work that you'll be alone."

"I *enjoy* working," he says.

"Obviously," I say, "but you don't have to forgo deep relationships to be an ambitious merchant. You don't have to travel alone. Imagine if you could go from market to market with *him*." My hands are still on Dolius's face, so I turn it so that he's looking at Cyrus. "Imagine that every night is like last night and every morning is like this one. Imagine sharing a booth and a passion for travel...sharing a bed that's no longer cold."

Dolius's face takes on a wistful expression. My words are making an impact. Is this the moment?

"Men can't marry," he says.

"Not by law, and that's unfair." I remove my hands from his face and place one palm over his heart. "But you can be married in here. Dolius, you can't let this promise of happiness slip through your fingers."

With a gulp, Dolius finally nods. Thank fucking hell.

"Can you watch my booth for a moment?" he asks me, not taking his eyes off Cyrus.

"Of course."

Dolius walks over to Cyrus. They're far away enough to where I can't make out the words they're saying, but I don't need to. Cyrus gazes at Dolius with such awe and affection. Then Dolius strokes the other man's cheek, and tears well in Cyrus's eyes. The two rest their foreheads together for a moment, and when they pull back, it's to give each other a sweet kiss.

Until this moment, none of the love-related quests has moved me. This, though? This is different.

My heart beats fast enough to feel like it might just fly out of my chest up to the heavens. I sniff back the tears that beg to escape the corners of my eyes. I'm just so *happy* for them. Dolius deserves this. Cyrus, too.

I lift my staff just an inch and whisper, "Near Future Vision." It's probably not what the spell is for. I should use it as an advantage for quests that require strategy, but I want to use it right now. This is important to me.

The world around me disappears as a swirling mass of stars surrounds me. A moment is projected before me, looking just like I'm sitting in a movie theater. Dolius and Cyrus snuggle against each other and hold hands by a campfire built between their two carriages. Something is bubbling in a pot over the flames, and they watch it with smiles on their faces. Dolius is the first to turn his attention from the dinner that's cooking.

"Cyrus," he says, "I love you."

"I love you, too," Cyrus replies in an awed whisper.

Their lips meet, gently at first and then passionately. It's long and beautiful. I think about exiting the vision so that I don't intrude on their privacy, though I'm not sure how to do it. While I search my menu for a way to end the spell, I hear Dolius say, "Let's spend forever together."

Finally, I find an X in the top right corner of my UI next to "*Concentration Spell.*" I tap it and, with a swirl, I'm back in the market.

Dolius is back now, too. "Thank you," he says. "Thank you so much."

"I need to go," I tell him. "Do you have this on your own?"

"Please, go," he says firmly. "You may be good at love, but you're terrible at sales."

With a chuckle, I walk away and wave at him. I hear a ping and see that my quest is finally complete. Then another quest pops up, my main quest: Rescue Princess Idaea.

"Here we go," I say. "Time to find my friends and save a damsel in distress!"

CHAPTER TWENTY-THREE

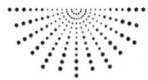

I find my friends wandering the market, helping Miko get some basic gear. It's a little difficult to choose the right items because no one is exactly sure how switching deities works. Does she stay the same class, or will Dionysus choose another for her? The temple here is closed for market day, so she likely won't know anything for a while.

When I find them, Miko is trying on cloaks. This is probably the smartest use of funds because just as I arrive, tiny snowflakes descend lazily from the clouds above.

"Winter is coming," I greet my companions, using my best Eddard Stark imitation.

"Yeah, no kidding," Cait says as she catches a few in her hand.

Tara tilts her chin up and sticks her tongue out. It's so childlike, so opposite of the shrewd rogue I know.

"Cheeses of Nazareth," Cait says with a sigh. "Don't eat the snow! That's so gross!"

I laugh. "Did you just say, 'Cheeses of Nazareth?'"

Cait crosses her arms and glares at me. "Yes, there are some ways to express surprise or frustration *without* using curse words."

She's so fucking cute right now. I wonder if she's just as adorable when she's having an—

A scream so shrill and distraught that it immediately wrenches my heart from my chest echoes around the market.

"Here we go," Guy mutters. "God, I hate this quest."

King Dardanus, the Greek mythological king whom this city is named after, marches into the middle of the market, dragging his daughter by her golden curls. He flings her forward, and she slides across the cobbled city square until she collides with a very surprised shopper. Dardanus has a thin clump of her hair in his grip. There's a small bloody mass at one end. I wince. Poor Princess Idaea.

"You're a stain on my honor, a blight in my lineage!" he yells at his daughter.

"I-I didn't lie!" she cries out, sobbing and holding the back of her head. "They really did—"

"You *dare* slander them again? After what you did to them?"

King Dardanus isn't having any of that. His face is the shadow that looms over you in your nightmares. I can only imagine how terrified Idaea is. How the hell are we supposed to save this woman?

"What did you do when you had this quest?" I ask Guy in a whisper.

"I offered the king a boon from Dionysus to make his vineyards the best in all of Peripeteia," Guy answers. "The land is *really* garbage here. He needed fertile ground more than revenge on his daughter."

"That's not really something I can do," I say with a sigh, then turn to the others. "What did you all do?"

"We pretty much all offered boons from our gods," Sylvia says. "You can only save her by convincing him not to do it, and he only listens to power, so..."

Well, fuck. What kind of boon can I offer from Aphrodite that a king would want? This guy can have any woman he wants simply because he's rich and rules this kingdom.

Dardanus walks over to a nearby stall that sells weapons. He grabs what looks like a sledgehammer that's displayed on the ground beside the merchant's booth, probably because it's too heavy to be on a table. It's about as tall as our tiny Tara, but somehow the king can swing it forward in an arc, causing the crowd to scream and back away.

"Bear witness to this," he says with a booming, commanding voice. "I will not suffer traitors, liars, and villains, even if they are my own blood."

There's no time to deliberate how best to bargain with Dardanus. I'll have to wing it.

I dash in front of Princess Idaea and hold up my arms in a pleading gesture. "King Dardanus, in Aphrodite's name, *stop*!"

The King's eyes widen with rage, but he lowers his sledgehammer. "How dare you contest me? I am your *king*!"

He's not really my king, but I don't press the subject. Semantics aren't helpful in this situation.

"And *I* am a goddess's emissary," I respond. "Do you want to hear what Aphrodite has to say, or do you want to piss off a goddess?"

As a silent moment passes, Dardanus's wrathful expression shifts in a stony, logical direction. "What does the Goddess of Love want with me?"

"She wants Princess Idaea to find peace in a land far away from your kingdom," I say, hoping that's enough to save the damsel in distress.

Dardanus shakes his head. "I am a king first and a man second. I will not neglect my duty to uphold the law and justice. Without that, my kingdom would fall apart, and my citizens would suffer."

"What if Aphrodite offers you a boon?" I ask.

This catches his attention, and he tilts his head. The strategy my companions all used works well so far, but I still haven't figured out exactly what my goddess can offer this man.

"What kind of boon?" he asks.

"Um...a boon of love, obviously," I respond.

Dardanus laughs. It isn't bitter or derisive. He roars so loud that I feel it vibrate through me. The man is absolutely delighted, entirely amused by my proposal.

"What need have I of love?" he says. "I've had more wives than I have money, and each of them has borne me many children. I can't even afford the love that already waits for my embrace each evening."

Yeah, this was the reaction I was expecting. But this is the only offering I can make him, as far as I know. So I decide to sell it. One of my skills is Negotiation. Time to use it.

"Yes, but have you ever had love like Aphrodite's?" I ask.

Now, I mean to say that I can help him feel true love or whatever. Like maybe make his bond with his wives stronger or whatever. By the way Dardanus is smirking at me, though, I feel like he's interpreted my words quite differently.

"I must admit, I'm tempted by a connection with the goddess," he says. "I hear a night with her can invigorate a man for the rest of his life."

Oh, fuck.

"Um, I'm afraid Aphrodite can't—"

"Dance for me," the king says, interrupting me.

I stare at him, totally stunned.

"Dance!" he commands.

You know how at homecoming events there were always the people who danced and the people who leaned against the wall wishing they could go home already? Guess which one I was. But that doesn't matter right now. When a man who's willing to bash his daughter's head in with a sledgehammer tells you to dance, you fucking dance.

I sway my hips in what I hope is a seductive motion. Dardanus strokes his beard as he studies me. He doesn't look all that impressed, so I twirl and leap about. My movements are clumsy, and twice I come close to twisting my ankle. The king looks bored now.

My thoughts race through every dance move I've ever seen on a TikTok video until I realize what actually might work, and I absolutely hate that this is probably the best choice. It's the one dance move I'm good at, and I've only ever done it privately because I'm not the kinda girl to do it publicly.

Turning my back to Dardanus, I bend so that my butt is clearly on display, and then I twerk. I mean, I *twerk*. I put every bit of effort I have into it, and I can feel my cheeks clapping perfectly. The benefit of not being a skinny chick is that my ass can do this. I try not to think about how my friends might react to this. If I gotta work it to save a princess, I'll do it.

"Stop!" Dardanus shouts.

I gulp and turn around to face him. This is it. I failed. He's going to tell me my dance was—

"That was the most alluring dance I've ever seen," he says.

Wow, he really is as perverted as I hoped he was.

"I will let you connect me to Aphrodite," he says. "Go to my servants. They'll bathe you and perfume you with my most expensive oils. I expect you naked and in my bedroom by sunset."

My stomach plummets like an anchor, and I break into a sweat. What the actual fuck? Did I just whore myself out?

"I-I think there's been a misunderstanding," I say.

"Are you not a Virgin of Aphrodite?" he asks.

"A what?" I look at my title in my menu. Sure enough, it's changed from Cleric of Aphrodite to Virgin of Aphrodite. Also, my quest log has updated to "Seduce King Dardanus."

"I'm honored that the Goddess of Love would send one of her virgins to perform a connection rite," he says. "I will deflower you most tenderly."

Deflower? I really want to puke. This man, this *monster* who kills his children, wants to spread my legs open and take my nonexistent virginity. I'm both seething with rage and quaking with fear.

Suddenly, Cait growls and then screams as she charges at Dardanus. "You disgusting old rapist!" she shouts.

King Dardanus growls, causing the shoppers and merchants to scream and run for their lives, clearing the market of everyone except Dardanus, Princess Idaea, and us.

Brandishing her great axe over her head, Cait leaps upward, ready to cleave the top of the king's skull. Dardanus dodges out of the way just in time, but that puts him right in the way of an icicle blasting from Guy's hand. It slices the king's cheek. Dardanus winces and presses his finger to the cut, but it hasn't stopped him. He glares at Guy and lifts his sledgehammer. Before he can swing it, however, Sylvia shoots a fire arrow, which pierces the king in the throat.

Dardanus grabs the projectile in his throat, but it's useless. Not only is he gurgling from the blood gushing out of his mouth and neck, he's also *on fire*. He stares at Sylvia as he buckles over and falls to his side. He's already dead by the time the fire reaches his royal garments.

We have no time to celebrate because his guards, who had been standing sentry at his palace gate, have finally arrived. They're brandishing spears while getting into formation. There are easily a dozen of them. We're well and truly fucked.

This doesn't seem to bother Joshua, who shouts with delight, "Finally! A battle!" Immediately, he gets his fiddle playing what I'm pretty sure is "Kiss with a Fist" by Florence + The Machine.

"Ares, bless my axe!" Cait shouts and fire leaps from its edge. The flame's light casts a devilish illusion on her face.

Cait charges toward the guards while Sylvia looses arrow upon arrow at them. With a wave of his staff, Guy creates a line of stone behind the men so that they're literally fighting with their backs against the wall. Then he rushes to my side.

Tara flings a dagger after dagger at the three guards on the right who are running toward Sylvia. I can feel Joshua's song energizing everyone in our party. He's dancing now, and I swear all of my friends' attacks are to the same beat as his skipping feet. Cait is actually glowing now as she slaughters our foes with wild abandon. In fact, *everyone* is glowing. I lift my hand to see I am, too.

I can't just let my friends fight without me. When I see a guard racing toward Guy, I dash between the two men and raise my staff. "Charm!" I shout.

The guard stops in his tracks, and his eyes take on a soft pink hue.

"Go kill the other guards!" I command him.

He pivots around and races back, lancing straight through one of his former comrades.

"Whoa," Guy says. "You're kinda scary."

I forgot all about Miko, but my memory is refreshed when she rushes forward with an armful of grapes from one stall. She flings them at the guards. This seems useless at first, but then the fruit drops to the ground at their feet, causing our enemies to slip around on the crushed grapes as they try to dodge our attacks.

"No one's hurting my new friends!" she yells.

One guard punctures Cait's side with his lance. My breath stops, but to my surprise, Cait doesn't fall. Instead, she grabs the spear in her side and head butts the guard. This knocks him out, and she pulls the spear out. This leaves a gushing wound, but she's still swinging her great axe around. Her barbarian nature is stronger than her pain, but it can't negate a life-threatening injury.

I lift my staff and shout, "Heal Major Wound!"

In an instant, the gaping hole in Cait's side is gone. She's so busy decapitating a guard that she doesn't even notice. Joshua also gets the sharp end of the spear, but this one is in his leg, and he howls in pain.

"Heal Major Wound!" I cry out.

Immediately, Joshua is healed and back to playing another song. I think it's Led Zeppelin's "Immigrant Song" this time.

How is he able to play all these on the fiddle? He's really bringing his A game!

One by one, our enemies fall until there's only one left, the guard I charmed. But now that all his comrades are dead, my spell has worn off, and he descends to his knees, screaming. He stares at his bloodied hands, knowing he took part in killing people who were probably his friends.

"Run," I tell him in the gentlest voice I can muster.

The guard shakes his head. "There is no running from my sin, you beauteous *monster*," he hisses at me. Then, he breaks his spear in half, turns it to face his chest, and drops himself onto it.

Now the market is quiet enough for the winter wind's keen to sound like a teakettle spouting off at my side. I stagger back, exhaustion slamming into me like a tractor-trailer as I do. "Holy fuck," I whisper. "What have I done?"

"You saved me," Princess Idaea says behind us.

We each turn to face her as she stands up on wobbling legs. Now that she's no longer curled up on the ground in pain, I can see her clearly. Her hair is a mass of knots, and her face is a landscape of welts. She's peeking at us through the narrow slits between her swollen lids. Her royal garb is in tatters, and she has to hold up a scrap to cover one of her breasts.

"I thought for sure he would kill me," she says. "When my stepsons raped me, my husband believed me at first. He blinded them for me. But their mother convinced him I'd lied and...and..."

Idaea stops to sob and then raises her head to the heavens. "Oh, gods, how you test me! First my stepsons assault me, then my husband threatens to kill me, and then my father nearly does!"

She's so pitiful, and my heart cries out for her. I can't leave her alone, so I take her in my arms and allow her to cry on my shoulder. "You're safe now," I whisper.

"But for how long?" she asks. "I thought I'd be safe coming home, but that wasn't true at all."

"Lauren's right," a familiar woman's soothing voice says.

I look up to see Aphrodite. *Aphrodite!* I didn't even know it was possible for a god to leave the temple or Olympus, but here she is, standing on the other side of the princess crying on my shoulder.

Idaea turns to see who it is and falls to her knees the moment she realizes she's face-to-face with a deity. "My goddess, I'm so sorry! I shouldn't have questioned the gods."

Aphrodite strokes Idaea's bowed head. "You're only human," she says. "Though, now, you are somewhat more. You are a queen."

"A *queen?*" Idaea asks and looks up at the Goddess of Love.

"You will sit on your father's throne in the city of Dardanus, and you will take his place as ruler of Mysia," Aphrodite says. "And if anyone questions that, they will know my wrath."

I wince, knowing that her wrath sometimes means genitals falling off.

"As for you," the goddess continues, facing me with a scowl, "you ignored my quest."

"I...I don't understand," I say. "I helped Dolius and Cyrus get together."

"You were supposed to seduce Dardanus," she says.

"But he's a monster," I argue. "I couldn't sleep with a man like that."

"Who said you had to sleep with him?" Aphrodite asks. "The next step in the quest was to poison him before he could have his way with you. That would have resulted in a lot less bloodshed. I should punish you for disobeying me."

On instinct, I slap one hand between my thighs and an arm over my chest. "Please, no," I whisper.

"It's my fault," Cait says, coming to my side. "I got emotional, and I didn't think."

Aphrodite appraises Cait with a calculating expression, and then a mischievous smile lifts the corners of her mouth. "You're the barbarian. My lover's chosen, I believe." She chuckles. "Yes, you got a little emotional, didn't you?"

"I'm so sorry," Cait says.

The Goddess of Love returns her attention to me, tilting her head inquisitively. With a nod, she says, "Forgiveness granted for the lot of you."

Our collective sighs echo through the mostly empty market.

"Thank you," I say. "I'm so sorry."

"Never deny my quests again," Aphrodite says in a stern tone. Then, she leans close to me and whispers, "Especially this next one."

Aphrodite pulls back and winks at me before walking away and disappearing like a slip of smoke on a breeze.

I check my quest log to see what she's talking about. "Kiss Her" is all it says, but that's all it needs to. The Goddess of Love took one look at Cait and one look at me and decided. As her cleric, I'm sure she knows my desires, but does she know Cait's?

Guilt and horror twist my stomach into knots. Aphrodite wants me to break Guy's heart—and potentially my own.

CHAPTER TWENTY-FOUR

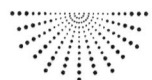

No one wants to be near the city anymore. Once Aphrodite left, we were left with the evidence of the horrors we committed. Yes, we saved a princess, but in the process, we killed a dozen people.

I had actually charmed one of our foes into killing his allies. He chose to fall on his spear after accusing me of being a monster. I can't spend a silent moment without that scene playing on a loop in my mind.

Beauteous monster. Beauteous monster. Beauteous monster.

I keep as busy as possible, hoping to drown it out.

We make camp far enough away from Dardanus that we can turn our backs to it and gaze ahead at the distant shoreline. One boat trip and we'll be in Thrace, and it will take less than a day to reach Khione in Ismarus. Will I be ready? Aphrodite had been clear that I needed to complete every quest I can before I give Khione Aphrodite's super secret message. Yet, I'm still only at level three.

Maybe tonight, I'll level up. After all, I took on a much higher-level monster while on an escort quest, completed the empusa quest peacefully, helped Dolius and Cyrus get together, and...No, I don't want to recall that last quest. It's complete; that's all that matters.

We're all eating stew for dinner, and Joshua keeps looking over the campfire and chuckling at me. It's because I still have "Virgin of

Aphrodite" over my head. I tried to revert it to say "Cleric," but I just keep getting an error message. *An error message.* I don't believe that for a second. Aphrodite's fucking with me because I disobeyed her.

I should be more annoyed with Joshua about his teasing, but I'm a touch grateful for the distraction from my intrusive thoughts. Cait seems angry about it, though. Every time he laughs at me, she gets redder and redder.

Finally, she snaps. "There's nothing wrong with being a virgin, you know! It only means you haven't had sex. That's not a bad thing."

"But she's like twenty-seven," Joshua responds, "and assigned to the Goddess of Love *and* Sex."

"Yeah, yeah," Sylvia says, rolling her eyes. Even she's tired of this. "The irony is terrific. Can we move past this already?"

"Actually, a Virgin of Aphrodite doesn't mean Lauren's never had sex," Tara says. "It just means she isn't married." She squints her eyes in deep thought. "At least, I'm pretty sure that's what I read in my western history textbook."

"Eventually my title will change," I say. "I just have to earn a new one or at least go back to the original one."

Guy leans close to me and whispers in my ear, "I can at least help you disprove it."

His breath tickles me pleasantly, and his words are seductive. I'd love nothing more than to let him, but guilt overrides desire. I want him *and Cait.* That makes me a cheater, right?

I've had "Opposites Attract" by Paula Abdul stuck in my head since we made camp, which is a really weird soundtrack to the occasional disturbing visions of the aftermath of our battle. "Two steps forward, two steps back" followed by King Dardanus's charred and smoking corpse is jarring to say the least.

But when I look at Cait, it all disappears. The song silences, and the memories sweep away, leaving her face and voice. When we first met, my swearing completely put her off. Sometimes, I annoy the shit out of her, too, and she's grumpy as hell. Despite that, she's listened to me more than any of my other companions, and her empathy is sincere. You know when Cait really cares because she doesn't placate anyone.

Fuck, I want to complete Aphrodite's new quest. The firelight complements her warm features, and without her leather armor on, the muscular tone in her otherwise slender arms stands out. I'd love nothing more than to kiss her—on her lips, her fingers, her everything. I want to touch her in such a way that I ease the tension she bears all day and pull a sigh from her.

I wouldn't do any of that without permission, though, and I'm uncertain I'll ever get that from her. She's spent her life being perfect for a family that had very conservative ideas about what a woman is and what a woman does. If they drilled into her that it wasn't ladylike to play sports or video games, I can only imagine how they'd feel about lesbianism.

Thankfully, there's no time limit on this quest. Maybe I can feel things out with her more, take my time, ease into a romantic moment, and ask for a kiss. And if she doesn't say "yes," well, maybe the quest will update, and the attempt will be enough to satisfy Aphrodite. I wonder what my goddess's stance on consent is. She was pretty vague about that whole quest to seduce King Dardanus. If Cait doesn't want a kiss, I won't force it on her, even if it angers Aphrodite. Love isn't about taking what you want from others.

Shit. Did I just liken this to love?

Guy yawns and puts his arm around me. "I think I'm going to sleep now."

I see the invitation in his eyes and know it's not for sex because nothing like that's going to happen in the tent we share with everyone else. He wants to spoon or something. However, I know that the moment I close my eyes, I'll think about today's battle.

"I think I need to take a night stroll away from the group," I tell him. "Clear my head and stuff, you know?"

He nods, understanding. "Just be careful. Who knows what's lurking out there?"

Guy stands up and walks over to the tent. Joshua, Sylvia, and our new member, Miko, follow him. Now, it's just Tara, Cait, and I left to tend the fire and observe the starry sky. I get up from my seat and let the group know I'm going on a walk.

"Did you tell Guy?" Cait asks.

"Yeah, I'm hoping it will help me sleep better tonight."

"He's right, you know," Cait says. "The dracaenae makes me think that there are some rogue monsters about."

"I'll be careful," I say as I get to my feet.

Cait stands up and walks over to me. "I'm not letting you walk alone."

I want to argue with her that I need to be alone. That was my intent, after all. However, I know she's making a practical decision for safety reasons, and I appreciate that. Also, I can't help romanticizing about a stroll under the stars with her.

For both reasons, I smile and say, "Sounds good."

Tara waves at us. "Have fun. I'll be up for a while making sure the fire completely dies out. Try to be back before it does."

Cait responds with a nod. "Will do."

Our camp is on a flat stretch of ground, high enough from the road that we can see in the distance but nowhere near the peaks that sweep the sky. It's all so beautiful. The developers did a good job with the landscape, but my heart sinks, knowing those stars aren't real. The sky isn't really even real because there isn't an entire universe beyond them. At least, I think. I would never imagine that someone like me could live in a video game, but here I am.

We walk along a path that occasionally forces us to climb upward. Though I've gotten used to trekking all over Peripeteia, this still wears me out, and soon enough, I ask Cait if we can sit for a moment and stargaze. She doesn't look tired, but she agrees.

The ground is craggy and uncomfortable, but it's nice to give my legs a break. We sit in silence, and that's all it takes for the horrific images to return.

Cait squeezes my hand. "It will get better."

I turn to her. "What will?"

"I know we're realizing NPCs can feel, but these quests are built so that if one of them dies, they respawn," she says. "I'm sure we weren't the first players to wind up in a battle there."

"What if we broke the quest, though?" I ask.

Cait gives me a consoling smile. "Remember when I said I was going back to get something I left at Dolius's stall?"

I nod.

"I was just checking on the quest," she says. "The shoppers and merchants were back, even Dolius and Cyrus. Everyone acted like nothing had happened. All those guards we killed were back, too."

"And Dardanus?" I ask.

Cait shakes her head. "He wasn't there, but I kept hearing people talk about how Queen Idaea was planning a festival soon."

My breath stops as my chest heaves, and a sob escapes me. Tears flow from me like river rapids, and Cait nudges my head to her shoulder. The sudden burst of grief makes Cait's touch seem like it's happening to someone else. It's like Cait is holding a different Lauren and letting that one cry on her shoulder.

"Go ahead," she says. "I cried a lot when I was new here, before I met Sylvia and Tara. I wish I hadn't been alone back then. I won't let you be alone right now."

Cait soothes me enough that I'm able to wipe my wet cheeks and lift my head to look at her. She's usually so *hard*, chiding one second and bringing down justice the next. She can be so kind, though. And now, she's so tender. This show of vulnerability is so rare for her, and I swear to myself I'll cherish it forever.

"Why are you so nice to me?" I ask her. "I know I get on your nerves."

Cait laughs. "You really do, but..." She quiets a moment and studies me. "You really make up for it. Your heart is concerned more about peace than romance. It's rare when you meet someone who cares for people the way you do."

We gaze at each other, and our connection is undeniable. I swear there's a promise of desire in the way she looks at me. I think about caressing her cheek and admitting that I long for her, but then a wolf howls.

"That wasn't all that close, but it wasn't far away either," Cait says.

I turn to look at our camp and have to squint to make out the glow of dying embers. "Yeah, we should go."

When we reach the tent, Tara has just wrapped things up and is heading inside herself. The three of us wish each other a goodnight, and I curl up under the heavy blanket I bought from Dolius when we were in Thebe.

Instead of the battle, when my eyes close, my mind wanders to what might have been if that wolf hadn't howled. Then, I hear the disembodied voice.

"Cleric of Aphrodite: Level 4. Spell Gained: Mass Healing. Skill Gained: Passive Insight."

Thank God. Well, thank Goddess, I suppose. I open my menu and see that my title has changed back to Cleric of Aphrodite.

"Appreciate it," I silently pray to the Goddess of Love. "I'll try my best. Promise."

CHAPTER TWENTY-FIVE

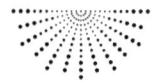

The walk to the coastline from Dardanus isn't long, so we take our time eating and packing up. After the tight deadlines we had helping Dolius, it's nice not having to rush anywhere. We even have time to chat and joke around.

"Good news!" Miko announces as she takes a bowl of boiled grains from Sylvia. "I got my new assignment last night."

"Oh, really?" Guy asks. "Please share."

"Well, I'm a *druid* now," she says, and we all gasp. "I know, right? Such a different class than a warlock. I guess it's because you all found me in the woods, and I fought off those guards with grapes."

"Makes sense," Guy responds.

"I got to keep my level five status, which was a big relief," Miko continues. "I don't have that many spells, but I'm sure rooting enemies to the ground and having elementals at our side will be helpful. Also, I can make grapes grow anywhere."

"That all sounds great!" Sylvia says. "We're happy to have you with us. You could have left us behind at Dardanus. It's nice to know we can call you a friend."

"Well, I couldn't leave my saviors in the lurch," Miko says and gives Guy a grateful look. "Without you, I would have been stuck wishing for the void's sweet embrace."

Guy blushes. "Aw, it's no big deal. I'm glad I finally got to use that favor. I thought I'd never use 'Convert Believer.'"

"We couldn't ask for a better druid," Joshua says, sounding genuine instead of creepily hitting on her.

Now it's Miko's turn to blush. "Thanks."

Hmm, are they into each other? Could Joshua be that lucky?

"Everyone seems so perfectly assigned to their deities," Guy says. Then turns to me and tucks a strand of my hair behind my ear. "Especially our Cleric of Aphrodite here."

His touch is so sweet, and I'm reminded all over again of all the reasons I want to be with him.

Cait stands and stretches. "I'm ready to pack up and head out."

"Yeah, me, too," Tara agrees. "I felt some snowflakes this morning. If we don't want to trudge to Ismarus during a blizzard, we should get going."

"Oh, come on," I say. "A blizzard? You think that's gonna happen so soon?"

Cait shrugs. "Probably not, but there's a big chance our trip won't be short. Conceivably, we could get there in two or three days, but sometimes stuff goes wrong."

"Wrong? Like what?" I ask.

Joshua laughs and points at the coast, just barely within view. "Here there be monsters!" he says in a pirate accent.

"What Joshua means is that sometimes players encounter Cetus on their journey," Sylvia explains.

"Cetus? What kind of monster is that?" I ask.

"Kinda like a whale, I think," Sylvia answers. "We never saw him, but we've come across a few players that have."

"Know what's weird?" I say. "I don't think I've ever really talked to any other players except for you all. I mean apart from turning down that other Aphrodite worshipper."

"Yeah, we kinda learned to keep to ourselves," Tara responds. "Getting to know people outside of our party can be...emotional."

"What do you mean?" I ask.

"Remember when I said people can really die here?" Cait asks as she packs cooking wares into a box. "Well, we know that firsthand."

Sylvia's eyes well, and she wipes away a tear. "The worst was that older couple. Remember?" she asks the group but doesn't wait for an answer. "They talked about how they'd taken up gaming together during their retirement, and they felt so lucky that they came here together. But they couldn't fight, not really, not like younger players."

The companions who took me in all look down with heavy expressions. Sylvia doesn't need to say anything more. I've wondered why all the players I'd seen so far were no younger than teens and no older than maybe their fifties. That's probably because the children and the elders didn't last long.

Aphrodite had said she wouldn't let me die. She'd said that some gods were fine with disposing of their worshippers, but she wasn't. I feel lucky to be so protected. I hope my friends share the same fortune.

I ponder this as we pack up camp and while we walk down the well-trodden road to the coastline. When the docks come into view, my mind turns to the quests ahead of us. Not only do I need to give a message to Khione, I need to complete the main objective of saving Orpheus from some Circones women.

This was a quest from the trailer for *Legends of Sacrifice*. I remember reading the beta forum threads about it, too. Seems Orpheus is another romanceable character, which feels weird to me, since the myth he's famous for is how he descended to the underworld to bring the woman he loved back to life. I remind myself for the millionth time that the game developers cherry-picked what they liked about Greece and its mythology and tossed the rest away.

As far as romanceable NPCs, I'm not as excited about them as I used to be. Alexander walks beside me with the same brooding look he's had since I first encountered him. I'm kind of tired of him, if I'm being honest. I mean, yeah, he's hot, but he can't fight. He didn't even opt to come to the market with us.

The outlines of boats form in the distance, and I grow excited. I can't wait to put a lot of water between me and Dardanus. I'm tempted to break into a sprint, but I know that I need to save my energy for whatever might happen once we get on our ship.

"That's her!" I hear someone yell.

I turn toward the voice and see a man on a hill pointing at me with rage in his eyes. "Oh fuck," I mutter.

Several other men appear from behind the hill, rushing to their friend's side. They all look ready to kill me as they run down the hill in my direction.

"Fuck, fuck, fuck!" I yell.

We all get into defensive positions for whatever battle is coming.

"Are those...*players?*" Miko asks.

I see what she means: one of them is wearing a ball cap; another's polo shirt collar is peeking out of his mage robes. All of them have titles I can't quite read yet above their heads. They *are* other players.

"What do they want with you?" Guy asks.

I want to say that I don't know, but I've been worried this might happen for a while. "I'm breaking the quests," I say. "Because of me, they can't level up."

"How do they know that, though?" Cait asks. "It's not like we're going around telling people about it."

"Well..." Joshua says. "We're not, but..."

"Out with it!" Cait demands.

"The gods know," he says. "Pan told me a lot of gods aren't super happy about it."

"But Aphrodite thinks it's great!" I say.

Joshua shrugs. "The gods are different people. They'll have different opinions."

"Enough!" Tara barks. "We can discuss all this *after* we deal with these dudes!"

But how will we? They're not NPCs. Fighting them could lead to their actual deaths. I'm still shaken from watching a guard fall on his sword, even though he apparently respawned moments later.

However, there's no time to think about an alternate solution because one player, a beefy orc wearing metal armor, swings a sword at Cait. He's slow, so it's easy for Cait to duck out of the way, but when she tries to shove him away, he doesn't even budge.

"Use your axe!" Joshua yells at her.

"These are real people!" Cait argues.

"So are we!" he responds.

Cait may have the temper of a barbarian, but I see the moral conflict all over her face. She knows there's no going back from the decisions she makes in this battle.

I've stared at her too long, so I don't react in time when an arrow comes at me. A sharp blow to my shoulder knocks the breath out of me, and my heart thunders in response. For some reason, I can't feel it anymore, though I'm hyperaware of everything else. Is this what Cait felt like when she had that spear in her side? Numb to the pain because of the chaos of the fight? I shake these questions from my mind.

Everyone's so busy with the fight that they don't notice my wound. Fortunately, I'm the healer of the group. Not feeling the pain of it is a boon I need to take advantage of. There are five of the enemy players and seven of us; most of us are higher-level, too. We can do this.

I call on my Strategy Under Duress and think through the situation. As a cleric, I'm the one who can keep the rest of the party alive, but I'm also the easiest to kill. We're up against gamers, so they're going to know this. They'll want to take me out of the equation immediately. I get behind the group like a smart healer should.

Regardless of whether I can feel my wound, I'm bleeding a lot and can't do my best with an injury. So, I yank the arrow out and cast Heal Major Wound on myself. Now I can concentrate on the battle at hand.

Our enemies have two soldiers, an archer, a healer, and a mage. Cait seems to be holding off the soldiers just fine, even if she's doing her best not to kill them. Joshua is playing something new. Is that the climax to "Live and Let Die"? Miko's brought a wind elemental into the battle, and the creature is whipping away every arrow the enemy archer looses at us. Unfortunately, this is also hampering Sylvia's archery as well. I'm not sure where Tara has gone, but she's a pretty shrewd woman. I'm sure she's figured out something smart. Guy is right by my side, trying to fling his magical icicles at the other mage, but every single one of them crumbles in his hand.

"That mage must have some kind of spell that negates mine," he says.

"Maybe not all of them," I tell him. "Try something else."

Guy nods. His eyes scan up and down quickly, and I can tell that he's looking through his spell menu. Then, he chuckles and says, "Of course." He lifts his staff and shouts, "Silence!"

Everything is just as noisy as it was before Guy cast his spell, but he's grinning ear to ear. I almost ask why, but he points, and I have to laugh as well. The mage is stomping his foot in frustration, and the healer next to him is shaking his staff like that will somehow make it work.

"I put the dome over them," Guy explains. "They'll have to get a lot closer to cast any spell now, and I don't think he wants to be anywhere near—" He stops, his eyes and mouth wide in horror, but I can't see anything wrong.

"Guy, are you all right?" I ask.

Guy turns his terrified face to me and grabs onto my cloak. He tries to talk, but he can only croak. I look down and see a dagger in his lower back, causing blood to bloom across his robes. Something whizzes by my head, and I turn to look at where it came from. Tara, half-hidden by a tree, has her hand poised to toss another dagger. Her eyes narrow in concentration as she looks directly at me.

That fucking bitch.

Before she can throw another, I fling myself to the ground, pulling Guy with me. "This is going to hurt," I whisper.

I don't wait for him to respond because I doubt he can, and I don't know how long it will take for another dagger to cartwheel toward me. When I pull the dagger from his back, Guy screams. I ignore that for the moment and glance up. Sure enough, another dagger is sailing in our direction. I roll away just in time, but the dagger still slices my earlobe before it buries itself in the dirt beside me.

"Heal Major Wound!" I yell, hoping that just having my staff on the ground near me will be enough to make that work.

It's not. Frustrated, I pull up the spells in my menu and tap on Heal Major Wound while concentrating on Guy's wound. Guy sighs, instantly healed. I don't even take the time to look up before rolling us over again. Thank God we moved when we did because this one actually pinned my cloak down to the ground.

I know I'm a healer, but I'm fucking pissed now. I grab the dagger that's piercing my cloak and stand up to fling it, but Guy grabs my wrist.

"Don't stop me!" I shout. "She's trying to kill us!"

Guy shakes his head, takes the dagger from my hand, taps on something on his menu, and flings it himself. It lands solidly in Tara's shoulder, causing her to stumble backward.

"What did you do?" I ask.

"True shot spell," he says. "With Sylvia around, I don't usually need it but—"

"Roots!" I hear Miko shout, and the tree beside Tara shifts. Its roots burst from the ground and bind Tara's arms to her side. Miko looks at us with some mixture of concern and mistrust. "Great friend you've got there."

Someone shouts, "Flaming Serpent," and I know it can only be the other group's mage. When Tara hit Guy with the dagger, it must have broken the silencing spell he'd cast.

Unfortunately, there's no time to react. Giant, undulating flames shoot across us all, friend and foe alike. The force of the fire spell knocks everyone but the mage down, since they're on the safe side of the blast. While the flame doesn't engulf any of us, we're surrounded by walls of it now.

The smoke blinds me and fills my lungs. Everything around me spins. I fall to my hands and knees coughing. The Soothing Grace favor calms me, but that's the last thing I need. Without my wits about me, I might die of smoke inhalation.

"Rain!" someone shouts. It's not Guy or Miko. It's...the same mage who cast Flaming Serpent?

A torrential downpour floods the road, dousing the fire immediately. I'm still weak, but I can breathe and see again. I scream when I see that everyone but the mage is laying on the ground, bleeding, burnt, and moaning. No one seems to be dead, as far as I can tell, but they're all pretty fucking close to it.

The mage runs to the healer, who has fallen like everyone, and shakes his shoulders. "Bruce, wake up! We need you! We—" He stops when he sees me approach and holds his hands up in surrender. "J-just kill me quick."

"I'm not going to *kill you!*" I shout. "I've been trying not to this whole time! You're the murderers!"

I see Cait at that moment. She's still—too still. The others are twitching and groaning in pain. There's no sign of life in her at all. I shouldn't waste time on this asshole mage.

"Stay here!" I tell the mage, then dash over to my staff. Raising it high, I shout, "Mass Heal!"

The strength of the spell nearly depletes my entire reserve of energy.

However, Sylvia, Joshua, Guy, and Miko slowly sit up, without even a burn or scrape. Cait remains still.

"Fuck!" I scream and flee to her side. "No, no, no!"

I press my palms to her chest and don't feel even the slightest stir of breath or a heartbeat. This close, I see the gaping wound in her stomach and the great axe still sheathed on her back. She hadn't wanted to kill a player, so much so that she didn't even defend herself. She was dead long before the fire.

"No, Cait..." The words come out of me high-pitched and pathetic. I pat her cheeks, like I can wake her up from a deep sleep. "Please, no! Please come back."

Guy puts his hand on my shoulder and tries to pull me back. "She's dead, Lauren."

I yank my shoulder away and glare at him, "Fuck you! I can bring her back!" Pressing one palm to her wound, I raise my staff. "Heal Major Wound!"

Nothing. She's still just as dead.

Maybe this takes a different magic. I'm a Cleric of Aphrodite. I can heal her with love, right? That works in anime. I just need a magic tear to drop onto her face. But my tears are already all over her. A kiss! Yes! Aphrodite wanted me to kiss her. This must be why!

I press my lips against hers desperately, but it's like kissing rubber. There's no life in her, no response. There is no life-giving magic in my touch. I collapse onto her chest and sob.

"There's another way," the other group's mage says. "There's a Revive Life spell."

"Fuck off!" I scream at him, not leaving Cait's chest. "If I had that spell, I would have used it already!"

"Our healer has it," he says.

This makes me sit up and look at him. "He does?"

The mage nods. "If you can heal him, he can bring her back."

I narrow my eyes at him. "How do I know you're not lying?"

"You don't," he says, "but you can kill me if I am. Without my party, I'm as good as dead anyway."

That's the best I'm going to get, and honestly, it's worth the risk if there's a chance to bring Cait back. I get to my feet and shuffle to the other healer. I lift my staff and say, "Heal Major Wound," my voice weak from grief. Exhaustion nearly has me buckling at the knees from the hit of the latest spell. I'm fairly certain adrenaline is the only thing keeping me on my feet.

The other healer takes a sharp, wheezing inhale and coughs. The mage helps his friend sit up and says, "Bruce, I need you to bring the barbarian back to life."

Bruce shakes his head. "Are you stupid? They're the—"

The mage covers Bruce's mouth. Then, he looks at me, back to Bruce, and over to me again. The healer turns to see me. I'm sure I look like a mess. My hair is probably both singed and matted with Cait's blood. If my face is even half as dirty from smoke as everyone else's, my tears must have left wide paths down my cheeks.

"Okay," Bruce says. He gets to his feet, and the mage hands him his staff.

Bruce doesn't need to ask who needs reviving. It's clear that it's the woman laying as still as a frozen lake. He staggers over to her and then lifts his staff. After a fit of coughing, he croaks, "Revive Life," then groans as he collapses into the mage's arms. I'm surprised such a powerful spell didn't make him pass out immediately.

Cait moans, and I rush to her side, sliding to my knees the moment I'm near her. "Cait, Cait, wake up."

"I hurt..." she whispers like she's sleep talking.

Of course, she hurts. She has a damn hole the size of a softball in her stomach. My healing spell didn't work before, but it should now that she's alive. I grip my staff tight as I say, "Heal Major Wound!" Dots pepper my vision, and I know one more spell will knock me out. When the puncture closes up, my whole body releases a tension I didn't realize it was holding.

Cait's eyes flutter open, and she looks up at me. It takes a moment for her to recognize me. When she does, she smiles and puts her hand on my cheek. Her eyes are hooded, and her soft voice is floaty when she says, "I had a dream that you kissed me."

CHAPTER TWENTY-SIX

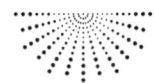

The other mage's name is Dan. Since he and Bruce helped us out, I decide to help heal the three other people in their party—*after* we tied them to some trees.

It doesn't take long for them to come to, since they were mostly out due to smoke inhalation. Like Bruce, however, they still have a nagging cough.

They likely attacked because I'm breaking the quests, but I want to know more. By their titles, I can tell they're all Zeus followers. Because of that, this feels like more than anger about the quests breaking.

I have even more questions about what the fuck is up with Tara. However, she's rooted and silenced by the tree's roots Miko summoned. If it weren't for her eyes watching us, I'd assume she was dead. She's lucky her tree didn't catch fire.

"Why did you attack us?" I ask. I'm directing my question to Dan, but I'm open to accepting answers from any of them.

"You're breaking the quests," Dan answers. "We can't get any of them done now. If we don't level up…" His throat bobs. "I just want out of here, you know?"

"So, you thought you'd kill me?"

Dan doesn't answer. He just focuses on the hem of his robes that he's fussing with.

"Yeah, well, I'm going to move past that, since you helped bring Cait back," I say.

"Don't let him off the hook so easily," Cait says. "They were all willing to commit murder instead of even just talking to you."

"It's not exactly like that," Bruce says. "We all met at the temple at Ephesus while waiting in line to talk to Zeus, so we're all bound to the same deity. We *have* to do what he tells us to do."

"Are you saying Zeus wants me dead?" I ask. If he does, I'm way more fucked than I thought I was.

"You either play the game by his rules or you're out," Dan says.

"And by out, you mean dead?"

"Yeah..." Dan gulps. "He's going to kill us."

"I'm sure he'll—"

"No," Bruce says. "He really will. He killed Lars when he said he didn't want to attack another player."

"Fuck," I mutter. "No wonder you came at us."

Miko elbows Guy in the side. "You gotta get the grapes."

Guy frowns. "I can only call on that boon once a day. So, like, I can convert one person now, but it will be days before they're *all* saved."

"Convert?" Dan asks.

"Yeah," Miko responds. "Guy can help other players switch over to Team Dionysus if they eat one of his magic grapes."

Dan and Bruce look at each other with hopeful astonishment. The three tied up men respond with a chorus of pleas.

"Like I said," Guy says, "I can only do this once a day. It's still a risk."

"Give it to Bruce," Dan says right away. "He can revive the dead. So if Zeus kills one of us, he can bring them back."

Miko shakes her head. "It's not like that. Dionysus gives you a new class, and you won't have any of your new powers until you go to bed."

Dan's face falls but then he shakes it. "Give it to him anyway," he says. "He's the one who just wanted us to knock the cleric out instead of kill her."

"Are you sure?" Guy asks.

"Yes," Dan says.

The other three party members shout, arguing that they each should have the first one. I wonder which one of them killed Cait. I'd love to shove my fist down his throat.

A magic grape appears in Guy's hand. With solemnity, Bruce plucks the grape and gives Dan a long look. "Maybe we can save you, too…"

Bruce bites into the grape, looking guilty the moment he does. He knows what all of us are trying hard not to. The moment Zeus realizes they've failed, everyone in their party *but* Bruce is dead.

Like Miko, within a few seconds of eating the grape, Bruce is moaning with pure rapture. He holds onto Dan's shoulder, locking eyes with him. "This is amazing," he whispers. "It's like…like…like you."

Oh, so that's why Dan wanted Bruce to have the first grape. These two are in love.

My gaze flickers over to Cait, and I see that she's already looking at me. There's no mistaking the expression in her eyes, on her lips. *I dreamed you kissed me,* she'd said it with a smile.

The "Kiss Her" quest isn't marked as complete, which isn't a surprise. Aphrodite would want it to be romantic, reciprocal, not a desperate attempt to bring someone back to life.

"Seems their mage and healer are also an item," Guy whispers to me.

I'm shaken from my reverie and brought back to the real world where we all almost died and I'm mentally cheating on Guy. All in all, today sucks balls.

"Should we trust them enough to untie them?" Miko asks Dan, pointing at the other three Zeus worshippers that are currently bound.

Dan and Bruce share an uncertain look, then Dan says, "You should get on the ship first. They're pretty desperate to avoid execution."

"You're not thinking of staying behind to untie them, are you?" Bruce asks.

"Someone has to," Dan answers.

"If Zeus doesn't kill you, they will!" Bruce responds. "We should travel with this group. If you can just make it to tomorrow, Guy can give you a grape."

"Isaac has a kid at home," Dan insists. "If there's a chance I can save him, I have to take it. Tomorrow isn't promised to any of us, but maybe Zeus will understand."

Bruce doesn't look convinced in the least. Zeus doesn't sound like a forgiving deity. Even if Dan travels with us, there's no guarantee that he'll make it to tomorrow. He knows that, knows that he may actually be putting the man he loves in danger.

Dan turns to us. "Can I talk to Bruce in private for a moment?" he asks.

We all agree. They need whatever time Zeus will allow them to say their goodbyes. I wish Aphrodite had given me the favor to convert. Despite their attack, I can see the good in them, and their desperation makes sense. I'm so powerless to help these two, and it's eating me up.

We make our way to Tara, who's still bound and gagged by the tree she'd once hidden behind.

"A literal back stabber," Miko hisses when we draw near. For someone so new to our group, she's certainly angry about Tara. I mean, we all are, but she hasn't had the time to form an emotional connection with our rogue. "When my friends betrayed me, all they did was pretend they didn't know me. At least they didn't try to *kill* me."

"Hold on a minute," Sylvia interjects. "We should at least hear Tara out. Maybe she was confused or something. She's always been there for us."

Miko rolls her eyes. "Fine, I'll unwrap the root from her mouth, but I'm sure all you'll hear from her are lies. She *is* a rogue after all."

One root uncoils, exposing Tara's face. There's a band of what looks like rug burn stretched over her lips and past her jaw lines. She gasps, gulping in as much air as possible. The root must have made it difficult to even breathe through her nose.

We give her a moment to collect herself and then Guy asks, "Why, Tara? Why did you attack Lauren and me?"

Tara's head droops with exhaustion and perhaps guilt, so when she looks at Guy, she's peering up at him from a down-turned face. Terror fills her eyes. Is she afraid we're going to kill her outright? No, there's something more.

"I-I don't know," she says. "It was like you were different people, like you were the enemy."

"You confused us with the Zeus worshippers?" Guy asks.

"No, I suddenly believed with all my heart that you all were evil or something." She shakes her head and then lifts it so that we can see that her cheeks are wet with tears. "I had no control over it. It was only after the battle that my mind cleared, and I realized what I'd just done. I don't understand it. It's...it's..."

"Horrifying..." Sylvia says, and Tara nods.

"I'm sorry," she says. "I'm so much more than sorry."

I'm ready to forgive her. Right from the beginning, she's been there for me. She was the first to tell everyone to slow down, that I needed time to adjust. She's so distraught that I want to wrap her in a big hug, but there's a tree keeping me from doing that. Though, even if she was perfectly free, I have no way of knowing she wouldn't plant a dagger into me the moment I got within arm's reach.

"Someone or something messed with her head," Cait says. "There's no way she would do this if she was in her right mind."

"She's lying!" Miko insists. "It's all over her deceitful face. How can you all be so *blind* to that?"

"You haven't known her as long as we have," Sylvia says. "She's my best friend! One of the Zeus worshippers must have done this to her. Once we're all on the ship, she'll be fine."

"No!" Tara shouts. "Don't take me on that ship!"

"Tara, we believe you," Sylvia says.

Miko crosses her arms. "I don't."

"I couldn't control myself, y'all," Tara continues. "I can't guarantee this won't happen again. You need to leave me behind."

"All by yourself?" Guy says. "You're bound by a tree!"

"I'll free her," Dan says.

We turn to see that Dan and Bruce have both joined us. Each of them has a look of resolve, and they're holding hands tightly.

"Once you're far from my view, I'll use one of my spells to unbind her from the roots," Dan continues.

"And she won't be alone," Bruce adds. "I'll be with her."

"*We'll* be with her," Dan corrects. "Zeus may let me live."

Bruce nods at his love, but there's no hope in his eyes.

"So you're both staying here," I ask Bruce.

"I want whatever time I can get with Dan," he answers. "Whether that's a day or a minute."

I think of Mom lying in her hospice bed, staring blankly at a TV show we used to love watching together. There was no sign that she had any idea I was there, but I took whatever I could get. I held her hand, talked to her, stroked her hair, laid my head on her chest so I could feel the comfort of her heartbeat...My whole motivation to bring Aphrodite her offering was so that I could get even a moment more with my mother. Lately, I've been pretty distracted by love, though.

Another stirring of guilt aches in my guts.

"I understand," I say.

"Take this grape at least," Guy says to Dan. "It might work while I'm gone, and Zeus might let you have tomorrow."

Dan nods and accepts Guy's gift. "Thank you. You had every right to slaughter us for what we did."

"We don't kill players," Cait responds. "They're not the enemy."

She's right, but now I don't think the NPCs are the enemy either. I don't want to admit who I think the villains are. I've already gotten on Zeus's shitlist.

Though I've only known Tara for a couple of weeks, it's hard saying goodbye. One less friend, one less comfort in this cruel game that we're all trapped in. But we still bid our farewells, we still walk away, and we still board the ship that will take us to Thrace.

CHAPTER TWENTY-SEVEN

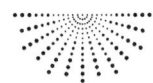

Normally, ships run on a schedule, but game logic means that when we get there, it's ready to go. That's an immense relief since it's been a long day, and we're a little afraid that something terrifying might possess Tara again. There's also a pang of grief that we have to part from our friend.

Hermes dubbed Tara a rogue, but she only ever wanted what was best for everyone, even if that slowed down her own progress. Now she's on her own, which isn't a safe situation for anyone in Peripeteia. There's a reason we don't see players wandering around alone outside of the starting village. Those people are all dead. Well, except for Miko, but she probably would have preferred death over what Hekate did to her.

Now, we're onboard a ship called the Argo. So of course the captain is named Jason, and he keeps rambling on about golden fleece to his sailors, which he named the Argonauts. It seems like a missed opportunity that we're not following his quest line. Did Jason even come close to Thrace in the myths? Well, that doesn't matter. Peripeteia's map looks nothing like a real map of Greece and Thrace.

Since it's nearly sunset when we board the Argo, we spend our first night on the ship close to Mysia's coast, and the water is calm. Our room is spacious, and our beds are soft, but sleep keeps slipping out of my grip. My mind finally drifts into slumber, only to have a dream about Mom.

I'm holding her hand and kissing our overlapping thumbs like I did way back when I was a kid. She whispers my name and dies. This wakes me with a start, and I decide I'd rather stay awake than risk a dream like that again.

I sit up and scan our dark room to see my companions are asleep. I can tell they're not enjoying a peaceful slumber as they toss and turn; some of them are even mumbling what sounds like pleading. There's one person missing: Guy. Did he have a bad dream? Did he even sleep? I decide to seek him out so we can at least offer each other sympathy.

When I get above board, I head toward the forecastle. What better place to contemplate our situation than near the figurehead, where I can stare at the inky waves and imagine I'm Kate Winslet in *Titanic*?

As I predicted, Guy had the same instinct. Maybe it's because of the roar of the ship or because he's so lost in thought, but he doesn't notice me approaching from behind. I decide to announce my arrival instead of getting close to him and scaring him. But when I say, "Hey, it's Lauren," he nearly jumps anyway.

After Guy catches his breath, he says, "Couldn't sleep either?"

I shake my head and move to his side where I place my hands on the railing. "Had a nightmare."

"Monsters?" he asks.

"No," I answer and let out a long sigh. "But it's a long story. I don't want to bother you."

Guy puts his hand over mine. "You won't bother me."

His fingers are so warm and comforting despite the icy wind whipping over the waves. Wrapping my legs around him would take my mind off all my fear and pain and confusion. It would feel like cheating on Cait, though. Meanwhile, thinking about Cait feels like cheating on Guy. But I still leave my hand under his because it's comforting, and I finally feel safe enough to share this about myself.

"Before I wound up here, I wasn't just dealing with a breakup." Just the thought of what I'm about to share forms a painful lump in my throat. I swallow it down and continue. "My mom, she...she's in hospice. Or she was when I left. She might be..." I can't finish. Fat tears fill my eyes. Wiping them away only causes them to splash all over my cheeks and blurs my vision. "Anyway, she's why I really need to get back. I just want a chance to tell her I love her one last time. In my dream, I didn't get that chance."

Guy pulls me into an embrace and kisses the top of my head. "Oh, Lauren, that's so much to deal with alone. I'm so sorry."

"I should have told you sooner."

"You told me when you were ready to," he says. "Any sooner than that wouldn't have been right."

God, he's so perfect.

"You should have been the cleric, not me," I say. "You've offered more healing with those words than I have the entire time I've traveled with you."

"That's not true," he says and sighs. "I'd lost any hope until you joined us."

Ugh. Here comes the guilt again. The other kind, the one that says I'll wind up breaking his heart.

Guy must see it on my face, because he says, "Not because of how much..." He clears his throat. "Not because of how attracted I am to you. You look at this game differently, and maybe you're the ticket to finding the right offerings."

"God, I hope so," I whisper.

A moment of contemplative silence passes and then Guy says, "I know, by the way."

I furrow my brow. "Know what?"

"You want Cait." He looks down at the waves, pain crossing his face. "It's okay. I promised you that there'd be no drama."

"Guy, I—"

"It wasn't even when you told me to fuck off before you kissed her," he says, ignoring my interjection. "I mean, that hurt, but I figured it was just the terror of knowing a friend died and there was nothing you could do to save her." He shakes his head. "No, it was when I mentioned that Bruce and Dan were another mage and healer dating. You didn't respond to me at all. You just looked at her."

"I'm sorry," I whisper.

Guy turns to look at me, concern across his tented brows. "Don't be sorry, Lauren. We barely know each other. You've spent a lot more time with her, and let's face it, she's a real knockout."

"She is..." I say, stopping just short of a literal swoon and then add,

"Not that you aren't. You're...Well, I was quick to take you up on your offer for a reason."

"Thanks," Guy says with a blush but then his face grows serious. "I should tell you I don't know if Cait swings that way. Her parents were very against LGBTQ rights, and she grew up pretty sheltered."

"I know," I say. "That's something I'm terrified about to be honest. I know I should just get over it and tell her how I feel, but I think I need to take my time. Even if she is attracted to me, I don't think she's the type of person who would jump into anything."

Guy laughs. "Unless it's a fight."

I chuckle in response.

"Look, this is probably really selfish of me but..." He chews on his bottom lip and shakes his head. "Never mind."

"What?" I ask.

Guy studies my face for a moment, then takes a deep breath. "If you think it's going to take a while to work up the nerve to tell her how you feel, will you give me that time to get to know you and see if maybe there really is something between us?"

A cloud shifts in the sky, revealing a bright moon that lights up his face. There's a seductive curve to his lips and a playful twinkle in his eye. He always makes me weak in the knees when he looks at me like this.

"I mean, we could at least have a little fun, right?" he asks. "We've only had one proper kiss so far."

Just a moment ago, I'd felt conflicted between my growing feelings for Cait and the temptation to fuck Guy just so I can forget my worries for a second. But something whispers across the sea, a familiar voice: Aphrodite. It's faint, and I can't quite make out all the words, but then there's a notification ping, and I have a strong feeling about what it is.

"Just a kiss," I say. "For now."

Guy nods. "For now."

He tilts my chin up, and his dark brown eyes lock onto my gray ones. Then his smoldering gaze lowers to my lips, and it's like he's kissing me already. Just a kiss, but I'm sure he wants more because I can almost see the night he'd give me if I gave him the go ahead. Can he work up as much magic in bed as he can in battle?

Finally, he lowers his lips to mine. We brush against each other, the touch of delicate wings before a butterfly leaves her petal. It surprises me how sweet it is, given that he'd looked ready to fuck me. But he doesn't pull away. Instead, he parts his lips so that he can gently tug my bottom lip with his teeth before deepening the kiss. And *oh my fucking God*, he really knows what he's doing with that tongue of his.

When Guy pulls away, I'm breathless and there's an ache between my legs. Another notification pings. I suspect I was right about what Aphrodite wanted me to do.

"Just a kiss?" he asks, tracing a finger down the side of my neck to the spot where it curves into my shoulder. How did he know that was my weakness?

I tremble, unable to respond with words, only a soft gasp. Guy chuckles in response.

"Maybe just *one* more?" he asks.

I can't help myself. I move in for another, but Guy shakes his head. "No, not like that," he says, then retraces that same line along my neck. "Right here."

Goddamn, am I getting wet?

"Yes," I say, so soft that it sounds like it will drift away with the ocean breeze.

He tucks my hair back before lowering his head to my neck. That skilled tongue of his flicks the skin there and then playfully nips it. Then he trails down my neck with soft, sweet pecks until he gets to that curve again and bites it. There isn't anything soft about it. It even stings a bit, but in the best possible way.

"Fuck," I whisper.

Guy places a sweet kiss where he bit, then pulls away. "There, two kisses." I pull him closer, wanting more, but he shakes his head and takes a step away. "No, I think that's good for now."

"But—"

"Maybe you'll stay with me; maybe you'll go with her..." A mischievous gleam lights in his eyes. "Maybe you won't even have to choose." Guys strokes my cheek. "But I'm not going to jump into bed with you. When I met you, I didn't see some Aphrodite sexpot. I saw someone who could very well win my whole heart. I'm willing to let you break it if that means I still get to have a handful of real moments with you."

"That felt pretty real to me," I counter.

Guy chuckles in a dark, seductive way. "If there's another kiss, I'll make it even better because I'm going to insist we get to know each other better before then."

I almost suggest we get started on that right away. I'm willing to talk all night, if I can get more of *that*. But when I open my mouth, a yawn escapes.

"Let's go back to bed," Guy says, taking my hand. "Something tells me neither one of us will have nightmares now."

I barely notice the third notification ping when I finally drift off to a deep sleep.

⇧

GUY KISSES ME ON MY LIPS AND DOWN MY NECK. THEN HE wanders lazily to my cleavage where he stops to flick a nipple with his expert tongue. I gasp and weave my fingers into his hair so I can hold him right there.

Long, elegant fingers fondle my other breast. But they don't belong to Guy. These belong to Cait, and her face is fierce with lust. She looks like she could break me in half with all the things she'd like to do to my body. I plead with her to do just that.

While Guy has his mouth on one nipple, Cait moves hers to my lips to the other, searing me inside and out. I close my eyes as I moan, knowing I've died and gone to Heaven. But it gets even better when I feel both of them push their hands between my legs where they begin to—

"Wake up."

I open my eyes to see Miko's sleepy face looking down at me.

I groan and then sulk. "No, I don't want to be awake! Let me go back to my dream!"

"Okay, I'll let everyone know you're not eating today."

My stomach growls at the very mention of food, and I sigh. "Fine," I say. "I'm getting up. I'll be there in a few minutes."

Miko doesn't say anything. She just turns around and walks out of the room, her mission accomplished. She must be as hungry as I am.

I run my fingers through my hair and straighten my chiton before putting on my cloak. That's really all I can do to get prepared. We can't summon our camp on board, so there isn't access to any of the stuff I'm accustomed to. What I wouldn't do for a bag of holding or something. Too bad this isn't *Dungeons & Dragons.*

The moment I open the door, I scream because Alexander is *right there* staring at the door like he was just waiting for me to leave the room.

This doesn't startle him at all, of course. Instead, he says, "I have a message."

"About Khione?"

"Aphrodite wants you to complete all the Ismarus quests and try to get level five before you talk to Khione."

I give Alexander a mock salute with two fingers and say, "Gotcha."

He blinks and looks slightly to his left like someone just whispered in his ear. Then he turns his attention back to me. "She also says, 'Check on your new quest already. I'm getting impatient.'"

"Oh, shit, that's right!" I'd forgotten about that third little ping I'd heard last night. I was too caught up in the moment with Guy.

I pull up my menu and tap on my quest log. Sure enough, there's another quest, and it seems I've already made progress. "Kiss Him, Too" is scratched through and a brand-new quest is in my menu.

"Why Choose?" I read aloud. "That's not a quest; that's a question. What does that even mean?"

"She says you'll figure it out," Alexander answers.

I shake my head. Much to my dismay, coffee doesn't exist in Peripeteia, but if it did, I'd tell him I couldn't decipher stuff like before I got a mug of the hot brew. Hopefully breakfast will clear my head a little at least.

I make my way to an area under deck that's open to anyone. There's a table there where we'd eaten the night before. There's no way that ancient Greek ships were anything like this one, but I won't complain about the game developers designing the one we're in. It's almost like they knew *real* people were going to have to actually be in this one for a couple of days.

Maybe they did know.

As I expected, everyone is sitting down to eat. My mouth pools with saliva at the spread before me. Sylvia is an excellent cook, so I've been very spoiled by what she can create over a campfire. But this? This is something from a foodie review about a five-star brunch.

I rub my hands together giddily and skip over to my seat. Sylvia chuckles as I approach. "Well, someone's excited."

"Morning, sleepyhead," Guy says, giving me a crooked smile. "Did you have pleasant dreams?"

Scoundrel. He knows exactly why I slept in.

"They got better," I say. "You?"

"Very enjoyable," he replies with a wink.

Cait doesn't look up from the food she's shifting around on her plate. "I had all these nightmares," she says. "About Tara..."

The mood darkens immediately.

"Yeah," Sylvia says. "Me, too. I just can't believe she did that. She and I met my third day here. We've been close for months."

"Yeah, well, traitors are like that," Miko says in a cynical tone before popping a bite of melon into her mouth.

Cait glares at her. "You don't know Tara like we do. She's not like this."

Miko swallows and looks Cait straight in the eyes, not at all intimidated by our fierce barbarian. "When I got here, I had 'friends,' too," Miko says. "We promised to make sure everyone got their deity's quests done while helping each other with the main storyline. We were all so *chummy*. But then Hekate gave me that quest to kill a giant, and they convinced me not to do it. When my goddess punished me, they didn't hesitate to call me a monster. Who do you think were the first players to hurl insults at me until I wound up in the black space?"

Jesus Fucking Christ.

We all stare stunned at her for a moment until I say, "Shit, that sucks."

Miko rolls her eyes, but I see unshed tears glistening in them. "You think? Guess Aphrodite doesn't care about brains if you've got beauty."

"Okay, you don't have to be a bitch about it," I snap. "We could have just left you in the woods, you know. Guy didn't even have to give you that grape. If you don't want to waste time with us, go try things out on your own."

Miko doesn't say anything. She just works her jaw and looks down at her plate before continuing to eat her breakfast.

"This isn't serving any purpose right now," Guy says. "There's a chance we might come across Cetus today or tomorrow. We should come up with a plan in case that happens." He looks at Cait. "You've been pretty effective with sea monsters in the past. While Joshua distracts him, I think you should hit him as hard and fast as you can."

"Sounds good," Cait says.

"Aye, aye, captain," Joshua says, then bites into a wedge of cheese.

"Miko," Guy says, "do you have any spells that draw on anything to do with water?"

Miko taps at the menu only visible to her and frowns. "Not really."

Guy sighs. "Well, that's not great."

"I can summon elementals, but I'm not sure a water elemental will be that effective against a monster that lives in the water."

"Maybe an earth elemental?" Sylvia suggests.

Miko tilts her head side to side in consideration. "Better than nothing, I guess."

"Okay, that covers that, then." Guy turns his attention to Sylvia. "Obviously, just keep the arrows coming, but this time I also need you to stick close to Lauren. She'll need someone to defend her from attacks. That's usually Cait, but we really need our barbarian pulling aggro."

"What about you?" Sylvia asks him.

"I'm going to get up as high as I can and blast as many ice daggers as possible before I run out of energy," he answers.

"No, I mean, why can't you stand with her," Sylvia says. "It would be best for me to have the high ground."

Guy looks at me, and I can see the answer in his eyes. After the kisses we shared last night, he's afraid I'll distract him during an attack. Just the feel of my body near his might be too much for him.

Might be too much for me, too.

"We both have really low strength," I say for him. "Having us together is a sure way to make sure we're both wiped out in one blow."

I know I've said the right thing by the relieved expression on Guy's face.

"Well, my strength isn't that high either, but I guess it's a lot better than yours," Sylvia says.

Alexander chooses that moment to walk over to the table. "Can I share breakfast with you?" he asks.

I'm not the only one whose jaw drops at the question. Not once has

Alexander eaten around us. I'm not sure he ever eats at all. He certainly never asks if he can hang out with us.

"Um...sure," I say.

Alexander nods in thanks and sits down across the table from me before taking a chunk of bread. We all watch in equal parts fascination and unease as he chews his food thoroughly. When he finishes, he wipes off his lips with a napkin and says, "I've decided I will fight by your side."

"Who *are* you?" I ask, not expecting an answer.

"I am Alexander," he says.

"But you can't fight," Cait says. "You're cursed to never lift a blade again, remember?"

"Yes, but Aphrodite says that this doesn't apply to other weapons," he counters. "So, I will use this." Alexander pulls a shotgun out of a pack on his back and holds it up.

We all scream and duck.

"Put that away!" Cait yells.

Alexander cocks his head in confusion, then shrugs and puts it back in his pack. With it out of sight, I feel safe to raise my head again.

"Where the fuck did you get that?" I ask.

"Aphrodite," Alexander answers.

"She gave you a fucking *gun?!*" I pull my fingers through my hair and shake my head. "What kind of fucked up game is this? They didn't have shit like that in Greek myths. Hell, they don't have them in fantasy RPGs!"

"Well, actually firearms are in many *Final Fant—*" Joshua starts.

"Stop," Cait says, holding up a hand at Joshua. "I *can't* deal with a 'well, actually' when there's an NPC sitting at the table with a Benelli M4 Super 90 shotgun in his pack."

"A Benelli what?" Sylvia asks.

"It's a kind of semiautomatic shotgun," Cait says. "One of my dad's favorites, actually."

Although Cait is our barbarian, she usually looks so prim and proper —maybe a little snobby. It's strange to hear those words. There's something absurd about it, really, causing a giggle to bubble up from my chest. I slap a hand over my mouth to stop. We *were* just discussing some pretty serious stuff after all. But it's too late; everyone heard it, and now everyone else is also laughing. Well, almost everyone else.

"What?" Cait asks. "He's a cop."

I don't know why, but that makes me laugh even harder.

Cait crosses her arms. "Stop making fun of me!"

I shake my head and swallow down another laugh. "We're not. It's just..." I don't know how to explain to her.

"It's just that if I was going to guess which of us knew that much about shotguns," Guy says, "I would have chosen Joshua."

"I would have said Miko," Sylvia says, pointing at our new teammate.

That *really* has me roaring with laughter because Sylvia is absolutely right. Miko would look completely natural with a gun. Hell, I wouldn't be shocked to see her with a machine gun.

Miko shrugs in response. "If I'd known they were an option in this stupid game, I probably would have tried to get one."

The entire table really is laughing together now, including Cait and Miko. That stops immediately when everything goes sliding off our table and crashes against the wall behind Alexander.

"Shit," I say. "What was that?"

An echoing grunt followed by an ear-splitting squeal rattles everything around us.

"Is that a pig?" Miko asks.

"A boar," Sylvia answers, then sighs. "And from what I've heard, this one has the body of a whale. Good thing we already have a plan for our fight with Cetus."

CHAPTER TWENTY-EIGHT

I have this to say about the ancient Greeks; they knew how to create some fucked up monsters. As Cetus slices through the choppy waves at us, I wonder how he was dreamed up. I imagine some Greek dude, high as a kite, making up shit to scare a friend. When he has to describe what his fictional monster looks like, he sees a whale rising above the waves and then looks at the roast boar cooking over the spit. So, he turns to his friend and says, "A boar fucked a whale, and they had a baby."

Or maybe he had a bad dream. Whatever. Doesn't matter, because this is the scariest goddamn thing I've ever seen in my life.

Cait and Joshua stand on opposite ends of the deck on either side of the monster's head. Miko is on a slightly elevated platform behind Joshua. As discussed, I'm on the crow's nest of the mainmast with Sylvia, while Guy has the crow's nest at the foremast. Yet, even from my high angle, I don't feel far enough away from this beast.

The closer it gets, the clearer its features become. Wild eyes roll around like unhinged marbles on a face made of hard leather and bristles. Blood-stained tusks, the height of Christmas trees, jut up from his lower jaw. That isn't what's causing a shiver of terror to creep up every cell of my body, though.

Under its snotty, snorting, crinkled nose, drool hangs from his lips like the pendulums on grandfather clocks. They're so viscous that they seem more like rubber than liquid. The drool's gelatin clarity displays the residue of its last meal—tail fins, fish skins, wood planks, intestines, and bones. We're going to wind up like that if we're not careful.

Cait stands just a few feet back from the railing on the starboard side, facing the monster and thumping her fist on her chest. As she roars in a completely unnatural way for such a pretty woman, she swings her great axe around. She's taunting the monster, a standard tactic tanks use, but one I haven't seen her use in the past. It's working.

Cetus directs all his attention toward her and veers his deadly path in her direction until he looms above her. He huffs, blowing her hair back and spraying her face with his fetid spittle. Her face remains a contorted mask of rage. She's completely unintimidated by her adversary, but it takes everything in me not to rush to Cait's side and pull her away from the beast.

From Cait's left, Joshua leaps upward and starts playing his fiddle. This gives Cait a chance to hack into the beast's snout with her axe. Once Cetus notices her attack, Joshua stabs Cetus's wrinkled temple with his sword. With acrobatic grace I never expected of him, Joshua uses that sword to swing himself up to the top of the monster's ear, where he finally pulls his blade free. It's a struggle, though, given Cetus's hide is so thick.

Cetus lunges forward and knocks Cait over with his slimy snout. This pushes her halfway across the deck, and now the whole ship is rocking like a spinning top that's beginning to slow down. I grab onto the mast nearest to me, but with water rushing over the deck, my feet are slipping away, and it's taking too much of my little strength to keep a firm grip.

My pinkie slips off the wet wood, then my ring finger. Heaving waves pull me away from the only thing keeping me on this ship.

"Sylvia, grab me!" I shout, but she's so focused on aiming her arrows at Cetus, she doesn't even notice my cries for help. I lose the battle to keep my middle finger in place and go sailing through the air.

Just as I'm sure I'm about to crash into the tumultuous waves below the ship, Guy shouts, "Lasso!"

Suddenly my body is no longer pulling away. Instead, it snaps like a magnet against the mast. Something invisible is binding me to the post. I can't even budge an inch on either side. I look up to see Guy is in a similar position, his head just a foot above my own. This lasso spell has proven itself to be pretty strong, and I'm surprised that Guy doesn't look tired at all.

"Are you okay?" he asks.

I open my mouth to say that I am, but the boat rocks in the other direction, causing my head to knock against the mast. A split second later, sea water barrels into my throat. I can't breathe. I can't...I can't...

My heart dances to a disco beat, and every piece of me screams at me to give it *air*. It's hard to think while experiencing this cacophony of panic, but I *have* to so my Strategy Under Duress skill activates. I'm not broken, only impaired. I just need to get all this water out of my lungs. I can't speak a spell, but I *can* mentally bring up my menu and look at my spells.

I tap on Heal Minor Wound and, before I even wonder what that will do, I'm vomiting. Seawater and bile erupt from me and fall to the waves below. My lungs grasp onto any oxygen they can get. My throat has suffered quite an assault, so every gasping breath feels like I'm swallowing flames.

My pain isn't important right now, though. I'm becoming more and more of a cleric every day I live in Peripeteia, so my instinct is to scan the area for my friends. If I barely got out of that, there's a good chance they're not faring well either.

Since Guy is so close to me, he's the first person I see. His eyes are closed, and there's a bruise on his cheek. But when I place my hand on his chest, I feel steady breathing. He needs help, but someone else might be in a more urgent situation.

To my surprise Joshua is still hanging onto the sword he'd driven into Cetus and is concentrating more on not falling off than using it as a weapon.

Miko has somehow created vines from the planks of wood that make up the deck. They're woven into a ladder, which she's clinging onto. I don't see any earth elementals, and I don't know if she's abandoned that idea or she just hasn't had a chance to cast the spell. Whatever the case, she's at least surviving.

Sylvia is no longer in the mainmast's crow nest. Somehow, she wound up on the forecastle, and she's crawling toward the bowsprit.

She's trying to get the high ground again. There's little an archer can do from the deck, especially under these conditions.

Cait is...Where's Cait?

I whip my head this way and that, scanning the deck, the masts, the sails, the waves, everywhere I can. I don't see her anywhere and fall helpless to visions of her lifeless body sinking to the ocean floor.

A pained, ear-splitting squeal draws my attention back to Cetus, where I discover Cait has somehow gotten back on his head and is burying her great axe into the beast's furry inner ear.

Holy fuck, she's impressive!

Cait growls back at the monster and gnashes her teeth as she yanks her weapon out. Rivers of blood burst from the wound. Joshua chooses that moment to drive his blade into the eye on the other side of Cetus's face, eliciting another shrill squeal from Cetus. Even with all this, the beast isn't even down to half his health bar.

How are we going to survive long enough to kill this guy?

I turn my attention back to Guy, who still seems half asleep. I decide to use my Heal Minor Wound spell again, and he rouses. He mumbles and slurs something that I can't understand as he blinks at me. Then he turns his weak head to look at Cetus.

"Ice blast..." he mutters with little conviction.

A spray of pebble-like ice falls from his palm and crashes on the deck below. He's too out of it to be much use in this battle. Still, he saved me with that lasso spell. Without him, I'd be shark bait by now.

The unmistakable whipping sound of an arrow draws my attention away from Guy. Sylvia is standing on the bowsprit now, with her bow in position to loose another arrow. This one zips a straight line from her fingers to Cetus's one good eye. The beast sputters a pathetic whine. It's not as loud as the last two, but not because this attack hurts. No, that barely nudged his health bar down. His whine is probably from his annoyance with Joshua and Cait, who are still hacking away at him.

Cetus swings his head wildly again, and Joshua loses his grip on his sword. Before he can crash-land on the ship deck, Cait takes one hand off her lodged axe to grab Joshua by the wrist. Their position is perilous. If they don't get off soon, who knows where their bodies will wind up? Wherever it is, they likely won't survive it.

As worries strangle me, Miko summons an elemental but not an earth elemental, an air elemental. That must have used up the last of her energy because she slumps against the vines that have her tied in place. If the ship keeps rocking like this, she might drown.

The wispy elemental flits in and out of my vision, frequently blending so seamlessly into the air that it's indiscernible. It's vaguely human-shaped but only in the most rudimentary way. It has no face or features; I can only make out what might be a head and two arms on a snakelike body.

The air elemental splits apart, creating a twin. The pair fly over the boar's head and extend their arms, one to Cait and one to Joshua. Though the elementals seem to have insubstantial bodies, they prove to be strong and reliable as they take our combat bard and barbarian into their arms and bring them back to the ship.

At this point, Guy seems a little more with it. He clears his throat and shouts, "Ice Blast!" He flings his palm with force at Cetus, and a devastating volley of icicles shoots forwards, piercing through the boar's hide.

Now Cetus has rivers of blood leaking from one ear, two eyes, and the wounds caused by ice sticking out from one cheek like porcupine quills. The monster is still alive, though, with a little less than half his health bar left. His whale tail thrashes, and large waves roll toward the ship.

"Close your mouth and hold on to something!" I shout for anyone to hear.

I shut my eyes and pie hole, and I feel Guy's hand pressing my head against the mast. He must have seen the way my head collided into it before.

As expected, the waves send the boat rocking back and forth wildly. Just when the deck settles, Cetus unleashes a mighty, echoing grunt. Though he's wounded, we still have quite a fight on our hands.

I open my eyes to see what the monster might do next so that I can prepare. The first thing I see, however, is Alexander standing on the dead center of the deck with his Benelli raised. With perfect aim, a bullet flies from the shotgun straight into the space between Cetus's eyes. Then Alexander shoots another and another after that, each one hitting its mark perfectly.

Cetus doesn't make a sound. It can't. It's dead.

The monster's head drops, breaking the railing beneath it. Its blood-covered snout drags against the side of the ship as he sinks lower and lower and lower until we can't even see one bristle.

None of us speak. We don't even gasp, scream, or cry. We only watch in silence, like if we look away or direct any attention at all away from it, the spell will end, and Cetus will return.

All that we've gone through just to survive Cetus, even just the rocking of the ship, and what ended the creature were a few well-aimed bullets. If not for Alexander, we would have all died.

The waves smooth out, and the deck settles. The only sound is a seagull cawing in the distance. Then an icy sea breeze slices through my thin, wet chiton, and a shivering shriek escapes me.

Guy wraps his arms around me to warm me. "Are you okay?" he whispers against my temple.

"Yeah," I say.

"We need help down here!" Cait calls out.

I look down to see her bent over Joshua, who simply stares at his leg. A bone has broken through the skin on his shin. How is he not screaming his head off?

"I'm going to release the lasso spell, okay?" Guy says.

I'm glad we're up in the crow's nest because I stumble backward the moment I'm no longer bound to the mast. The wall of our station keeps me from plummeting to the deck.

My legs wobble when I climb down the ladder, but adrenaline and determination help me get to Joshua, regardless. The closer I get, the more grisly his leg looks. He's still just staring at it in shock. I can only assume that his pain isn't registering yet.

It's only because of game logic that my staff is on my back and not halfway across the sea right now. I take it from its magically magnetic position and clasp it tight as I say, "Heal Major Wound."

The bone shifts inward until it's no longer piercing the skin. It pops into place, causing Joshua to wince at last. It's too covered in blood and muscle for me to see, but I can sense the bone knitting together. This is when Joshua screams. It seems his healing hurts more than the wound itself. Then his flesh repairs as well, until his skin looks just like it would on any normal day.

Joshua looks at me through the slit between his heavy eyelids.

"Thank you," he whispers before he closes his eyes and falls asleep against Cait's chest.

"We should get him to bed," Sylvia says. "Even with Lauren healing him, it's going to take a long rest for him to get any energy back."

At this point, the vines holding Miko release, and she wakes up. Her eyes find Joshua right away. "He...he was amazing," Miko says to no one in particular. She stares at him like he took on an entire army by himself. "I've never seen anyone fight like that."

Cait hoists him up and drapes him over her shoulder. "Our room better not be flooded."

"It won't be," Sylvia says. "I mean, look at the deck."

We scan our surroundings. The planks are as straight and unbroken as they were when we boarded. The railing is intact. It's not even that slick with water.

"This ship respawns fast," Guy says. Then he looks at the smooth ocean surface. "I hope Cetus takes at least a while longer."

Another icy gust whips across me, and I rub furiously at the goose-bumps on my arms. Then I notice how I look. I hadn't bothered to throw on a cloak when we moved to the deck for the battle. There wasn't time. So, I've been wearing the thin fabric of my chiton this whole time. The wet, white fabric is almost sheer now and clings to every curve of my body. I might as well be naked.

I clasp my arms over my breasts and whip my head up hoping to see that my friends are all too distracted by Joshua to notice me. Sylvia and Miko are already sluggishly walking away. Cait is half turned from me but has stopped in her tracks. Her eyes linger on mine, and her mouth parts in awe. Guy stands next to her, his complete focus on me as his eyes wander down my body, hunger furrowing his brow.

I've never hated my body, but I've never considered it attractive. Doug enjoyed fucking me for the first ten years of our relationship, but I don't think he was picky about stuff like that. When I met Aphrodite, I had the option to change my body any way that I wanted to, but it felt strange to walk around in something unfamiliar. These curves are mine, and by the looks in my friends' eyes, they're sexy as fuck.

Dropping my arms feels like an act of bravery, but I do it anyway. I'm a goddamn Cleric of Aphrodite. I shouldn't feel ashamed if people want me.

"Cait," I say, tilting my head at her. "Let's get Joshua to our room."

She blinks, suddenly remembering she has a grown man hanging over her shoulder. "Uh, yeah, I-I'll go do that."

As Cait walks away, Guy approaches me. He finger combs my sodden hair away from my face, then places his lips on mine. He's not trying to impress me like he did last night. There are no playful nips or trails across my body. Instead, he presses us into a deep, ravenous kiss, only pulling away to give me a sweet peck on each of my cheeks and my forehead.

Guy rests his forehead against mine and says, "I need to get to know you. I need...Oh, God, I need you, Lauren." Before I can respond, he clears his throat and turns around. "Let's get you dry and warm," he says before walking away, sure that I'll follow him immediately.

I let a winter breeze slice across me first, hoping the discomfort will clear my head. That's when I feel a hand on my shoulder and startle. It's Alexander.

"You are most fair and brave," he says. "Aphrodite wants you to have this."

With his free hand, Alexander lifts a pink gem, similar to the one on my staff. Then he presses it to the bronze laurel on my head I'm wearing to increase my wisdom score. In an instant, the two fuse, and I feel... different in a way I can't describe.

"What is this?" I ask.

"This gem ensures you'll only attract those you romance first," he answers.

"Holy fuck! Really?"

After all the drama over Cait and Guy, I needed this. I couldn't handle another person complicating things.

Alexander nods.

"That's a *huge* deal." I shake my head, confused. "Why would she give this to me? I didn't really do anything to deserve it."

Alexander looks over his shoulder to some invisible entity and then back to me. "She's saying you've done more than you think and that you need to talk to your friends."

"I'll do that, then," I say, then make my way below deck.

⇧

JOSHUA IS IN A DEEP SLEEP ON HIS BED, BUT THE REST OF US SIT around the table, leaning over it with our elbows propped on the surface and our weary heads resting on our palms. It's hard to believe that we ate breakfast only an hour ago. It's even harder to accept that not a platter is out of place on the table. It's all exactly how we left it.

I didn't get to eat until I was full before Cetus attacked, but my throat is so raw that I can't even think about finishing breakfast without wincing. At least I'm warm. When I arrived, Guy already had a blanket and my cloak waiting for me.

"Of all of us, you really got the short end of the stick with gear," Miko says. "I don't know how you can get around in all this cold weather in such light fabric."

"Once she gets to level five, she'll be able to update her gear," Sylvia says. "Surely, there will be warm clothes in Thrace."

"Speaking of level five," Cait says. "How does anyone that level survive a battle like *that*?"

Guy shakes his head. "I wish I knew. It's really bothering me. Most of us are around level thirty, and I wasn't sure that we were going to survive."

"Remember that dracaenae?" Cait asks Guy. "Way too high-level for that area, and she attacked when it was just you and Lauren."

Miko rumbles with a bitter chuckle. "Attacks from OP monsters *and* Zeus worshippers coming after you. Lauren's breaking the game, and it's trying to break her back."

Everyone turns their questioning eyes on me. Miko's right. Everything was normal until I broke that spider village quest. Since then, none of it has followed its programming. Some of that's been nice. The people of Sardis can rebuild and have real lives now. NPCs who were only ever supposed to be in the background now have fulfilling love lives. Princess Idaea no longer has to suffer her father's blows.

But now I'm fighting battles way outside of my level as well as fending off players sent by their god to kill me. If not for my friends, I would definitely be dead.

If not for me, they'd be perfectly safe.

Sylvia is such a kind soul. Miko has suffered enough at the behest of Hekate. Cait and Guy? I hate to admit it, but Aphrodite's magic is working on me. I look at Cait's beautiful, determined face, knowing she'd slaughter anyone to keep me safe. Guy's gentle hand rests on mine, and I remember all he's done to make me feel pampered and adored. They don't deserve to be targeted like this.

"I need to leave the group," I say. My friends protest, but I raise my hand to stop them. "Things are just going to get more and more dangerous. The game doesn't want to break me, but there's at least one god who certainly wants me to stop fucking with the system."

"Lauren, the gods are just NPCs," Cait says.

"You mean like Alexander, who just killed a monster by firing bullets into its brain?" I ask.

"NPCs or not, not all the gods are working against you," Guy says. "You said yourself that Aphrodite is thrilled with your progress. Dionysus isn't ordering me to do anything to hurt you."

Cait nods. "Ares made it clear he's not going to do anything to make Aphrodite unhappy."

"Artemis is only ever concerned with how I'm helping nature," Sylvia adds. "So when you aided Arachne's children, she was pleasantly surprised."

"Yeah, but there are a lot more gods than that," Miko says. "And even if it's just Zeus, you don't really want to piss off the *King* of the Gods."

Cait sends Miko a cutting look. "Please don't tell me you agree with Lauren that she should leave."

Miko leans back in her chair, frowning. "It would be the smart choice, but..." She sighs. "Lauren was the first person in months to show me kindness. So...no, I don't think she should leave."

"Then what do we do?" I ask. "You'll never get your offerings if we're always running for our lives."

"I don't run from *anything*," Cait says with an arched brow, like I'd just challenged her bravery. "If the gods want to target us because you're making a few NPCs happy, then they're going to have a fight on their hands."

"We all almost *died!*" I tell her. "You were so adamant about that when I met you. Playing by the rule book is kind of your thing for a reason."

"Yeah, well, sometimes you have to break the rules for people who are special to you," she says, keeping her unwavering stare on me.

Cait's tone is unyielding, and her stance is intimidating, but her words are true. There's a hard glint in her fierce eyes, but there's the promise of tears as well. She's hurting. I want to hold her to me, let her curl against my chest while I stroke her beautiful red hair and promise her everything will be okay.

"You're special to me, too," I say.

"Then please don't go," Cait whispers as every hard line of her face and body softens. "The moment you leave us is the moment you die."

I'm condemning them by staying, but selfishly, I take their refusal to let me go as my excuse to stay.

I nod and say, "As you wish."

Sylvia sighs. "I know it's not even noon yet, but I think we all still need a long rest. That battle used everything we've got."

She's right, so no one pushes back. We all just get up from our seats and climb into our beds. When I close my eyes, I hear, "Cleric of Aphrodite: Level Four. Spell Gained: Kiss of Life, to be used no more than three times before leaving the spell list."

Well, at least there's that small comfort.

CHAPTER TWENTY-NINE

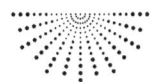

It's our second morning onboard the Argo, and if I squint really hard, I can make out a thin black line on the horizon that's supposed to be land. According to Sylvia, my feet will be on it by late afternoon. I'm so ready to get off this fucking ship and make progress on my Thrace quests.

Until then, I need to hang out *somewhere*, and it's too stuffy below deck and too cold above. I take a while to choose, but I decide to idle away the hours where at least I can breathe, even if it means I'm trembling the entire time. Fortunately for me, Guy is following me around like a lapdog and is eager to do whatever he can to keep me warm.

He's sitting with his back against the outer wall of the captain's cabin and I'm straddling his lap so that we're comfortably face-to-face in the tight space.

I imagine that whoever designed this part of the game was like, "Screw Greek mythology! Let's make Argo a pirate ship!" Right now, I'm grateful for that flagrant disregard for accuracy because the structure of our little spot is blocking me from most of the winter wind. It's also giving Guy and me a little privacy, which we're taking full advantage of.

Guy holds a lock of my hair to his lips and kisses it. "Tell me more," he whispers. "What other classes did you take?"

I laugh. "I'm not sure we have that much time."

"Well, just the best ones," he says. "I've never known someone who almost had so many degrees."

"You realize this makes me a flake, right?" I ask. "This isn't an attractive quality."

"I don't know what you're talking about. A thirst for knowledge is sexy as hell." By the look on Guy's face, he means what he's saying. His dark brown eyes light with curiosity, and his mouth crooks into a wicked grin. "Besides, whenever I learn something new about you, I get to kiss you."

"That was your rule, not mine," I say. "If it were up to me, we'd break into the captain's cabin and go to town."

Guy lets a low moan escape in response to that but shakes his head. "No, I meant what I said. I want something real, even if..." He trails off, pain shadowing across his face.

He doesn't need to finish that sentence because we both know my feelings for Cait. These moments might be all he gets with me. Sex is great, but he told me he was getting plenty of that before I came along with other Dionysus followers he met in cities all over Peripeteia.

"Studies of Arthurian legends was a fun one," I say, directing our conversation back to his question. "I also really loved the class about the history of jazz."

"Are you a musician?" Guy asks.

"God, no," I say. "Just sounded like a fun class. My turn."

"After I get my kiss," he says.

I'm all too happy to comply. I cup his face in my hands and lick his lips, teasing them apart so I can do more clever things with my tongue. He moans against me and bucks his hips a little beneath me so that I can feel how hard I'm making him. I glory in the power I have with such a simple trick, one that I realized a few kisses ago works *really* well on him.

When I pull away from him, he takes a moment to open his eyes. "Ask your question," he says breathlessly. "I need another one of those."

"Well, I'm always telling you that you're hot like Ryan Reynolds," I say.

"Hot?" Guy responds. "I mean, you've told me I look like Ryan Reynolds, but I didn't know you thought I was hot."

"It was implied," I say and continue, "When you all told me how I can change my appearance, you said you didn't really change yours. Is that true?"

Guy nods but slowly. He's hesitating a bit.

I lean away from him to get a better look at him. "Are you lying?"

"No!" Guy says. "I was telling the truth. I only changed one thing about myself. It...it made me look a little different, but...this is pretty much me. *More* me, really."

"Okay, that's not a good enough answer," I say. "I need details."

Guy looks down. His previous elation has darkened. He looks sad—scared, too.

"It's pretty serious," he says. "If you're just looking for a fling before you move on to Cait, I think I'd rather keep it to myself. Even if that means we stop the kissing here."

Oh, shit. I definitely hit something deep there.

"I didn't know," I say. "Honestly, I was just using this as an excuse to tell you that you're sexy, but..."

"It's okay, really," he says, but he can't look at me.

There's nothing okay about this. I didn't just touch a sore topic; I'd reminded him that this is likely a temporary situation. Though, the more we talk and kiss, the less I want to end this. Yes, I want Cait. I want her *so* bad. But Guy? The more I learn about him, the more I care, and the more my heart flutters when he looks at me.

"You're not disposable, you know," I say. "Not even a little. If I wind up with Cait, what you and I are sharing right now matters to me, and it will always matter. You're not just a distraction while I wait for someone else."

Guy responds with a soft, sad smile. "Thanks."

"You don't have to tell me anything else about that situation," I say. "In fact, three kisses for you because you put up with me just now."

I press my lips gently to his, and he leans into it, but when I come in for a second kiss, he pulls back.

"No, I-I'll tell you," he says. "You told me about your mom. You deserve the same trust from me. But please don't tell anyone else."

We lock eyes, and I know whatever it is, I better wrap my heart around it and keep it safe. "If that's what you want," I say. "I'll give you whatever you need."

"Right before I came here, I was drinking. A lot," he says. "I was in my bathroom, chugging down all the booze I could find in my liquor cabinet."

I nod, remembering what he'd said about why he thinks Dionysus chose him.

"It wasn't because I was partying or that I'm an alcoholic," Guy says. "I just thought it would numb me when I..." His throat bobs. "I was going to kill myself."

My fingers press against my lips instinctively as I gasp. "Oh, God, I'm so sorry."

"There's more," he says. "There's why." He looks at me with pleading eyes. "Please, please don't hate me. Please don't think I'm gross or..."

"Of course, I won't!" I say, shaking my head vigorously. I wipe his messy brown hair from his forehead so that I can see his face better. "Guy, you've been an absolute godsend to me ever since I met you."

Guy offers me another smile that's gone all too quickly when he returns to his explanation. "My dad wasn't a nice person," he says. "He didn't want kids. My mom got pregnant and refused to abort me. Instead of getting mad at her, he got mad at me. One night I said something, I don't even remember what, but he got so angry that he shoved me against the stove and pressed my face to the burner. Every day, I noticed the way people winced at me, from clients to coworkers. Even people I thought of as friends. I just couldn't take it anymore."

"Guy..." I can't think of anything else to say, but my heart hurts for him. How could anyone do that to their kid?

That must be all over my face because he strokes my cheek and says, "I'm okay now. Really. I'm *here*, where my face is *my* face again, and I'm around people I actually like. People like you."

People like me...

Those words and this secret are an honor I don't deserve to carry, but I will do so anyway because he needs me to.

I don't wait for any more questions to exchange. This moment isn't part of the cute little game he's concocted for us. *This* is real, and that's what he really wanted from me.

"Where did it burn you?" I ask.

Guy traces over the right side of his face. "From my scalp to my chin," he says. "I actually didn't have hair on that side until about an inch behind my ear."

His hair. His beautiful hair. I comb it back delicately and then press a kiss to his forehead. I tread a gentle path with my lips across his eyebrow to his temple and down his cheek and jawline. At his chin, I leave a sweet, lingering kiss. Then, I loosen his wizard robes at the collar so that I can kiss his heart because I'm sure there's a scar there that hasn't magically healed like the others.

As I do all of this, Guy responds with soft sighs and moans. When my lips leave his chest, he grips the sides of my face and buries his fingers in my hair. It's a shock, but a pleasant one. He claims my mouth with his own, and oh God, I don't think I've ever been kissed like this, like he'll die if he can't get more of me.

Guy pulls away, and tears spill down his cheeks. "God, Lauren," he whispers. "What am I going to do when you leave me?"

My heart shatters at the question because I don't want to leave him, but...Cait. When I look at her, I can't even think straight. She's so powerful and determined. My hero. But now, after all our time on the ship, something big has shifted between Guy and me.

Why Choose? That's one of my quests. A question. There are too many of those right now and not enough answers. Why choose? Because of Cait, because she's...what? Uptight? Rigid? Until recently, I would have thought she was one hundred percent straight, but her gaze lingers on me more and more deliciously every time we come across each other.

"Let's just think about what we have right now," I whisper back and take one of his hands in mine. I think about how best to show him the depth of intimacy I want with him. I consider my breast, my ass, my pussy. None of those are good enough, not after what he's shared.

I place Guy's hand over my heart and say, "You're special to me. Very, very special."

CHAPTER THIRTY

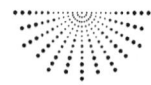

The ship had been bitterly cold, but now I wonder if it was actually blessed with a magical heated bubble because Thrace's chill bites into my bones. A *cloak*? That's all Aphrodite thought I'd need here? It's fucking snowing! And not just like it has a few times on our journey. No, it's coming down hard. Not quite a blizzard, but not far from that either. I'm from Atlanta, not the North Pole!

It's late afternoon, too, which means soon it will be dark and therefore even colder. That's why I'm grateful when Sylvia suggests we camp for the night. Now that we're off the ship, we can finally call on our camp, and all our creature comforts are back, including mountains of blankets and the means to make a nice campfire.

With every awful thing that's happened since we ran into the dracaenae, we don't dare all sleep at the same time. We make the choice to pair up and rest in shifts. Joshua and Miko will go first. After that will be Cait and Guy, followed by Sylvia and me. And Alexander has stated he'll be nearby with his Benelli whenever we need him.

Sylvia was the one to come up with the pairings. Guy had been really obvious with his sulking, but she put her foot down. She believes we'll be too busy making out to pay attention. Plus, it's not a good idea to isolate the two low-strength party members. Honestly, she probably made the right move. I just wish she hadn't stuck Cait and Guy together. But what argument can I make against that? It would be awkward if the two people I'm romantically interested in spent time alone together?

While Sylvia cooks up a savory soup over the campfire, the rest of us set up our camp in the best defensive position we can. We figure we can back it up against the tall hill we spotted near the road. The campfire is set on the hill's flat top, so whoever is on watch will be warm and have an excellent view all around.

I really hope we're going overboard with these protective measures, but something tells me that even this might not be enough. Aphrodite told me she won't let me die, though. I wonder if she knew Cetus was going to be much tougher than usual. Why else would she give Alexander a shotgun right in the nick of time?

Except for Miko, my friends are all around level thirty. What level did that make Cetus? Even if they were matched in level, it shouldn't have been such a close call. We shouldn't have needed an NPC to plant bullets in its brain. So he would have had to be at least close to a level forty, and most players who take that ship are level four or five. I shiver, and it's not just because of the drifting snow stinging my bare cheek. What if he respawns and is still that OP'd when newbies travel on the Argo?

I'm testing the tentpoles near the hillside when Cait approaches me. Despite being clad in heavy leather armor, the cold air turns her pale skin and pink lips nearly purple. I must look even worse with only my flimsy chiton and cloak to keep me warm.

As uncomfortable as Cait must be, she still has a smile for me when she reaches my side.

"Hey," she says. "Is the Heart of Ares helping you out?" She points at the locket clasped around my neck, the one she gave me out of the kindness of her heart.

I touch it, feeling its eternal heat beneath my fingers. "Honestly, it's probably the only reason I don't have frostbite."

"Yeah, I wanted to talk to you about that," she says. "I know healers are only supposed to wear cloth only and any other armor class might hamper your energy levels, but you could actually die of exposure. Let me help you try on some of my lower-level leather stuff I haven't sold off."

Laughing, I say, "Something tells me we're not the same size." I gesture at her tall, slender frame and then my short, curvy one.

Cait rolls her eyes. "C'mon, a gamer like you knows armor is one size fits all."

She's right. This isn't like real life where I need to be concerned about what size I am.

"Okay, thanks," I say. "Show me the way."

Cait takes me by the hand. It's meant to be innocent, what an excited friend would do when giddily leading you to a fun surprise. But the moment our fingers touch, a pleasant, thrumming heat flows through me. She must feel it, too, because her smile softens, and she looks at me with half-lidded eyes.

It's fucking cold. I'd love nothing more than to rush into our magically warm tent and put on *real* clothes, but we're alone in this spot. Everyone else is on the other side of the tent. Once we're inside, we may not get another moment like this for at least a day.

I grip Cait's hand in mine and tug her toward me, not enough to actually move her. I'm not strong enough to do that. It's just a message, really. I want her closer. Cait closes the distance between us, standing no more than a foot away, so that I have to tilt my head to look up at her.

"What's up?" she asks, like she doesn't know.

Maybe she doesn't. Maybe this is all in my head, but...No, I see the tenderness in her eyes and feel the brief and subtle stroke of her thumb across my knuckles.

"You were dead," I say. "And then with Cetus, you were *almost* dead. I can't tell you how much that scared me, how that...broke my heart."

Cait's throat bobs. "It did?"

I nod. "Remember how you said you dreamed I kissed you?"

Her eyes widen. "I said that? Out loud?"

Ignoring her panic, I continue, "Well, I did kiss you. You were very, *very* dead, and I thought maybe if I just kissed you, it would bring you back. But it didn't. It took that Cleric of Zeus to do it."

"But you tried," she says. "That means a lot to me."

"Aphrodite has granted me a spell called the Kiss of Life," I tell her. "I only get to use it three times, and then it's gone for good. But still, that's three times I'll be able to bring someone back with a kiss."

Cait gasps. "Oh my God, really?!"

"Total game changer, right?"

I sigh, knowing that I can't beat around the bush any longer. I have to tell her how I feel, even if I don't know how it will pan out in the end for her, me, *and* Guy. Because not being honest might hurt us all more in the end.

Swallowing down my anxiety, I say, "The thing is, if I kiss you again, I don't want it to be because you're dead. I want it to be reciprocal, a *real* kiss."

Cait stares at me, stunned as a doe facing a semi. Her hand slips from mine.

I've just fucked up big time. I must have misread all the signs. She's little Miss Prim and Proper. What I took for attraction could have simply been friendly affection on her part.

Despite the freezing weather, my face feels like an oven, and I turn to hide my blush from her. "Um, I think I heard Sylvia say dinner is ready."

When I take a step away, Cait reaches out and grabs me by the wrist. "Wait!" she cries out. Her eyes are wild, shining with confusion and the promise of tears. "But you're with Guy."

"I am," I say.

"Are you saying you want to break up with him?"

Oof, now there's a question.

Things are going really well with him now, much better than I ever expected them to. There's nothing in me that wants to leave Guy, but I also can't deny my feelings for Cait.

"No, I don't," I answer truthfully.

"You want to *cheat* on him?" she asks. There's a hint of accusation in her tone, and I get it. Guy was her friend long before I ever entered the picture.

"I would never cheat on him," I tell her. "Just because I want to kiss you doesn't mean I would betray either of you. I told you how I feel because I want to be honest. Guy already knows."

"But...the two of you..." Cait shakes her head, mystified. "I mean, you've both been pretty obvious lately. Your kisses aren't as secret as you think."

That's a little embarrassing, but it's not the point. I don't know exactly how to describe what's going on between Guy and me. Still, I'm going to try my best.

"I feel myself growing closer to the both of you the more I get to know you," I say. "And he said he wants to get whatever time he can with me in case I decide I only want to be with you."

"In case you decide you *only* want to be with me?" she asks. "What does that mean?"

"He's open to me being with both of you," I answer.

"I...I..." Cait can't seem to form any other words. Pain contorts her features, and her tears fall at last. "All three of us could...?" She shakes her head and then looks at me with pleading eyes. "No, I'm being—"

She can't seem to complete her thoughts out loud. She's clearly not ready for this conversation.

"It's okay," I say. "I understand. I won't push you into—"

Cait lets go of my wrist but not to walk away. She grabs my face with both her hands, and her lips crash into mine. Her kiss is as fiery as her temper and just as deep as her heart. I lose all sense of where and when we are. There is no snow or winter wind, just the heat of our bodies pressed together.

Then, just as suddenly as the kiss began, it ends. Cait parts from me, gasping from arousal, her features twisted with confusion.

Eventually, her expression settles into a cool but friendly mask and, in a tone that implies nothing at all passed between us, she says, "You're going to freeze to death. Let's go get you into some of my old clothes."

Cait walks to the other side of the tent, not waiting for me to follow. The ping of a notification prompts me to bring up my quest log. "Kiss Her" is crossed out and "Patience" is added. No explanation needed. I'll give her all the time she needs and respect whatever decision she makes. I just hope I didn't fuck everything up.

A snowy gust slams into me, pulling my cloak away so that the ice crystals can cling to the thin fabric of my chiton. I don't waste any more time thinking about my romantic life. I need to put on some real fucking clothes.

⇪

It's a few hours before dawn when Sylvia wakes me. I only know what time it is because that's what my game menu tells me. How did guards know their shifts were over before there were clocks? If these were the actual days of ancient Greece that inspired the game developers, I would have absolutely no concept of time.

It's that point in the middle of the night when the temperatures have reached the lowest they'll get for twenty-four more hours. I'm *so* grateful that Cait lent me some of her old armor because, even though I'm dressed head to toe in leather, my joints ache from the cold.

Sylvia seems remarkably calm about the weather, though. I suppose her cloak made of heavy fur has a lot to do with it. But when I sit beside her next to the campfire, she actually hands it over to me!

"Oh, no, I appreciate it, but I don't want you to go cold just for my sake," I say.

"I'll be fine," she says in her typical sweet tone. "One of the favors Artemis gave me is the ability to feel comfort in any weather."

"Damn, that's really handy."

"Definitely," she responds and uses a stick to move the logs around. When the flames don't get bigger, she frowns. "Can you go back in the tent and grab another log?"

"Sure thing."

I do exactly as Sylvia asked, but when I exit the tent, I hear someone whisper something unintelligible to my right. I turn but see no one.

I'm about to write it up as my imagination, when it happens again, but this time I hear, "Lauren."

Nausea creeps up me. It's dark, and the only people around are either asleep or next to the fire at the top of the hill. I scurry to climb up the hill but stop when I hear, "It's Tara with the other earrings."

I remember we got matching earrings in Thebe so that she and I could communicate from a distance. I'm impressed that they work from this far away.

"Tara? What's going on?"

"Don't trust Sylvia," she hisses urgently.

It hits me then that Tara's actually whispering. Why? She's in my ear. Even people close to me can't hear what she's saying.

"What do you mean? Sylvia wouldn't hurt any of us."

"Yeah, *our* Sylvia wouldn't," Tara whispers, "but that's not her."

Panic thunders in my chest. This is even creepier than if it had just been a strange voice whispering my name in the dark. "Why are you whispering?"

"I don't want the Zeus worshippers to hear me," she answers.

"They're alive?" I ask.

"All of them except for Bruce and Dan," Tara responds. "When they were freed, they killed Bruce and Dan. I had to pretend I was still possessed and on their side."

"Holy shit! They killed Bruce and Dan?"

"Yeah, Zeus is letting them live because of what their warlock did," she says. "The reason I lost control of my mind in the battle is that he possessed me with an eidola. I just heard him bragging how he got me and Sylvia. Once Miko trapped me, mine must have left. I'd already served my purpose but Syl—"

Tara breaks off, and for a heartbeat, I think she's gone, But then I hear her let out a low sigh. "Shit, I gotta go. I hear them talking about how I've been gone too long. I'm going to stay with them as long as I can to keep tabs on what Zeus has planned, okay?"

"Okay," I reply. "Thanks, Tara."

She doesn't respond. I guess she's gone now.

Sylvia possessed by an eidola? What the fuck is an eidola? And if she is possessed, why hasn't she tried murdering me in my sleep yet? She's had plenty of opportunities. Maybe Tara's wrong. Maybe the warlock's spell didn't work on Sylvia.

Whatever the case may be, I can't stand at the bottom of this hill any longer. I need to help with the fire.

When I reach Sylvia, I see that she's talking with Alexander. I'm behind them, and I guess she doesn't hear me because she doesn't turn to see me. I pause, considering Tara's warning and then I pick up on Sylvia's conversation.

"So what exactly does Aphrodite want Lauren to tell Khione?" she asks. "Is this something that maybe Zeus would want to know?"

Why the hell would an Archer of Artemis give a fuck about what Zeus should know? More than that, why is she concerned with pleasing the god who is actively trying to kill me?

"That is between the cleric and her goddess," Alexander says.

Sylvia reaches forward and strokes his knee in a blatantly seductive manner, "Come on, you must know something."

That is *not* Sylvia. She's not a seductress. Hell, she's not even into dudes. She's got a girlfriend at home that she misses. Tara's right. Probably the only reason she hasn't killed me yet is because the eidola possessing her wants to find out more for her god.

Fuck, what am I going to do?

I take a long, steadying breath and plaster on what I hope seems like a genuine smile before I get within view of Sylvia. "Sorry, I took so long," I say. "As an Archer of Artemis, I'm sure you know when nature calls you gotta answer."

Sylvia laughs, just as sweetly as ever, but this time I hear the saccharine in it. I pretend I don't, though. If I don't play along, she may decide to cut her losses and stab me right now. Better to let her think she's collecting intel for Zeus.

The urge to feel hopeless about the whole situation threatens to take hold of me, but I shove it aside. If she can lie through her teeth to lead me astray, I can return the favor. If Zeus wants information, he can have as much as he wants, but none of it will be at all reliable.

I put the log into the fire and watch as the flames climb along the length of it.

"Mmm, that's better," Sylvia says, holding her hands up to the flame. "I'm not cold, but there's nothing like feeling heat from a campfire on your palms."

"Hopefully, being in Ismarus will give us some shelter from the cold weather," I say. "I mean it's a city under a winter deity's protection, right?"

Sylvia nods. "Boreas." I can see the eagerness in her eyes. I've just handed her the perfect opportunity to get information out of me. "You know, Khione is his daughter."

I shrug and try to sound nonchalant when I say, "Oh, really? That's interesting."

"I wonder why Aphrodite wants you talking to her," she says.

Here's where I need to poison the well with a lie. Why would Zeus want to know about this quest? What does it matter to him that Khione claims her son? Aphrodite wanted me to keep my lips zipped about it for a reason, though. Perhaps, she doesn't want anyone knowing where Khione's son is headed.

"She just wants me to tell Khione that her son is lost, and she needs to go search for him," I say.

Something crosses over Sylvia's eyes. It's mechanical, like when Alexander goes blank and waits for his programming to tell him how to respond.

"Well, I hope she finds him," Sylvia says at last. "Maybe when we're done in Ismarus, we can escort her."

"Yeah," I say. "Maybe."

CHAPTER THIRTY-ONE

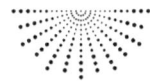

Not getting a full night's rest definitely left its mark on us. Poor Cait and Guy both look completely bone weary. Although, I wonder if they're more than tired. Did they talk about me at all? I never had a chance to spill the beans about the kiss to Guy.

Whether or not he knows, I need to get him alone right away. Not just to discuss the kiss, but also to share what Tara told me. He's shared his deepest secret with me. I know I can trust him.

I'm grateful that the sky is clear, and the icy gale is calm. Yes, it's still cold as fuck, but at least I can get a little away from the fire without turning into a snow sculpture. I want to be as far from the others as possible when talking to Guy.

When he gets up to put his bowl in the bucket for washing, I motion for him to follow me. He responds with a sad smile and then heads my way.

"Hey," I whisper to him when he gets near. "I want to talk with you about some important stuff far away from everyone else."

Guy gulps but nods. He probably thinks I'm about to end things.

We get far enough away that I can't hear anyone at the campfire, but not so far that they get concerned that we're leaving. Maybe they'll just assume we're out here to slip in some kissing. Though that might not be the best thing for Cait to dwell on right now.

"What's going on?" Guy asks.

"A lot, actually," I say. "Honestly, I don't know where to start."

"Is this about Cait?" he asks. "I noticed you talking yesterday."

"Well, yes, she's part of it."

Guy's lips vibrate with a frustrated exhale, and he says, "Wish there was some place dry to sit. Seems like I might need it."

Ugh, I can't have him in disaster mode before I get into things. He'll read into everything Cait-related as some sign that I'm bound and determined to leave him. That will make the news of Sylvia's betrayal even harder on him.

I brush back his dark hair and press my lips to his. I meant for it to be short and sweet, a quick "things are good between us" message. However, Guy deepens the kiss immediately, wrapping his arms around me as he does. I don't know if it's because he's scared it's the last one we'll share or because he's grateful I didn't straight up break up with him. I'm not complaining, though.

When one of his hands slips down from the small of my back to cup my bottom, I almost forget why we're out here alone. God, why do his hands always have to feel *so* good? I can't think. If we weren't past our ankles in snow, I might take our physical relationship to a whole new level.

No, there are way more important things than getting into his pants right now. I pull back from our embrace and take a deep breath, letting the bite of the winter air clear my mind.

"I'm sorry," he says, his face turned downward.

"Sorry?" I laugh. "I started it. You just made it better."

With his head still slightly bent, Guy looks up at me with a playful smile and mischievous eyes. "There's an inn in Ismarus, you know..."

Visions of a long night spent tangled up with Guy distract me for a moment, but I shake my head. "We'll talk more about that later. There's a lot I need to say and not much time to say it."

I guess Guy hears the seriousness in my tone because he straightens up and studies my face. "Go on."

"Two things," I say. "I did talk to Cait last night. I told her about my feelings, and well...she kissed me."

Guy blinks. "Wow, just like that?"

"Well, sort of," I tell him. "She's definitely confused about the whole thing. Her parents brought her up to believe in one man being with one woman. Not a man and a woman and a woman."

"A man and a woman and a woman?" Guy asks.

"Well, she asked me if I wanted to break up with you, and I was honest," I say. "I don't want to break up with you, but that doesn't make me want her any less. You'd mentioned maybe me being with you both, so I brought it up as an option."

Guy's eyes widen. "You don't want to leave me?"

I stroke his cheek. "You're not just a placeholder to me," I tell him. "I have genuine feelings for you." I sigh. "But my feelings for her run just as deep. Honestly, I'm not sure what will happen. She may not be into the idea at all, and you may get jealous of her."

"No, never," he says. "My brain doesn't work like that. If you really care about me, that won't change if you care about her, too. I want to be with you, not *own* you."

"Goddamn, you're so sexy right now," I whisper.

I should really get on to the *truly* important conversation, but I indulge myself with another kiss. If there wasn't a god trying to kill me, I would spend days in bed with this man.

When our kiss ends, I pull away again and let out a long sigh, "Now for the other thing I need to talk about."

I tell Guy everything about Tara's sudden warning and the suspicious behavior Sylvia displayed. His features press together as I speak, growing more concerned with every word I share.

"So, she hasn't killed us because she's trying to send information to Zeus?" Guy asks. He presses his fingertips to his forehead. "Oh God, this is terrible."

"What are we going to do?" I ask.

"I guess what you're doing already," he answers. "Pretend like we're clueless and give her enough believable lies to keep Zeus off track."

I cross my arms and look up at the blue sky, wondering once again just how far that barrier in the programming extends. "Peripeteia seems less like *Legends of Sacrifice* every day I'm here."

Cait approaches with a clenched jaw and stern eyebrows. My immediate reaction is that she saw Guy and me kissing and is freaking out. But why would she? She's not even sure she wants me like that.

"Is everything okay?" I ask.

"No," she answers. "Miko thinks she saw a chaos dragon in the distance, close to the water. We need to put as much distance between us and that monster as we can."

I nod. "Got it."

Cait studies me for a moment, her face still all business. Then she gives Guy a long look. "You told him," she says. It's not a question, but I nod in response. Cait crosses her arms. "The kiss was...a mistake."

The words twist like a knife in my heart. When I opened up about my feelings, I knew her rejection was the likely outcome. I didn't know it would hurt this much though.

"Yes, I'm attracted to women," she says. "But I'm attracted to men, too. Sometimes. And all my life I've been told it should only be men and women together. Now? Well, let's just say I don't believe that anymore, but kissing you should have been about my attraction to you, not a way to deal with my confusion."

My quest log told me to be patient, and I plan to be. I'll respect her feelings in this matter.

"Your choices are your own," I tell her. "Whether you're with me is up to you, but I hope your heart guides you to me."

Cait gives Guy another long look. "And you're okay with this?" she asks. "Sharing your woman with someone else?"

"She's not *my* woman," Guy answers. "She's the Cleric of Aphrodite. How selfish would I have to be to deprive anyone of the love she offers, when she has an endless supply of it?"

"Hey!" Miko yells in the distance. "Hurry! The chaos dragon is getting closer to land!"

"We'll talk more about this later," Cait says, looking from my face to Guy's and back. "All three of us."

"You need to know something first," I tell Cait. "Don't trust Sylvia."

⇧

THE CHAOS DRAGON HAS A BODY LIKE A SNAKE AND THREE HEADS. In every other regard, it looks like your typical European dragon—a giant fucking nightmare that can fly. Its black scales sometimes shift to smoke, but that does nothing to lessen the intensity of its six glowing red eyes.

As if that isn't bad enough, it's moving in spirals on its path toward Ismarus so that it can carry a cyclone of sea water with it.

"Do you think this is a level five chaos dragon or a 'Zeus is trying to kill Lauren' chaos dragon?" Miko asks. "Because it seems to be catching up to us."

"Really missing Dolius's carriage right now," Joshua responds. "That would get us to Ismarus in no time."

"Being in Ismarus doesn't guarantee that we'll be safe, though," Cait says. "What if it's bringing that cyclone this way to *attack* Ismarus? I know we're tired of fighting, but I think we might have to."

Sylvia groans, giving the impression that she hates the idea of that. Cait glances at me just long enough for me to know she's thinking what I am. Sylvia isn't all that sad that we all might die fighting a chaos dragon. Well, at least the eidola possessing her feels that way. Our actual friend might be screaming in terror deep down.

"Cait's right," Guy says. "We need to put ourselves in a position where we might stand a chance against it, though. We're in the middle of snow-covered hills. That doesn't seem like the best tactical position."

Miko taps her chin. "I could summon some fire elementals to melt the snow."

"Good idea," Joshua says, bringing an uncharacteristically shy smile to Miko's face.

"Yeah, that will help a lot, but we'll still be an open target," Guy says.

"We'll just have to go full offense, then," Cait says. "Hit it as hard and fast as we can. Hopefully, we can weaken it before its first attack." She turns to Alexander. "You still got your shotgun?"

Alexander pulls it out of his pack and gives a nod.

"Good, if it gets close enough, try to get it in the eyes or the brain," Cait says.

"Wait, does that gun need to be reloaded?" Sylvia asks. "Or is this like a magical game gun with endless ammo?"

In response, Alexander points his pistol toward the chaos dragon, who's too far away for an actual attack to land. He fires off round after round. Even with my hands clapped tightly over my ears, every shot feels like thunder in my brain. Then he opens up the magazine to show us it's still full of bullets.

"Well, that's helpful," Sylvia says and turns to me with a smile. "Aphrodite must really want you to succeed in this Khione mission."

My fist is begging me to punch her in the face. But my strength score is pitiful, and it's the eidola, not Sylvia trying to stab me in the back right now.

Instead, I say, "Or she just wants me to stay alive."

Miko scrolls at the menu only visible to her. "God, I can't wait to get some druid gear so I don't have to use my menu for spells," she says and then taps in the space a few inches from her face.

A fire elemental shows up. Much like the air elemental, it looks like the vague outline of a person, with an undefined head and arms and a body but no legs or feet.

"Double up," she commands it.

It splits into two copies of itself. At Miko's behest, the two fire elementals wander around our area, melting the ice in their path.

All the while, the chaos dragon is getting closer. "Sorry, but how are we supposed to fight that?" I ask, pointing at it. "It's so high up. Either Cait needs to learn how to fly so she can clobber it, or we need to figure out how to kill a fucking water cyclone."

We all share a moment of grim silence. Even Sylvia seems genuinely concerned, though it's probably just the eidola wondering if she'd survive something like this.

"I have a spell that might help," Guy says, "but it's going to use up all my concentration and energy."

"What is it?" I ask.

"Magnet," he answers. "It magnifies gravity on the target of my choice so that it can't fly and can only move with great effort. But it only lasts for maybe fifteen minutes, and the last time I used it I wound up passed out for several hours."

Joshua nods. "Yeah, I remember. You used that on the harpies in the Strophades, and we had to take a long rest so you'd have time to recover."

"That's a huge gamble," Cait interjects. "If we're not able to kill the chaos dragon in time, you'll be defenseless."

"Doesn't matter," Miko says. "Lauren's right. You and Joshua pack the biggest punch, but you won't be able to do that unless the chaos dragon is within reach."

I wish my Near Future Vision worked on battles instead of just life stuff. That would be pretty handy in this decision process.

"I'll stay by Guy," I say. "I know I'm weak, but I should still be able to alert someone in case he's in danger while passed out."

Cait's mouth twists in hesitation. There's no perfect solution to this problem, and she hates the idea of her friend being helpless in a situation like this. But after a moment of consideration, she nods at Guy. "If you think it's a risk worth taking, I will do whatever I can to make sure your plan succeeds."

"Here's hoping," he responds with a nervous laugh.

I squeeze his fingers and whisper to him, "I'm here for you."

The words were only meant for him, but Cait adds, "I'm here for both of you." The look she gives Guy and me is so sure, so warm, that I wonder if it comes with the promise of *us*—not just her and me, but the three of us together.

God, I hope we don't die.

We don't rush formulating a plan. As fast as the chaos dragon is traveling, it will still be several minutes before he reaches us. Better to spend all the time we have making sure we can do our best than to panic and fuck everything up.

Just like on the ship, Joshua and Cait will be far ahead of the rest of us but even more so than before. There will be a full football field length between them and us. This is so that there will be room for the chaos dragon's body and cyclone to land, but our heavy hitter will also be able to melee immediately while Joshua keeps up a sleep song on his fiddle.

Alexander, Miko, and Sylvia will provide ranged attacks from the left. They'll be closer to the monster than Guy and me, but far enough away that they shouldn't have to resort to melee. Sylvia will use her poisoned arrows in her rapid-fire assault. Miko will see if she can wrest the cyclone away using water and wind elementals to reverse its churning so that it spins back to the ocean. Alexander will keep up firing his endless supply of bullets.

Meanwhile, Guy will cast this huge, terrifying spell, and I'll make sure nothing attacks him while he's out. Of course, I'll also be casting healing spells if needed. I remind myself that I can only use the Kiss of Life three times before it's gone. Hopefully, using all my energy on healing spells will prevent me from needing to use anything like that.

Once we're all in place, I ask Guy, "Are you scared?"

He lets out a nervous chuckle. "Terrified." He keeps his gaze on the approaching dragon but laces his fingers with mine. "But I know you'll keep me safe."

"I'll try," I say. "But I'm only level four."

"You do more at level four than most people do at level forty. You're the gamebreaker." Guy turns his attention from the dragon so that I can see how serious he is with his next statement. "You're the most likely to figure out your offering out of all of us, and I'm not letting anything keep that from happening."

A sound like the overlapping of a roar, a thunderstorm, and a shrieking eagle sends waves of energy rippling through us. The chaos dragon is so close now that the black smoke leaving its nostrils drifts to the ground at Joshua's feet.

Guy lifts his staff high and shouts, "Magnet!" Then, he drops to the ground.

The chaos dragon falls with a thud that topples me over despite it being more than a football field away. That's no surprise given that this creature is easily fifty feet long, and its scales look as hard as rock. Even Cait and Joshua get knocked down, but they jump to their feet as fast as rabbits and pounce on the monster at once.

Having three heads means it will be hard to kill it, but Joshua fiddles his sleep song, and the third head passes out. Then, our melee duo gives it all they've got on the two other heads. Joshua strikes at one of the dragon's throats, and blood flows like a river from the wound. Cait cleaves the skull of another head with her great axe. But the two heads remain conscious. Game logic, I suppose. At least its health meter went down by a fifth with those two attacks.

Though Alexander is at a distance, the sudden bang of his shotgun startles me. He just keeps going, concentrating on the head not targeted by Cait and Joshua. The monster's health bar creeps lower and lower... but not by much. I guess three heads means it's three times as hard to kill it.

Despite secretly working against us, Sylvia keeps the arrows coming, and most of them strike true. That doesn't mean I'm not scared to death that one of those will "accidentally" wind up lodged in Joshua or Cait.

Maybe she understands that by killing them, she lowers her own chances of surviving this encounter.

Miko puts her water and air elementals to work. It looks like they're playing ring around the rosy with the water cyclone—so effortless, so playful. Their minimal effort seems to be making more progress than anything the rest of the party is doing.

I'm crouched beside Guy with my hand over his chest so that I can feel the steady rise and fall of his breathing. All the while, I keep a careful watch over our surroundings. The dragon and its cyclone seem to be the only threats to us now, but I'd rather be overly cautious.

The whole situation is terrifying enough with how little our attacks are chipping away at the chaos dragon's health bar. I check the time on my menu. Five minutes have passed. The monster is down to three-fifths of its health bar. That seems like it would be a big deal, but there's only ten more minutes until the magnet spell ends. Then, we'll have to fight a pissed off, high-powered dragon who can fly, and Guy will be helpless the whole time.

Cait uses all her might to swing her great axe down on the same spot she's been attacking since she jumped on the chaos dragon. Broken pieces of the chaos dragon's scales look like onyx chips when they spray all over her. Dozens of little cuts across Cait's face bleed, and she roars in agony with her eyes sealed tight.

Fuck, she's been blinded. Heal Minor Wound or Major Wound? Heal Major Wound is going to zap more of my energy than Minor Wound. That's a big deal given that my spell casting energy is limited while I wear Cait's leather armor. Also, with an enemy this lethal, there are likely to be many wounds for me to heal. But Heal Minor Wound might not be enough and, well, it's *Cait*.

I lift my staff and shout, "Heal Major Wound!"

Usually, when I cast my first spell in a fight, I don't feel it that much. The energy drain creeps up on me. This time, it feels like someone's siphoning it out of me with a syringe because I never changed out of Cait's old leather armor.

Jesus Christ, I'm going to have to be really careful, especially if I have to use one of my Kiss of Life spells. I wonder if there's a time limit on that. Would I be able to take a long rest and then use that spell afterward? The idea of kissing a corpse that had been lying around for hours makes me want to gag.

Fortunately, my spell seems to have at least done its job. Cait blinks her eyes open again and returns to whacking the ever-loving fuck out of the dragon, this time with even more rage in every swing.

I check the time again. We have seven minutes left to get in as many hits as possible. Its health bar is somewhere between three-fifths and two-fifths. Except for Miko and me, these are level thirty plus players! Why aren't their attacks doing that much?

To everyone's surprise, the chaos dragon screams in a serpentine accent, "Ssssssmoke!"

Just as it had several times in the sky, the dragon's scales shift to black smoke. Before, I'd thought it was maybe a trick of the light or a new way to cover its mass. Now I know that's a sign that its entire body has turned to smoke. Joshua and Cait plummet. It's not a short drop. When they hit the ground, their bodies make a loud crack.

I panic, wanting to flee to them and check for serious injuries, but I can't afford to leave Guy alone. The two heroes get up on their shaky legs, and I cry out with relief. How the fuck do you attack a dragon made of smoke, though?

Six minutes left. Fortunately, just before it shifted, Sylvia and Alexander got in some well-placed shots. The sleeping head they'd worked on together now lays limp on the ground. It didn't even turn into smoke with the rest of the body, probably because dead parts of the body can't function like the living parts.

Its other two heads sing a duet of "Sssssmoke, smoke, smoke..." It repeats the word like a chant, probably because that's the only way to keep the form. The moment it stops, it will be solid again.

Physical attacks can't hurt a creature like this, it seems, at least not for long. If only Guy was awake, he'd probably have magic that could take on something with a spiritual form, or at least prevent it from using its magic.

Wait. The silence dome. Guy has used it twice now. I remember how upset Dan the mage was when he couldn't speak his spells. It rendered his magic useless.

Guy isn't awake to cast that spell right now, but maybe I could try it with his staff? It probably won't work, but it's worth a shot. I grab his staff, and it feels *wrong*. Not immoral or anything, more like I've got a new limb, and it doesn't fit my body. Still, I can feel its power thrumming through me. This definitely is an item that belongs with a much higher-level spellcaster.

I take a deep breath and hold the staff up high. "Silence," I shout, pulling up the word from the depths of my lungs hoping if I'm very loud, I'll succeed.

To my surprise, it does. The chaos dragon is voiceless now; its body solidifies. But this one spell has sucked every bit of energy from me. It belongs to a mage, and not just any mage, a level thirty mage. The world goes as black as the chaos dragon's scales, and the last thing I feel is my body falling to the ground.

Before I lose consciousness altogether, I hear that disembodied voice again.

"Cleric of Aphrodite: Level 5. Spell Gained: Sun Ray - the cleric calls on a ray of sunlight to dispel any magical darkness, including creatures made of darkness. Second Class Unlocked: Mage of Aphrodite: Level 1. Spell Gained: Silence - the mage creates a dome that prevents all enemy creatures and effects within it from making sound. Favor Gained: Shielded Slumber - When the player sleeps or loses consciousness, they cannot be targeted by an enemy. Stats Updated: Strength - 8, Dexterity - 14, Constitution - 15, Intelligence - 17, Wisdom - 18, Charisma - 16, Faith - 15."

CHAPTER THIRTY-TWO

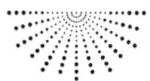

Have you ever been so cold it felt like you were burning? That's my current situation. Or am I actually on fire? I need to open my eyes. Why is this so hard? What's that stench? Is someone cooking?

My eyelids are like old, stiff leather, but I fight them open. The first thing I see is the black sky and the bright stars. Then I let my gaze lower to my body. The leather that Cait let me borrow is charred in places. My hands are red and welted, with blackened tips. I try to move my fingers, but they're numb. Frostbite? Or did I get so burnt, my nerve endings are dead?

Guy! He was right beside me when I passed out. If I'm burned, he may be, too. I roll onto my side. My back pop-pop-pops as I do, and I swear I can hear my muscles groaning from the effort. I'm in tears by the time I get into place. He's there, but I'm a little further away than he was when I was fighting, and it's hard to see in the dark.

I take a deep breath, knowing this is going to hurt like fuck. Using my numb hand, I pull myself forward inch by inch through the fresh snow. When I get close enough to touch him, I scream, not from the pain but from the sight of him. His clothes are little more than ribbons and ash. His skin is as black as onyx and as knotted as a tree root. The smell...It's him.

My stomach lurches, and I know I'm going to vomit from the realization that he smells like dinner. It's agony to move, but I refuse to puke on him or myself, so I force my body to a sitting position and turn my head away from him so that all my bile falls on the snow on the other side of my body.

Guy...I failed him. All I had to do was make sure no one hurt him. Instead, I tried my hand at DPS. I've never been content to be a support class. That's why I never played a healer, why I was upset that the game classed me as a cleric. But this isn't a game, not to us, and now it's killed someone that I...

I shake my head. I'm not even ready to think that, especially not now.

Kiss of Life! I have a spell that can bring him back. I wanted to save those up as long as possible, but this is Guy. If I have to, I'll use up all my kisses. But where are his lips? His face looks like a lump of bleeding coal. In order to save him, I have to press my mouth to *that*.

I swallow down another wave of nausea and lean forward. The closer I get, the more he smells like last night's barbecue. I tap the Kiss of Life spell on my menu and squeeze my eyes closed. Maybe if I can't see him, I can pretend my other senses don't work either. Thank God my lips have lost all sensation; I don't want to know what kissing a burnt corpse feels like.

My lips press against some unknown part of his face. I hope it's his lips, but I'm not sure it has to be his lips to work. It's a peck, hardly the romantic notion that played in my head when I gained the spell. There's nothing sweet or yearning about this moment, just grim desperation.

A croak rumbles from him, and I know he's alive, but for how long? He can't talk or even open his eyes like this. There's no telling if there's damage to his organs. Just the Kiss of Life spell sapped me, but I know I need to cast Heal Major Wound. So I do. As soon as I tap the spell on my menu, I watch Guy's flesh renew, and he sucks in a sharp breath which he coughs out at once.

Tears burn down my frostbitten cheeks as his eyes open. Relief floods me because he's back, but also, I grieve. Guy almost killed himself because he couldn't bear to look at his burn scars in the mirror anymore. He wants to stay in Peripeteia so he never has to go back to that again. My healing spell wasn't enough to heal him completely.

Guy sits up and grunts from the pain. Squinting, he looks around. "It's night. What happened?"

"We fought the chaos dragon, but it was going too slowly," I say. "None of the attacks did much damage at all. Then it turned to smoke by chanting a spell. I thought if I could silence it the way you did the Zeus mage..."

"You took my staff?" he asks.

I nod.

"Did it work?"

"Yes, but it took all my energy, and I passed out," I say. "I'm sorry."

Guy shakes his head. "Don't be sorry. That was smart. We could have died if he wasn't in physical form."

I lower my gaze, because I can't bear to see any grief in his eyes when I tell him the rest. "You did die. You...you burnt to death."

Guy gasps and presses his hand to his face. I still can't look at him, don't want to see the pain at his realization, but I can hear him cry.

"Not again," he whispers through a sob.

"I tried to heal you, but that's the best I could do," I say.

"You should have left me dead," he says.

I snap my head back up to look at his face, which is contorted by his genuine horror. He's barely recognizable, but those are still his beautiful brown eyes, and they're filled with unimaginable pain.

"No," I say. "I regret a lot of things I've done since the chaos dragon attacked, but I will *never* regret using one of my Kisses of Life to bring you back."

Guy shakes his head and snarls in disgust as he looks at his hand. "What life can I lead as some *creature*? I'm hideous! Disgusting!"

"Hideous? Disgusting? How can you say such things about yourself?" I ask.

"Look at me!" Guy tries to shout, but the last word comes out in shreds from his still raw throat.

"You want me to look at you?" I ask. "I can see more of you than you can."

I cup his face. My hands are too numb from the cold to feel it, but that doesn't matter. I need to touch him. And though my lips are also frostbitten, I leave a trail of kisses across his scarred face.

"You're beautiful," I whisper between kisses. "Sexy." I kiss either side of his mouth. Then I lean back a little so that he can see me say the truth I've been avoiding. "And I'm pretty sure I love you."

I tremble, not from the cold but from those words. It's like I've cast a spell that's far too high for my level. Is that what the truth is? The most powerful magic, older than time itself.

Guy stares at me for a moment and then sobs. I wipe away his tears and press my lips to his. I've kissed him so many times, many of them the best I've ever had. There's nothing passionate or skilled about this one, but I know it's the truest because of the magic that passes between us.

A song pulls from me, sweet and lonely. A plaintive melody unravels from him. They braid together, forming a duet, and all the sadness in their tender notes disappears as our heartbeats fall into the same rhythm.

When the kiss ends, we pull away, but our eyes stay locked in wonder. There's no denying what I admitted. Not with a song like that coming together. Like a scarf in the breeze, the notes drift away into the distance, leaving us in silence. That is until I hear a groan of pain.

"We're not alone," I whisper. I don't know if I'm relieved or scared.

Until then, I hadn't seen anyone. I was so focused on making sure the person next to me lived. Did my friends survive? Or is that a death rattle? Or is that the waking sounds of an enemy?

I start to get up so that I can see who it is, but pain radiates through me, and I wind up falling onto my back instead.

Guy leans over me, panic written on his wide eyes. "Lauren, did you heal me and not yourself?"

I nod.

"What were you thinking? Heal up!"

Casting Kiss of Life and Heal Major Wounds on Guy sapped a lot of my energy, and I may have to cast some pretty major spells before long. If I can just take the edge off the pain, though, I can make the rounds with my healing spells. So, I tap on Heal Minor Wounds on my menu.

I wince at the sting of sensation returning to my frostbitten parts. My body still feels broken, but I'm no longer in agony whenever I move a little. I call on my Strategy Under Duress. We may not be in a battle, but that doesn't mean we aren't fighting for our lives under difficult circumstances. If I want us all to live, we'll need more than my healing spells.

"I think our staffs rolled down the hill," I tell Guy. "Can you get them while I try to find who's hurt?"

"Of course," he says. "I'll also shed a little light on the situation."

Guy taps on his menu, and a faint span of light about fifty feet in circumference hovers in the sky above us. It gives a cold, fluorescent quality to the scene. Everybody on the ground looks even more grim than they would have in a natural light. Still, it gives me hope because one of those bodies is the chaos dragon, and beside it is Cait, rubbing at her head while sitting up.

I know I need to heal everyone, but I hobble toward her immediately. As I get closer, I see the dried blood on her various scabbed up wounds. I cry with relief because they must not be that bad.

Cait's eyes grow wide with a similar relief when I reach her. Wincing, she gets to her feet and takes me into her arms. "Thank God," she whispers against my temple. "I saw you lying on the ground, and I thought you'd died."

"I just ran out of energy," I tell her.

"Oh, Lauren..." Cait's tears slide from her eyes onto me and then she pulls back to soak me in. "I thought I lost you. I thought..." She stops and presses her lips against mine.

There's nothing tender about this kiss. It's hungry and desperate, like she doesn't know if we'll ever share another. Desire uncurls deep within me, and it's only the sound of Guy's approaching steps that helps me remember the terrible situation we're in. Our lips part, and I allow myself a moment to look at my fierce barbarian.

Cait's gaze shifts from me to beyond my shoulder where Guy stands. She smiles at him. "You survived," she says. "I thought with Lauren down, you might not." Then she squints. "Guy, what happened?"

I turn to see him with his hand covering part of his face, looking downward. Maybe he knows I still think he's beautiful but hates anyone else looking at him.

"He...he died," I tell Cait. "I guess the dragon..."

"Oh God, I remember," Cait whispers. "Right before I got in my last blow, the magnet spell ended, and the chaos dragon got high enough to breathe fire. I think Joshua was riding it when he took the last bit of its health bar."

Cait's eyes get wide. "Joshua! He must have fallen when the dragon did!"

"We'll find him," I say. "I'll do whatever I can to get everyone healed up, but we'll need our camp to get a long rest in."

"I'll call on it and set it up," Cait says. Then she takes another look at Guy. "I'm so glad you're alive." Without another word, she moves past me and wraps Guy in a hug. "I don't know what I'd do without you."

Guy leans into the embrace, crying while Cait rocks him. When they part, Cait wipes away his tears.

"I'm going to take care of the camp," Cait says. "You two do your thing and call out to me if you need my help."

I nod in response as she walks to an area that's far enough away from the dragon for comfort but close enough that the wounded won't have too much difficulty getting to it.

"I found our staffs," Guy says. "Looks like Miko grabbed them. I guess she saw we were passed out and thought she might need them."

"How does she look?" I ask.

"Like she's sleeping," he answers. "She must have used up all her energy, but I don't see any wounds."

"Well, that's a small blessing. Let's go look at the rest."

Joshua's bones are broken, but he's breathing. I cast Heal Major Wounds on him and feel like I might slump to the ground right then, but Guy positions me so that I can lean on him. After Cait carries a sleeping Miko to camp, she guides Joshua there as well.

Guy and I make our way to Sylvia. Like Miko, she's unharmed, simply asleep from her energy draining out. *Traitor.* I'm so tempted to leave her there to die from exposure, but I remind myself that Sylvia isn't at fault. She didn't make that chaos dragon attack us, and she's as much a victim as the rest of us. The eidola is to blame. *Zeus* is to blame.

I'm tired of playing along like it's not trying to get us all killed, though.

"Let's get her to camp," I say when Cait joins us. "But we're tying her up. I don't trust her. When she wakes up, she'll have a lot to answer for."

CHAPTER THIRTY-THREE

W e've spent two nights in Thrace while Ismarus is within a day's hike. I'm *so* close to completing this big quest for Aphrodite, but Zeus is throwing everything he can at me. At this point, I would turn off my ability to break the game if I could, despite how pleased Aphrodite seems to be.

Usually, Sylvia makes breakfast, but she's still asleep, and we're afraid to untie her. So Miko is trying her hand at cooking but failing spectacularly. I consider taking over, but Joshua beats me to it. Apparently, he's a pro at toast in a pan.

Miko watches Joshua with an appreciation that I've noticed growing more and more every day. It's almost comical, someone so serious and standoffish as Miko getting along so well with a goofy horndog like Joshua. Yet, they make sense, too. They balance each other. I can't help but matchmake them in my head, even if I've only seen friendliness and respect between the two of them.

Aphrodite is really making her impact on me. Love, love, everywhere. A few weeks ago, I would have cringed at who I've become. Love? *Really?* Ew.

Yet I can't stop smiling as I watch Cait and Guy walk toward the chaos dragon. They're chatting and laughing, like they have been all morning. There's almost a flirtatious element in their postures, but I can't tell how deep that runs. We should feel exhausted, defeated. Guy died, after all. I had to use up my first Kiss of Life to bring him back.

In addition to that, Sylvia's been compromised. Our group mom getting possessed isn't a great morale booster. I hope there's something we can do to fix that, otherwise we'll have to leave her behind the way we did with Tara. God, if we'd known about the eidola leaving her, she would be with us now. However, she's using this as an opportunity to spy for us, and we can use all the help we can get.

Aside from the beautiful moments I shared with Cait and Guy, there's only one good thing that's happened. The long rest healed what I wasn't able to, and Guy looks like he did before the chaos dragon attacked. I would love him even if he was permanently scarred from head to toe, but I know how much it would hurt him if he had to live with the stares he used to get in the real world.

"What are they hoping to get from that dead dragon?" Miko asks as she grabs the first piece of toast Joshua made.

"They're wondering if there's any magic in the scales that made the dragon turn to smoke," I say. "I don't think they'll find anything, though. It was chanting a smoke spell, which stopped working once I silenced it."

"Why did you do that?" Joshua asks. "You had to have known that it would wipe you out."

"We only had a few minutes left to kill it," I answer. "Besides, you were right up there clobbering away at it when you're a *bard*."

"A *combat* bard!" Joshua corrects as he hands me a piece of toast. "My specialty is to entertain and *annihilate*."

"Annihilate" is a strong word for what he's spec'd for, but I'll let him have it. He did kick ass last night, even with all the odds stacked against him. I hate to admit it, but the person who I judged as a perverted loser in the beginning is actually a brave and loyal person. Interesting that Miko, the person slowest to trust anyone, saw who he really is right away.

The three of us are eating when I hear a groan coming from the tent. Sylvia's awake. Great.

I wish Cait and Guy were here with us eating breakfast. Having their support while I do what I need to would make a world of difference. Maybe I can finish eating my toast first. Interrogation will probably be easier on a full stomach.

"What's going on? Why am I tied up?" Sylvia says. Being in the tent has muffled her voice, but she's loud enough that I can't pretend I didn't hear her.

Joshua and Miko give me a questioning look. They want to know what I'll decide. Earlier this morning, I brought them up to date on the troubling revelation. It broke Joshua's heart but strangely softened Miko. Perhaps it's easier for her to deal with a possessed party member than one that would gladly betray her with no supernatural interference.

I set my toast on my plate and get up. Miko grabs me by the wrist.

"Maybe you should let me do it," she says with an empathetic expression. "She knows you've got a big heart, but I'm a bitch. She'll believe threats easier coming from me."

She's right. Sylvia will play on my sympathies. I'm the one who made friends with Arachne's spider children and brought an empusa into our little group. Would an eidola prey upon that?

Nodding, I say, "Yeah, let's do that."

Joshua gets up and walks into the tent before I'm even done with that sentence. Maybe he thinks Sylvia might overpower me because of my pitiful strength score. I'm counting on her underestimating me, though. I'm a Cleric of Aphrodite, not a mastermind. Except I'm *also* a mage now, and my intelligence score is quite high, but she doesn't have to know that.

Actually, I haven't told anyone about the level up yet. We've been busy with important matters, and I don't want them giving anything away on accident. That eidola could have a direct connection with Zeus, and he'll want to know any of my strengths he'll need to overcome. Not that a low-level secondary class is a high hurdle to jump. He's throwing monsters at us that not even veteran players can handle with any ease.

Joshua drags Sylvia out to the campfire. Her eyes are wide with terror and confusion. When she's face-to-face with Miko, it's even more exaggerated. Our druid still has all the intimidation of a warlock.

"What's going on?" she asks again and then turns her pleading eyes to me.

I cross my arms. She's not getting anything from me.

"Why don't you tell *us*?" Miko responds.

274

"Wh-what do you mean?" Sylvia turns to Joshua now. "Why are you treating me this way? I've always taken care of you, haven't I?"

"*Sylvia* has always taken care of me," Joshua answers. "You're an entirely different story."

"You've all gone crazy," she whispers, tears rolling down her cheeks. The innocence in her big brown eyes is so convincing. I want to believe her. It would be such a relief if we were wrong. But it's hard to ignore the smirk she's trying to suppress.

"There's something that's seemed odd to me since our battle with the Zeus worshippers," Miko says. "When I met you, there was a wolf by your side. Quite a loyal animal. Joshua told me you found him on your first day as a puppy, and he's been at your beck and call ever since. Yet, I haven't seen him since we were in Dardanus. Surely, he'd want to protect his friend."

"Maybe the Zeus worshippers did something to him," Sylvia says.

"You don't seem too heartbroken over that," Miko says.

"Of course I am!" Sylvia says.

"Liar," I mutter, causing her to face me.

"Don't tell me you believe all this, Lauren." Sylvia's tone is so pitiful. She's definitely trying to prey on my kindness.

"Who do you think was the first to know you're an eidola possessing my *real* friend?" I ask in response.

Her plaintive expression drops to a scowl so intense that I can feel the hatred rolling off it. This isn't just a mission from Zeus for her. She actually wants me dead.

"If you kill your friend, I won't die," she says.

"Then we'll have to find some other way to get rid of you," Miko responds.

Sylvia scoffs. "Good luck. Even if you manage that impossibility, Zeus will just send more monsters after you."

At that moment, Cait and Guy return. They seemed so pleasant when they left, but now their features twist in anger. They heard enough as they approached.

"You *bitch*," Cait hisses.

As one, the group gasps. Even Sylvia.

"You...you just cursed." Joshua squints at her. "Are you possessed, too?"

Cait crosses her arms. "It's the best word for what she is. And maybe I'm learning that some rules don't make much sense." She drops her crossed arms so that she can lift Sylvia by the ropes binding her and growl in her face. "For example, I'll do *anything* to protect my friends, including torturing you."

I say nothing, but I doubt there's a way to hurt or kill an eidola. Then I see the momentary lapse in Sylvia's expression, one that isn't an act. She's *scared* of Cait. If we can't hurt her, then she should smile or laugh.

"You know," Miko says, "I may not have the powers of a warlock anymore or have access to Hekate, but that doesn't mean all the knowledge she gave me is gone." Sylvia flinches, and Miko laughs. "Oh yeah, gotcha there, didn't I?" Miko turns her attention to Cait. "You won't be able to beat the eidola up. Just like the chaos dragon, it's a creature of magical darkness. We need to find a spellcaster with a light spell. That would basically eviscerate the eidola."

A light spell? Often, the spells I receive from Aphrodite come after I need them. When I received the Sun Ray spell, I assumed it had to do with the chaos dragon. Maybe it did, but Aphrodite *had* to know about the eidola possessing Sylvia. She must have wanted me to have it for this purpose.

"I leveled up," I say, causing everyone to look at me. "I also got a secondary class as a mage. That got me a new spell called Sun Ray. It can dispel any magical darkness, including creatures made from it."

Cait, Guy, and Joshua stare at me with mouths agape. Sylvia squirms away from me closer to Miko, seeing me as more of a threat now. And Miko? She's smiling wide. It's unnerving, a reminder of who she used to be before we saved her.

Miko turns to Sylvia. "Do you like being alive, little eidola? Would you like the chance to leave this body without harm?"

Sylvia nods frantically.

"Then, it's probably in your best interest to tell us everything you know about what Zeus wants with us."

THE EIDOLA WEARING SYLVIA'S FACE SPILLS THE BEANS A LOT MORE easily than I thought she would. You'd think someone who serves Zeus would show at least a second of hesitation before divulging the secrets kept by the King of Gods. However, the demon laid it all out there, and what everything boiled down to was that Zeus was losing power over the game.

It seems he made a deal to play a game with the other gods about whose followers could get them the right offering first. Only, he didn't know until recently that the others had worked with the developers to make the winner of that game the new ruler of Olympus. Since any deal a god makes is binding, he's terrified of losing his crown, and he's pretty sure Aphrodite is his biggest threat.

Why? Well, her little cleric is breaking the game with almost no effort. There's nothing special about me as far as anyone can tell. I'm not some chosen one that's been prophesied. So, obviously, Aphrodite must have gifted me with some unknown power. Except, why wouldn't she have done that for one of her veteran players? Or all of us? An army of game breakers would be a terrifying and unstoppable force.

I'm *not* special, not like that. I'm just like any other player who landed here. No one knows why I'm able to do it, and it's not like I woke up one day and decided I would break the game. It's unlikely that Aphrodite granted me some favor I'm not aware of that unravels coding. If that was the case, I don't think she would have been so pleasantly surprised when I helped Arachne's children and their villager neighbors.

There have been hundreds of questions about this place swimming in my head since I got here. Every day, I do my best to ignore them so I can focus on finding the right offering and getting home to Mom. But what if that's been a mistake? Solving these mysteries might help me survive Zeus's attacks or even find the right offering for Aphrodite. She said I was the closest anyone in the game has ever been, but the only thing that separates me from the other players is that the NPCs around me act like real people now.

As we take down our camp, Alexander broods on the hill, his gaze on the middle distance. He's pulled out some surprises, for sure. He stayed with us despite his programming to leave when we reached a certain point in our main quest line. He brought me food, called me Lauren. Then there was the fucking Benelli M4 Super 90 shotgun. Yeah, he's changed a lot. Sometimes, I wonder if Aphrodite recoded him.

That thought intrigues me. If she can recode, the other gods probably can, too. Are they the real programmers? Wouldn't that be interesting? You create a fantasy RPG and incorporate enough elements from Greek mythology so that you can comfortably settle into a godlike role, and the players never question that they should do whatever you want. Not sure why they would want to live like that, but it makes more sense than all the other ideas that float through my brain.

I walk to Alexander's side and touch his arm to get his attention. "Hey, it's time to go," I tell him.

Alexander turns to me, his haunted eyes even darker than usual. "There will be many dangers in Ismarus."

"Yeah, well, that seems to be the case everywhere we go." I point at the chaos dragon's corpse, which is now missing so many scales that we've left yards of bare skin. "If we can take that thing down, I think we might have a chance in the city."

He shakes his head. "Danger doesn't always attack. Sometimes it comes in a drink or an embrace. It can shine in a friend's eyes and offer comfort at night."

"Yes, we're aware of the eidola," I say.

"But you cannot predict the danger that doesn't know itself," he says in an ominous tone.

"Well, that's vague and unnerving, but I still have a quest to do for Aphrodite," I tell him and grab his arm to pull him toward the group. "Let's go talk to Khione."

Alexander shirks out of my grip. "You need to do all the other Ismarus quests first."

"Dude, we don't have time," I say, my voice now clipped with irritation. "Zeus is trying everything he can to kill me. The only chance I might have to survive is to get this done for Aphrodite."

"That won't save you," he says. "You *need* to complete the other quests. You *need* to help Orpheus."

"Oh my fucking God," I whisper as I bury my fingers into my forelock and try not to pull all the hair out. "Okay, *you* try telling everyone that. I'm sure they'll all be on board with doing another quest when Zeus is sending actual fucking chaos dragons after us."

Alexander marches over to the rest of the party. Of course, he took me literally. That's what an NPC does. His coding may be different, with way more advanced AI, but he can't understand that I'm telling him there's no chance in hell we're doing the Orpheus quest, because my statement was too nuanced. I chase after him.

"Hey, Alexander," Guy says when the NPC approaches him. "Ready to head out?"

"You must complete the Orpheus quest and all the other Ismarus quests if you can," Alexander says, ignoring Guy's question.

"Afraid we can't do that yet," Guy responds. "We have a bit of a tight deadline for Lauren to talk to Khione."

"She will fail if she does that now," Alexander insists.

Cait comes to Guy's side and crosses her arms. "Yeah, well, she'll *die* if we don't rush things, so..."

"You're wrong," Guy says. "Aphrodite won't let her die. Pretty sure Lauren is her chosen."

Miko finishes packing up and walks over. Rolling her eyes, she says, "Are you fucking kidding me? Her chosen? I knew this game was missing some overdone trope."

Joshua holds up a hand and looks at the party with an uncharacteristically serious expression. "No, let's hear him out. Being chosen doesn't mean she's some prophesied hero. We were all *chosen*, after all." He turns back to Alexander. "What about the rest of us?"

Alexander shakes his head. "The rules of the game prevent her from aiding or harming anyone other than her players."

I cock my head to the side. "So, you're aware this is a game? Do you also understand your part in it?"

"I'm a player, as well," he answers.

Did I really expect him to understand he's just a string of code? Of course, he thinks he's one of us.

"Forget about this being a game for a moment," Miko says. "If Aphrodite can't help or harm other players, then how come Zeus can?"

Sylvia, or rather the eidola possessing Sylvia, laughs darkly. She's still bound and sitting where we interrogated her. "You can do anything you want when you're the King of Gods," she says. "He holds so much power that he could snap his fingers, and you'd all die."

"Okay, well if Mr. Thanos can do that, why hasn't he?" Cait asks. "Why go through all this trouble?"

The eidola tilts Sylvia's head. "Like I said, he wants to know what

Aphrodite is up to. Unlike you pawns, she's a god and knows enough to hurt him."

"You must finish the other quests," Alexander insists again. "If you don't, you will fail, and Aphrodite may not be able to protect you."

Once again, I feel I'm a burden to my group. If they weren't with me, they wouldn't be targets. Can Aphrodite truly prevent me from dying, no matter what? I think about when I woke up next to Guy. He'd been dead, charred to a crisp. Except for passing out and experiencing some frostbite, I was perfectly fine. I was close enough to Guy that the dragon flames should have killed me, too.

Going alone would be better for everyone. There's no reason to protect me because I can't die. They should worry about getting their own offerings.

Guy and Cait stare in silence at Alexander. They're almost leaning against each other, finding comfort in their friendship. Well, maybe *more* than friendship by the sounds of their conversation this morning. I love them. I'm sure they'd miss me, but they would still have each other. And most importantly, they'd be *alive*.

"Fine," Cait says. "We'll do the dumb quests." She turns a pointed gaze at me. "And you! I can see the gears turning in your head. You better not be thinking again about ditching the party."

I hold up my hands in surrender. "I'm not leaving."

Not yet, anyway. Not while they expect it.

We'll get the Orpheus quest done, maybe even the other quests. But when it's time to talk to Khione, I'll slip away and go alone. Whatever Aphrodite's up to, it scares Zeus. If I were him, I'd kill me and any witnesses as soon as I told Khione she needs to claim her son. I don't know why this is so important, but I'm taking it seriously, and I won't let my friends die.

CHAPTER THIRTY-FOUR

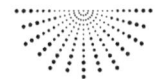

A fter what seems like a century, we finally arrive at Ismarus. So far, this is the biggest town we've encountered on this trip. That makes sense given that the game chose it as the capital of Thrace.

There's a line of NPCs and players at the gate, waiting to be let in. The city guards are interviewing each person, looking for any threats, but they're also judging whether each person has anything to offer Ismarus in return for its protection from the wilderness. All the NPCs look pretty desperate to get on the other side of the gate, and I don't have to wonder why for long when I overhear a conversation behind me.

"Did you see the chaos dragon?" a man's voice whispers. "I'm not sure what happened to it, but I would rather let my farm fall apart than risk becoming its prey."

"I saw it," a woman answers. "I was sweeping the front porch like I do every single day, no matter how clean it is. Then the dragon showed up, and I...I don't know how to say it. It felt like I woke up and then realized nightmares don't just exist in my sleep."

Looks like I broke some of these NPCs without even meeting them. This is a big city, and the streets will be crowded with many more of them possibly having epiphanies like this. God, I wish I had my headphones.

Some players a little ahead of us are arguing with the guards.

"What do you mean I'm too far behind in the main quest line?" asks a woman wearing first-level plate armor. "We've tried to do every quest, but they're all *broken!*"

I'm not sure if any of the players here are like the Zeus worshippers and would know me on sight, but I pull at the hood on my cloak, hoping it will cover enough of my face to hide my identity.

Guy leans close and whispers, "Turn off your title."

Oh, shit, that's right. I've gotten so used to everyone having a title over their heads that I don't even notice them anymore. If I'm lucky, no one will see mine before I turn mine off.

"Cleric of Aphrodite?" a man's voice says from some point behind me just as I'm bringing up my menu. Guess I'm not so lucky today.

I turn to look at him. He's a big guy, probably because he chose to be an orc. His tusks kind of remind me of the ones Cetus had, except they're small enough to fit in a normal-sized mouth, and they're not covered in drool.

"You're not *that* Cleric of Aphrodite, are you?" he asks. His furrowed brows and squinting eyes could be the angry mask most orcs wear, or he could be really pissed at me. Or both. I'm betting on both.

While I consider whether I should lie and say it's a coincidence, I see a familiar arm waving at me from far behind the orc player. Fuck, it's Dolius. Maybe I can pretend like I don't notice him, and no one—

"Cleric!" he cries out, waving and smiling like I'm a good friend he's finally getting to see again after years apart. "Lauren!"

Oh, great. He said my fucking name. An *NPC* said my goddamn name.

"I knew it!" the orc shouts.

Fuck, fuck, fuck.

Dolius comes rushing toward me. He was such an all-business type in Thebe, but now he's bubbly. Love really changes people. My attention ping-pongs from the orc to Dolius on repeat, trying to gauge whether I should deal with the immediate threat the player brings or the possibility that my merchant friend could make this situation a whole lot worse.

Maybe if I break off the conversation with Dolius now, I can focus on charming the orc.

"Um, fuck," I say, scrambling for the best way to get my friend to go back to his spot in the line for now. "Shit. Look, I can't really—"

The orc makes a dash at me, and I fumble with the staff on my back. I've never had trouble getting this thing off, except for now when I desperately need to. It's too late. He's almost here. I squeeze my eyes tight and hope that one of my friends is prepared for this encounter.

To my shock, instead of beating my face in, the orc puts his arms around me. Is this a *hug*? He's rocking me back and forth like you would with a big bear hug. It feels like...like...the way *Doug* used to hug me.

"I wondered if it was you when I heard there was some Cleric of Aphrodite named Lauren," he whispers. "But that could have been just a coincidence. Then someone described how you look, and it sounded like you. But as an elf, you look different enough that I couldn't be sure. Not until you spoke, and no one swears as much as you! It's *you!* It's really *you!*"

"Lauren," Guy says from over my shoulder. "Do you know this person?"

"Apparently," I say.

The orc finally lets go and laughs at me. "I guess I look pretty different, huh? You must know who I am, though."

I don't want to know, but I'm pretty sure I do. That hug is much too familiar and, despite the way the tusks make him lisp, he sounds a lot like Doug.

With a sigh, I say, "Of course I do, Doug."

Guy comes to my side. I can see now that he's crossing his arms, and there's a stern expression on his face. "Doug?"

Cait comes to my other side. "*That* Doug?" she asks, looking at me.

"Yeah," I answer them both.

"She talked about me?" Doug asks.

"A little," Guy answers. He weaves his fingers with mine and rubs the back of my hand with his thumb.

Cait does the same with my other hand. "Honestly, not much. Just mentioned she had an ex named Doug, but it didn't seem that important to her."

Do they think they need to protect me from Doug? He's like a golden retriever, a dumb one who never figured out how to do anything useful.

I realize I don't have any ill will against him. Sure, I was mad at him in the real world, but I've barely thought about him since we started our journey to Thebe. If I really think about it, I can admit we'd been breaking up for years. We pulled that Band-Aid off slowly, but it's still off.

I squeeze their hands, then slip away from their grasps. "It's good to see you, Doug," I say, extending one of my hands to shake his.

Doug seems confused by my formality, but he shakes my hand all the same. "Is...is everything okay?"

The answer to that is "No, nothing's okay," but he won't understand. He just wants to know if he's in trouble.

"We're good," I say. "They're just protective of me, and, well...Guy, Cait, this is my ex, Doug. Doug, this is my boyfriend and girlfriend."

If Doug was confused by my handshake, he's gobsmacked now. "Your *what?*" he asks.

I open my mouth to explain, then Dolius interjects in a voice so loud that I'm sure everyone can hear him, "You're together? Oh, how wonderful! The Cleric of Aphrodite finds her own love! And she's been doubly blessed!"

"Fuck me," I whisper, knowing how much attention he's probably brought upon me. I get the staff off my back and look at Doug. "You may want to run. Pretty sure you don't want to get in the middle of whatever smackdown the other players are going to bring."

"Why would they—?" Doug starts, only to be interrupted by several outcries of rage.

Cait readies her great axe, and Guy grabs his staff. Joshua grips his short sword, and Miko brings up her menu. Goddamn it, we were *so* close to getting her druid gear.

Players from all over the line run at us with their weapons at the ready. They're much lower-level than my friends, but there are also easily over twenty of these people.

Doug pulls a great sword out of its sheath. "You think I'd run from this? I'm an orc with a lifetime of gaming under my belt!"

Cait gets in front of me, while Guy casts a spell that creates a sparkly fog between us and the players heading our way. Joshua and Miko stand behind me, with Sylvia at their side. Because we're not sure we can kill the eidola without hurting Sylvia, she's still bound and unable to fight. However, Miko summons a wind elemental, and Joshua hurls out sick burns.

Really, this game has a mockery spell, and now's the first time he's using it?

"Was it your mother or father that gave you those ugly frog genes?" he asks.

The painful groan coming from the attackers behind me tells me that this insult was enough to knock down that person's health bar a little.

"Untie me!" Sylvia calls out. "You need me in this fight!"

"Not a chance!" Miko responds.

While Miko's elemental splits in two, Alexander whips out his shotgun.

"Whoa, whoa!" I say. "Don't get trigger-happy! I'd like to make this fight nonlethal if possible."

"Emphasis on *if possible*," Cait says as she kicks a player to the ground. "I learned that the hard way."

The memory of Cait dying tightens my chest. We took down a chaos dragon. Surely, she can survive this. Right?

A few players pass through the sparkly fog, looking dazed as they stumble toward us. Whatever spell that was, I sure wish Guy had tried it out much earlier. Maybe it's a really high-level one and zaps too much of his energy. Hopefully, I won't have to guard him as he sleeps during this fight.

One by one, they come at us. Some are slow and clumsy, some are fast and tricky, and some are downright terrifying. No matter how they approach us, though, we knock them back too easily, and they grow tired quickly. How low-level are they if I'm a level five and doing okay still?

Within a few minutes, our attackers are either passed out or have given up altogether. They sit on the ground, their heads bent downward in both defeat and exhaustion. I feel sorry for them. Of course, they think I'm their enemy. They're trying to survive, to get back to their lives, and they can't.

Because of me.

Most of them are wearing the armor and gear that's for sale in the starting village. If the quests are broken, they may not be getting paid, or they may not qualify for updated items. Fuck, no wonder they're all desperate.

"It's not fair," I say to no one in particular.

"What isn't?" Doug asks, putting his sword back in its sheath.

"It's not fair that we're stuck with the choice between NPCs having real lives and players getting the XP they need to play the game the right way," I answer.

"Why choose?" Doug asks.

Why choose? I check my quest log. It's been a while since I did so. I've been so preoccupied with making sure no one died, I haven't checked on my progress. Hell, even if a notification pinged, I doubt it would even have registered.

"Why Choose?" is still on my quest log. I assumed that because Guy, Cait, and I were together now, I'd completed that quest. Could it be that it has nothing to do with love? Am I supposed to help the players as well as the NPCs?

"Doug, why aren't you mad at me?" I ask him.

"I think we both saw our breakup coming for a long time," he answers. "But we've always been friends, and I don't want to give that up."

"That's really sweet, but that's not what I mean," I say. "All the other players are pissed because I keep accidentally breaking the quests, and they're not getting any XP."

"That's because they're not grinding," Doug says. "When I got to Sardis and there wasn't a giant web for me to get rid of, I realized I needed to find another way to level up. So I went into the forest and killed a bunch of monsters."

Cait's eyes widen with realization. "Oh my God, of course. Everyone's so focused on figuring out their offerings that no one goes off the beaten path."

"But none of them can get into Ismarus unless they've made progress with the main quest line," I point out.

"Seems like you need to break some guard coding, then," Guy says with a wicked grin.

"Smart thinking!" Cait tells him, and they high five.

"Maybe a charm spell?" I ask. "At least so I can convince them to relax the rules a little."

"Can't hurt to try," Doug says.

I leave our spot in line and approach the guards while my friends hold my place.

One guard holds up his hand to stop me. "No cutting."

I lift my staff and say, "Charm" in a syrupy sweet voice.

The guard's eyes turn pink, and his head bobs like he's dizzy.

"You're feeling generous today," I say. "Ismarus needs more people, *new* people. It needs them from every walk of life and every level. You want to take in everyone from the line."

The guard nods. "Yes, we need all of them."

He waves in the NPCs standing in front of him, and they rush in like they expect him to change his mind.

"What are you doing?" another guard hisses at him. "We have to vet everyone!"

The charmed guard shrugs in return. "We need all of them."

"Why?" the other guard asks.

The charmed guard turns to me so that I can supply the answer.

"Because of the chaos dragon, of course," I say and decide to exaggerate. "I saw *three* of them on my way here. Ismarus will need as many people as possible to defend the city from an attack."

The other guard makes a choking sound and stutters out, "Th-three?"

"Yes," I lie.

"Everyone in!" the other guard calls out. "One by one in an orderly line. No pushing or running but make it quick!"

A few of the weary players approach me.

"Did you just break the guards?" a halfling player asks me, her eyes full of hope.

"Yeah, they shouldn't be any trouble now," I tell her. "I'm sorry the quests are all breaking. It's an accident, but my orc friend over there says he knows a way people can still level up."

I point at Doug, and he waves in response.

"He does?" the halfling asks.

"If you spread the word, maybe we can all meet somewhere tomorrow after everyone's rested and figure out a solution," I say.

The halfling beams. "Yes! Where!"

"Good question." I turn to the charmed guard. "Where's a good place for a lot of people to have a meeting?"

"The courtyard next to the temple," he answers. "There's a podium between the fountains."

I turn back to the halfling. "Did you hear that? Let's say noon tomorrow?"

She nods. "I'll let everyone in my group know to tell all the others."

Why choose? It doesn't have to be one or the other. Freedom is for the taking—players and NPCs alike.

A notification pings, and I check my quest log. "Why Choose?" is scratched out, replaced with "Meet With Players."

CHAPTER THIRTY-FIVE

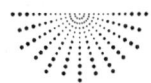

They didn't have inns in the other towns I've been to. For that reason, and because we're not made out of money, we always slept in our camp. But Ismarus has plenty of inns, and getting in and out of the city is a real pain in the ass. Even with the guards happy to let anyone in that asks politely, going through that mess again is the last thing we want.

So, we get two rooms: Miko, Joshua, and Sylvia in one room, Cait, Guy, and me in the other. I would be more excited about sharing a bed with my boyfriend and girlfriend tonight if Doug hadn't somehow secured the room next to ours.

There isn't much space in our room. There's a full-size bed in the middle. In the far right corner, there's a table big enough for the two chairs pushed into it. As far as a bathroom? This isn't like some American hotel. No, there's a shared bathroom downstairs, and it doesn't smell all that great.

I let out a long, exasperated groan as I set my staff on top of the table and plop down face first onto the bed. Warm hands stroke my back.

"It's going to be okay," Guy whispers. "Tomorrow we may wind up with a lot of allies to get through all this."

I unbury my nose from the mattress and turn to peek at him from the corner of my eye. "I'm not stressed about *that*," I say. "It's Doug."

Cait laughs and sits down next to me. "His personality is so wrong for you. How did you two wind up together?"

"We played an MMO together in high school," I answer, "and we never questioned whether we worked as a couple. Well, until we broke up."

Guy lies on his back on the other side of me. "High school? Wow, that's a long time."

"Yeah, too long," I say. "It took me eleven years to realize we were better as friends."

Cait lies down beside me. This prompts me to flip over so that I don't have to scrape my nose against the bed every time I want to look at one of them.

Guy and Cait reach for each other's hands over my stomach. They share a knowing glance.

"You two seem awfully chummy lately," I say.

"We've been spending time alone together talking," Cait says. "Some things started to make sense."

"Continue," I say.

"Guy was right before. I was jealous," she says. "Of you, of him. I-I wanted to be with him before you arrived. I thought maybe he'd want to settle down some day and have something real with me. He was the first person I've wanted to date. And, well, I was tired of being a virgin. I figured if I might be stuck here for the rest of my life...Anyway, then you came along, and he was ready to be with you from the start."

"Oh," I say, lowering my gaze. "That's why you didn't want us dating."

"Not just because of that," she continues. "I understood why he wanted to be with you because when we all sat down to discuss you joining us, I felt something *new* looking at you that I've never felt with a real person before. While I've been crushing on Guy from day one, I only have a little physical attraction to him. But you were sitting there with only a bra to cover your upper half, and, well...I wanted you."

"So, that was you!" I exclaim. "My first Aphrodite quest was to Inspire Lust, and before I could try, it was scratched off. All this time I thought it was Guy."

Guy laughs. "As hot as you are and as much as I love touching you, I was more attracted to you as a person at that point. I was trying to be a gentleman and purposefully didn't look at your breasts. After that, though? No comment."

"I was definitely the person you were turning on," Cait says. "It scared me. My family told me some really horrible things about women who want women. I grew up believing they were right about everything. I felt *guilty* just playing video games. But Guy convinced me that love is love, and..." Cait's fierce eyes grow soft as she drinks me in. "I love you, Lauren."

The words reach into my heart and pull at something deep within, something that's been hungry for love all this time. Like it did with Guy, when Cait presses her lips to mine, a magical duet forms between us. It's different from the one I shared with Guy. While the previous one was like a sweet sigh, this one is like a thrumming beat.

When our lips part, we gaze at each other in wonder. There's no question that we love each other. Our magic together is palpable.

Before our duet can fade away, Guy kisses me on the neck. I gasp in bliss. His plaintive melody joins our duet, creating a perfect trio. The music sweeps me up into heaven, and I ache for more, but reality hits home hard when I hear Doug burping from his room.

Jesus, these walls are thin.

I sigh, knowing I'll be sexually frustrated all night.

"What's wrong?" Cait asks.

"I want us together, you know?" I point at the wall we share with Doug. "But..."

Guy smiles and gets up from bed to grab his staff. "Silence," he says, and I can no longer hear our song. In fact, I can't hear anything at all, apart from Cait and Guy, since the spell doesn't silence party members.

"Silence," he says again. He winks and nods toward Doug's room. "I cast it on his room, too. He won't be able to hear us, and we won't be able to hear him."

After leaving his staff leaning in the room's corner, Guy takes off his robe. It's the first time I've seen his torso. Because he's always wearing loose clothing, I never knew what to expect. He could've been rail thin or had a six-pack. I'm pleasantly surprised to see he's got a slight dad bod.

I know many people would love a partner with a movie star's honed appearance, but I've always been a fan of *real* bodies. Guy's body reminds me he's human, that we're not just part of a game. I want to touch him *everywhere.*

Cait sits up next to me and takes off her top. I've seen her in the nude before, back when we went to the bathhouse together. Her lean frame and toned arms amazed me then, but now that I'm closer, I can see every freckle and the way her nipples on her small, perky breasts are such a light pink that they're barely darker than her pale skin.

"Are you sure?" I ask her. "I mean it's your first time, and your par—"

Cait presses a finger to my mouth. "Like I said, Guy and I did a lot of talking, and I've realized so much of what I thought I *should* want isn't right for me. We discussed what could happen when we all had time alone together. *This* is what I really want."

Guy climbs into the bed behind me, now fully undressed. He kisses along my shoulder until he gets to that glorious spot on my neck he knows stirs me up.

"Do you want this?"

"Oh God, yes," I whisper.

"Do you, Cait?" he asks.

Cait bites her bottom lip. "Can I just kiss Lauren for a while first?"

Guy gives her a wicked grin. "Of course."

The thought of making love to Guy while kissing Cait has me pooling with desire. I'm ready to shred apart my chiton if it starts things even a second sooner. I cup her cheek and kiss her. Then I kiss Guy. They also kiss, with as much love as they share with me.

Guy turns his lustful gaze to me. "Let's get these clothes off you. Immediately."

Holy fuck! This is actually happening!

I pull my clothes off as fast as possible and toss them across the room before lying down between them.

"Fuck," Guy whispers as his eyes swallow me up.

Cait doesn't chastise him for swearing, probably because she's too busy kissing my jaw.

Guy strokes Cait's back at the same time he weaves his fingers with mine. "We'll take this slow. Only do what you feel comfortable with. If it's too much at any point, tell us. There's no judgment."

"I'll be fine," Cait says.

"I'm talking to both of you," Guy says. "I'm a Mage of Dionysus. Half my side quests involved group sex with other followers. I plan to use everything I know to make this a magical night for the two women I love."

The two women I love.

I'd been so worried that I would break someone's heart by loving them both. Instead, we know love threefold with each other.

Our first time is magical. As though we've always done this, our bodies work together to show our love with every touch and taste. I'd thought that group sex might be too much for Cait's first time, but with Guy's directions, she seems like a natural. It's like she's been saving herself for the two of us because nothing less would have been good enough for my Viking queen's first time.

There's nothing forced about it; it's actually sweet. Our kisses are promises; our caresses are worship. When Guy puts his head between my legs, it's after he's made sure both Cait and I are comfortable with it, and then he pulls out every trick in the book. His sole focus becomes giving me an orgasm while Cait explores my body with light touches and kisses.

I want to touch her back, but I'm so afraid of making this too much for her that I hold back. She's never done anything before, and now suddenly she's in a threesome. And then, she does something unexpected.

Just as Guy's fingers hook inside me, making me moan as he brings me close to the crest, Cait whispers, "Good girl." I'm not sure she meant for me to hear it, but that's all it takes to rip a scream of pleasure from me as I have probably the best orgasm of my life.

That's when everything changes. Her feather-light kisses deepen as I come down from my high and she asks, "I want to watch him move inside you."

Well, fuck. How can I say no to that?

"What about you?" I ask.

"Touch me here." She takes my hand and places it on her breast. "While I, um..."

That's when I realize, she can't say it. She can't say she wants to watch him fuck me and that she'd like me to play with her breast while she rubs her clit. She can *do* these things but is too shy to say it out loud.

That makes this even more special. She's braving a past riddled with guilt because she *wants* this that much.

"While you finger yourself?" I ask.

Cait nods.

"I'd love that," I say as I tease the nipple on her small, perky breast. "I'll touch wherever you want me to touch. Just name it, and my hands will be there. If it feels good, say 'yes.' If it doesn't, say 'no.' If you want to stop at any time, just say 'stop.'"

Relief loosens Cait's features. I've taken away the burden of her demanding things of me. While I think she may turn out to be a natural Domme later, she's still a virgin, and she feels self-conscious about it right now.

When Cait lowers her hand between her legs, Guy slowly pushes himself inside of me, and I almost come apart right then. He hisses with pleasure and praises me for how good I feel. I'm incredibly full, but there isn't a hint of pain. It's hard to feel anything other than bliss with Cait's breathy moans against my ear.

Guy picks up speed, pressing his thumb against my clit and bucking wildly into me. His smile should be next to the definition of "ecstasy" in the dictionary, and just knowing I'm doing this to him is bringing me to new heights of pleasure.

Cait moves her hands between her legs to the same rhythm as Guy's hips, like she's the one inside me and not him. Her eyes are focused on where Guy's body joins mine. All shyness is gone from her expression. She's that lost to the heat of the moment.

Cait grabs my hand and places it between her legs. "Please," she begs.

While she furiously rubs her clit, I lower myself between her legs and hook my fingers inside her. I've never done this with a girl before, but I at least know what *I* like. She's beautiful and smells incredible, and I know I need to taste her. I lap the wetness now pouring out of her pussy and all over my hands. The faster Guy moves within me, the greedier I am for Cait's sweet tart flavor.

Apparently, I'm doing things right because Cait's moans turn high-pitched and breathy as I move my fingers the way I do on myself. Her eyebrows pinch together over her now-closed eyes.

"Yes!" Cait calls out just as Guy shouts out the same.

Cait's walls clench around my fingers as she orgasms, and I come again right before Guy releases inside me. As the three of us reach our crescendo, this becomes so much more than sex. We're joining souls as much as we are bodies. My head collapses onto Cait's abdomen, and Guy spoons me. We stay like that for a long moment, soaking in the afterglow.

"I love you," I say after a minute of contented silence. "I love you both so much."

Guy kisses my temple. "We love you, too."

Cait strokes my hair. "So much."

CHAPTER THIRTY-SIX

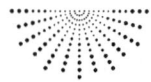

For the first time since I entered Peripeteia, I wake up happy. At best, I've felt hopeful, even eager to get going. But happy? No. Even in the real world, I can't remember the last time I woke up in such bliss. Maybe I never have.

With only a full-sized bed for us all to sleep in, Cait, Guy, and I have to fit together like puzzle pieces to stay on the bed. Fortunately, I'm squished in the center. There were several times when Cait and Guy started slipping off. Of course, that always wound up waking us up, and the sensation of our naked bodies pressed together would get us going again. I'm exhausted in the best possible way.

Cait and Guy slumber peacefully with their limbs draped over me. I enjoy the steady rise and fall of their chests against my sides—Cait on my left and Guy on my right. Cait is usually so perfectly groomed when not in battle, but right now, her hair is completely loose, with tendrils stuck to the sweat on her forehead. Guy sighs dreamily in sleep, clearly having some lovely dream.

This is Heaven. It's got to be.

However, daylight has no patience for the weary, and there are important things to do, things that could very well save us all. After last night, I know how ticklish Cait is and how much she loves it. So I dance fingers across the side of her waist, a spot I learned was one of her favorites. She giggles in such a sweet, girlish way that it makes me forget what a Domme she turned out to be during our third go. Her lashes flutter open, and her beautiful green eyes caress me.

"Good morning," I whisper.

"Good morning," she whispers back before giving me a long, soft kiss on the lips. She tastes like me.

Guy nuzzles against my breast and mumbles, "No, morning. Only sleep." With his eyes still closed, he smiles. "And sex."

"I'd be up for that if you both can give my arms back," I tell him. "They lost sensation hours ago."

"Oh, you poor thing," Cait says and sits up. She raises my now free hand to kiss my fingers better. "I'm sorry."

"If that's the price for sleeping next to you, I'll gladly pay it," I say.

Guy opens his eyes and yawns before sluggishly sitting up too. "Next time, we'll demand a bigger bed."

"We should get our own tent," Cait suggests, giving him a big smile.

The idea of multiple nights like the one we just experienced has me ready to go for another round but then I remember how important today is. Bringing up my menu to see the time, I bolt upright. "Fuck!"

"What's wrong?" Guy asks.

"It's already eleven o'clock!"

Guy's eyes widen. "Oh, shit!"

Cait jumps out of bed and scrambles for her clothes. Guy and I do the same. As soon as we have on our clothes and armor and grab our gear, we fly out the door. I'm the first to our friends' door. Before I can knock on it, Miko opens it.

"We're coming," she says, beckoning Joshua forward. He grabs Sylvia by the bindings and takes her along with him. Then, I see Doug get up from the shadow of the far-left corner. I never knew an orc could look embarrassed, but the pink blush on his green cheeks is pretty pronounced. Oh, no...Did he...?

"By the way," Miko says, directing her gaze to Guy. "Your silence spell doesn't work when you're concentrating on something else. Like teaching Cait how to make Lauren moan like that."

Guy goes pale, and Cait ducks her face behind her hand. I squeeze my eyes shut like maybe when I open them again this whole horrible moment wouldn't have happened. But when I do, I see Miko's unamused face focused on me.

"Tonight, I'm getting a full night's sleep," she says. "Got it?"

I offer her an apologetic half-smile. "Sorry. We'll be quieter."

Miko leans close, a stern expression on her face. "You will be silent as the dead unless you want me and Joshua to get loud, too."

My eyes dart over to Joshua, who is covering up his mouth. His chest is bubbling with a laugh he's trying desperately to hold back.

"You and...?" I point at Joshua.

Miko shrugs. "A woman has needs."

"If we want to eat, we should get something on the way," Doug says, ending this terrible interaction. Thank fucking God.

Just as in Thebe, there are street vendors, but they're pretty much on every street, not just near the temple. So, we have plenty of time as we walk to eat our toasted almonds. I hold my bag of them close to my chest so that my cloak can capture the heat and keep me cozy. The others take after my example, so by the time we make it to the courtyard by the temple, we're smiling at each other like sleepy kittens.

Just like everything else in Ismarus, the temple is bigger than any I've seen yet. Even as spacious as the courtyard is, it's completely dwarfed by the sky-brushing structure devoted to the gods. I'm tempted to go there and talk to Aphrodite first, but there's not enough time. Players are already congregating.

This morning, I turned off my title. Even if the players coming here are willing to give me a chance, there's still a chance I'll pass by some that want my blood. This gives me a chance to watch them without feeling watched in return.

They all twitch with anxiety, but their chatter is excited, even hopeful. Despite having difficulty getting past level two or three and making little headway in the main quest line, they're here in Ismarus. And the Orpheus quest is still in their menus because I haven't broken it yet.

"It's time," Miko says.

I walk to Doug's side and whisper, "You go first, okay? You've got the info they really want."

Doug responds with a solemn nod and makes his way to the podium. "I'm glad to see so many of you here," he shouts a bit too loudly, getting everyone's attention right away. "My name is Doug, I'm a Fist of

Hephaestus, and quests haven't worked for me for a really long time. But that doesn't matter because I'm level six."

I gasp. *I'm* not even level six, and every single quest has worked for me so far.

"The further I got from the main quest line path, the more chances for gaining XP I found," Doug says. "There are monsters all throughout the woods and mountains. There are even other towns with NPCs who have side quests. Because we're all in a rush to find the offerings our gods want, we don't take the time to explore. This is a *sandbox* game, guys! We're *supposed* to wander! Jumping straight to the big quests means you'll probably be underpowered, anyway."

I glance at Alexander, who's watching Doug speak. As always, he has his brooding romanceable NPC look thing going on, but he's also nodding. *Nodding*. Why would there be any programming for him to agree silently with a player who isn't even in his party? No, he's having his own thoughts on the matter, and they align with Doug's. He's broken like all the other NPCs.

Alexander is also right. What Doug says makes sense. It overlaps with Alexander's own insistence that we not jump straight to the Khione quest. I barely got to level five when I got here because I was in such a rush to press ahead. But how many days are left until seeing Mom again isn't a possibility?

"Anyway, there's more to this," Doug says and beckons me to join him on the platform. "Hear what my friend here has to say."

Suddenly, I wonder if everyone who has arrived would love to see me dead. All the players carry their weapons on them wherever they go. It would only take one well-aimed arrow to take me down right now. This is too important to wimp out on, though. Swallowing down my nerves, I get up to the podium.

"My name is Lauren," I tell them. "But you probably know me better as the Cleric of Aphrodite."

A wave of grumbling in the crowd tells me they know full well who I am. Most of them were probably those who attacked me when we were all in line to get in.

"I didn't mean to break any quests," I say. "I just saw another way to handle a situation and then...Well, it changed the outcome of that quest.

After that, no matter what I did, the quests started breaking because the NPCs are becoming aware."

I look across a sea of stony faces. I'm not telling them anything new. In fact, I'm reminding them of how much I've fucked things up for them. What I'm about to say will probably piss them off more.

I clear my throat and continue, "I'm sorry that it's made things so difficult for all of you. You're all just trying to figure out how to appease your gods. I assume most of you are like me and want to get home to the people you love. My mom is dying, and all I want to do is..."

I duck my head and pinch the bridge of my nose. I don't have time to cry over this. After a few sniffs and a deep breath, I decide I'm ready to get back to it.

"I'm sorry that this is making things so difficult for all of you," I say. "But I'm not sorry that I'm breaking the NPCs."

Gasps ripple across the crowd. Some mouths are open in shock, others bare teeth in rage.

"If you've talked to an NPC, maybe you see what I do," I tell them. "They're *people* like us. I believe they've been able to feel things all this time, but it's like the game put them in this dream state where they have to do and say the same things over and over. They have to deal with any kind of abuse a player might throw at them. They respawn after grizzly deaths, and after we 'save' them, they're back in the same horrifying situation the moment we leave."

Some of the audience is nodding, but far too many still look upset.

"In Sardis," I continue, "I saw an opportunity to broker peace between Arachne's children and the villagers. The spiders only spun that web because they wanted to reclaim their home. They weren't bad people, just scary looking. They never wanted to harm anyone.

"I thought I'd found an alternate way to complete the quest. I didn't realize I'd broken it until I walked through the village and saw the shell shock on the NPCs' faces. Children cried, and people searched for their missing loved ones. That's how real people respond to trauma. And if I hadn't broken the quest, they'd have to experience that nightmare all over again."

"So what?" a man calls from the crowd. "They can figure things out after we leave!"

"You think we're all going to leave any time soon?" I ask him. "Seriously? My beta player friends have been here for *months* and haven't found their offerings yet. My goddess told me no one has. But I'm getting off track."

I take a deep breath, hoping that they'll take the olive branch I'm about to offer.

"I haven't even touched the Orpheus quest yet," I say. "If you all join my party, we can do it together. Even if you're low-level, there are so many of us, we should be able to knock it out easily. That will get you on track with the main quest line, and you'll probably get some good XP out of it."

There are dozens of players in the courtyard. Most of them are gawking at me. I see a couple shake their heads and walk away. A few approach the podium.

"Do you think it will work?" a young woman asks. She's small and shy, not the kind of person you think would get this far, but her title says she's a Blade of Hades. Even if she's low-level, she's probably a complete badass.

"I do," I answer. "Even when I complete the quest in an alternate way, it's always marked as complete, and all of my party members get XP for it. Though, they're in their thirties now, so it takes a lot more than beginner quests to help them level up."

"Even if it doesn't work," Doug says. "I'm willing to help any players that want to earn XP like I do."

"I-I want to join your party," the young woman says.

"Me, too," says a burly man. He's a cleric like me but for Hera.

Several other players come forward, offering to join our party. There are some folks in the middle of the courtyard watching all this go down, weighing their options. After a while, though, they straggle over. In the end, we wind up with a party of twenty-two.

"I think we're more than prepared to help Orpheus get away from some scorned women," I say, almost laughing.

It's going to be nice to have a straightforward mission for a change.

CHAPTER THIRTY-SEVEN

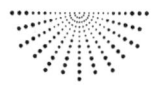

W e weren't even *remotely* prepared to help Orpheus escape these women. This is like keeping a heartthrob singer safe from a horde of raving fans. They all want a piece of him—literally. After failing to save his love, Eurydice, from the underworld, he didn't have it in him to pursue romance ever again. The Cicones women of Thrace didn't enjoy hearing that.

Even if he'd accepted their advances, he'd still be in deep shit. At least fifty women surround us right now. What was he supposed to do? Take every single one of them on a date? And what if they weren't into the idea of sharing? I'm in a throuple, but polyamory on that level sounds like a recipe for disaster. So, it was either get throttled for saying "no" or for saying "yes" to someone else. Poor guy.

When we spotted Orpheus, he was playing his golden lyre near the northern gate, the one we didn't use to enter Ismarus. Like Alexander, he has a brooding expression. The game devs copied Alexander's template and pasted it to create Orpheus. The only actual difference is that while Alexander has dark hair and eyes, Orpheus has a mop of red hair, and his eyes shine like copper.

When I got his attention, he wasn't startled in the least by the throngs of other players behind me. His programming wasn't made for noticing anything other than the player directly interacting with him. As soon as I greeted him, he looked past me toward the distance and his eyes widened in panic. He exclaimed something about how they'd found him and then all these angry women with rabid expressions came stampeding down the streets.

Fortunately, we got him through the northern gates out into the wilds pretty fast. *Un*fortunately, this has given the Cicones women enough space to surround us. There are so many more of them than us, and I suddenly wish we'd helped the newbies level up a bit before tackling this.

Us casters and healers stick close to Orpheus so that we can hurl our spells from a distance and heal him quickly if need be. It's also because we're the easiest to kill. The DPS and tank players circle around us. There are fewer of us than the Circones, but we have enough that Cait isn't within my reach, and I hate that. What if she gets hurt? It will be hard to heal her when there's so many people between us.

"It'll be okay," Guy whispers, noticing the trembling of the hand I'm using to hold my staff. "This was pretty easy when I did it."

"Oh, yeah?" I respond. "Sure seems like we have to murder an army of angry ladies."

Guy frowns. "Well, you have a point there. At the time, these were just NPCs, but we know now that they're far more than that. Nevertheless, it's kill or be killed."

Why choose? That question echoes through me again. I completed that quest, but its truth haunts me. Once again, the game wants me to choose between saving the NPCs or the players. Is there a way to do both?

So far, no one has attacked. The women are wise enough to know they can't just lunge past a bunch of people with weapons, but their eyes are as manic as ever. It's only a matter of time before they figure out a way to push through our defenses. Maybe they'll just wait until we're tired and distracted.

That will be a while, though. This should give me enough time to think using my Strategy Under Duress skill. If there's another solution, maybe I can find it in time.

I consider using my staff to charm them into going away, but this only works on one person at a time. They're going to notice if one of their friends suddenly changes her mind and probably attack sooner to avoid being charmed themselves.

Find a way for both Orpheus and the women to both get what they want? This isn't like Sardis, when Arachne's children and the villagers could share resources peacefully. The only thing these women want is this man's body, heart, and soul.

If I want to get rid of them without anyone getting hurt, I have to convince them they don't really want Orpheus. That means figuring out what they actually want, though.

I use my Insight skill to study them. Each woman looks bloodthirsty. They've curled their fingers like talons, ready to claw him apart. Their hair and clothes are in complete disarray. Their eyes have the feverish shine of violent mania, but there's something behind that: loneliness, disillusionment, heartbreak.

"Orpheus, how did you meet these women?" I ask.

"I was playing a concert dedicated to my Eurydice in the temple," he answers. "These women were all part of the audience and approached me to talk about how much my music inspired them. After that, they became...well, like that." He gestures at the throng of Circones women.

"So, you were playing your lyre?"

Orpheus nods.

"And you were playing your lyre when they found you later?"

"Yes," Orpheus says. "I had been hiding in a storeroom for days, but I couldn't take it anymore. I thought if I could get a little light, it would give me the will to live on. The sunshine on the snow so moved me I *had* to play my lyre, and—"

"What were you thinking about when you played the lyre in the temple?" I ask him.

"Eurydice, of course," he answers.

"And you were just a moment ago thinking about the sunshine on the snow?"

Orpheus starts to nod, then shakes his head instead. "The sunshine on the snow inspired me, but it reminded me of when Eurydice and I threw snowballs at each other. That was the day we first kissed."

I remember reading in high school that his lyre is magical. It can soothe beasts and bring peace to hearts. Can it also cause heartbreak? Or at least reopen old wounds? If so, he really fucked himself over by thinking so much about the dead woman he still loves.

"When you play, your emotions cast spells on others," I say. "You've broken every heart here just by thinking about how you've lost the love of your life while you're using your lyre. What would you do if Eurydice was back and didn't want to be with you?"

"Not kill her!" he answers.

"But would you kill someone who was keeping you from trying to be with her?"

Orpheus's eyes widen. "Oh, no..." he whispers.

"Get out your lyre now and play a song that makes them happy or some shit," I say.

"But I don't know how to make cheerful music anymore," he says, his penny eyes gazing forlornly into the middle distance.

"Jesus Fucking Christ," I mutter. "You emo romanceable NPCs are going to be the death of me. *Literally*."

Wait...Romanceable. Just like Alexander, he's heartbroken over a deceased lover, and he also has his own romantic quest line. This means that the game developers always meant for him to get over Eurydice, as long as the player willed it.

I lean close to Guy and whisper, "This means nothing, okay. You and Cait still have my whole heart."

Guy opens his mouth, probably to ask me what I mean, but I don't wait to hear whatever it is he wants to say. I grab Orpheus's face and turn it toward mine, then look up at him with what I hope is a seductive expression and plant my lips on him. Pretty sure a peck won't do the trick, so I give it all I've got. If I want to shortcut through what is probably a slow burn romance, I need to pull out all the bells and whistles. I even silently call on Aphrodite for help.

May my lips be soft and warm, I pray, *my tongue be skilled, my touch sear him with lust. Let this kiss be one for the record books.*

When I pull away, Orpheus stares at me, stunned. His jaw is slack, and his hair is mussed from where I grabbed him. And there's a spark in his eyes that wasn't there before. It's not love; it's awareness. I've broken Orpheus.

A growl rumbles through the crowd of Circones women

surrounding us. It must have pissed them off seeing me kiss the object of their violent desires.

Orpheus brings out his lyre and plays a new tune. This wasn't bittersweet like the one I heard when I approached him. It isn't sad at all. The only emotion emanating from this instrument is *hope*. Orpheus is experiencing a real, unprogrammed emotion.

As his notes drift across the throng, the women's scowling visages soften in wonder. Their eyes become clear, alert. They gaze at each other, as if waking from a dream.

"What's happening?" a newbie caster near me asks.

"They're snapping out of their spell," I answer and inwardly add, *and breaking their code.*

The Circones women mumble at each other, casting embarrassed glances at Orpheus occasionally. Then, without any parting words, they walk back into Ismarus like nothing had happened at all.

A notification pings, and I check my menu. "Save Orpheus" is scratched through. Being a main quest, it bumps my XP up significantly. I'm a quarter of the way to level six now. By the sounds of squeals, shouts, and laughter, this might have been enough to level up the newbies.

"It worked!" cries out a soldier near Cait.

Doug walks out of the ring we've formed around Orpheus and turns to face all of us. "We plan on helping all of you with side quests and such while we're all in Ismarus," he says. "Visit your deity, and tomorrow, we'll figure out who will tackle these quests together."

The low-level players clap. Doug blushes from the praise. He's *good* at this! I think of all the time he wasted lounging around our apartment when he could have been doing great things. Perhaps coming to Peripeteia was the best thing to happen to him.

Or maybe it was the worst.

I think of all the photos I saw online of him with his beautiful new girlfriend. He seemed so happy.

I should talk to him, catch up on all that's happened. There's a chance he might know what's up with Mom, too. What are the odds of someone I know this well winding up in such a strange situation? I suspect it isn't a coincidence.

"That meant nothing, huh?" Guy asks, playfully elbowing me in the side.

I laugh. "Look, I had to try something!"

"It worked," Guy responds. "Your kiss can do anything."

He leans forward to claim my lips for himself, but before he can, Cait inserts herself between us. Her stern eyes are on mine. Am I in trouble?

"Look, I'm all for our little threesome," she says, "but we're not bringing an NPC into this."

"It was just one kiss," I say. "All it did is break his programming. It's not like we're dating now or—"

A hand slips into mine, one with calloused fingers from playing his lyre for so many years. "Lauren," he says, "your love has saved me from a terrifying death. Let me repay you by worshipping your body tonight."

"Fuck," I whisper.

Cait crosses her arms. "Take care of it," she says, then she grabs Guy's hand. "We'll be doing our own thing until you sort out Mr. Romanceable NPC."

Guy looks at Cait with puppy dog eyes. "But I wanted a kiss."

"Fine," Cait relents like she's giving in to a child that wants candy. "We'll both get a kiss first."

Smiling, Guy wraps one arm around my waist and cups the back of my head with his free hand. "I better make this good," he whispers against my ear, sending pleasant tingles up and down my body. "If Orpheus is even half as smitten as I am, he'll be hard to shake off."

Guy's kiss is slow, skilled, and deep, purposefully making me weak in the knees. When we part, the first thing I see is Cait's lustful gaze.

"God, that's so hot," she says. "You better get rid of this guy so we can have another night like last night."

Cait doesn't take her time. Her lips crash against mine, causing an inferno of desire to spread throughout me. Her hands seek every delightful spot she discovered in bed, and I sulk when she pulls away.

Guy and Cait lock hands. "We'll see you later," Cait says with a wicked grin. She knows she's given me enough incentive to launch Orpheus to the moon if necessary.

The lyre-playing hero leans for his own kiss, and I hold up a hand between us. "Look, Orpheus, you're a really nice guy, but I think we should just be friends."

Orpheus nods. "Friends works for me." A seductive grin crooks up. "You should see what I do with my 'friends.'"

I groan in frustration. "Dude, weren't you just so heartbroken over Eurydice that you couldn't be bothered to accept a date with all those women we just fended off?!"

"None of them were like you," he says.

Orpheus tries to put his arm around my waist, but I step away in time.

"Sorry, but the feeling isn't mutual," I tell him. "I'm sure you'll find a lovely girl who likes lyre music and grabby hands."

"But I only want *you*!" Orpheus insists. He steps toward me again. "How can you kiss me like *that* and say you don't want this? Every time you say 'no,' all I hear is 'yes.'"

I press a hand over my mouth, certain that I'm going to puke. *This* is what the game devs thought made for a romanceable NPC?

"Look, there's this thing called consent," I tell him, "and you don't have mine. Now, back the hell off."

My words mean nothing to Orpheus. He grabs my hand and pulls me toward him. I'm sure he's about to lay a disgusting kiss on me, when suddenly something yanks him away. No, not something. *Someone.*

Joshua grips Orpheus by the back of his collar. He has his mouth close to the NPC's ear, but he doesn't bother to whisper when he says, "Don't be gross. The woman said 'no.' You need to respect that. Got it?"

Orpheus nods frantically. "Y-yes!"

"Now go board the Argo like you're supposed to after this quest," Joshua says as he releases his grip.

Orpheus doesn't wait to talk more. He dashes into the woods and out of sight.

"Joshua, did you just save me from a pervert?" I ask him.

"Look, there's a difference between being a pervert and forcing people to be with you," he responds. "I will *always* respect a woman's boundaries."

Miko comes to his side and puts her hand in his. She looks at him with heavy-lidded eyes and a sexy smile. "That was hot," she tells him in a husky voice.

Joshua blushes all over and ducks his head as he smiles. He whispers something to her that makes her giggle. Then he clears his throat and turns to me with a failed attempt at nonchalance on his face.

"Miko and I are...going out for a while," he says. "We'll see you later."

Just when I'm about to run back into Ismarus to find Cait and Guy, Doug approaches. Goddamn it! I just want to have mind-blowing sex with my partners! Why does everyone want to talk to me right now?

I will myself to remain patient and smile at Doug when he reaches me. "Good job," I tell him. "You make quite the leader."

Doug laughs. "Yeah, I never saw that coming." He sighs and then says, "Look, there's stuff we need to talk about. Important real-world stuff."

I nod slowly. He's right. As much as I want to jump into the sack with Cait and Guy, I can't neglect everything else that matters.

"Yeah," I say. "While everyone else is busy in the temple, let's find a place to sit and chat."

CHAPTER THIRTY-EIGHT

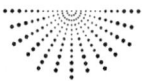

Finding a place for a deep conversation has proven difficult. The sun started setting when we reentered Ismarus, so all the taverns filled up with hungry NPCs and players alike. Newbie players who helped us with Orpheus filled the temple. The markets are teeming with players looking for new gear.

Finally, we wind up sitting at the table in Doug's room. As incredibly awkward as this is, I'm glad that I can go straight to Cait and Guy right after this conversation ends. I told them I was right next door beforehand as well. I don't want them to see me leaving Doug's room and not know why.

The polyam thing is new to all of us, and we're still figuring out our rules, but I'm pretty sure we're all on the same page about honesty. Doug is my ex. It's not unheard of for two former lovers to hook up. But I will *never* do something like that behind their back. Besides, there's no spark between Doug and me, hasn't been for years. This is a meeting of old friends in a strange situation.

While I caught Cait and Guy up on where I would be for a bit, Doug grabbed some drinks and food from downstairs. Now, I'm sitting at the stained, weathered wooden table in the corner of his room, toying around with food I really need to eat, but my appetite is nonexistent.

"So, when did you wind up here?" I ask.

"After you," he answers. "I was watching the news, and there was a missing person story. About you. They found your abandoned car at the store with your wallet inside. When I woke up in Peripeteia, I knew this must have been why. I tried not to get my hopes up that I would find you, but...I just felt it deep down. You were really hyped about this game before it came out."

"Well, you were right," I say. "I was shopping and realized I'd left my wallet in my car. When I left the store to get it, there wasn't a parking lot or store anymore, just a forest. You said you woke up?"

Doug scratches the back of his neck and looks away. "This is going to sound pretty creepy."

"Can't be any creepier than Orpheus."

"Well, I'll let you be the judge of that," he says. "I still had the keys to your apartment and decided to look for clues there."

"Okay, that *is* a little creepy," I say. "But I can't say I wouldn't have done the same. Doesn't explain how you wound up here, though."

"When I didn't find anything, I remembered about how obsessed you were with *Legends of Sacrifice*," Doug explains. "You must have just started playing when you disappeared. So I took it home and played your save, thinking maybe there was a moment that made you decide to walk away from your life. Man, you sure put a lot of effort into that Alexander relationship."

"Ugh, yeah, I totally did." It's so weird thinking about it now. Alexander? That guy? Really?

"Anyway," Doug says. "I fell asleep at the computer, and then I woke up in this farmer's house, and...yeah. Here I am."

"How did you become a Fist of Hephaestus?"

"When I woke up in a stranger's house, I punched my way out of there."

I gasp. "You *punched* the farmer? Celeas?"

"Look, he was acting all weird! Repeating the same stuff over and over!"

Remembering back to my experience with him, I can't help but agree. "Yeah, he was pretty disturbing." Posing with my arms bent like a robot, I mimic Celeas. "'I haven't had a guest in a long time. I'm not used to making myself presentable.'"

Doug laughs. "Yeah, he said that a lot when I asked him why the hell he was still smiling."

"But why Hephaestus?" I ask.

"I don't really know," he says. "I have a theory, but it's not a strong one."

"Go on," I say.

"Because you're the Cleric of Aphrodite, and you dumped me."

Doug looks hurt, actually *in pain*, inside and out. He'd shown nothing but indignation when I'd told him to hit the road, and since then, all I'd seen of him were photos of him with his new girlfriend.

"But you're with someone, right?" I ask.

"Melissa?" Doug asks. When I nod, he says, "We just started dating."

"All over town, it seems," I say. "And with a ring on her finger."

Orcs have interesting features. Their resting face is angry. So when Doug winces with embarrassment, it looks like he's baring his tusks at me.

"So, that was a joke," he says. "Did you notice the date we posted the ring pic?"

I shake my head.

"April Fools' Day."

"Oh, my God," I mutter.

"Don't get me wrong," Doug continues. "Melissa's a wonderful person, but we barely know each other. I'm not just going to jump from an eleven-year-long relationship into something serious within a few weeks. That's not who I am."

I look over his shoulder at the wall he shares with mine.

"Hey," he says, bringing my attention back to him. "I'm okay with you being with Cait and Guy. Am I surprised? Yeah? I never thought of you being bi or polyam, but there's nothing wrong with you being in a romantic relationship with anyone else. And I get it, too."

"What do you mean?" I ask.

"In the game, you put in all that work into leveling up your relationship with Alexander because he was giving you all the romance I probably never gave you. I'm not that kind of guy, but you have *always* been that kind of girl. You've waited a long time to be loved the way you deserve to be loved."

My eyes mist. I didn't expect to hear such thoughtful words pass

Doug's lips, but I guess he's grown a lot since the last time we saw each other.

"But I'm beating around the bush about something I'm sure you want to know," Doug says.

I wipe my eyes. "What's that?"

"Before I went to your place, I thought I'd try seeing if you left anything with your mom," he says.

My heartbeat and breathing halt for a second too long, and my chest aches from it. "Mom? H-how is she?"

Doug looks down, but I can still see the tears in his eyes. He's known her since we were both teenagers. She's always been so kind to him. I'm sure it hurt him to see her like that. Even just thinking about the way she said "Lauren" the last time I saw her makes me want to sob.

"Lauren, her room was empty because...because..."

I shake my head. "No! You went to the wrong room or maybe they moved her to a different facility or—"

"They asked me if I'd heard from you," Doug continues. "They... they tried calling to tell you, and they needed you to sign some paperwork...to figure out which funeral ho—"

I bolt upright from my seat. "No, you're wrong. She was saying my name the last time I saw her. I'm getting out of this game and going to see her. She *can't* die before I see her again. *She can't!*"

Doug reaches up to grab my hand, but I shirk away. "I'm sorry, Lauren. I wish you were right, but she's dead."

"Fuck you!" I shout. "Fuck *you!*"

I storm out of his room and slam the door behind me. Guy opens our room door and rushes out to hug me.

"What was that bang?" he asks. "Are you okay? I heard you shouting at Doug. Did he hurt you?"

This is too much. His touch, his questions. Cait comes out to join him with her own words, colored with concern. I don't comprehend any of them. My head swims with the chaos of their affection. I know I'll need it soon, but I can't handle it right now.

"I need to be alone," I whisper.

"What?" Cait says. "Sorry, you're whispering. What did you say?"

I push away from Guy's embrace. "I need to be alone."

Cait's face shifts from confusion to anger, and her eyes dart to

313

Doug's door. "Did he do something to you?"

I shake my head. "No, he just gave me some bad news, and I need to go process that by myself."

"Bad news?" Guy asks.

"Lauren, is it...about your mom?" Cait asks.

The word "yes" can't seem to pass through my lips, so instead I say, "I promise I'll talk about it when I get back."

"I'm not sure it's safe for you to be alone," Cait says.

"Is there really any time I *am* safe?" I ask.

I don't wait for an answer. I just turn and walk away.

DOUG AND I MUST HAVE TALKED FOR MUCH LONGER THAN I thought we had because the streets are dark and empty. Cait's warning about it not being safe for me seems ominous now. Anyone or anything could hide in these shadows. Still, going back to my room and trying to explain how much everything hurts to Cait and Guy feels like too much.

A few blocks away, a building radiates a comforting glow.

The temple.

If the streets are empty, maybe the temple will be, too. Even with Zeus's statue there, I'll probably be safe. Temples are sanctuaries, right? Aphrodite is there, and she'll protect me. I wonder how much she knows about Mom.

I wrap my cloak tight around me so that the icy breeze doesn't cut through my chiton and no one recognizes me. I'm not sure having my title turned off is enough to hide my identity anymore, not after the speech I gave earlier today.

When I enter the temple, I'm tempted to take my cloak off. It's so warm, almost too warm, like they have the heat turned up to 75° to overcompensate for the weather outside. I don't dare do it, though.

Despite the emptiness of the temple, I can feel the statue of Zeus staring at me. It's probably just my imagination or an optical illusion, like one of those paintings where the eyes follow you everywhere. Just in case, though, I use my hood to obscure my face.

I make my way to Aphrodite. This statue of her is even taller and grander than any I've seen of her before.

"Hi," I say simply. "I don't need anything. Well, nothing big, anyway. I just thought maybe we could talk? Please?"

It isn't a prayer, but Aphrodite answers anyway. She pulls away from her statue, and the entire world shifts. It no longer looks like we're inside the temple. Instead, we're once again standing on her pink sandy beach. It's got a tropical climate here, causing sweat to pool up under my cloak immediately.

My discomfort must be evident because Aphrodite says, "You can take off the cloak for now. I've shielded you from the rest of the temple."

I let out a long breath of relief and untie my cloak. It goes into the mysterious inventory, pocketed away into nothingness using game logic.

"What's on your mind?" Aphrodite asks.

"Too much," I answer.

"Do you want to sit?" Aphrodite asks.

When I nod, she sweeps her arm to her side, and two chairs appear. They're surprisingly simple—white wicker rocking chairs, the kind Mom used to have on her back porch. Wait, they're *exactly* like them. I look from the chairs back to Aphrodite, unable to hold back the tears pouring from me now.

"You know about Mom," I say, and she nods.

"Please, have a seat," she says, settling into the chair nearest to her.

Sitting next to a goddess is weird. She's so close that I can feel the energy coming off her. It's like that subtle, fuzzy static that came off old television screens. It's also so much more casual than feels comfortable with someone so powerful. Then again, I did come to the temple asking if we could just chat.

"I'm sorry," Aphrodite says.

"How long have you known?" I ask.

Aphrodite's lips flatten in empathy. "Since right before you came to Peripeteia."

I shake my head. "What? How?"

"Do you think everyone here came by coincidence?" she asks. "Are you like some of those who think we're just NPCs?" She shakes her head. "No, we watched all our players once they received the game."

"I'm sorry, what?!"

"We're not supposed to tell any of you this, but after all you've been through, I feel like I must," she says. "We are the *real* gods. The ones passed from myth and legends all over the world, the ones just as changeable as the weather. No one can ever really know us, not even the developers who created this world on our instruction."

My mouth feels dry, and I realize it's because it's hanging open.

"You look thirsty," Aphrodite says. "Here."

With another wave of her hand, a white wicker coffee table sits before us. On top is a pitcher of lemonade and two glasses. Aphrodite fills a cup and serves it to me. A *goddess*—a real one, apparently—is serving *me* lemonade.

"But this world is so inaccurate!"

Aphrodite responds with a soft, half chuckle. "Who's to say what's accurate? Even within the Greek pantheon, no one can agree on what stories are the original ones. And we've overlapped with so many other cultures throughout the centuries, adapting to a changing world." She shakes her head. "No, it doesn't matter what's accurate. We wanted *this* world because this is where we can be worshipped in today's culture."

"By trapping people here?" I ask.

"What? No!" Aphrodite says, genuine shock on her face. "The worship comes from people buying the games, playing them for hours upon hours, talking about them with each other, sharing videos and fan art that reach people all over the world. Your worship is different. It's reciprocal."

"I don't understand," I say.

"Of course you don't. Why would you? You don't have enough information yet." Aphrodite sighs. "When we saw that some beta players were destined to die soon, we brought them here instead. Then the game came out, and we did it again."

"Wait, so...Cait and Guy and Doug and *everyone*..." I gasp. "*Me?* We were all going to die in the real world?"

"You all would have if we hadn't brought you here," Aphrodite answers. "Now, you can live forever."

"And then something we did caused us to be assigned a class and which deity to serve?"

Aphrodite nods. "Although, with you, I knew before I even brought you here."

"Because of my breakup?"

Aphrodite looks at me with proud eyes. "Because you're my granddaughter."

I already felt like the world had turned upside down when I learned Mom died. This news makes time stop, too. For a long moment, I'm sure my heart has ceased beating. Finally, I say, "No, you can't be."

"My son, Eros, your father—"

"Abandoned my mother."

"Couldn't stay with your mother," Aphrodite corrects. "Eros loved her, but he always knew he'd have to leave. He's a god. It wouldn't have taken long for people to realize something wasn't normal about him. He felt it was better for you to never know him than to lose him."

"Well, I *did* lose him, didn't I? And now I've lost *her*!" I shake my head. "I can't believe I thought you actually cared about me."

"Lauren, you're my granddaughter; of course I care about you!" Aphrodite reaches to squeeze my hand, but I shirk away. "I only govern the power of love. I had no way of making anything better for you or your mother. However, I knew you were going to get in your car, grab your phone, and see that missed call. I *knew* you would get in a car accident on the way to the hospice. I had to rescue you, and I hoped this could be my chance to have you in my life."

"You just delayed my death, though. Zeus is out to get me."

"I won't let anyone hurt you," she says. "I've already broken so many rules to keep you safe. Just the fact that I brought my own blood into the game isn't allowed."

I squint. "Why?"

"How else could a player break this game?"

"Fuck." The word croaks out of me, barely audible, just a sob framed in consonants, followed shortly by a torrent of tears. I curl my legs up onto my chair, bringing my knees up to my chest, then lean my elbows on my thighs and rest my face in my palms.

Aphrodite rubs my back. "I'm so sorry, Lauren."

Her apology means nothing when she's provided an excuse for *everything*. She's been lying to me from the get-go.

I snap my face up and cast my burning eyes on her. "You knew about Mom this whole time and didn't tell me! I've been fighting for so long to get you that offering so I could go home, when there's no one to go back to!"

"I was afraid you'd hurt yourself if you knew."

"If you just wanted to keep me safe, then what's the point of promising to grant me a wish?" I ask. "Of the offering? Of any of it?"

Aphrodite stares at me in silence, studying me while chewing on her bottom lip. "I can't tell you everything. Yet. I've already told you too much, but if you succeed, I'll tell you what you want to know. All of it." She strokes my hair. "Cait and Guy are waiting for you. Let them care for you. They deserve that. *You* deserve that."

"The Why Choose quest," I say. "I thought it was about them, but it was about the NPCs."

"Who says it wasn't about both?" Aphrodite asks. She kisses my forehead. "In every instance, you've chosen well. You definitely did with the two of them." Getting out of her white wicker chair, she adds, "Grab your cloak."

I take it out of my inventory and tie it on. Aphrodite waves away her beach, and I have my hood covering my face the moment the temple surrounds me again.

"Good night," she says before returning to her statue.

Though she isn't there, I also wish her a good night and exit the temple.

All the information Aphrodite gave me swims around my mind, and I struggle to keep my heart from shattering into a million pieces. Mom's dead. She's been dead this whole time. I never stood a chance of saying goodbye, not even before I came here. The last time I saw her, she said... she said...

I don't want to relive that moment, but I can't stop it. In my mind, I'm in that hospice. Mom's staring blankly into nothingness, but she still takes a moment to look at me, and she remembers my name. She said *Lauren*. She still knew me in the end. Was she like the NPCs, trying to say goodbye but could only say my name?

An icy breeze whips the hood of my cloak from my face, shaking me out of my reverie. I realize I have no idea where I am, just a random dark alley. I look up to spot the light from the temple several blocks away and use it to reorient myself. I'll pay better attention to where I'm going now. I just need to head—

Sparks overwhelm me, whether from my vision or in reality, I have no idea. They're gone soon enough, though, because now I'm swimming in inky black. There is nothing. I am nothing. It's all...nothing.

CHAPTER THIRTY-NINE

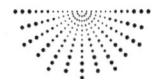

I don't know where I am, but it's dark. I don't mean like someone should light a candle. There's nothing but black. There's nothing to smell or feel or hear. I even try opening my mouth to see if I can *taste* something, but all I get is the lingering taste of my dinner with Doug on my tongue. The lack of everything and the strange peace of the environment disturbs me.

Where the fuck am I?

I think back to the last things I remember. I went to the temple to talk to Aphrodite. About what? Khione? No, if I did that, Zeus would overhear. She told me to stick to talking with Alexander about that stuff. Maybe it wasn't important.

My heart *hurts* for some reason. Not physically. Except for the agony on the back of my head, the rest of my body seems unharmed. However, it feels like someone broke my heart. Did Guy or Cait break up with me? Is that why I went to Aphrodite? She is the Goddess of Love, after all. Maybe I wanted her to help me get over it.

Wait! We drank lemonade. We sat in white wicker chairs and drank lemonade. It was just like—Mom? Why does the thought of her hurt so much? It's hurt ever since she had the stroke but nothing this bad.

Then it hits me. This isn't heartbreak; it's grief.

She's dead.

Doug's words come back to me. I remember shouting at him, refusing to stay with Cait and Guy, and running to talk to Aphrodite. I don't know why I chose her to confide in. She's the Goddess of Love, not the Goddess of Loss.

'Tis better to have loved and lost than never to have loved at all.

Who said that? I swear I used to know this. Tennyson! That's right. Mom used to say it when I would ask her about my father, why she wasn't mad or sad that he'd left before I was born. There's something I know about him, something new. What is it?

I sat drinking lemonade with a goddess. She was friendly, casual, and sympathetic. We were talking about Mom and...She knew before me, way before me, before I even came to Peripeteia. But how? Mom's in the real world.

Because Aphrodite was watching her, watching us, before I'd even played *Legends of Sacrifice*.

I'm her granddaughter.

My head pounds from the swollen bump on the back of my head, but I force myself to think through every step of that painful conversation and then to my journey home. That's where everything went dark, but not as black as here. "Here" is just nothingness, like the space beyond the playable areas of a sandbox video game.

Didn't Miko say something about how Hekate put her into a world like this? Miko would play her part as an empusa, and when it was time to pause, she returned to her own little pocket of nothingness.

Aphrodite would never do something like that to me, but Zeus would. He'd known I was at the temple right beforehand. The streets of Ismarus were teeming with players, many of whom were pissed at me for breaking the game. How many of them are his worshippers?

Wait, no, not worshippers, not really. The players in the real world are worshippers. All the players in here would have died in the real world like me. The gods brought us here so we could live and bring them an offering.

"I'm so fucked," I whisper to myself.

"You woke up!" says a familiar voice. It's the first thing I've heard since I roused into this blank world.

"Hello?"

There's a shuffling sound. It comes close enough that I know I should see whoever it is, but it's too dark. I can't even see my own hands, more or less anything else that might exist in this space.

"I was afraid you'd never wake up," the person says.

There's a perfect warmth and sweetness to this voice and I realize who it is—Sylvia.

I back away, even though I have no idea if there's anything or anyone behind me. "Leave me alone!"

"It's me, Lauren!" Sylvia cries out. "The real me! I promise!"

"That's exactly what the eidola would say," I respond.

"It's gone," she says. "It escaped Miko and Joshua when they were distracted. Some Zeus worshippers took off my bindings, and the eidola helped them attack you. Once that was over, its job was done, and it left me."

"You could be making all this up."

"Why would the eidola want to be trapped in here with you?" Sylvia asks. "Zeus got what he wanted from both of us."

"What could he have gotten from me he didn't have before?" I ask.

Sylvia sighs. "The eidola told him about Khione's lost son. Its job was to tell him what you knew of Aphrodite's plan and help him kill you."

"Well, she failed on both counts, then," I say. "The thing about Khione's son was a lie, and I'm not dead."

"Lauren..." Sylvia lets my name hang there for a moment and then continues, "Are you sure about that last point?"

"Dead? If I was dead, we wouldn't be talking!"

"In a world of nothingness?" Sylvia asks.

"I heard you shuffle to me," I say. "That's not nothingness. You have enough substance to create friction and produce a sound. I'm in pain on the back of my head. If I was dead, I wouldn't feel that."

"Then where are we?"

I don't fucking know, but I offer her my best guess. "I think we're in that little pocket that Miko told us about. The storage closet where gods put us when they don't want us wandering around Peripeteia."

"But that was because Hekate turned her into a monster," Sylvia says and then gasps. "Do you think *we're* monsters?"

"Fuck, I hope not."

As if in answer to Sylvia's question, all the black around us melts away, revealing a snowy field. In the distance, I can just about make out Ismarus.

Sylvia screams from my left. I turn to see what's frightened her and jump backwards in terror. There's a horse with sharp, bloody teeth and wild, red eyes staring back at me. Every impulse in me is to run away, but I can't leave Sylvia behind.

"Sylvia!" I shout, backing away from the beast. "Sylvia!"

Oh God, did it already eat her?

The horse cocks its head to the side in the creepiest way imaginable and slowly approaches.

"Sylvia!" I shriek, my voice breaking from the effort. If she doesn't answer this time, I'm bolting.

"Lauren?" the horse asks in Sylvia's voice.

Oh. Fuck.

"Sylvia? Y-you're a horse."

Sylvia nods, which looks odd with her equine head. "You, too."

"Your teeth—" I start.

"If they're anything like yours, I don't want to know about it," Sylvia says.

We're monsters. *This* is what Zeus is doing to us. It wasn't enough to kill us. No, he has to torture us by having players kill us over and over, with our only respite being time spent in nothingness.

"What the fuck are we going to do?" I ask Sylvia.

"Run," Sylvia says.

"Yeah, but where?"

"No! *Run!*"

Something like a war cry grows louder behind me. I turn to see a swarm of players stampeding our way with their weapons raised high.

"Fuck!" I shout.

Sylvia is off like lightning, and I race behind her. There are endless fields of snow around us with nowhere to hide. As I wear out, I realize I can only run for so long and then I'll be just another objective scratched through on these players' quest logs.

Now, I understand why Miko was so resigned to us murdering her. Better to get it over with and let them kill me. Maybe if I don't put up a fight, that will give Sylvia a chance to get away. Hopefully, their quest says they need to kill *a* horse and not both horses.

I stop running and turn toward my approaching attackers. These faces are familiar to me. They're the newbie players I'd helped complete the Orpheus quest the day before. At their lead is Doug. He's helping them grind for XP. Well, I said they should do whatever they could to level up. How poetic that my first death should be at their hands.

Taking a deep breath, I will my body to hold stock-still. I tremble violently anyway, both from fear and the biting chill in the air. The thought of watching Doug beating me to death terrifies me, so I lower my head to the ground. Maybe if I don't see it happening, it won't be so bad.

Their feet rumble closer and closer. Their shouts of violence and preemptive victory grow louder and louder. This is when I realize horses don't cry. If they did, there would be tears flowing over my muzzle right now.

"Wait!" Doug shouts.

The stampede halts, and the voices lower.

Crunch, crunch, crunch, Doug's footsteps grow closer. Does he plan to land an incapacitating blow so that it's easier for the level two and three players to kill me?

"Why aren't you attacking?" he whispers.

I lift my head to look at him. Doug shudders. I can't blame him. If I look anything like Sylvia, I must be terrifying. However, he settles and lifts a hand, not to hit but to *touch*.

"You're not a monster, are you?" he asks.

"It's me, Lauren," I say.

Doug shakes his head. "I don't speak horse, fella," he says.

Ugh, of course, I sound like a fucking horse. Just because Sylvia and I can communicate with each other doesn't mean we make sense to anyone else.

"Can I pet you?"

Pet me? That's something I never expected my ex-boyfriend to say, but it's an easy way to show him I'm harmless, maybe appeal to his sympathy.

I rub his palm with my muzzle to show him, "Yes, pet me, I'm totally a nice horse. *Please* don't kill me."

Doug strokes my nuzzle and then scratches behind my ear. "Wow, you're surprisingly soft for a man-eating mare." He frowns and tilts his head to study me. "Something tells me you've never eaten a person in your entire life, though."

"Miko, can you come here?" he calls out.

Excitement vibrates through me. Miko is here? Someone else I know. Maybe this is a good sign.

The Druid of Dionysus joins Doug, keeping a wary eye on me the whole time. "What's up?" she says.

"This is a really tame monster, wouldn't you say?" Doug asks, as he scratches behind my ear.

God help me, I hate how good that feels. Like, I *really* needed that. Do you know what it's like to have a random itch and not have hands to scratch it?

"Could be a cursed player," Miko says. She steps closer to me. "Hard to tell."

"You got that new Speak with Animals spell when you leveled up this morning," Doug says. "Ask it."

Speak with Animals? I shake free of Doug's hand so that I can nod.

Miko shrugs. "Sure." I guess she finally got that shopping trip she wanted because she whips out a brand-new staff and holds it up. "Speak with Animals," she says nonchalantly.

I don't even wait for her to say anything. "Miko! It's me, Lauren!"

She squints in response and turns to Doug. "She says she's someone named Lauren."

Doug scratches the back of his neck. "Why does that name sound so familiar?"

"Because I'm your ex-girlfriend, you asshole!" I shout.

Miko's eyes widen. "Whoa, she's got quite a mouth on her! Says she's your ex-girlfriend."

"What?" Doug asks. "I don't have an ex-girlfriend. I mean, unless you count Melissa. But we didn't break up. I just wound up here when I...Why can't I remember how I got here?"

"Maybe you were drunk like Guy," Miko responds.

"Guy!" I cry out. "Is he okay? Is Cait okay? Joshua?"

"How do you know all those names?" Miko asks.

"Because it's *me,* Lauren," I answer. "And that other horse is Sylvia!"

"Sylvia?" Miko asks.

"She's the Archer of Artemis," I say, "and I'm the Cleric of Aphrodite."

Miko laughs. "Okay, yeah, and I'm Santa." She turns to Doug. "She says that she's the Cleric of Aphrodite."

This gets Doug laughing as well. "That old legend?"

"Legend? No, I'm your friend!" I insist. "Miko, I convinced the party to let you live when you were an empusa, and that's why Guy gave you the grape so that Dionysus would adopt you. Remember?"

Miko's laughter stops. Instead of looking at me curiously, she takes me in like I might deserve her rare sympathy. "That's not something many people know," she says. "When Hekate turned me into an empusa, my friends acted like they'd forgotten me. I thought they were pretending but...could it be?"

"Tell Doug that he has a bad habit of leaving empty chip bags on the desk after playing video games all day," I tell her.

"Ew," Miko grimaces and turns to Doug. "You leave your trash next to your computer? That's how you get a gunked up cooling fan!"

"Exactly!" I shout.

Doug looks at me like I'm a mystery. "How would you know that?"

"I think we actually might know this Lauren person," Miko says. "Probably whoever Sylvia is, too. Whatever god did this to them made everyone forget."

"But she said she's the Cleric of Aphrodite," Doug says, shaking his head. "That's just a quest line for people who didn't get to finish those broken low-level quests."

"*I* broke those quests," I say. "That's why Zeus did this to me. Well, I *think* Zeus did this."

"Zeus?" Miko says. "If you belong to Aphrodite, another god can't hurt you."

"The rules don't apply to him," I say. "He's the King of Gods."

"Oh, shit..." Miko whispers.

"What is it? What's she saying?" Doug asks.

"Zeus did this," she answers. "He can hurt any player he wants, regardless of who their deity is."

"Please, is everyone else okay?" I ask.

"Yeah," Miko says. "Joshua is resting after a battle. I think Cait and Guy are on a date."

A date. So they really love each other. They're not just pretending for me. This warms me from head to toe. What we have is real, not just a byproduct of being one of Aphrodite's players. Well, what we *had*. If they've forgotten me, too...I don't even want to think about that.

"What am I going to do?" I ask myself aloud.

"There's a cleric in town who can remove hexes, but that would just return you to human form," Miko says. "I have no idea how to help anyone regain their memories of you."

That will have to be good enough. I can probably start these relationships over from scratch, but I'll definitely need my human form to complete the Khione mission. Now that Zeus has done this to me, I want nothing more than to succeed where he hoped to see me fail.

"Please bring him," I say. "I'll get Sylvia and let her know. She'll be so relieved."

SYLVIA AND I STAND SIDE BY SIDE BESIDE THE ROAD LEADING TO Ismarus. Doug stays by our side to prevent players from killing us. He's had to tell many players that we're not the monsters they're looking for, so I feel like sobbing with relief when Miko and the cleric show up. I can't cry, though. I'm a horse.

The cleric trembles at the sight of me. "Are you sure this isn't a monster?" he asks Miko.

"Yes, I talked to one of them at great length," she says. "If she was a man-eating monster, she had plenty of opportunity to chew us to a pulp."

"Well, then, I must do what I can to save them both from this curse," he says.

The cleric stands in front of Sylvia and me and presses his palms on our muzzles. Then he closes his eyes and whispers a prayer to Apollo. God, I hope Apollo pulls through. Zeus is his father. Maybe he'd prefer for me to stay like this.

My body shifts, and agonizing pain radiates from every inch of me. It's like someone is breaking all my bones and tearing apart my skin all at once. But soon, I slump forward in human form, my hands and knees buried in the snow.

The little protection from the cold my horsehair had provided is gone. The freezing gusts burn against my nude body. I look at Sylvia, who's curled up on her side, naked and shivering.

"Oh, God!" Miko shouts. "I didn't realize it was going to make you naked! Um, um..." She brings up her menu and taps furiously at it until her old warlock robes are in her hands. "Put this on," she says, offering it to me.

I almost refuse and ask her to give it to Sylvia, but Doug is already passing some old armor of his to her. With shaking arms, I pull on her robes. Unlike my white cleric chiton, this is black and hugs me in more of a witchy seductress way.

"Damn, that looks better on you than it did on me," Miko says. "And I looked *incredible*. I guess you really do belong to Aphrodite."

Ignoring her lovely compliment, I get straight to business. "I need to get to Khione."

Miko shakes her head. "You *need* to eat a warm meal and figure out what else you're missing. I already sent a message to my friends—*our* friends—to expect a guest soon."

"A message?" I ask, but I don't wait for an answer. "Fuck, this could be all it takes for Zeus to—"

"Relax," Miko says. "I'm a druid. I sent it with a bird. No one's going to know what's going on but *us*."

"I really could use that meal," Sylvia says, leaning against Doug. She's still shaking, but I'm pretty sure it's not just because of the cold. She looks gaunt. How long were we in the nothingness? It doesn't look like she's had a bite to eat in days.

I nod. "Okay, but as soon as I can, I need to figure out a plan. There's a reason Zeus did this to us, and speaking to Khione may be my only way to prevent it from happening again."

"Got it," Doug says. "Recover, plan, and then talk to someone named Khione."

We walk back into Ismarus, leaving the endless snow behind for a city full of people who would like to see me dead.

CHAPTER FORTY

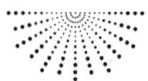

Sylvia and I sit at the table in Doug's room, eating the stew he purchased for us in the tavern below. It's hot but not scalding, and everything about it is excellently prepared, making it the perfect comfort food.

Yet, I find no solace sitting exactly where I was when I found out Mom died. The awkward stares from all my friends don't help either. It's so strange that I can share so many happy memories with them all and yet they have no clue who I am.

Cait and Guy squint at me like I'm the weirdest creature they've encountered. I haven't told anyone yet that I'm in a relationship with the two of them. Or I was, at least. I suppose them not remembering me means that we're over. In which case, I'm sitting in a room with three friends and three exes. Because I'm not a horse anymore, my ability to cry is back. I couldn't hold back these tears with a dam.

"This all must be so traumatizing for you," Guy says.

"Honestly, turning into a horse isn't close to the worst thing that's happened to me since I got here," I say and squeeze Sylvia's hand.

"I can't believe you all forgot us," Sylvia whispers. She looks at Guy. "I met you the second week we were here. I was with Tara. Do you remember Tara?"

"Of course I remember her! She—" Guy winces and presses his

fingers against his temple, scowling in agony. "God, why can't I remember where she is?"

"Because of why she isn't *here*," I say. "We were all attacked by some Zeus worshippers so they could kill me. She got possessed by an eidola during the battle and didn't trust herself to remain safe around us after that."

Guy rubs his back right where her dagger hit him. "Something sounds familiar about a battle with players but nothing else."

"I guess that's something," I say with a sigh.

Cait remains squinting at me but with distrust this time. "Why would Zeus want you dead? Did you do something horrible?"

Sylvia pipes in for me. "She treated the NPCs with compassion, and they came to life. Zeus wants them to remain NPCs."

Cait arches an eyebrow. "The NPCs came to life? That's more unbelievable than her being the Cleric of Aphrodite."

I drop my spoon into my now-empty bowl. "Fine. You want proof that we know each other? I'll give it to you. Cait, you like video games and sports, but your parents don't think it's ladylike, so you've been doing it in secret all this time."

Cait's jaw drops, but I don't wait for her to respond to me with words. I look at Guy.

"I don't want to say this out loud, because you told me in confidence," I say. "But I'll say that you have always been beautiful, even before I met you, even if you hated your own face. I'm glad you made it here, and so are you."

Then I turn to Joshua. "I'll admit that I don't know that much about you," I say. "I didn't attempt to because when we met, you made some lewd suggestions about me, thinking that I might be a romanceable NPC. What I know is that you and Miko have something going on, and I hope you feel extremely lucky that a woman this hot is even tolerating you."

If they were all gawking at me before, it's even more apparent now.

"How do we not know you?" Cait asks, looking mystified.

Miko answers, "Because a god turned her into a monster. It's like when Hekate turned me into an empusa, and my entire party forgot I existed."

Cait winces just as Guy did a moment ago. Then she shakes herself out of the moment. "It's almost like I can remember her talking to you about that."

I wonder if I can break through this spell by pushing their memories to that brink. It might give them all migraines, but it's worth it to me.

"Sylvia used to cook all our meals," I say. "Her boiled grains with honey were the bomb!"

They all moan in pain at that. I guess good food leaves a long impression. I think about reminding them an eidola possessed her. That's a big memory, but that would mean potentially causing them to distrust her.

"She has a wolf companion, but we haven't seen him since we boarded the boat for Thrace," I say.

Sylvia droops her head. "I really miss Marshmallow."

As my friends cry out in pain, I continue. I talk about herding the cercopes and the girls' day out. I remind them of Dolius and Cyrus. I tell Guy that he saved the day for me when he silenced everyone outside of our party so my social anxiety wouldn't get the better of me.

I save the most impressive memories for last, at least the ones that involved most of my party. "We battled a dracaenae on the road from Thebe to Dardanus," I say. "She was way OP'd. Then there was the fight with the Zeus worshippers. Cait, you didn't want to hurt a player and wouldn't fight them. That got you killed, but fortunately *their* cleric brought you back to life. Cetus attacked us on the ship to Thrace. If not for Alexander shooting him in the head, none of us would be alive. Alexander also helped us take down the chaos dragon. And Guy..." I look at him, my heart hurting all over again. "That's when you died, and I used up one of my three Kisses of Life to bring you back."

Guy touches his lips, and I think I see some flicker of familiarity there, but it's gone in an instant when Sylvia says, "Where is Alexander, anyway?"

Miko rolls her eyes. "I told him to hit the road. He kept going on and on about how we needed to find—" She grabs her head and screams. "Ow!"

I bolt up from my chair and look around at my friends. "Do you know where he went? How long ago was that?"

Everyone but Joshua shakes their heads, who nods and says, "Alexander went to the temple. I saw him there earlier today just standing around Aphrodite's statue. That NPC is super broken. Someone needs to take him out of the game."

"Absolutely not!" I cry out. "He's supposed to help me with the Khione quest."

"What is this quest you keep talking about?" Doug asks.

"Aphrodite has a message for her," I answer. "A *secret* one. She doesn't want Zeus figuring it out."

"Zeus again?" Cait asks. "What a dick." She slaps a hand over her mouth, and her eyes widen in embarrassment.

I giggle. "You swore."

"I-I didn't mean to," she says.

"That's the second time I've heard you do it," I say. "Believe it or not, you've changed a lot since I met you. Only in the best possible ways. Everything that I lo—liked about you stayed the same."

"What do you mean?" she asks.

"We need to get to Alexander," Sylvia chimes in, giving me a knowing look. She knows I'm not ready for that conversation with Cait yet.

"First, you need to check your stats and inventory," Miko says. "When you shifted, you didn't even have clothes on. Remember?"

THANK FUCK FOR GAME LOGIC. OUR CLOTHES, OUR GEAR, everything was in that mysterious space that all player inventory goes to. I guess it was too much trouble to clear it out when Zeus could just turn us into monsters instead. Our stats, spells, skills, and favors are all the same as well.

After confirming that we had all of that back, I was eager to get to the temple immediately, but then I remembered that's the worst place for me to go. Zeus is there. The moment I step inside, hood up or not, he'll know I escaped his monster curse. Sylvia couldn't go in for the same reason.

So we have to leave this up to the people who don't even remember us. Sylvia and I have been waiting in Doug's room for what seems like forever. I'm pretty sure my tapping toes have made a groove in the wooden floor. Sylvia's nails may never grow back with how much she's been biting them.

I just hope that Alexander understands Guy when he sees my cloak. They can't exactly tell the NPC that I'm in the inn waiting to talk to him. Not with Zeus right there.

The door clicks, and I jump from my seat at Doug's table. It creaks open so slowly that I wonder if the inn is haunted. I'd rather deal with a ghost than one of Zeus's worshippers. Neither of those options walks through the door, however.

Doug and Cait drag a wounded Alexander through the door while Guy, Joshua, and Miko walk behind them. They keep looking over their shoulders like someone might be following them. God, I hope they're just being paranoid. I don't want to be any more fucked than I already am.

As they enter the room, I see Alexander isn't conscious. His head lolls on his right shoulder. A dark bruise is just visible on his hairline. Someone must have knocked him out. But why? He's just a stray NPC.

"What happened?" I ask Guy as Cait and Doug stretch Alexander over the bed.

"There was a really long line to see Ares when we were talking to Alexander," he explains. "And the worshippers there wanted to stretch into Aphrodite's area since no one needed to talk to her, but Alexander wouldn't let them. So one of them hit him on the head with the hilt of his sword."

"Jesus Christ..." I whisper.

Miko's already-black eyes seem to darken as the rest of her features flatten into grim lines. "When all the NPCs wake up, I hope they take care of players like that." Her tone doesn't leave any doubt in my mind that she's serious.

"So you believe me about breaking the NPC coding?" I ask her.

"That dude was so insistent that he wait for *Lauren* to show up," she says. "Kept saying that you were meant to free people. He also put up a fight. The game's story has always been that Alexander is cursed to never lift a blade, but he said that Aphrodite granted him permission to defend you in other ways."

"Whoa..." Doug says as he pulls a shotgun out of Alexander's pocket. "Where did he get this?"

Cait blinks in surprise. "That's a Benelli M4 Super 90 shotgun!"

"Benelli what?" Miko asks.

"It's a shotgun, and Cait's cop dad used to have one," I answer. "As for where Alexander got it, Aphrodite gave it to him because Zeus kept sending OP'd monsters after us. Now, step aside. I need to heal him."

They all create a clear path between us. He's not bleeding, and that bruise doesn't look all that bad, but that doesn't mean there aren't terrible injuries underneath all that. So, I decide that Heal Minor Wound won't do the trick.

Lifting my staff, I say, "Heal Major Wound."

Nothing. I tap my staff with my palm like it's an old TV set that will work if I give it a good smack. Then I lift it again and repeat the spell. Absolutely, nothing.

"Maybe my staff is damaged," I say.

I put my staff back on my back and bring up my menu. I tap the Heal Major Wound spell. Still, nothing.

"Is he alive?" I ask Cait, who's standing closest to him.

She presses two fingers to his neck and then nods her head. "He's got a pulse. So, I assume so."

Joshua doesn't look convinced by this answer. "You know how sometimes NPCs will still twitch and stuff after they die? What if his pulse is just a glitch?"

I hate that his answer makes sense. Alexander is a level two NPC. Some players here are high enough level that one hit could actually kill him. Fuck, if he's dead, we're all screwed. He's the only one who can communicate with me about what Aphrodite needs regarding this message to Khione. She'd even said I needed to keep him around just for this.

If Alexander is dead, there's only one thing I can do, and it terrifies me because if I'm wrong about this, it may mean someone else dies and stays dead for no good reason.

"I'm going to use one of my Kisses of Life," I say.

"How many do you have?" Guy asks.

"Two," I answer. "One after I kiss him."

Sylvia comes over and puts a hand on my shoulder. "Are you sure about this, Lauren? After being stuck in that nothingness, we both know what Zeus is capable of. We might need those two kisses for players."

She's right. There's a solid chance that one or more of us will die trying to get this message to Khione. Even if we survive that, who's to say Zeus won't try to get us afterward?

"You know Alexander started showing signs of sentience a while back," I say. "I asked him if he knew what he was, and do you know what he said?"

Sylvia shakes her head.

"He said he did." I swallow, remembering how easily I dismissed that moment and how important it is now. "He said he was a player like us. Alexander thinks he's one of us. He *cares* about us. Deep down, he wants to be one of us."

Tears well in Sylvia's eyes, and she nods. "Do it."

I look at Alexander. When I played *Legends of Sacrifice* in my old apartment, I longed to kiss him then. I have no interest in him now, not with *real* people like Cait and Guy to love. But as I press my lips to his, I channel old Lauren, the one who swooned for the romanceable NPC. I'd rather think of it like that than as a gamble on a vital and limited spell.

Alexander's skin starts off so cold and stiff, but as my lips brush against his, his warmth returns, and his mouth softens. I pull away slowly, wanting to make sure he's really alive before returning to Sylvia's side.

His eyes flutter open, and he smiles at me. Cupping my cheek, he says, "Lauren, you're alive. I was so worried about you."

I can't believe the immense relief those words bring. It's not just that he's alive when I need him. For the first time since Sylvia and I came back, a friend remembers me.

Alexander winces and removes his hand from my face so that he can clasp it over his bruise.

I stand up and whip out my staff. "Heal Major Wound," I say.

A long sigh escapes Alexander, and he smiles. The NPC sits up and takes a good look around. Then his eyes land on Sylvia, and he screams.

"Eidola!" he shouts as he points at Sylvia.

I shake my head and push his arm back to his side. "No, the eidola is gone. It's really her. Zeus punished her just like he did me."

Alexander squints at me with disbelief. "Truly?"

"Yes, I promise," I say.

"Then I won't shoot her." At that, Alexander pats his pocket and gasps.

"Oh!" Doug hands the shotgun over. "I was making sure you didn't have any other injuries and found it."

As Alexander puts it away, I say, "Look, Alexander, we need to get to Khione now before Zeus throws anything else at us."

"No, you need to get to level six first," he responds.

"*What?* Now I have to get level six?!" I throw my hands up in frustration. "First it was I needed to do all the quests on the way to Ismarus. Then it was complete the Orpheus quest. Now, I need to level up again?"

"You could die if you—"

"I almost did!" I shout. "Because I got caught coming back from the temple. Zeus planned on having me killed over and over again as a monster! Me and Sylvia both!"

Alexander lowers his eyes. "Then, I suppose we can do no more to prepare for this, except pray to Aphrodite we all survive."

"How dangerous is this mission?" Miko asks.

"Apparently, more dangerous than anything else we've done," I say. "Which is really saying something after defeating that chaos dragon."

My friends share looks. I know what they must be thinking. Why should they help some woman they just met with the mess she's landed herself in? For Cait, this is probably like one of those horrid escort quests.

"You don't have to come," I tell them. "I offered in the past to do this on my own. It's a big ask to put your lives on the line when I can't even tell you much about what this mission even is."

"No, I'm coming," Cait says. "I...I don't remember you, but I feel like I do."

Guy nods. "I feel that way, too, and I couldn't let you do this in good conscience."

Miko crosses her arms and looks down at her shuffling feet. "Honestly, I don't know. I've stuck my neck out before and pissed off a god."

"Then you understand better than any of us just what Lauren is risking right now," Joshua says. He moves to stand by Cait and Guy. "I plan to help my friends, even if I don't remember some of them."

Miko nods. "You're right. I'm just...I'm just scared." She reaches over and squeezes Joshua's hand. "I'll help."

I look at Doug, the man I'd dated since our high school days. Even as angry as I was when we broke up, he's still someone I share years of memories with. Except all of his have been erased, and he's already done plenty to help me already.

"Are you coming?" Sylvia asks him.

Doug scoffs. "Of course I am. You think I'd be the lone coward of this group?"

"Okay, let's go!" I say and walk to the door.

Guy grabs my arm. "Not after all you've been through today. It's late, and we all need to get as much energy as possible. We can do this tomorrow."

I cast my eyes at the window. Sure enough, the sun is setting. "Fine."

"I'll head downstairs to get everyone dinner after we sort out our sleeping arrangements," Doug says.

"Well, last time, I shared the same room as Joshua and Miko and Lauren slept with Cait and Guy," Sylvia says.

The four people mentioned look at their partners with disappointment.

"Maybe this time, we do something different," Joshua suggests.

Doug shakes his head. "No, this is better. This way you're not keeping each other up all night with your mo—" He winces and holds his hand up to his head. Then he looks up at me, his mouth slightly open in surprise. "I-I remember something. Something vague but...I think I remember hearing you, um..." He swallows, visibly uncomfortable. "I remember you making noises from Guy and Cait's room."

My face is a thousand degrees right now. *Of course*, the one memory that all this prodding has unlocked are my loud orgasms. Not any of the nice or interesting things I've done. Just how loud I get when I come.

"What kind of noises?" Miko asks, a curious, almost mischievous, spark in her eyes.

Doug glances down. "I-I don't want to say."

The looks Cait and Guy are giving me burrow right into my soul.

"What does that mean?" Cait asks. "Are you saying she—?"

Cait groans in pain and clasps her head, burying her fingers in her red hair. She crumples sideways onto the bed, next to Alexander. Guy rushes to her to comfort her, but when he touches her, he looks at me, and it's his turn to shriek in pain and slump over. These reactions are by far the most dramatic of them so far.

"Jesus, what kind of memory did they touch up against?" Miko asks.

I look at Sylvia and shake my head. I don't want them to know. If she tells them and Cait and Guy still don't remember me or study me like I'm an alien, I won't be able to handle it.

"The three of them are in a relationship," Alexander says.

God fucking damn it.

"They love each other," Alexander clarifies. "That's why she was in their room. So that they could—"

"Okay, that's enough of that!" I interrupt.

Cait pulls herself to a sitting position, panting as she recovers from the pain she just endured. "But...you're a woman. I'm—" She winces again, then blinks and looks me up and down, realization lighting up her features. "Okay, yeah, I'm into that."

"Do you remember her?" Guy asks. "Because I don't, but I can see why I would be interested in her. I just don't recall anything happening with the three of us."

Cait shakes her head. "No, I just remember feeling that way about a woman."

"Maybe Sylvia should sleep in Cait and Guy's room instead of Lauren," Doug suggests.

Cait and Guy protest as one. "No, no, we're fine with—"

"I really don't want the two of you suddenly remembering every-thing while Lauren is in there," Doug says. "Not when I'm trying to sleep next door."

Cait pouts, and Guy sighs.

"Fine," Cait says. "Sylvia can stay with us. Let's get dinner now."

CHAPTER FORTY-ONE

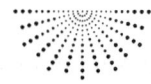

Last night wasn't as awkward as I assumed it would be. I guess Miko and Joshua like to keep things private because they didn't even flirt while I was in the room. I was more than happy with that, but I still had difficulty sleeping.

I couldn't stay asleep for long. Intrusive thoughts shook me awake every time I drifted off. *Mom is dead. Remember the harpy's dead eyes? Remember the dracaenae's decapitated body? Cait doesn't remember you. Guy doesn't remember you. They don't remember that incredible night when the three of you became one. Alexander thinks you're unprepared, and you're going to die.*

You're going to die, Lauren. Just like Mom, and you never got to say goodbye.

I'm haunted by them even now, fully awake and walking with my friends toward the palace where Princess Khione lives. We asked the innkeeper this morning how to get an audience with her. He told us that we simply had to attend the daily court she sat in.

Since there was a blizzard overnight, there aren't many people out and about today. I expected this from the players. Who wants to quest in shin-deep snow? I thought there would be more NPCs out, though. They're programmed to ply wares. However, there are very few out here, and those outside are silent as the grave.

"They're broken, aren't they?" Cait asks as we pass by a mostly empty market street.

"Seems that way," I answer.

Cait clears her throat and with a blush asks, "So, um, we did stuff?"

"Yes," I say, not holding back the longing in my voice.

"H-how much?" Cait asks.

"You and I know each other's bodies intimately," I tell her.

"Did you and...?" She points her eyes in Guy's direction.

I nod in response.

"Did he and I ever do things?" she asks.

"Not as much as with me," I answer. "You're not into him sexually. That's what you told me, at least."

Cait let out a sigh of relief. "I don't," she admits. "I mean, I love him, but I don't feel any sexual attraction."

"You love him?" I ask her.

"Yeah," Cait answers.

I smile. "That makes me so happy." It really does.

"We're here," Alexander says, pointing at the steps into the palace. "I will ensure we can join the court audience when we—"

An arrow whips through the air, narrowly missing Alexander.

"Fuck," I mutter. "Haven't even made it into the palace, and this bullshit is happening."

Cait and Joshua have their weapons out immediately. Sylvia knocks an arrow into her bow. Guy, Miko, and I get our staffs from our backs. Alexander had his shotgun out before any of us were ready to defend ourselves.

Sylvia spots the player who shot at Alexander and lets an arrow loose. The player dodges out of the way. Before any of us can throw another attack at him, though, he gags on something and slumps sideways into an alleyway. Then, from the shadows, out steps Tara.

She smirks at us, showing off the daggers in her hands. "Like 'em? Just bought them yesterday. Ismarus really has the best stores."

Sylvia runs to Tara and wraps her in a bear hug. "Oh God, you're alive!"

Tara laughs. "Of course, I am. I'm like a cockroach."

"We need to head inside," Alexander says. "There could be more players ready to attack us."

"Oh, there are a *lot* more," Tara says. "Out here *and* in there."

"Shit," Miko says. "How outnumbered are we?"

"Oh, if it's just y'all, maybe five to one," Tara answers.

"What if it's *not* just us?" Doug asks. He turns to Miko. "What if we call in a favor from the newbs we just helped level up?"

Miko crosses her arms and tilts her head. "Do you really think they'll do it?"

"Can't hurt to ask," Doug says with a shrug.

"How will we even get them here in time?" Miko asks.

"Oh, don't worry about that," Tara says.

She snaps her fingers and around every corner come the players we've helped since coming to Ismarus. But it's not just them. NPCs step out of their homes, carrying knives, canes, and all manner of tools that could be weapons in certain contexts. There are easily forty people approaching us. Their voices overlap as they tell us they want to help.

"I hear a lot more than you think through our earrings," Tara says, tapping at her earlobe. "When the Zeus worshippers I was spying on got here, I took care of them and gathered the allies you've made while here."

"Wait, do you remember me?" I ask her, deciding I don't want to know how she "took care" of the Zeus worshippers.

"Of course," she says. "I was in your ear, even when you and Sylvia were in the nothingness. There was never a moment when I could have forgotten you."

I tapped on my ear. The earring was still there. I guess whoever disrobed me to become a horse didn't bother to take off that piece of jewelry. Maybe they didn't even notice it was there.

If we didn't need to get into the palace right away, I would fly over to Tara and hug her, just as Sylvia did. However, we have to press on. If we all survive this, I can give her all the hugs she'll tolerate.

"Okay," I say, some hope filling my chest at last. "Let's do this."

I move past Alexander, but he grabs me by the wrist. "You must stay by my side. Aphrodite insists."

Dear old Grandma must be worried about my safety since I was kidnapped after our last meeting. She said she wouldn't let me die. I'm not dead so far, despite her king's best efforts.

"Fine," I tell him. "I promise, I'll stay with you."

Alexander, my companions, and dozens of players and NPCs join me in climbing the stairs to the palace. I hope that whatever waits on the other side of the door doesn't kill all of us.

⇧

DESPITE THE FLOOR AND WALLS BEING MADE OF MARBLE, THE interior of the palace is almost dead silent. At the end of a long hallway is a large, closed door. More than a dozen people stand in line at it. I hear loud, overlapping voices when the guard beside the large door opens it to let in the person in the front.

There are people on the other side talking over each other. The conversations seem quite intense by the volumes coming from then. However, as soon as the guard closes the door, the library quality of the room resumes.

"How can one door block that much noise?" Miko asks.

"I think they have a type of silence spell connected to it," Guy tells her.

"The silence spells are your favorites," I say.

Guy turns his attention to me. "They are."

"I'll get us a spot in line," Cait says. "The rest of you stay out of sight. Especially you, Lauren. We don't know who might know you by sight here."

When she walks off to talk to one of the guards, Guy comes to my side and leans in to whisper, "Earlier, you said I was beautiful. Did you mean..." He looks down. "Actually, don't worry about it."

"I meant what you shared with me," I whisper in response. "About what happened before you came here and why you'd had so much to drink the night you wound up here. About what you hated when you looked in the mirror."

Guy lifts his eyes to lock onto mine. "I told you that?"

I nod. "When you told me, I realized I love you because it wouldn't matter how you looked. I'd still want to spend hours sharing parts of ourselves with every kiss."

His throat bobs. "You would?"

"Are you *kidding* me?" Cait shouts from the line.

We turn our attention to her conversation with the guard. He says something, but we can't make it out because he's talking at a reasonable volume.

Cait's response isn't even-toned at all. "I don't *care* if court ends soon, this is vital! We have a message for Khione!"

At the mention of Khione, every guard in the hallway readies his weapon. Even the people in line have pulled out daggers. Cait's temper has given away who we are. Well, I guess this fight was coming at some point. Might as well get through these folks before we move into the actual court area.

Guy, Miko, and I whip out our staffs. Cait raises her great axe, ready to bring it down on anyone who gets too close. Joshua's short sword sings when he unsheathes it, and Doug's bastard sword reflects the candlelight brilliantly. Tara's expert fingers help her hold several daggers in both hands. Sylvia has already knocked an arrow. Alexander seems quite pleased to bring out his shotgun. All the newbies and NPC allies get their weapons ready as well.

The guards are the first to lunge at us. Cait makes quick work of the ones near her. When they fall, they slip on their own blood on the slick marble floors. Sylvia looses arrows at the guards near the exit doors, and Tara flings dagger after dagger at the ones at the other end of the hallway.

Meanwhile, the NPCs that were in line rush over to Guy, Miko, and me. They're all dressed like proper nobility, regal and groomed. This makes their savagery almost comical. *Almost.* It's hard to enjoy a good chuckle when people are trying to kill you.

Guy lifts his staff and shouts, "Ice Blast!" Dagger-like icicles shoot from his palms, planting one into the forehead of a rabid nobleman. Miko summons an earth elemental, which splits into two. Both copies pummel anyone who tries to get past them to us. Our new allies fight off the stragglers and help finish the guards who got past the worst attacks we can throw at them.

I stand beside Alexander, ready to heal anyone who might need it. He takes precise shots at any enemy who stands still long enough.

I bet this guy would love a good old-fashioned spaghetti western.

There are so many of us, far more than our enemies here. It seems too easy when we finish up our battle, especially since I only had to cast a couple of Heal Minor Wound spells on the newbie players in the room. Tara said there are tons of people waiting to kill me in the palace, though. I can only assume most of them are in the court, which sounded quite crowded when the door opened.

"Are you ready?" Alexander asks me.

I don't answer. Instead, I take a deep breath and walk toward the large door between us and the court. Alexander's steps match my own as he walks just behind me. Guy comes to my right side and Cait to my left. They still don't remember me, not really, and yet they seem just as committed to helping me as before they lost their memories. Is that because I'm the NPC breaker or because they want to know more about our relationship? Maybe it's just that they're good people. That was the first thing I liked about both of them when we met, after all.

When I open the door, I'm immediately hit with a cacophony of raised voices. No one even blinks at our entrance, which is surprising. There are dozens of us, and we're all covered with signs of battle. No one in our group is free from blood, sweat, and grime. I suppose our presence isn't enough to distract everyone away from their arguments.

Every noble in this court looks ready to stab each other. The only calm people sit at the other side of the court in their thrones. King Boreas and his NPC daughter, Khione. Boreas, God of the Winter Wind, is a giant of a man, pale with a cloud of white hair, marble white skin, and ice-chip-blue eyes I doubt ever held a flicker of warmth.

It's strange seeing a god like this, sitting in a palace instead of inhabiting some world outside of the game until a player prays to his statue. He isn't a major god, however, so maybe the others didn't think he was worthy of a spot in Olympus.

Khione looks like deep snow on a moonlit night. Like her father, she has white hair. She wears it over her left shoulder in one long thick braid that reaches her hip. Her eyes are as blue as her father's as well. That's where their similarities end, though. She has a dark tan and a spray of freckles across the bridge of her nose and cheeks.

Both the king and the princess stare right through us like we aren't even there because we haven't initiated contact. Once I do that, I'm sure all the attention in the room will finally turn our way. Given the reception we received out in the hall, I doubt it will be pleasant.

This room is smaller than I thought it would be, and it's so crowded that my social anxiety is peaking. I clench and unclench my fists while I try to regulate my breathing. Then peace washes over me. Thank God—no—thank *Aphrodite* for that Soothing Grace favor.

"You said Aphrodite wants you by my side?" I ask Alexander.

"Yes, she wants me to protect you," he answers.

"*Right* by me though?" I ask.

"Yes," is all he says, not having any further information to give me, I suppose.

My lips vibrate from the nervous puff I let out. "Well, I guess, let's do this, then."

CHAPTER FORTY-TWO

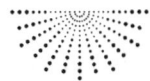

A lexander insists on holding my hand as we weave through the crowd to Khione. I don't know if it's because he's afraid someone will get between us or he thinks I'll try to run off and do it on my own. I seriously don't understand why he has to be *right* next to me. However, I'll be doing whatever the hell Aphrodite wants me to since she's not just my most powerful ally but also my grandmother.

Boreas and Khione still stare stone-faced when I get within a couple of yards of them. I wonder how best to greet a king. It's certainly not how I did when I encountered King Dardanus. I should probably bow and lavish him with compliments, but frankly, I don't have time to bullshit around. I decide on a straightforward approach.

"King Boreas, Princess Khione," I say, and they both turn their cold eyes on me. I gulp and continue, "I come at the behest of Aphrodite."

The bickering around the court quiets to listen to me closely. Oh Jesus, I better get this all out before it comes to blows.

"She has a message for you, Princess Khione," I say and rush the rest of the words. "Your son is on his way to become the King of Thrace. You must claim him as your own."

Khione's eyes widen before turning them ever so slowly toward her father. The God of the Winter Wind's deathly pale cheeks pinken, and his eyes take on an icy rage.

"You have a son?" he asks Khione with a growl.

"N-no, of course not!" she cries out. "This is just some cleric. Obviously, Aphrodite is playing a game, and—"

"Was it Poseidon?"

Khione's chest shakes with every ragged breath. "Of course not, Father! I'm still a maiden!"

"Khione, you *have* to claim him!" I plead.

"*You!*" She points a long, trembling finger at me as she sneers in disgust. "You will call me *Princess* Khione and will stop lying!"

I ignore her rage. "This is imperative! I've come from far away to give you this message. Aphrodite was clear that it's urgent."

"Then she toyed with you," Khione responds. "She's jealous of the unwanted attention her lovers give me. I've never given up my maidenhood."

Alexander squeezes my hand and speaks up, "Aphrodite isn't lying. She isn't jealous. She is concerned for you and said that Poseidon wasn't able to prevent this from happening."

Wow, it seems he knows a lot more about this whole deal than I do. I suppose that makes sense. He can be programmed to keep a secret until it's time to reveal it, while I might run my mouth off on accident.

Khione's bottom lip trembles. She looks like she's on the verge of tears, but it's not out of fear or anger. No, this is heartbreak.

For as distraught as Khione looks, Boreas is the definition of rage. He's the current King of Thrace, and he probably expected he would always be that. But if there was a prophecy that his grandson would kill him, then he would do everything in his power to prevent Khione from having a child.

Boreas grabs her by the wrist, causing her to gnash her teeth in pain. He twists her arm and flings her to the ground, all while keeping the tight grip on her wrist.

"You *whore!*" he shouts. "You've brought ruin on this house!"

"Father, please—"

With his free hand, he slaps her across the face. That's when Alexander lets go of me and raises his shotgun. "Get your hands off her," he growls at Boreas. I have *never* seen him angry, but his face twists in rage now. Where did this come from?

Boreas bares his teeth at Alexander. "A human cannot kill a god, boy."

Alexander blinks and shakes his head. His eyes ping-pong between Boreas and Khione. Then, his features widen with realization. He lowers his Benelli, and his jaw drops.

He's fully broken now.

"Are you okay, Alexander?" I whisper.

"I'm not Alexander," he says. "I'm Eumolpus, immortal son of Khione and Poseidon." He turns all his attention to Boreas. "Prophesied to kill my grandfather when I come to take his throne."

Fucking what? He was Khione's son all along? No wonder Aphrodite wanted me to stick to his side like glue.

But for Boreas's throne, though? I know that the reason given to me was that Aphrodite cared about Eumolpus as the son of her friend, Poseidon, but that feels lacking. Why wouldn't she have simply sent him on his own, instead of with someone so closely monitored by Zeus. If anything, I'd made it more difficult to deliver Khione's son to him. No, there's some bigger reason for this to be my mission, and I think it somehow has something to do with me being her granddaughter.

Khione gasps. "You're him?" The tears that threatened to spill before trail down her cheeks. "I see Poseidon in you now. He's done so well raising you."

With a roar, Boreas lets go of Khione and charges at Alexander. He doesn't even get a chance to unsheathe his sword. Alexander simply raises his shotgun and fires into his grandfather's chest and then his head. The God of the Winter Wind had been so certain that Alexander couldn't kill him. He hadn't counted on him being the product of divinity himself.

I don't have time to process the ease of Boreas's death. A chorus of swords and daggers unsheathing draws my attention. Every noble in this court has their violent eyes on Alexander and me.

Khione jumps to her feet and holds up a hand. "Stand down! This is my son! The new King of Thrace!"

She claimed him. This must mean my mission is over. Everything should be good—

My breath stops when I feel a sharp sting on my lower back.

Suddenly, I feel something warm and wet saturate the back of my chiton.

"Wh-what's happening?" I ask, my voice slurring as I see the sneering face of one of the noble NPCs right behind me. Will one of these minor NPCs be responsible for my death after I survived several of Zeus's OP'd monsters? Really?

"Lauren!" Cait calls out and rushes to cradle me before I fall to the floor.

A nobleman raises his dagger to attack her while she's distracted with me. However, Guy shouts, "Ice Blast!" and an icicle punctures the man's forearm, causing a bone to protrude through his bloody flesh.

"I-I c-can't move my hands," I say, every vowel stretching like silly putty. My entire body feels cold and stiff now; my tongue tingles like I'm experiencing anaphylaxis.

Khione beckons at Cait. "She's been attacked with a poisoned dagger. Pick her up and follow me!"

Cait hoists me over her shoulder. If I didn't feel like I was turning into stone, I would appreciate how sexy it is that she can do this so easily. Guy rushes to her side.

"I have your back," he says. "Just concentrate on getting her through this crowd."

My body is so out of my control now that my head bobs up and down with every step Cait makes. It causes my vision to go from the red carpeted floor up to the battle between my allies and my enemies, down to the floor again, up to Alexander chasing after us, and back to the floor.

A door creaks open from Khione's direction, and we all step through to a shadowy room.

"Lock the door," Khione whispers, and Alexander does so.

"Can you heal her?" Cait asks as she sets me down on something soft.

It's hard to feel much, but I can tell whatever surface I'm on gives under my weight. I try to look at my surroundings, but I can't turn my neck, and I can barely move my eyes.

"No, I'm sorry," Khione says. "If she's who I think she is, then she should be able to heal herself now that she's out of harm's way."

"Heal herself? She can't even move!" Guy shouts.

Khione shushes him. "Keep your voice down. I don't know who might hear."

Cait yanks my staff off my back and places it into my hand, curling my fingers so that I'm cradling it with her help. "Just say the words, okay?"

"Ressss..." It's hard to move my tongue in the right way to create the "T" sound. I try again. "Ressssteraaaaa..." My tongue is so swollen that it's hard to breathe, much less form words, but I have to keep trying. "Resssssss...terrrrr...aaaaaa...shhh...shhh...on." I did it. I got the word "restoration" out. It sounds like I'm passing out at a bar, but it was the right word!

Sensation returns to my body, assaulting me with the prickles that come when your limb has fallen asleep. My fingers grip my staff without Cait's help, and I'm slowly able to turn my head to take in the room.

This is a room for worship but to whom? Boreas was a god, and Khione is his daughter. Why would they pray to anyone?

I look down at the surface I'm lying on. It's a raised table, as long and wide as a tall man, and covered with pillows and blankets.

I turn to Khione and ask, "What is this?"

The princess looks downward, whether from guilt or despair, I can't tell. So, I don't know how she feels when she answers, "It's where a hero must be sacrificed."

"What?" I ask and try to sit up, but the pain of the dagger in my back returns, and I cry in agony.

Guy touches my back. "I'm going to yank this out," he says. "When I do, cast a healing spell."

There's no countdown, no warning at all, just a wall of white flooding my vision as pain lances through my entire spine.

I roar from the pain but somehow tighten my grip on the staff and shriek out the spell, "Heal Major Wound!"

My Soothing Grace favor washes its peace over me during the excruciating process of healing the open gash over one of my lower vertebras. If not for that, I wouldn't be able to control myself. Even with this, I have to fight the urge to thrash around and scream at the top of my lungs.

Then, the pain is gone. Well, mostly. It still feels like there's a sore spot on my back, but nothing worse than what I'd feel if I fell too hard.

Cait helps me pull up to a sitting position, and I take a moment to even my breathing. Then I look at Khione.

"Who the fuck are you sacrificing?"

Khione raises her hands up in surrender. "It was my father's doing, but we haven't sacrificed anyone *yet*."

"Yet. So, you still plan to?" Cait asks.

"I-I have to," Khione says. "But only if the hero asks to make the sacrifice."

Oh, God. I understand now.

"Legends of Sacrifice," I mutter.

"What?" Guy asks.

I look up at him. "The name of the game is *Legends of Sacrifice*. The offering we're supposed to make is ourselves. *We* are the legends that must be sacrificed."

Guy's eyes widen in terror.

"No, no," Cait says, shaking her head furiously. "That can't be right! They said they would give us what we truly desire if we give them the right offering. They can't do that if we're dead!"

Guy's shocked expression shifts to grief-ridden resignation. "But they only ever wanted to give us something that would keep us in the game," he says. "Because they know we won't make it to the real world alive."

"No hero has offered themselves as a sacrifice before?" I ask.

Khione nods. "The first hero to sacrifice themself will be the last," she says. "That hero's god will become the one to rule over all the rest."

"Aphrodite told me I was closer than any player so far to getting an offering to their deity," I say. "That's because I had Alexander—I mean, Eumolpus—with me. She knew he would bring me here, get me close to Khione, and lead me to this room. She *knew* I would give her that crown."

I hate how *sad* this makes me. I should feel angry or terrified. Instead, it feels like my heart is going to shatter. Aphrodite promised me she wouldn't let me die, when all along that was exactly what I had to do. But I still get to make a wish, and she will have to honor it.

As much as the concept terrifies me, Aphrodite will give me anything I wish for. I know exactly what I want, too. This is my only way to save my mother and keep my friends safe from Zeus. I *have* to do this.

"Okay," I say. "I'll do it."

Cait turns my head to face her. "Lauren, don't do this. It's not worth it. Obviously, this is why Zeus wanted you dead. If you refuse to sacrifice yourself—"

"He'll keep coming after me," I say. "Just in case I change my mind."

"What if I do it instead?" Guy offers.

"No! You're the only one who can save Zeus's followers." I turn to Cait. "And before you say it, Aphrodite would never forgive me if I let one of Ares's chosen do this."

Guy sits beside me on the sacrificial altar. "We can hide. It won't be that hard."

"I have a god-killing gun," Alexander—Eumolpus—says, holding up his Benelli.

I give Alexander an exhausted chuckle. "Not sure that's going to work on someone as powerful as Zeus."

"You can't do this," Cait whispers. Tears spill like diamonds from her green eyes.

Guy squeezes my hand. His brows tent together in what looks like grief. "I don't remember you, but I was hoping to get to know you again."

I stroke his cheek. "That would have been lovely," I say. Then I turn and cup Cait's cheek with my other hand. "It would have been perfect."

"Then stay with us," Cait says. Her voice hitches with a sob so uncharacteristic of my fierce barbarian.

I shake my head. "You don't understand. I want what Aphrodite can give me, even more than I want to live." I drop my hands to my waist and turn to Khione. "How do we do this?"

Khione approaches me, her every step somber. She motions for Guy and Cait to leave my side. Cait crosses her arms, and Guy inches even closer to me.

"Go," I tell them. "This is what I need to do, what I *want* to do."

Part of me wants them to fight me on this, but I know I'm dooming them if I don't make this sacrifice. They love each other. Sure, Cait isn't sexually attracted to Guy, but she's loved him romantically for months. Maybe they'll even find a third person, someone a lot like me. If I truly love them as much as I say I do, then I have to do this. I'm sacrificing myself for them and Mom, not for Aphrodite.

Finally, Cait and Guy back away, and Khione rests me along the altar. I'm a short woman, and this was built for even an orc to fit on. So, there's plenty of room for Khione to lay the sacrificial cup and dagger beside me. She gets a piece of parchment and a quill pen out.

"First, slice down your arm with the dagger over the cup," she says. "Don't cut too deep. This can't be what kills you. Just make sure all the blood collects in the cup." I do so and then she dips the quill into the blood and hands it to me. "Sign this."

Words appear on the parchment, stating that I am willingly making this sacrifice.

Sign it in my own blood? How trite.

I sign it.

Khione takes away the parchment, pen, and dagger. Then she pours a sparkling, golden liquid into the cup and mixes it with my blood.

"Just drink from this," she says. "Your death will be soft and easy. You'll feel no pain, only peace."

As I lift the cup to my lips, Cait shouts, "Wait!"

I lower it and sigh. "Cait, I made my decision."

"Can I at least know what your kiss was like?" she asks.

"Yes, can we have that?" Guy asks. "Before you leave us for good."

Their faces mirror each other with pleading eyes, tented brows, and lips that perhaps remember what their minds cannot.

I nod. "Can you hold this for just a moment?" I ask Khione.

Khione takes the cup, and I sit up so that there's room on either end of the altar next to me.

Cait sits on my left and Guy on my right. Cait's the first one who lowers her lips to mine. The song that lifts from us surprises her, and she gasps against me. Our music is bittersweet, a goodbye melody. Guy brushes his lips with mine, and his notes intertwine with ours, making the song even more beautiful and even more poignant.

Guy opens my mouth to deepen the kiss, while Cait kisses my jaw and then Guy's cheek. Then Guy lets her claim my mouth again so that he can kiss my ear, while weaving his hand into my hair.

Our song swells, the plaintive notes of a lone violin climbing above it all. I'm so glad that the last thing I'll experience in my life is this beautiful moment.

Cait pulls away, her face even wetter than it had been before. She swallows and whispers, "I remember now."

"You do?" I ask, hoping it's true, willing myself to believe it even if it's not.

"The kiss..." Guy says. "Our kiss, our song. The two of us and the three of us. We shared that before. We..."

Guy wipes away the tears now trailing down his cheeks. "I love you, Lauren."

Cait nods and echoes him. "I love you, Lauren."

I reach up and cup each of their cheeks. "I love you, too. And I'm so glad you'll have each other to love as well."

"Are you ready?" Khione asks.

Swallowing back a sob, I look at her. "Yes."

Cait and Guy resist again at first, but eventually they give me room to drink the poison from the cup. Once I've emptied it, they help me lay down and hold my hands as I enter a state of bliss. Then I drift away but not into the dark this time. No, it's somewhere else entirely.

CHAPTER FORTY-THREE

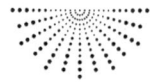

The beach is still as beautiful as before, with pink sand and waves that reach into the sunset. Mom used to call it a tie-dye sky when there were this many colors on the horizon. She would never want to leave this beach.

Aphrodite walks past swaying palm trees to reach me. Atop her head is a crown made of starlight that emanates raw power. Flickers of white magic cover every inch of her skin. She has the overwhelming aura of total authority, the most important god of them all.

Well, her promotion happened fast. Did Zeus even put up a fight?

"You won?" I ask.

"If by won, you mean the code gave me Zeus's crown and control, yes," Aphrodite answers. "But this isn't a game or a war, so I don't consider this a win."

"Don't give me that bullshit," I say. "You literally made a video game for this."

"I told you before," she says. "The worshippers are the people playing the game in your original world. *This* world is where we live and where players who were about to die in the real world can live forever. What happens to you here isn't a game; it's life."

I refrain from rolling my eyes. "None of that matters. I've brought you the offering you most desired."

Tears well in Aphrodite's eyes. "I never desired your sacrifice. It was just too dangerous to let Zeus keep control, not when he's so quick to kill. The reason the game *Legends of Sacrifice* exists is that this was the only way to get him to give up his crown. I would have been happy for any other god to become our new ruler."

"But I'm sure you were *really* glad it was you," I say and sigh. "Let me have my wish, please."

Aphrodite wipes at her eyes and nods. "Of course, anything you want."

"I have two wishes to choose from," I say, "so I need to know something first. Now that you're wearing the crown, can Zeus still attack any player he wants?"

"No, he's lost any power outside of that which he uses with his own worshippers," she says.

"Sucks to be them," I mutter.

I consider wishing for Zeus's death, but that might cause unforeseen problems. And this other wish? It's what I *really* want.

"Okay, then I know what I want," I say. I take a deep breath and then lock my eyes on Aphrodite's. "Take me back to the day Mom died, right beforehand. Let me say goodbye and let me give her my last Kiss of Life."

Aphrodite's eyes widen. I can't tell if it's shock or terror.

"Please tell me you can do this," I say. "Please tell me this wasn't all for nothing."

"I can do that," Aphrodite says. "But are you sure that's how you want to spend your last kiss?"

"It's not like there will be any other opportunities to use it," I say.

Aphrodite studies me for a moment. She opens her mouth to say something, then shuts it and shakes her head. "No, this is your choice. You deserve the wish you asked for."

She waves her hand, and the beach disappears, revealing my city. I almost choke on the stink of gasoline in the polluted air. I guess my lungs got used to the pristine air and water in Peripeteia.

Across the street is the hospice where I last saw my mother. Aphrodite stands beside me still. She's dressed like any woman would in my world. We both are. I guess she figures people can see us here.

"I can't stay outside of the game for long," she says. "The longer I'm here, the less power I have."

"Okay, well, then go," I tell her, not holding back a bit of the resentment I feel toward her.

Aphrodite purses her lips at my backtalk, but then her face softens with regret. "Lauren, I don't let my worshippers die."

"Then, I wish you'd let me stay on this side," I say. "After all, it's the players in front of the computer screen who are your true worshippers."

"Lauren, please listen to—"

"*Go!*" I shout. "Let me be alone with my mom now."

Without saying another word, Aphrodite walks away. With every step, she fades more and more, until she's not there anymore.

I take a deep breath and cross the street, ready to get what I've wanted most for so long—a chance to say goodbye.

THE HOSPICE IS EXACTLY HOW I REMEMBER IT. IT HAS THAT SAME smell, a mixture of cleaning products, vanilla-scented wall plugins, and death. The reality of this building and these people is so clear that I'm tempted to believe I'm waking up from a dream about Peripeteia. I'm not, though.

There are two big reminders of where I come from. Even though I'm dressed like I was before I went to Peripeteia, I can still see the UI on the edges of my vision. I guess that's part of the magic I need to give Mom the Kiss of Life.

"Hi, Mom," I say the moment I enter her room. I've longed to say those words for so long that, when I finally get to, my heart threatens to burst through my ribcage.

It doesn't even matter that she doesn't say it back, that she continues to stare at the television. I sit in the chair beside her bed and look at what show is on.

"Ooh! Our favorite soap!"

I put her hand in mine and squeeze it. Her thumb brushes affectionately against the side of my pointer finger, and I try not to cry. I fail.

If there's one thing I want everyone to know, it's that you should hold hands with the people you love as often as possible. Their fingers may gnarl, and their skin may loosen, but it will still feel the same. I've missed Mom's hands so much.

"I love you, Mom," I say. "So much. I wish I could talk to you again. I wish..."

Wait. Maybe I *can* talk to her. I bring up my menu. All of my spells are there, including Restoration. Dementia isn't a poison or hex, but it can't hurt to try. I tap on the spell, close my menu, and hold my breath.

Mom blinks. The movement is slow and labored, like a rusty gear trying to click along. Then, without turning her head, she looks at me.

"Lauren," she says.

A guttural sob tears from me. It's loud, ugly, more like a scream than crying. I didn't expect to respond like this. But she said my name. She remembers me.

"Are you okay?" she whispers as I fight to even my breathing.

Finally, I reach a state where I can talk again. Wiping away my tears, I give her my brightest, most genuine smile. "I'm okay. I've just really missed you."

Mom turns her head toward me and grins. "I've missed you, too. You should visit more often. Let me get you a treat."

She starts to sit up, but her IV pulls at her, and she winces and then breaks into a coughing fit.

Another bout of pneumonia. That must be what killed her.

That's when she notices where she is. I watch her face shift from pleased to see me to the realization of what's going on. "Oh, I'm...I'm dying. That's right."

"You don't have to die," I say. "Not really."

Mom squints at me. "What do you mean?"

"This is going to sound like a big lie, but I have a spell," I say. "It's a gift from Aphrodite."

I expect Mom to laugh, but she tilts her head to the side. "You met her?"

"You believe me?" I ask.

"When your father ran off, this beautiful woman came along," she says. "She had all these baby things and money. It was suspicious. What stranger just comes along and gives you all that stuff. I thought maybe she was his sister or wife or something. So, I asked." Mom shakes her head. "She told me point blank that she's Aphrodite and your father is her son."

My jaw drops. "What? Why didn't you ever tell me this?"

Laughing, Mom says, "You would have thought I was crazy. Besides, I never saw her again." She strokes my cheek. "But you saw her."

"Mom, I have this spell called the Kiss of Life. Aphrodite let me come back to this moment because soon you're going to die, and if I kiss you, then you can come back."

Mom gasps and tries to sit up again. She grimaces from the IV's pull and lies back on the incline of her hospital bed. "You can do that?" she asks. "I can live, and we can watch our soaps and stuff? Maybe you could come live with me again!"

I shake my head. "I can't do that, Mom."

"Okay, I can live at your place, or we can just see each other more often," she says.

Ugh, this is going to hurt so bad. I wish I could just lie, but that wouldn't be fair to her. "No, you don't understand. It's not that I don't want to. That would be lovely, actually."

"Then why not?" she asks.

"Once I give you the Kiss of Life, I'm going to die."

The faint color that was still in my mother's pallid cheeks drains away. Her eyebrows press together, and her mouth hangs open. "No, Lauren," she whispers. "I don't want your Kiss of Life."

"Please," I say. "It's my dying wish to do this for you. Please, let me have this."

"I don't want to be alive, missing you," she says. "I can't think of anything worse than outliving my precious baby."

Mom shifts to sit up more. This time, she pushes through the pain until she can move the IV into a better position, then kisses me on the forehead.

I back away from her touch and shake my head. "If you die, then everything I did will be for nothing."

"Lauren, I'm going to die," she says. "Whether or not you give me the Kiss of Life. I've had multiple strokes. I could have another one tomorrow or the next day or a few years down the road. But I don't have long to live, regardless of what you do today. I would rather just spend the little time I have with you and then go wherever I'm meant to go when I die."

I want to scream. I want to have a full-on tantrum. *No, Mommy! You will* not *die! You will stay here with me!* But she's right.

Cait and Guy respected my wishes enough to let me choose my death. I should give her the same thing. That's what people do when they love you. So, I nod.

"Okay, Mom."

"Promise me, you won't give me that kiss."

"I promise." The words croak out of me, but she nods to show they're sufficient.

Mom glances at the television. "Oh, look! It's our favorite soap! Climb up here with me, and let's watch it together."

She scootches to one side. There's a ridiculously narrow amount of bed next to her, but I force myself in anyway and lay my head on her chest while we watch. She and I badmouth the trashy and evil characters. We laugh at the jokes and swoon at the good-looking doctors.

The credits roll, and I reach for the remote. "Let's see what's on the other channels. What would you like to watch, Mom?"

Silence.

"Mom?"

I set the remote down and look at her. Her eyes are fixed on the television, but they don't blink. There's no life in them.

Oh, no. Not yet.

I can't breathe. My heart pounds so hard that it's all I can hear in my ears. Tears and snot flow from me. There aren't enough tissues in the world for this.

There's still a smile on her face, and I look at her lips. I could go back on my promise. All I have to do is press my lips to hers. This is the way she wanted to go, though: cuddling with me and watching our favorite show. Do I really want her to find my dead body and then die lonely someday soon?

Fuck.

This is so much harder than deciding to sacrifice myself—harder than anything I've ever had to do in my life. But I have to because I love her.

I lay my head against her chest again as I hold her limp hand in mine. "I love you, Mom. Goodbye."

Then, like I used to do as a kid, just like a dreamed about in Peripeteia, I kiss our overlapping thumbs. It's time to die now, so I squeeze my eyes closed, waiting for that final moment. It doesn't come. I open my eyes again and look around.

"Um, I...I kinda got my wish, so..." I say to the sky, like that might be where Aphrodite is.

There's no response at all.

"If this is about the Kiss of Life, she didn't want me to give it to her," I say.

Oh God. I *have* to, don't I. Otherwise, I'll be in this "almost dead" state forever. I sit up and look down at Mom. Will she understand? Goddamn it. I bring up my menu to see if there's a way out of using the spell or *something*.

The spell isn't there. What the fuck?

A disembodied voice says, "Cleric of Aphrodite: Level 6. Spell Gained: Speak to the Dead - one use before leaving the spell menu. Mage of Aphrodite: Level 2. Spell Gained: Portal - one use before leaving the spell menu. Skill Gained: Forgiveness. Favor Gained: Immortality."

CHAPTER FORTY-FOUR

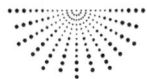

I don't know why I'm not dead or why I leveled up. Yet, here I am. I only have one use of the two spells I just gained. As far as the Speak to the Dead spell goes, that was a pretty obvious choice.

I tap on the spell and turn to smile at Mom.

"Hi," I say, stroking her cheek.

"Hi," she says, but her lips don't move. There's no sentience in her face. Her voice is as disembodied as the one that gives me leveling updates, but it's filled with as much emotion as if she were alive.

"I really loved talking and watching TV with you," I say.

"It's our favorite soap." She giggles. "Wish it had been the Paris special, though."

I groan. "Ugh, I *hate* the travel episodes."

"Yeah, well, it was *my* last episode, so I should have gotten to choose."

I squeeze her hand and tell her, "I would do anything to get you that episode."

"I know," she says. "I'm glad you saved the Kiss of Life for yourself."

"What do you mean?" I ask.

"Look where your right hand is," she says.

My hand still holds hers. Nothing has changed about it. What is she talking about?

"Remember how you used to kiss our thumbs as a kid? You'd hold my hand and kiss it, but you *always* kissed your thumb, too. That's all it took."

Oh, God, of course. "I gave myself the Kiss of Life."

"They're telling me I don't have much longer to talk."

"They? Who's they?"

"That's for me to know and you to find out. Or not."

"Really, Mom?" I ask. "Pulling out that old chestnut?"

"Do you want to spend these few seconds discussing my turns of phrase?" she asks.

I shake my head. "I wanted to tell you goodbye."

"You are the sweetest girl," she says. "I'm so damn proud of you."

Though her body doesn't move, I swear I feel her caress my cheek and kiss the top of my head, just like she used to do when I got on the bus to school.

"I'm proud of you, too," I say.

"It's time for me to go," she says. "I love you. Goodbye."

"I love you, too," I say. "Bye, Mom."

The air grows heavy, and my chest deflates with the last bit of hope I had to talk to her again. Mom is gone now—really gone. I'm beyond lucky that I got the chance to speak with her *twice*.

Then there's the whole "I accidentally gave myself the Kiss of Life" thing. I hadn't even realized I could do that. Is that why Aphrodite acted shocked when I said I wanted to give it to Mom? She'd told me she doesn't let her worshippers die. Was that her way of trying to hint at what I could do with that spell? Why didn't she just tell me?

Really, there's no use asking why the gods do anything. They're always vague as hell, and it always turns out we're just their pawns.

Yet, Aphrodite visited Mom when she was pregnant with me, just so that she wouldn't feel lost after my father left. She escorted me to the hospice, knowing that any minute she spent outside of Peripeteia weakened her. She *cried* when she saw I'd sacrificed myself, even though she knew I must in order to defeat Zeus. Even more than all that, she'd brought me into the game to save me from a car wreck she saw as a consequence of receiving news of Mom's death.

Is that how you treat a pawn?

Speak to the Dead is no longer on my menu. There's still one use of the Portal spell. I could really go anywhere, but really, isn't it obvious where I should go? Not back to my apartment or my job or even a vacation somewhere exotic.

I click on the spell, and a computer screen big enough for me to fit through appears before me. On it is the starting screen for *Legends of Sacrifice*. There are three buttons: New Game, Load Game, and Exit Menu.

Smiling wide, I press my hand to the screen.

EPILOGUE

T hank God Guy saved all that money before I came into his life. There's so much room in our new tent that he, Cait, and I can lounge about and cuddle. It's even woven with silencing threads so that no one outside can hear a single peep from us. We've been relying on that heavily these days.

Last night was heaven, but we were up way too late. I'm loath to leave the satin sheets and greet the day, but it seems Cait and Guy have already left. So, reluctantly, I open the tent flaps and exit.

I sigh with delight at the sight of a bright blue sky and swaying palms. The Strophades are so gorgeous once you convince the harpies that live here to cash in on the tourist trade instead of attacking innocent people.

"Get your swimming clothes!" Cait calls out to me from my left. "Tara, Sylvia, and Miko invited us to go swimming!"

"What about Guy?" I ask.

Cait laughs. "He didn't wait for swimwear. He's there buck naked!"

"Are you fucking kidding me?"

Cait shakes her head. "You should have seen Joshua's face when Guy came splashing into the water!"

"Oh, my God!" I exclaim. "Okay, I'm coming!"

"Wouldn't be the first time in the last twenty-four hours," Cait says.

"Perv, you're just as bad as Joshua now," I tell her.

"I blame you," she says and skips away to the beach.

I throw on my swim clothes and run into the crystal blue waters where everyone's waiting for me. Cait and Guy unlink arms so that I squeeze between them. A song, happy and bright, swirls around us. We don't even need to kiss anymore. It happens with any touch, or even look, that reminds us of how much we love each other.

"I love you," Guy whispers against my hair. Then he strokes Cait's hair. "I love you, too."

"Love you back," Cait says. "Both of you."

I kiss them both on the cheek. "Love you forever."

And since we can live for eternity in the game, that's a promise I can make.

THE END

ACKNOWLEDGMENTS

There are so many people who believed in this story and were part of its creation. But I want to spotlight one person in particular: my editor, Gabriel Hargrave.

Gabe is a talented writer who also has an impressive editing record. I'd wanted to work with him for some time. Fortunately, he felt the same way about me, and our schedules aligned for this project.

From the beginning, he was my biggest cheerleader. He loved the concept of the book and couldn't wait to dig in. Once he began work, he would send me little excited notes about what he loved. Writing a LitRPG like this was a big risk since it departs somewhat from the subgenre's typical tropes, so his encouragement muted the whispers of self-doubt in the back of my mind.

Gabe saw the potential in this story and beautifully guided me on what needed improvement, while also making sure that it was still in *my* voice. I'm sure if Lauren existed in this world, she would be just as grateful as I am for the hard work Gabe put into *Cleric of Aphrodite*.

ABOUT THE AUTHOR

ARK Horton is a small woman made of round shapes and long sighs.

She's deluded herself into believing she's descended from selkies. Convinced that selkies need frequent dips in water (like the mermaid in *Splash*), ARK squeezes in ridiculously long baths as often as she can. This can be difficult since her husband, children, and pets seem to like having her around for some reason.

When she's not writing fantasy novels and short stories, she's gaming or dying her hair funky new colors. You can also find her posting nonsense on Instagram, Threads, Facebook, and TikTok under the handle @arkhorton.

You can learn more about her and her work at arkhorton.com.

ALSO BY ARK HORTON

The Telverin Trilogy

An epic fantasy about one woman's struggle to control her dangerous new powers so that she can seize back the country her family lost to invaders.

Secret of Pantheons

An urban fantasy series about two teachers at a magical public school who must protect their Chosen One student from the quest given to her by the gods.

www.ingramcontent.com/pod-product-compliance
Lightning Source LLC
Chambersburg PA
CBHW072339020726
47506CB00004B/938